# IRISH LUCK, CHINESE MEDICINE

*Molly Mahoney Matthews*

Printed in the United States of America
Published in the United States of America by Creative Cache, L.L.C.



Interior design: JERA Publishing



Second Edition
ISBN: 978-1-7321109-2-2

*Dedicated to my great grandmother, Johanna Kennedy,
and the millions who endure a tempest-tossed
life so their children can breathe free.*

# CONTENTS

## About the Molly Maguires

In the latter half of the 19th century, Schuylkill County, Pennsylvania, was an area rife with violence. Between 1861 and 1875, a series of violent assaults, arsons and murders was blamed on a secret society of Irish immigrants known as the Molly Maguires. The group had originally emerged in north-central Ireland in the 1840s as an offshoot of a long line of rural secret societies including the Whiteboys and Ribbonmen, who responded to miserable working conditions and evictions by tenant landlords with bloody vengeance.

Laura Schumm, *History Stories*

# PROLOGUE

**Nanticoke, Pennsylvania, 1882**

Johanna Kennedy locked her knees to stay upright. The banshee of grief would not engulf her, at least not until her children were out of sight. She watched her sons walk away from the warmth of her kitchen toward the purple monolith. She wanted to run after them and drag them home. Just five and seven years old, they soberly trudged ahead, shoulders hunched, to the mouth of the mine. The lunch pails she'd packed minutes before—a meager offering of bread and cheese—clanged against their skinny legs. The mountain might not swallow her lads today, but the menace was there, obscured by clouds. She had no means to protect them from the Lehigh Valley Coal Company.

As "breaker boys," her sons would sit, their legs on either side of the belt until the coal was released and came thundering down the chute. Small hands were better at sorting shale and debris from newly harvested coal. Johanna could not lift even one piece of coal in their stead. It would be ten hours before she would know if they had made it through the day. Unlike the miners, who spent their shifts buried alive, at least the boys toiled above ground. She felt hollow, with a chill deeper than the near-freezing mist that blanketed the valley.

When the children's silhouettes vanished, Johanna walked into the larger of the two rooms in their post-and-beam shack. She looked in on Connor. Her husband was sleeping, his mouth a wide O. In the silence, she worried he'd stopped breathing, but then his rhythmic wheeze started up again. He reeked of stale beer. Her throat tightened with revulsion. At least the boys didn't have to tiptoe around their father sleeping off the drink today. If she shook Connor awake, he would just sit there, sullen and defeated.

She poured boiling water on depleted tea leaves. Despite the steam rising from the watery brew, she shivered, remembering the waves that battered their ship on the voyage from Liverpool to New York. She thought of Thomas Michael Flaherty. In the weeks before she left home in Ireland, she had spent afternoons stretched out on his grave. Grief is love with nowhere to go. When she stood to leave the cemetery, she always expected to find a puddle of tears, but not even a damp spot acknowledged him. His life melted away in the soil, meaningless. Thomas left nothing except the child growing inside her. It was at the grave that she realized she would have to marry Connor to give the baby a name. They would go to America to keep her secret, and hopefully Connor's jealousy would fade. True, she had loved Thomas, chosen him over Connor. But he was gone, and she was married to Connor now.

Her secret no longer mattered. All she could think about was how to keep a roof over their heads and food in the boys' bellies—her dear sons, who had already faced such hardship in their short lives. Perhaps a mine boss would beat them today, or they might suffer one of the freak accidents that happened too often to be called accidents. She would have buried herself beneath the quilt and wept, except if she woke Connor, he might roll over on top of her—one more disgusting chore.

"Okay," she said to herself. Somewhere between leaving Ireland and landing in New York Harbor, she'd picked up American slang. She searched for the strength of heart and the spirit of this new land to discover a way to get her sons out of the mine.

She managed to slip past her husband, pull a fresh blouse from the wardrobe, and change, so close to Connor that she could smell his sour, beery sweat, the odor of defeat that permeated the room. She pulled her cape from the peg by the front door, fastened her braid, and tucked it under her bonnet. As she opened the door and stepped on the path, she didn't know if today she would find a way to rescue the boys. She could only count on the luck of the Irish.

## San Francisco, California, 1865

En had just turned seventeen—old enough in his mother's eyes that she could finally let go. She took to her bed and three days later died of an undiagnosed condition; surely her broken heart was a contributing factor. The day after her burial, En lay in bed until dusk, when hunger drove him to the streets. He purchased a bowl of rice, a packet of roasted melon seeds, and sugared coconut shavings for four cents. He wandered around San Francisco until he found himself standing on a pier, gazing out at the Golden Gate Strait and beyond to the Pacific Ocean. As light vanished, he walked toward the market district. The gas flame on a streetlamp illuminated a billboard:

*WANTED: Chinese Coolies to Build Railroad: $15 a month.*

There was no reason to stay in their Chinatown flat. He would leave Jinshan, the "gold mountain," just as his family had fled China after the rebels attacked their rural village. En was twelve, his sisters only five and four, his baby brother two, when they departed Guangdong Province in southern China. All seven Chang family members had survived famine, living on meager portions of rice, peanuts, and sweet potatoes grown in the Pearl River Delta. They were robust then; even his eighty-year-old grandmother, Nai Nai, had been vigorous, able get a full day's work done hobbling on her lotus-blossom feet. It was only as they packed up their belongings that she began to shrink. Even so, she stoically climbed up the ship's gangplank in Hong Kong, refusing En's arm. As soon as they sailed, Nai Nai fell ill. Her body was the first of many hoisted overboard into the dark Pacific Ocean. Then, almost as if a pitiless god had devised a timetable, one Chang was snatched from the Earth each year the family lived in San Francisco.

One of the Six Companies, a local Chinese benevolent society, arranged for the funerals, but because their bones were not returned for burial in China, En's mother lamented, "They are doomed to roam, searching for the land of our ancestors." The day she took ill she said, "I must go to them." Three days later, she joined the family pilgrimage seeking timeless peace.

En returned to the flat, walking around the rooms his family had shared. He took down the food basket that hung in the kitchen; the rats could eat what was left. In the shadows, he could see his little sisters, An and Ai, playing in the corner. He turned and saw a faint apparition of his mother stirring a pot at the stove, his father sorting out his medicinal powders. A watery image of baby Ji, sitting on a pillow at the kitchen table, was so real En could hear the boy's jabbering and the dull banging of the chopsticks he slammed against the oilcloth.

En could see Ji, when he was learning to walk, his chubby hands flat against the doorframe to steady himself. En smiled, remembering the look of surprise on Ji's face each time he landed on his padded bottom. Baby Ji had an engaging laugh. His brother's death had been the most heart-wrenching. En recalled holding the limp body and the crushing weight of grief squeezing against his chest. Consumption, flu, or communicable diseases—never named but rampant and deadly—took them one by one. After each death, En waited, alone on his mat at night, until he could hear the steady breathing of his family members still alive. He allowed himself silent tears. When only his mother remained, En held back because she might hear him sob. After she died, the room was silent. En had no tears.

En packed an extra cotton tunic and two pairs of loose-fitting pants in a bamboo basket and strapped a bedroll on top. He pulled the money box from the shelf, counted out coins he would leave for the landlord, and pocketed what was left. He replaced the empty box next to his parents' leather bag of tinctures and needles. His father had been a bonesetter, his mother an acupuncturist: both useless. None of their medical interventions had prevented illness from taking his loved ones. En took a wide-brimmed hat from a hook and walked the few short steps to the front door. He paused before twisting the doorknob, turned back, and reached for the bag. He held the rope handle tight as he closed the door behind him. Chinese medicine and herbal remedies had not saved his family, but it was all he knew.

# CHAPTER ONE

# EN

**Nanticoke, Pennsylvania, Spring 1883**

Johanna sat at the hotel's front desk, enjoying the morning light flooding the room until she noticed the murky windowpanes: how long since she'd had them cleaned? She added it to the maintenance list. Guests wrenched towel bars from the wall, stained carpets with ink, and plowed suitcases through plaster but rarely mentioned the damage when they checked out.

Guests—living with them was difficult, but living without them was unthinkable. She listened for the clink of teacups and the quiet murmur of breakfast conversation in the dining room. The hum of voices sounded like money to her. She was about to continue with her list when Kathleen, great with child, and the Celestial man entered the lobby. She sighed. The last thing she needed was to manage someone down and out. He probably couldn't understand directions and would require more of her attention than he would return in labor. If anyone but her dear friend,

Kathleen, had asked she would never have agreed. She forced herself to put down her pen. It took will to resist spitting out, "What now?"

He was the first Celestial she had ever seen—nice looking, with a broad face and a square jaw. He wasn't tall, but he was solid. He stood before her in an ill-fitting Western suit. When he removed his wide-brimmed hat, she got a better look at his thick pigtail. The shiny black plait reached halfway down his back. His skin wasn't yellow, like people said, but burnished gold.

"Johanna, Michael's on his way to the mine and asked me to introduce his friend from the railroad," Kathleen said.

"So, this is the man who saved your husband after the explosion?" Johanna said. "Good morning. Is it Mr. En or Mr. Chang?"

"They called him Doc Coolie at the camp," Kathleen said.

Johanna saw the Celestial draw back. Perhaps he didn't like that name.

"Well, you won't be practicing medicine. How about we'll just call you by your first name? Is it En?"

"Yes, ma'am," En said.

"You are just in time to help while Kathleen is out with the new baby," she said. "You're willing to do whatever we need?"

"Yes," the man replied. His black eyes met hers with a potency she would not have expected.

"What type of work can you do?" she asked. Something in his demeanor made her hope he might be capable of managing tasks without much supervision. That would be a relief.

"He's been in medical school," Kathleen said. "And practices acupuncture and bonesetting."

"I've heard, but this is a small hotel. We also operate the three rooming houses on this street, but no hospital," Johanna said. "Your work will be domestic tasks."

"Oh, he understands," Kathleen said. "I'll show him what I do upstairs, but there's no need to waste both of us on the same job. Is there anything special that you might want him to do before the stork calls?"

Johanna looked at her list. "Let me see."

"What about the death-defying back porch?" Kathleen said.

"Good idea, we could replace the floor," Johanna frowned. "Hmm, not even on the list. And the screens are falling out."

She looked up. He was clearly uncomfortable, sad even, and she had been so curt. She wanted to seem more hospitable and added, "You'll get your wages every other week. Do you need an advance?"

"That won't be necessary," En said.

Just then Johnny bounded into the room. In the two years since they came to Nanticoke, he had grown taller, but he was still small for his seven years.

"Ma, I've finished my boots …" Johnny's jaw dropped.

"Johnny, close your mouth. You'll catch flies," Johanna said. "En, let me introduce you to my son, Johnny, who evidently is unaccustomed to people who are not from around here."

En turned to Johnny, knelt down to the boy's eye level, and said, "I'm pleased to meet you."

Johnny stuck out his hand and said, "Likewise."

She was happy to see this new man seem to immediately draw Johnny out of his shell.

"Johnny, En is a friend of Uncle Michael's. He'll be working here," she said. "Would you show him to the shed we fixed up, the one behind Butterwort House?"

"Come with me, Mr. En," Johnny said with great solemnity. "And I like your ponytail."

Johanna called after them, "Johnny, show him the work clothes he can borrow and the toolbox."

After they left, Kathleen said, "Not much of a talker."

"I can see that. Maybe they don't have women where he comes from?" Johanna said.

"I hope he's not too much trouble."

"At least he won't gossip like Tilly, the new cook," Johanna said, although she was still worried the Celestial might turn out to be more trouble than he was worth.

"I'm so sorry we're asking one more thing of you," Kathleen said. "Johnny also liked him. That's a good sign."

"It's fine. After seeing how Johnny reacted to a Celestial, we'd best prepare the other servants."

## Sierra Mountains, Winter 1868

En stood up from behind the rock wall, testing his legs—shaky but nothing broken. There was a loud ringing in his ears. Small granules of soot burned his eyelids, but the blast had not blinded him. As the dust settled, the terrain came into focus. The snow-capped Sierras rose, majestic and imposing. In the foothills, he could see a tree line of dark green pines spiraling the trail, sagebrush and endless prairie. He couldn't make it out, but he knew that somewhere below him the railroad camp squatted at the mountain's base like a coward hiding from a bully.

En rubbed his watering eyes and looked around. The Irishman was gone. The explosion must have sent him flying. He made out the form of the man, lying face down, about five feet from where the blast had toppled heavy rocks. The big body lay still. The arm jutting above the Irishman's head was twisted backward like the broken limb of a puppet. En scrambled over the rubble, picked up the good arm, and felt for a pulse. It was rapid, but he was breathing. En started counting, as if calculating how fast the pool of blood could pump out from the man's wound. En slid a practiced hand beneath the blood-soaked curls, methodically examining the scalp and neck for the source.

En tried to think back so he could understand how he ended up on the side of a mountain, coated in dark ash, his hands covered in the blood of a man he just met. He remembered waking in the Chinese camp. He recalled the ice crystals cracking under his feet as he navigated the rutted path. It was just after dawn and the sun—a flat orb—emerged off and on from smoke-blue clouds. Like most mornings, snow-covered mountain peaks were veiled in haze. He had finally adjusted to the high altitude and spring was just a few weeks away. The brutal blizzards, wind, and frigid temperatures would end soon. He'd eaten breakfast: congee, sweet-and-sour pork, dried oysters, abalone, fruits, mushrooms, seaweed, crackers, and a handful of candies. Most of the ingredients were shipped from China. En relished meals that tasted of his childhood. The railroads provided lodging and food for the Irish who camped near the work site, two pounds of rations per day per man.

The food was plentiful—well-fed laborers could work harder—but the rest of the Chinese camp was substandard compared to the Irish camps. The Chinese reported to middlemen who arranged for meals and transport for a cut of their wage. They slept in canvas tents fixed to wooden slats, used a crude privy, and everything was spattered with mud. In the center was a long tent, built low to the ground with slits for entry. It served as an office and mess hall. The showers and latrines were outside. The Chinese workers were meticulous about cleanliness, washing each other down after work each day, no matter if the water pounded their bodies like icicles. Unlike the Irish camps, there were no infestations of fleas or bedbugs.

Wooly Wools was the foreman responsible for laborers, stable men, engineers, contractors, masons, carpenters, and what little medical personnel was available. Named for unidentifiable animal skin that kept him warm, he was a walking specimen of vermin infestation. En stood as far away possible when the boss man handed out work assignments because Wooly also spewed bugs. Some days Wooly's commands sent men to their deaths. For the first six months, Wooly ordered En to wicker basket. En spent the day dangling against the

Sierra mountain face, chopping away rock with a pickax. A week earlier, Wooly had moved En to the explosives crew.

"You eat too much," he'd told En. "You're no longer one of them skinny Celestials we can lug in a basket."

En was no pyrotechnic expert, having only observed Chinese New Year fireworks from the roof of his family's flat, but he was glad to get out of the wicker carrier. It wasn't necessarily safer, but En had never liked swinging on ropes controlled by others.

It was only this morning that Wooly, pushing a fermenting pelt off his face, had confronted En outside of the mess hall.

"Takin' you to the Irish side today. Figured you must have some experience with fireworks, all that Chink New Year madness in San Francisco. They need more guys who can handle powder."

This was not good news. The Central Pacific Railroad work, mostly Chinese laborers, had advanced from the west and recently converged with the Union Pacific Railroad, predominately Irishmen building track from the east. The work areas were parallel, and the line work was segregated. En had been around enough Fan Gway, the white folks, to know the depth of their hatred, making this assignment more dangerous than most. Even if he didn't become a target, the Irish would control the hook up and the detonator. He could only keep an eye out to prevent his body mingling with pulverized mountain.

Instead of getting into the wagon with the Chinese workers, En had followed Wooly to a smaller wagon. It appeared he would be the only Chinese laborer on the Irish side of the camp, which meant either Wooly liked his work so far, or they needed someone expendable that day. The foreman escorted En to where two bearded men stood over a table, deep in conversation. Both men had the broad faces and ruddy skin of the Irish, with thick beards and shoulder-length hair. Maps covered the tabletop. Boxes of explosives were stacked behind them. The bigger man, with the blue-black eyes and hair of the Spanish Irish, looked up.

"Is this the wee Chinese lad we've heard is fond of blowing up the world?" En had only recently learned to understand the brogue, but he still wasn't certain if the words were friendly or threatening.

"I'm Michael Farrell." The man turned to his buddy. "This guy here is Duff."

"I'm En. En Chang, sir." En's stomach felt tight. It didn't take much to set off the Irish, especially if they'd been drinking the night before.

"Pleased to meet you." Michael stuck out his hand.

En had never shaken the hand of a white man. He hesitated.

"You should reach out your meat hook, young coolie. Your life's in my hands today."

En took Michael's hand. His own was clammy with sweat.

"We're gonna blow that northeast ridge to smithereens. Okay by you?"

En nodded.

The man called Duff had a wad of tobacco swelling in his cheek, his mouth was lined with wet brown liquid, his skin withered and ageless.

"Sent us the runt of the litter," Duff slurped.

He gave En a slap on the shoulder. It wasn't a friendly nudge.

"Did you run away from mommy to build the railroad?"

En surprised himself by speaking. "My kin built the Great Wall of China."

He instantly regretted the outburst—it was foolish to speak unless necessary. Still, these men had probably never heard of the Great Wall. He could see the ignorant one fuming and was glad he'd struck a nerve.

Duff pulled his fist back and aimed for En's jaw.

"Ha, that's a good one, Great Wall of China!" Michael lifted his arm and blocked Duff's assault.

"You've heard of it, sir?" En said.

"Read all about the Qin, Han, and Ming Dynasties." Michael's laugh was like a balm. "I like history books. I blame the priests."

"Never did get why in the hell you cart all those heavy things around," Duff said, glaring at En.

"Keep your opinions and your dukes to yourself, Duff," Michael said. "We need this Celestial."

"I'm saying I never heard of no Chinese wall, and I'm against the Chinese element." Duff jammed fists into his pockets. "Wear baskets on their heads for God sakes."

"I'm told he knows his stuff," Michael said.

"You know they drink tea like little old ladies and eat rats for dinner? Opium dens and pleasure houses, too." Duff spat a wad of tobacco near the spittoon. "You gotta admit, Michael, it's downright unchristian. With all these Celestials, no wonder this job is such slow going."

"Laying track has gone a lot faster since the Chinese showed up. They're working circles around the Irish, and you know it." Michael put his hand on En's shoulder. "We'll have a lot to talk about, Mr. Great Wall, and keeping Duff pissed off is part of the fun." He pointed to a pile of gear and some boxes.

"You know how to line up wire and fuses?"

"I do, sir," En said.

"Good, we worked the rock face yesterday, marked a place about four feet down. The hole is about fifteen feet deep, add the right amount of powder, we should spring a crack," Michael said. "We can adjust the final rigging up the mountain. No more riding around like the Queen of Sheba for you."

They gathered their packs and left Duff muttering.

The map was not well marked; they lost their way twice. It took an hour to hike the mountain.

"Okay, here's good." Michael wedged himself in a crevice and pulled out wires and the box. "When it's too narrow, just turn sideways—no screaming or losing your shit in tight places."

En knew how to crawl away from explosives without setting anything off. Hadn't he done it nearly every day for a week now? This guy, Michael, was better than the one called Duff, but he couldn't wait to rid himself of these pasty characters. For Chinese laborers, working with the Irish held as many hazards as those posed by the mountain.

"This is my last job before I go back to meet my sweetheart, Kathleen. She's coming over on the boat next month. I'll get work in the coal mines of Pennsylvania—she'll be my wife by the new year," Michael said, unwrapping the sticks. "You got a gal back home? She got a pigtail longer than yours?"

The questions were intrusive, but collegial. Michael spoke to En as a man and wasn't put off when En remained silent. En spoke so little at the camp that normal conversation didn't come easily, nor did he wish to disclose anything that might evoke hostility.

Once the wires were laid out, they hiked downhill with the detonator. The angle was steep and there was no footpath. They stopped talking to focus.

The fissure in the rocks where they would lay the final wires was tapered and better suited to En's slight build. En was surprised and pleased that the Irishman signaled him to complete the installation. He slipped through, attached the fuse wires, and returned to where Michael was waiting. Michael attached the charge wire to the detonator and signaled En to squat behind the jagged rocks.

"Let's hope the engineers got this one right," Michael said.

The last thing En remembered was Michael plunging the stem on the black box, and now he could see that Michael's body had taken the greater force of the blow. The man was losing a lot of blood. En's parents had well prepared him to treat traumatic injury, and there was no option but to act as his parents would have. They had risked their own lives many times to help others.

En put his ear against Michael's chest. The Irishman's heart was pounding—a good sign. En uncovered several deep lacerations on the arm. He took off his shirt and ripped off a piece of fabric. He tied a tourniquet above Michael's elbow. En felt around Michael's head and this time located a long gash. He remembered his father saying even shallow head wounds bled profusely. Thankfully the laceration was not deep. He placed what was left of his shirt between Michael's head and the dirt, at an angle so pressure would slow the bleeding.

He judged Michael was in shock. It had been a thirty-minute walk to this section from the mountain's base. Rescuers should be there within that same amount of time. It would help if Michael could be resuscitated and conscious for the trip down the mountain. For the first time in months, En wanted the medical bag that he'd stuffed under his cot at the Chinese camp. If he had his bigger bloodletting needles, the sanling zhen—three-edged needle—he would prick all ten of Michael's fingertips to release a few drops of blood and bring him around. He didn't even have a regular acupuncture needle. His only option was to put pressure on the renzhong acupuncture point. He pressed the tip of his finger into the small indentation right below the man's nose. Nothing. He put one hand behind Michael's head, pushing even harder into the crease of the philtrum. Michael's eyes opened. Although he wasn't fully conscious, he was at least responsive. En's pressing would probably leave a bruise or mark at the acupuncture point, but that would be the least of Michael's medical problems.

Where was the rescue party?

En stood to survey their location. The explosion had cut a hole in the mountain, and heaps of rubble severed the trail. Even if men were on the way, he and Michael would not be easy to spot. He moved stones in hopes of creating a passageway and crawled to a perch high above the valley. He saw Irish workers searching the mountain below them.

En frantically waved to get the men's attention. He took off his pants and dragged them above his head like a flag. He was about to give up when a man pointed and signaled. Soon the search party was clambering toward him.

En sat back down with Michael. After a few minutes, he could hear men on the ridge. He saw two in the lead, recognizing Duff.

"We meet again, Mr. Great Wall," Duff shouted.

They hiked to where En sat next to Michael's prone body.

"Engineer overestimated this one—too much explosive, I guess. Michael's too good to have made this big a mistake, even if he was dumb enough to take you with him," Duff said. "Or maybe you had something to do with this fiasco?"

Duff pushed past En without waiting for an answer. "He's still breathing," he said. "Let's get him down the mountain."

Other men arrived and loaded Michael onto a makeshift stretcher. One of the men looked at En and sneered, "Where are your clothes, Chinaman?"

En realized he was, indeed, standing in his skivvies.

"Looks like he made a tourniquet," another said.

Duff said, "Wooly was talking about this Celestial being a medical man, but it's hard to believe he knew what he was doing."

"Doctor is two work camps away. It'll be hours before he gets here. Do you think Michael will last that long?"

"I don't," Duff said. "Hey, Mr. Great Wall, can you stitch him up when we get back to camp?"

"If you have the medical supplies."

"He's Chinese," the other man said. "Don't be daft. He can't do much more than tie rags."

"Not much of a choice, it's him or nothing," Duff said.


When they got back to camp, the men put Michael's stretcher down on a cleared table. En examined the head wound and was relieved to find it was an easily stitched flap. The arm would need stiches, too. He hoped he was good enough to save a vein that might be punctured. Duff showed En a table covered with medical supplies. En's hands were shaking as he threaded the needle.

"Carefully," he heard his mother's voice echoing inside his head. "You have the gift of healing, En. Always remember to calm yourself and go slow to make precise stitches."

En took his time, and when he released the tourniquet, the sutures held. He asked Duff and another man to hold Michael still. En carefully felt along the triangular edge of the shoulder blade: dislocated shoulder, maybe a torn shoulder muscle. This time, it was his father's words guiding him.

"To set the bone, hold it gently, as if the bone were your child, guide it firmly, then one swift movement."

En felt Michael's flesh around the displaced bone and ran his fingertips along the muscle. He touched the socket and, with one quick jolt, forced the shoulder back in place. Michael drifted in and out of consciousness. His body sprang up when En jerked his arm. After En taped Michael's shoulder to his chest, he tended to the smaller abrasions. Then he assessed his patient. Michael lay white faced—nearly a corpse—but his breathing was regular. En felt the pulse, and it was no longer racing.

Duff handed him a mug of water. "Take a break, coolie," he said. "The real doctor will be here soon."

The others drifted out of the tent. Duff brought in two crates. He stumbled down on one and offered the other to En. They sat in silence until Michael stirred, opened his eyes, and said, "What the hell?"

En stood and put his face in Michael's line of vision.

"You've been in an accident. You're back at camp now. You will recover."

"You're my doc?" Michael's voice was barely audible.

"Yes, for the time being."

"I remember you," Michael said. "Did we blow the mountain to kingdom come?"

"We did." En smiled.

"Hell, yeah," Michael said. "My shoulder hurts like a son of a bitch."

"One minute." En opened the box of medical supplies. Nothing was labeled, but he pulled out a powder that he guessed was a narcotic. He found a teaspoon and mixed it with some water. Michael licked it off the spoon and fell asleep instantly. En hoped he hadn't given too high a dose.

The camp doctor arrived a few minutes later.

"Who would have thought the Celestial had this capability?" he said to Duff after examining Michael. "Michael will make it. Not much I can do. This guy did what mattered."

The doctor left the tent without acknowledging En.

En slept next to Michael that night. In the morning, his patient, although groggy, was aware of his surroundings. He lifted his head and grinned at En.

"Got any grub?" Michael said. "I'm starving."

"I will ask," En said. "How do you feel?"

Michael grimaced. "Like I've been run over by a team of horses."

"It was a pile of rocks," En said. "Here, I'll give you something for the pain."

"It's the luck of the Irish that I had you there—I owe you my life," Michael said through cracked lips. "When I get back to Pennsylvania and marry my Kathleen, I want you to stand up with me at my wedding."

"That is very kind," En said, wiping Michael's mouth with a towel and dotting salve on his chapped lips and the broken skin on his face. "But I have no plans to be in Pennsylvania."

"She's gorgeous, Doc," Michael mumbled. "You and she will get on."

Michael drifted off, groaning each time he shifted positions.

The next morning Duff sat next to his friend as En changed Michael's dressings. Wooly walked into the tent. En moved to the wall, partly to show respect, and also in an attempt to stay downwind.

"How is he?" Wooly scratched beneath his wool cap. Tiny black specks—likely insects—rained around his head.

"I gave him something to help him sleep," En said.

"I hear you are the one who put him back together," Wooly said. "Finish up with those bandages now, and we'll get you back to your camp."

"But, sir—" En said.

"Questioning an order, Chinaman?"

"No, sir," En said. He bit his lower lip and then made another attempt to speak.

"Shut up." Wooly scratched his back, this time with the barrel of his rifle. En had a vision of Wooly's brains splattered on the canvas. There was not much he could do to put a man's brain back in his skull.

"Wait, Wooly. He saved Michael," Duff said. "Let 'im talk."

"God damn it, I'm busy," Wooly said, adjusting his pelt. En saw a few more dark seeds fall from the tangled fleece. En hoped nothing would take up residence in his patient.

Duff took a menacing step toward Wooly.

"Oh, all right, what do you want?"

"His dressings will need changing." En stared at the dirt floor. "If it's not done properly, the wounds could get infected."

"Wooly," Duff said. "I don't like this Celestial any more than you do, but he seems to know what he's doing. Maybe just for a few more days?"

"Men will think I'm soft in the head if I don't get this Chinaman back," the foreman said.

"It ain't soft if it keeps Michael alive," Duff said. "In the war, the men mostly died days after surgery, of infection, not bullets."

"True enough."

"And you could arrange so's you get a good day's work out of him. Make him clean up the chamber pots, latrines. Chinese are good at laundry, too."

Wooly sighed. "You take charge and make sure this goddamn yellow bastard sleeps outside of the tent. They aren't bunk mates."

En questioned whether he should have escaped from the Irish, but he was accountable for the care of a man he had treated, and his fortunes were tied to Michael's recovery. They knew where they could find him if Michael died. Besides, the guy had offered En his trust and deserved En's in return.

That night, En did all he could to make Michael comfortable and then took a bedroll outside of the tent and lay down. The temperature would go below freezing. En had tucked the heavy blankets around Michael, leaving only a sheet and tarp for himself. He woke, shivering, a frigid rain pelting against his thin covering. He tried to stay awake to prevent hypothermia, but he eventually dozed. Later, he would think that without the beating, he might have frozen to death.

He woke the second time in sharp pain; his body was rising and crashing against the hard dirt. Blows were coming at him from at least three directions. En curled in a fetal position so that most of the punches landed on his back and legs.

A voice said, "You better get your Chinese ass back to where you belong."

There was a final kick, the metal toe of the boot pierced En's flesh mid-thigh, and then quiet.

En forced his breathing to a slow rhythm. Pain knifed between his ribs. He felt a visceral anger that comes with unexpected injury. He choked back tears of pain and rage.

"You're fine," he told himself. "Just inhale."

He would have advised a patient to lie still. He took his own advice and slowly flattened out against the frosty earth. They likely wouldn't be back, at least not tonight. He dozed off. He woke to chirping birds. The swelling flesh around his eyes limited his sight, but he could see the rising sun.

En rolled over to his knees. He pushed himself up and found he could stand, but his ribs hadn't fared well. He gingerly touched the area on his rib cage where the pain was sharp. After a quick assessment, he determined the ribs were just bruised. The laceration on his thigh was the only external injury that required care. He may have avoided internal injuries and would keep a watch for bloody urine or stool.

En limped to the bucket of water by the tent. He washed the blood from his mouth and nose, got the medicine box and bandaged up his leg. He managed to wrap his ribs, but without help he couldn't get enough traction. Perhaps he could ask Duff?

En kept his head down when he entered Michael's tent. He busied himself straightening the medications on the crate by Michael's cot.

"You're soaked, shiverin' like a junkyard dog." Michael grabbed En's arm. "Don't you know enough to come in out of the rain, Chinaman?"

"Lie still," En said. "Let's take a look at you."

Michael watched him as En examined his stiches.

"After these heal you may not get much feeling back for a while," En said. There would be scars, but they likely would not be too noticeable in a few months' time.

Michael's eyes followed En as he moved.

"They're making you sleep outside, and you're limping."

"Just a little stiff," En said.

"And look at your face. You run into a spike driver in your sleep?" Michael said.

When En didn't answer, Michael said, "Don't bother. I can guess. They're treating my doc like an animal."

"It's nothing," En said. "A small disagreement."

"That bloomin' shiner isn't gonna be small."

With his good arm, Michael pulled En toward him.

"You saved my life, and they're knocking you around?"

"Please, there is no problem." En extricated himself from Michael's grip.

"You're afraid if I raise hell about it that it'll get worse?" Michael lifted his head and looked around. "This is my tent. I'm in charge, so listen up. See that corner? Tonight, you will sleep there, inside the tent. That's an order. And over there—my duffel? I have some extra clothes; they may not be clean, but they're better than those skanky things you got on."

En wasn't sure what to say.

"And I don't think Mr. Great Wall is the right name for you. Seems like from now on you should be Doc Coolie, the doc who saved me."

Duff stuck his head in the tent, gave a thumbs-up to Michael, and then saw En. "Looks like you're makin' a lot of friends."

Michael demanded Duff get Wooly, who arrived faster than En would have expected. En could see that Michael had a lot of clout in the camp. When Wooly entered, he pointed at En and Duff and said, "Get out."

En followed Duff outside.

"Knew you was trouble," Duff said under his breath.

It was windy, and En could only hear a few of the heated whispers—mostly Michael's angry rumbling. After Wooly emerged from under the tent's flap, he pushed En toward the tent. "You will sleep inside from now on. Your duties would be limited to nursing."

En returned to a drained Michael. His patient managed a smile.

"Welcome back, Doc. Men will be on notice to leave you alone, or they will get to know the hot end of Wooly's rifle."

## Sierra Mountains, 1868 and Pacific Ocean, 1860

During Michael's convalescence, En had more time to rest than he'd ever known. Growing up on a farm in China, and during the years in San Francisco, when he and his mother had struggled to feed themselves and look after his sisters and baby Ji, there was always more to do. Nursing Michael required minimal time and skills. The camp's kitchen sent meals, and Michael insisted on delivery in large bowls so En's portion was not contaminated "accidently." After he attended to Michael and tidied their quarters, En was idle.

"I'm not good company quite yet," Michael said. "Do you like to read? I have a trunk full of books. Help yourself."

"Thank you," En said. "When you feel better, I will read to you."

En started exploring the books each afternoon while Michael slept. Reading in English was slow going at first. He struggled with George Eliot and Anthony Trollope but liked Robert Louis Stevenson and Thomas Hardy. Sometimes when his mind wandered, he put the book down and watched the bear-like Irishman, his barrel chest inflating with each breath. Who was this giant who treated him with such kindness and respect? There was a temporary closeness between the two. En would not think of this as a budding friendship, although it did remind him of the one childhood friend who gave him hope that, one day, he would find another.

Grief and physical exhaustion had suppressed memories of Woo, the boy he met on the voyage a few days after they left the harbor in Hong Kong. His first friend. In the comfort of Michael's tent, En allowed himself to think back to his first relationship outside of his family.

En was eleven the day Woo flew into his life. Huddled below deck, with his family sliding back and forth against one another, En could see through the hold's opening directly to the deck above. Two sailors, white bellbottoms flapping in the ocean breeze, held a limp child by the arms and legs like a human hammock. The boy, who looked about his age, would appear during the seconds when his body was elevated over the hatch.

"On my signal," a sailor yelled. En's eyes followed the sailor as he hoisted the boy above his head. "Anchors aweigh."

The sailor tossed the child, like a sack of rice, into the dark interior of the ship.

"Watch to see if he bounces," the other sailor said with a laugh.

The boy landed catlike on all fours, seemingly without injury. The sailors slid a wooden slab over the opening. Everything in the hold went dark except for the rectangle of light outlining the trap door.

En's eyes adjusted to the dark. He saw Woo staring at the Chang family, as if he were about to choose traveling companions.

En cared for his three younger siblings, but he wanted a playmate—one his own age; it would be wonderful to play challenging games. En watched the boy sizing up the Chang family. En's heart galloped; he wanted to make friends with this brave boy. But even if the boy picked En, would his parents allow it? En's eyes entreated his mother, Lian. She sat cross-legged in the bunk across their partitioned compartment, Baby Ji asleep on her lap. Lian saw her son searching her face for permission. Her husband, Tan, would make the decision.

"Perhaps we might share our space with this boy? His misfortune—" she whispered.

Tan cut her off. "Only until we get to America."

Lian nodded at her son. En moved toward the boy, but Ai and An, aged four and five, who had clung to him since getting on board, refused to release his arms. They were sober little girls in matching tunics, bordered at the neckline and sleeves with a panel of piping, red in the sunshine, now black in the darkness. Their polished black hair was parted in the middle, braided and coiled over their ears. Before they could crawl, the two sets of ebony eyes had surveyed him with wonder. Once they could toddle, the girls trailed En like baby ducklings. A stranger might think their serious expressions indicated a melancholy, but En could elicit giggles or tickle them until they fell in a heap of laughter and his parents told them to behave. The girls learned early to cover their mouths to hide their smiles. They smiled with delight and love when they looked at him. En's heart yearned to protect them.

His mother was always telling him, "En, save your sisters," but he was not abandoning the girls, just helping this young boy.

"I'll be right back," he repositioned his sisters to rest against each other.

He scuttled across the pen and assisted the boy to his feet.

"Are you hurt?" En asked.

The boy shook his head.

"Your knees are skinned."

"They're okay," the boy said.

"I'm En, what's your name?"

"Woo," the boy said.

"We've been at sea for days," En said. "Where were you until the sailors tossed you in with us?"

"In one of the lifeboats," Woo said. "I ate more cheese than the rats. They figured there was a stowaway ... and it was me."

En could just make out the boy's huge grin.

"We don't get cheese down here," En said.

"Sailors get cheese, and one of 'em must love it. He was mad as a flea-bitten dog. I ate almost an entire wheel. He tried to throw me overboard," Woo said. "But then Captain pulled me away. Now I guess I'm going to be here, with you."

"We get only rice and some pork fat down below."

"I'm starving. Can I have some?"

"Not now, only when they lower the cauldron. They will hang it on the pulley tonight."

"That sounds delicious," Woo said.

"It's boiling, so stay back; if it tips, you'll get burned."

Woo nodded. In the strange light, En thought Woo's head looked like a coconut, his emaciated cheeks sunken into too-deep eye sockets. En's queue was long enough that he could almost sit on it. Woo's hair was short and too uneven to braid; it looked as if it had been chopped with a stone. Yet Woo's jubilant spirit absorbed his undernourished face and too-large features. Ai and An responded to Woo's big smile with their own shy ones and a few giggles. The girls had been uncharacteristically quiet since the family had escaped their burning home.

"Will your parents meet you when we get to San Francisco?"

"I don't have parents." Woo looked around at Tan and Lian. "Do these grown-ups belong to you?"

Tan was on the floor, pulling packets of herbs, needles, bandages, and small jars from a leather bag. He tossed the packets of cinnamon, hawthorn, gardenia, clove, licorice, and chrysanthemum to his wife. Lian, still holding the baby, used her free hand to sort leaves, roots, pods, and blossoms.

"Yes, these are my parents, and my two sisters and baby brother," En said. "We are going to Gold Mountain."

En wasn't sure if this talk was how to make a friend, but his curiosity got the best of him, and he said, "If you don't have parents, then who named you Woo?"

"I've just always been Woo. The other boys called me Woo as long as I can remember. Like Woo Who, where are you?"

"This was before the ship?"

"On the streets of Shanghai."

"In those big houses on the Bund?"

"No, in a crate."

"A crate?"

"It was good fun, especially on Chinese New Year when I got dumplings and egg rolls."

"How did you get the money to buy food?"

"Not buy, from the trash heap."

En could not imagine eating trash, except maybe if he got any hungrier on this voyage. At first the sloshing waste buckets tied to the beams had curbed his appetite, but now En was starving—thirsty, too. He ate anything put before him, despite odors that had once turned his stomach.

"But only on Chinese New Year," Woo went on. "After that, there was nothing to eat, and it was freezing. It will be warm in America. There will be gold and food. I will grow stronger when I have endless dumplings."

"I need to grow, too. My mother says I should be taller for eleven. Are you eleven?"

"I might be ten, or twelve."

"You don't know how old you are?"

Woo shook his head.

En felt sorry that this boy was all alone in the world. He himself had never known a day when he wasn't surrounded by family. Their village had been small, sixteen families sharing walls between identically designed dried-brick homes. Chicken and pigs ran free in the courtyard, and despite summer and winter monsoons, there was always something to harvest in a climate that allowed year-round farming. En's belly was full. Poor Woo, no food, no parents.

"Maybe the captain will be your father?"

"Captain will sell me."

"You can sell a boy?"

"Boys are sold all the time," Woo said. "Don't look sad. It is a good thing to belong to somebody. Not as much danger. You see, En, my dreams are coming true. In America, I will grow rich and powerful."


On board, Woo was always the first one ready for a game. They played Woo's choice, warriors and emperors, more often than En's favorite, leapfrog. En hardly noticed that Woo made the decisions because he drew En into his expansive imagination and make-believe world. When the sea was calm, En's mother let them run about as warlords, slashing through the air with invisible swords and burning pretend villages. When they got too rowdy, En's father would shake his head or clear his throat, and they would retreat to quiet games like knucklebones. En had no idea how Woo found the stones and treasure they used for knucklebones. They stashed them under a loose floorboard.

Woo usually woke first, but on what would turn out to be one of the most important days of En's life, he was awake long before his friend. En sat next to Woo. His friend's eyes were closed, his breathing raspy. En lost his patience by the midmorning light and decided it had been long enough. He shook the boy's shoulders. Woo opened rheumy eyes, barely shifted his body, tried to speak and only managed to croak a jumble of words.

En put his hand on Woo's forehead. Fever. He held his friend's wrist between his thumb and fingers. He'd learned how to assess a pulse long ago. His parents saw their work as bonesetter and acupuncturist as a calling, and they intended to pass it along to him. En was raised to honor the patients who came to their farm for treatment, no matter when they interrupted the family. En knew his parents saw their ability to heal as a gift that demanded allegiance and reverence. The leather medical bag was as precious to them as their children.

Woo's pulse raced. En called to his father.

Tan came to En's side. His felt for the fever and also took Woo's pulse. He lifted the blanket that covered Woo's legs to reveal angry welts, green-white with pus.

"Rat bites," Tan told En. "It is good you were paying attention, son. This boy needs immediate care."

En's heart nearly burst with Tan's rare praise.

Tan called Lian to bring the leather bag, and together they prepared the treatment.

"Do you want to mix, En?" His father handed him packets of medicinal herbs. En looked at his mother and saw she was as surprised as he. En had overheard her suggest to her husband that the voyage was a perfect opportunity for En to begin his apprenticeship, but up until that moment, Tan had refused.

"If a patient dies during the crossing, and I fear some will, we can't let them blame En," his father had told his wife.

Now Tan looked at Lian's questioning face and said, "The fee for a boy as scrawny as Woo won't be large enough to trouble the captain. This is En's opportunity."

Tan opened the bag and gestured for En to take the medicine bowl in his palm.

"Do you know what we need for this poultice?"

En nodded. "We could use skullcap?"

"Yes, that is the bearded scutellaria," his father said. "Smell."

En sniffed. His nostrils tingled.

"Bitter," En said.

"Yes, skullcap and rhubarb root are pungent, but they are good for infection," his father said. "But if you prefer sweet and fragrant for your friend, we'll use these too."

His father selected several herbs. "Can you name them?"

"Chrysanthemum flower," En said as he inhaled, "and honeysuckle flower." The honeysuckle was his favorite; he remembered vines growing profusely over the courtyard walls and crawling up the thatched roof.

"And how do you use them?" Tan said.

"One part bitter herbs, the skullcap and rhubarb, to three parts fragrant herbs?"

"Yes, son,' Tan said. "You are exactly right."

En placed the powdered herbs in a bowl and moistened them with water. Tan put the bowl to his nose and sniffed.

"Ah, the moisture, the dryness, a good balance of cleansing and heat. You did well, son."

En had never felt prouder. He decided to add a few more drops of liquid.

"Do not presume," Tan corrected him. "You must always smell and test. Dried herbs lose potency over time."

En's spirits fell. He could never quite please his father, but he took some solace, glancing at his mother—she was beaming.

Tan took the bowl from En and added drops of lard. He stirred it with chopsticks until the mixture formed a thick paste. He showed En how to lather the white medicine over the fluid-filled wounds. The bites had formed yellow craters, their edges outlined in red, defining infection. When Tan finished, Woo's legs looked like they were covered with egg drop soup.

Tan moved away from Woo so his wife could take over. En had been absorbed in the treatment, but during the minutes it took his mother to set up her needles and the mugwort, he studied Woo. En had hoped Woo was asleep—he now realized his friend was awake but in pain. Woo's eyes were squeezed shut; his fists were clamped tight. En pushed away his awareness of Woo's pain. His mother always admonished him that a healer must be compassionate but detached.

He took a deep breath.

"We need to strengthen his qi," Lian said. "Your father's work is done, but moxibustion requires the patience of a woman, or someone with a gift of patience for healing. Perhaps you would like to help?"

"Yes, Mother," En said, eager to demonstrate he was worthy. He could tell he had earned Lian's confidence when she handed him a clumpy fibrous mass of mugwort. He knew it was high quality mugwort because his mother didn't give him a knife to cut it. He was able to pinch it into a cone shape by hand.

Lian lifted Woo's shirt, placed a slice of garlic and then the mugwort cone on the boy's abdomen, and lit it. He and Lian watched it burn down to a pile of ash and Lian wiped up the remaining powder.

She then expertly applied the needles. En would need years of apprenticeship to learn the right placement. She completed the treatment and instructed En to cover Woo with a blanket. En watched over Woo the entire day. His mother brought him a bowl of rice and some broth for Woo that evening. En tried to spoon the liquid into Woo's mouth, but Woo turned away.

"Don't force him to eat tonight," his mother said. "He will wake tomorrow with an appetite."

En placed his bedroll next to Woo. They both drifted off to sleep. The next morning, Woo was hungry and feeling better, yet never quite the same playful boy. He was listless, quiet, and not as much fun for the rest of the journey. En had never had a friend like Woo and worried that he had done something wrong. He waited each day for Woo to initiate one of their make-believe games. Finally, he learned they would land soon. He wanted at least one more adventure banishing imaginary rebels, so En begged, "Please, Woo, your xi is strong now. Let's play warrior. I made a new sword from a piece of wood while you were sick."

Woo said, "There is no more time to play now."

"Why not? We have a few more days," En said, hoping Woo didn't hear the catch in his voice.

"I need to think. We are both small. Many who leave China have women back home to ask the goddess, Songjiu Funu, to watch over their man overseas. I am not yet a man. I do not have a woman, and no one prays to the ancestors for me. You will be a doctor because your parents will train you. I will not have training, and the poison from my legs has weakened me. Without strong legs, I may not be able to use swords. I must spend my days thinking. Perhaps there is another way for me in America? I must become clever," Woo had told En. "I'm sorry, En. I thought when we got to Gold Mountain that we would fly kites, sing loud songs, or kick a jianzi, but even if we find a shuttlecock there, I will not have time."

Make-believe was over. A few days later, they stood together on the dock. En's family gathered around their possessions. Woo was alone, with all that he owned in a rolled-up handkerchief.

"There is glorious happiness ahead," Woo said. His body deflated by illness was frail, but his spirit seemed stronger than ever. "We must separate, but I will see you soon in this great land. Goodbye, my friend. Fill your belly with food and your pockets with gold."

Woo walked away with the captain. The too-big shirt the captain had given him nearly reached his knees.

En watched until the man and boy disappeared around a corner.

En's mother had put her hand on En's shoulder, "Your father and I treated that boy, but it was your care that healed him. A true physician knows that healing starts with compassion. You, my son, possess the healing gift of Chinese medicine."

## Sierra Mountains, 1868

Michael's snort brought En's thoughts back to the tent. He looked over at his patient. Michael had taken good care of him, and he had done his best to treat Michael. Two days earlier, an explosion had killed ten men on the crew En would have rejoined. His knowledge of Chinese medicine and days here with Michael had kept En alive.

Michael's head wound took two more weeks to heal. En wanted him to remain in bed, but as Michael felt better, he grew impatient. In an attempt to entertain his patient, En read to Michael during the day, and at night, they played cards. At first En let Michael win, but over time, he discovered that Michael wanted a fair fight. They were both competitive and avoided conversation. After the game, they took swigs from a flask of whiskey that Michael's friends always kept topped off.

One night, a tipsy Michael told En about his childhood.

"I was a kid—maybe eight or nine—when the potato famine took my family, one by one."

"They died of starvation?"

"We called it the Great Hunger, but it was slow—hard to know what killed them. First, the young ones got weak, then they'd get dropsy or the fever," Michael said. "I bet you could name what killed 'em, Doc Coolie, but we didn't. There was no money for medicine anyway. We just kept digging small graves."

"Poor nutrition makes a body weak," En said.

"My sister and I hung on. I was seventeen; she was fourteen. One day, she walked into the cottage. We all walked kinda slow by then. She looked funny, stooped over like my grannie. Her mouth was green."

"Had she vomited?"

"No, ate grass. I guess it didn't agree with her," Michael said. "Died the next day."

"I'm so sorry."

"Fourteen. Sometimes I pretend she's somewhere in the world. I dream I'll get a letter, or she'll find me here in America."

"I can't really imagine my sisters grown up," En said. He told Michael about Ai and An. "My parents told me, 'En, save your sisters,' but I failed."

"You were a kid too," Michael said.

They both got drunk that night. They took the next day slowly— En's hangover potion was not particularly effective.

Once they began, and especially when the liquor loosened their tongues, there was no topic off limits. One night, Michael said, "Ever been with a woman?"

En decided he had nothing to lose and told the truth.

"No, in San Francisco I was too young," En said. "And there are no Chinese women here at the camp."

"Some of the whores will go with the Chinese."

"I've treated those women. No, thanks," En said. "I hope you avoid those ladies, too."

"Don't worry. They're not my type," Michael said. "But I sure do miss the smell of a woman. There was a girl before Kathleen. Then I met Kathleen, and, Jesus, Mary, and Joseph, I only wanted her—big problem."

"Sounds like a good problem."

"Nope. We couldn't keep our hands off each other. But we couldn't risk making a babe either, not with our plans to come to America."

"How did you manage?"

"I've never told anyone this." Michael lowered his voice. "We found ways. I'll tell you about it, might come in handy for you some day."

Michael briefly described parts of female anatomy that were new to En. Despite assisting in the delivery of several babies, En had been focused on the crown of the infant's head.

"Is this true for Chinese women?"

"I think they're all built alike." Michael was drunk.

"Most interesting." En tried to visualize what Michael described, but his imagination failed him utterly.

"File that away, Doc Coolie, and when the women can't get enough of you ... then we'll be even for you saving my life."

They laughed.

"I can't wait for you to meet my Kathleen—so beautiful—and her eyes, blue like the sky, and her hair, dark and curly. Best feeling in the world, touching her hair."

En could almost picture this woman and although he would like to meet her, he would probably never get as far as the place Michael called Pennsylvania.

"If you ever decide to come east, you can take one of those prairie schooners to Chicago, then get a train," Michael said. "When I'm well enough, I'll get back through that town near the Platte River. Those towns dry up when the railroad moves on, so I hope it's still there."

"Be careful," En said. "Those men are all liquored up. I hear there's a murder nearly every day in pop-up railroad towns."

"I won't be there long. I figure it'll take about the same time for me to get from here to Missouri by wagon as from Chicago to Philadelphia by train. Those trains are fast as bullets. Sure wish we got the rails this far. That wagon will be slow, but I'll be sailing across the grass as Kathleen is sailing over from Ireland. I hope I get to Nanticoke before she does. Get us a nice place."

Once Michael was well enough to travel, En accompanied him to meet the wagon train going east. At the shack that served as the train station, Michael gave En a bear hug.

"You're the reason I'm still on God's Earth and on my way back to Kathleen," Michael said. "God bless, and remember you have a home with us anytime."

"I won't forget you, Michael," En said. "You have been a good friend to me. I wish you every happiness."

"Send letters to me care of the postmaster in Nanticoke," Michael said. "I'll just write 'end of track' on the envelope and hope that they find you, my friend."

En was astonished that Michael expected they would stay in touch. Inside the tent they had forged a kind of friendship, but outside in the real world, what was the possibility that loyalty or attachment would remain? En was saddened, but he doubted he would ever see Michael again.

## Sierra Mountains and Promontory Point in Utah, 1869

When En returned to the Chinese camp, Wooly Wools gave him a medical bag and provisions and set him up in a tent.

"I hear tell you'll do more for us as a doctor than up the mountain," the foreman said.

En treated dysentery—the most common problem—along with colds, stomach trouble, lice and the lesions the men contracted from the whores. For men with nervous or wood emotions, he remedied liver imbalance with a brew root of Chinese licorice, the fruit of the jujube, and common wheat kernel tea. The men used tobacco and opium; he dispensed neither, but he did keep cloves for belching, and white peony and gardenia, cooling herbs to treat the hot tempers of laborers living without the influence of women. He occasionally delivered a baby for one of the few women who followed the camp. He worried about the burden children would add to their already dismal lives.

En had enjoyed storytelling, rice wine, whiskey, and gaming around the campfire and remained friends with several. One man was chosen to be among a special team of Chinese and Irish laborers to lay the last ten miles of the track and invited En to join. Figuring his days as a paid employee of the railroad were numbered, he accepted the invitation and came along to celebrate the Wedding of the Rails. He packed his toothbrush, rice bowl, chop sticks, a wok, kettle and soup ladle, and matches in a box. He would carry the oil lamp, bedroll, herbs, and his medicine bag on his back. During the trip to Utah, En was awed by the magnificent high country and the variety of terrain: mountains, valleys and basins, dust-dry deserts. The lush springs and wetlands were fed by groundwater from the snowmelt feeding the Snake River. En lingered to enjoy nature's bounty, hoping he wouldn't miss the events at Promontory Point. He might never be in this part of the country again, and he didn't want to rush. Fortunately, bad weather, bad blood between the Union Pacific and Central Pacific rail companies, and labor disputes delayed the ceremony for two days. En got there in time, and after four years of working on the railroad, stood in the crowd that included Mormons, miners, Mexicans, and Indians to watch California's Governor Stanford of the Central Pacific Railroad and Thomas Durant of the Union Pacific Railroad pound the Golden Spike. The cross-country rail line was completed.

En wrote a letter and posted it to Michael.

*June 10, 1869*

*Dear Michael,*

*By the time you receive this letter I hope you are completely healed and are happily reunited with your Kathleen. I am well and no longer with the railroad.*

*I wish you could have been with me a month ago, on May 10th, at Promontory Point in Utah, to watch them drive the Golden Spike. Did you know about the message "DONE" that was sent by telegraph from San Francisco to New York City? Did bells toll or cannons blast the news in Pennsylvania? It's thanks to the men we knew and worked among that the nation is connected by rail and a dangerous journey of three months will now take a week.*

*After the ceremony, I managed to get invited to join other Chinese laborers at a special dinner aboard foreman J. H. Strobridge's private railroad car. You may remember Strobridge lost an eye after an explosion. He wears an eye patch. I heard the men calling him One-Eye-Bossy man, but not to his face. He and the other bossy men hailed us laborers, even the Chinese, and it was a wonderful night indeed. Had you been there I know you would have been cheering the loudest.*

*Unfortunately, it was short-lived praise. Almost overnight, the gratitude of the American people toward us is gone. This may not be true for the Irishmen, but the fact that we Chinese built the railroad no longer matters.*

*The Railroad Chinese have been tossed aside. So many are unemployed and nearly starving. I have been fortunate, finding odd jobs and providing medical treatment to my fellow country-men. I often get paid in chickens and vegetables, so I am among the lucky ones who eat regularly. Chinese laborers greatly exceed demand and the people here are calling for us to go home. Recently I have seen violence and experienced certain hostilities myself.*

*Of course, China hasn't been my home for nearly half my life, so I have decided to head east where I hear towns like Philadelphia have a growing Chinatown. Hopefully it will be better than getting run out on a rail in a cowboy town. I will let you know where I settle next. Perhaps I shall find you in the town of Nanticoke someday?*

*Are you married yet? Are her eyes still blue?*

*Your friend and doc,*
*En*

# CHAPTER TWO

# JOHANNA

**Nanticoke, Pennsylvania, 1882**

The town of Nanticoke ended abruptly at a row of miner's shacks flanked by the blacksmith's barn. Behind that last building, chicken coops backed to open fields. Johanna found the sudden termination of civilization unsettling, as if her family lived precariously on the Earth's edge and might topple off. The boys would not be back from the mine until dark. She had several hours to find some way to save them; maybe she could find a job?

Pulling her shawl tight against the wind, she set out to walk the six blocks to the business district. The dingy shacks looked pathetic against the expanse of gray-brown dirt rolling flat toward the domineering mountain. Today the landscape was forbidding, the drizzle suffocating. When life returned in the spring, Johanna hoped fresh pastures would one day ease her longing for Ireland. Only five months ago, they had boarded the *City of Rome*, but her old self was a lifetime away.

The light rain became a heavy downpour as she got closer to Main Street. She was soaked to the skin when she came upon a Victorian building that the locals referred to as a hotel because it was the largest of four rooming houses on the street. Johanna had to tug hard to open the door against the driving rain. She struggled and finally pulled the door open just as three men pushed past her. Standing her ground to avoid getting knocked over, she stepped inside, slammed the door shut behind her and rested her back against the wood.

The lobby was shabby. The front desk to her right took up a good portion of the parlor, which contained beat-up chairs circling a sofa. On her left were a few tables scattered around a bar. She guessed the man sitting on a stool behind the front desk was the proprietor. He resembled an owl, his nose protruding from two piercing black eyes and white hair matted like feathers around his ears.

"Don't care who you are or what you want, we're not open till three," he said. "Now, leave."

"I thought perhaps you could use some help?" She forced herself to speak. "Chambermaid, cook?"

"Got no jobs," he said. "Now, get the hell out of here so I can have some peace."

Before she could respond, the door lurched open again. Rain blew sideways through the opening, and two men dressed in the blue uniform of the Coal and Iron Police stomped in.

She swallowed panic. The Coal and Iron Police, technically employees of the town, worked for those Welsh mine supervisors who hated the Irish. The job of this police force was to hunt down anyone associated with the Molly Maguires. As a new Irish immigrant, was she suspect? She thought she'd left these vigilantes behind. Now she was in the clutches of the exact hostilities she'd hoped to leave in Ireland.

She stood to one side and watched them shake water off their slickers like dogs. Both were stocky; one was a head taller than the other.

"Walsh, you're in trouble again. Why don't you give up on the Mollies?" The taller policeman bounded toward the old man and pinned him against the bar.

Johanna cried out, "No," as the other man lunged at her. He grabbed her upper arms, pinching flesh to the bone.

Johanna winced. "Please, sir."

He lifted her off her feet, her toes dangling above the floor. She threw her weight to one side, and the goon, losing his balance, released her.

"You behave, missy, or we'll take you in." The officer grasped her again and pushed her down. She was on all fours. He curled his body behind hers. With one arm around her waist, he jabbed his free hand between her skirts.

She looked down on his frayed blue trouser legs that puckered over slick black boots. Rough fingers were sliding under her bloomers.

"Not today, you idiot," the other policeman yelled from across the room. "Keep it in yer pants, will ya?"

The policeman stood up, his arm still around her waist. He yanked her up to her knees.

"You'll hafta wait until another day to get a taste of what you Irish sluts crave." He grabbed his crotch and leered at her before letting go and moving to the bar.

Her eyes followed the black boots, her body weak with relief. Her assailant walked up to the old man, and with no warning thrust a hard punch into his stomach.

"So, we hear you got some of those fookin' losers from Ulster staying here. Where are they?" he said.

Johanna flashed back to the three men who had rushed out of the bar as she entered. She'd recognized thick Irish brogues. She didn't know who or where they were, and even so, if they had spent the night, renting a room wasn't a crime. The old man was doubled over. He was no match for these brutal policemen. She stood frozen, unsure what to do, regretting her decision to leave the Kennedy hovel where she had been safe. Only minutes before, her chief worry had been looking like a drowned rat and, of course, that Connor wouldn't understand her need to find work. She had not appreciated the safety of the fog that had enveloped her and wished she had a cloud around her now. These policemen were going to beat an old man to death before her eyes, and perhaps she would be next. They still might rape and kill her, but since one had said, "not today," perhaps she should press that advantage.

She straightened her skirts. She might have some bruises and the shame of that man touching her there, but she was not seriously injured. She clenched her teeth, walked to the bar, and planted herself between Walsh and the Billy club.

"Gentlemen. Aren't you both too strong to be manhandling my elderly uncle?"

She did her best to smile. She doubted she was alluring. She was too thin; motherhood and the voyage had aged her. Still, Thomas had always said she was the prettiest girl in County Mayo, and maybe some of his blarney was true.

The policeman who seemed the more reasonable let go of the old man and turned his attention on her.

"We're investigating," he said. "Looking for some of those vigilantes, the Molly Maguires. The old man harbors them."

"I don't," Mr. Walsh said.

"What about you, missy?" The policeman put his face close to Johanna's. "You swear on your Virgin Mary—that statue you folks are always praying on—you didn't see any men here last night?"

The other policeman looked directly at her bodice, the wet fabric clinging to her. He ran his tongue over his lips.

She shuddered. How dare these men act like they owned the place and her? She forced an innocent smile and placed her hand on the arm of the least offensive officer.

"Last night? I saw no one here last night."

She supposed that was technically a white lie, and she might have to mention it in her next confession.

Seeing they were unsure, she said, "Gentlemen, this is a hotel, and we want you to feel welcome." She gestured to the bar stools.

"Perhaps you would like something to drink?"

The policemen looked at one another. "Suppose one drink would wet our whistle?" They sat down. Walsh walked behind the bar, trembling, and poured each policeman a pint.

"I'll get you officers something from the kitchen," Johanna offered. She had no idea how to find the kitchen.

Walsh pointed to a corridor with his eyes. He seemed like he might keel over, but he kept his head. Even if he had been rude to her, she felt for the old man, and together they had a better chance against these intruders. She ventured down the hall, and a rotten smell assailed her before she entered the kitchen. She pushed the swinging door open and was overwhelmed by the stench. How could a room where food was prepared be so disgusting? The sink was piled high with dirty pots, and plates caked with food were everywhere. The main source of the stench was an overflowing garbage pail.

There was a fresh sandwich sitting on the counter—probably the old man's lunch. She rinsed and dried two plates, cut the sandwich in half, and added pickles she found in the pantry. She found an apron hanging on a nail and put it on, deciding she may as well look like she belonged here.

The policemen ate heartily, accepted another round, then stood to leave.

"Sorry to trouble you and your uncle." The taller one said. "Didn't know Walsh had any family left. Good he has you looking out for him, lady. He'll need it."

Johanna suddenly felt drained and could not hide a flash of fear as the other man moved toward her.

"And my partner here is a bit off today," the policeman said. "He'll not be bothering you again, ma'am."

They left. Johanna sank into a chair. Walsh poured two shots of whiskey and put one in front of her. He sat down next to her.

Johanna assessed the man. He operated this house, which he insisted was a hotel, and three small rooming houses, the only lodging in town. He apparently had customers despite his bad temper, the stench in the kitchen, and the disarray in the rooms.

Johanna had learned about Walsh from her dearest friend, Kathleen. They had grown up together in Ireland, and after Kathleen left for America to marry Michael, the couple had welcomed Johanna and Connor to the town. Kathleen once worked at the hotel, before her first baby and said Walsh was the meanest man in the world. One of her duties—Kathleen's nose wrinkled when she told Johanna about it—was bringing Walsh's coffee each morning. He drank while giving her instructions for the day and trimming the white thicket of hair in his nose and ears.

"I had to watch," she said. "He's finicky about his grooming but not as fussy when it comes to the hotel. I guess he thinks a clean-shaven face assures his customers that the place is tidy. But he rarely had us change linen between guests. There are sticky rings on furniture and dust balls under beds."

Walsh unstuck his glass from the tacky surface of the table and took another gulp. Kathleen might be right about his housekeeping, but Walsh didn't seem mean to her. She felt sorry for him. His forlorn face reminded her of her father the day she'd said her final goodbyes.

She took another sip of the syrupy liquid. It burned her throat.

"They seemed to know you," she said.

"Strike's been over for nearly a decade, but they'll never forget I was with the miners back in '76." Walsh coughed. "Sometimes they haul me in for questioning. Last time they got me bad. Still can't breathe right."

"I hear it was a terrible time," she said, glad she had been here to defend him but sickened that the ugliness she hoped to escape was here in Nanticoke.

"We turned into skeletons, especially the children," Walsh said. "The company never cared if they reopened the mine. They were more intent on destroying us and the Mollies ..." Walsh shuddered. "I should shut up. They are not to be named."

"The Molly Maguires?"

Walsh's face darkened. "Never speak it aloud, girl."

"It's just us." She motioned to the empty room. She wanted him to confide in her.

If he kept talking, perhaps she could assess if he was haunted by the past or whether the Molly Maguires or other secret vigilante societies had migrated from Ireland and were establishing their terror groups among America's immigrant community in Pennsylvania.

"I remember other names, too, from back in Ireland," she said. "The Ribbonmen, Ancient Order of the Hibernians, Whiteboys. It's true there are horrific working conditions in the mines, but violence and murder only cause more misery. Even so, please tell me none of these groups are around here?"

"The Peep o' Day Boys, one of my favorites," Walsh said, chuckling. Perhaps it was the alcohol kicking in or was he intentionally avoiding answering her?

Johanna gazed past the bar to the entrance hall and lobby. At one time, someone had kept this place nice. Holes in faded fabric revealed stuffing beneath the horsehair sofa, but the dilapidated furniture was still elegant. She guessed that person, probably a woman, was no longer around to talk about the Mollies, and there would be no answers from this man, who was reaching for the bottle.

"Whatever the name, I hate them. I'm sympathetic, truly, but someone I loved died because of the Mollies."

"Sorry for your loss." Walsh poured himself another shot. "A sweetheart?"

"Yes. His name was Thomas." She was a little surprised by the personal question, that this old man had figured it out. Or maybe her love for Thomas was obvious to anyone.

"To your Thomas, and my Mary," Walsh said. He downed the shot.

Johanna took another sip. She felt warm inside for the first time since she'd come to coal country.

"Bad things happen in the dark of night, as the Mollies say," Walsh said. "We Irish with our bitter but, unfortunately, justified grievances."

"Thomas said the mine bosses deserved everything they got."

Johanna couldn't resist the pleasure of talking about him, saying Thomas's name out loud. She thought about Thomas every day, but she could hardly discuss him with Connor. She'd learned to live with the reminders. The most difficult was seeing him in her eldest son, his father's eyes, the same impish smile.

"Oh, he's right. They deserved it, and more. Low pay, black lung—miners go to battle for better working conditions and get only retribution," Walsh said. "Ever hear of that dastardly fellow, James McKenna?"

"The Pinkerton detective?" Johanna said. She wasn't sure she wanted to know any more about the man who sent men to the gallows.

"He was here, at my bar. He'd stop by, stay a few days, win their trust, then he'd disappear. Reporting back to his Pinkerton bosses, he was. He'd buy the Irishmen a round, then gave 'em ideas. They carried out his schemes. What did they get? Arrested, some of them hung."

"He turned them in then?"

"And testified. A stinking spy, he was." Mr. Walsh pounded a fist on the table. "No way McKenna had personally witnessed all those crimes, although he sure set the men up to commit 'em."

Johanna shuddered. Her mother would have said a ghost had walked over her grave.

"I was there, innocent bodies twisting in the wind, hung in public so everyone could watch how long it took 'em to die."

Johanna didn't want to picture Thomas with a noose around his neck, but the image invaded her thoughts. She couldn't will it away.

Walsh stood up and walked across the room, his back to her. "My Mary, skin and bones when she died. That was her apron you put on."

"I'm sorry. I didn't know. I hope I didn't upset you."

"And my son George, he took off," Walsh muttered, steadying himself on the bar.

"I'm so sorry," she whispered.

"Left town a week later, couldn't bear his mother's death. Maybe didn't want to live with me either. I'll never know."

Earlier that morning, Johanna had seen the same defeat in her sons' hunched posture, surrendering to the burdens this world placed on their young shoulders. She put her hand over Walsh's withered one.

He swallowed and cleared his throat. "I guess I could use a bit of help here after all," he said.

"And are you offering me a job?" she said.

"Not much money, but you can get meals and the place could use some sprucing up." He downed his beer. "When can you start?"

## Nanticoke, Pennsylvania, 1882 and
## County Cork, Ireland, 1874

Johanna walked home, unsure whether she should be relieved or terrified. Despite an ocean between herself and the Molly Maguires, would that cowering old man somehow connect her back to the very thing that had ruined her life? She prayed that she wasn't making another mistake like the day, almost a decade ago, when she'd made Thomas her husband. One day later the Molly Maguires lured him back to Ulster.

Bright sunshine had illuminated the haze on the day Johanna linked her fate to Thomas and the Molly Maguires. It was the first warm day of spring, and she decided to become Thomas Michael Flaherty's wife that very afternoon. It was April of 1874. Thomas had returned to Claremorris, County Mayo, from working the mines up north in Ulster. He came south each spring and fall to help with planting and harvest on the family farm. He always stopped to see her before going to his uncle's farm outside of town.

Three years earlier, when she was twenty-one years old, Johanna had met Thomas when she'd picked up their weekly order of provisions. Johanna and Connor grew up on the same street. Connor's parents owned the dry goods store, and he had been her childhood friend and confidant. Eight years old when she was born, he had looked out for Johanna as a toddler and carried her on his shoulders when she was too little to see over crowds at the May Day and Advent festivals. He always saved her extra cheese or a special piece of Irish cream cake from the store. Her sisters teased Johanna that Connor was sweet on her. She had noticed but gave it little thought. When she thought of him, if at all, he was an older brother.

"Good morning, Johanna," he stammered.

"Morning, Connor."

"Your order is all packed up. I bet you want to see the new fabrics that just came in?"

"I was thinking about a new dress for spring."

"Already pulled some bolts out for you, just want to bag up some fertilizer for Frank's nephew." Connor gestured to the handsome russet-haired man standing in the aisle.

"Have you met Thomas? He's getting to be a regular customer."

"Uncle Frank needs the help with spring planting," Thomas lifted a bag of seed to the counter. He had strong shoulders, his chest nearly splitting the buttons of his shirt.

She knew every young man in town but this one. A fringe of his tousled hair dipped over bushy eyebrows, the same wonderful color as his beard. His earnest green eyes drew her. When he flashed a smile, every part of her smiled back.

"Johanna is a close friend of the family," Connor said.

"You're supposed to be my friend. Why did you never tell me about this fetching lass? She may be the most beautiful sight County Cork has to offer."

Johanna flushed.

Connor cleared his throat. "I'll get your order, Thomas. Be right back."

She gathered the parcels Connor had left on the counter. Thomas took a step toward her. It made her jittery, but she hoped he wouldn't move away.

"That's too much for you to carry," Thomas said. "How about I help you?"

"Thank you, I can manage," Johanna said, instantly regretting it. Why hadn't she accepted?

"I didn't say you couldn't manage, but I would like to escort you. How about it? I'm in no hurry, and it's a lovely day for a walk." His baritone was deep, masculine. His hand brushed hers as he picked up the bags. He smiled. She felt a rush of happiness and longing.

"Then, yes, thank you," she said, thrilled with the second chance. She handed him the largest sack.

"But I thought you wanted to look at fabrics?" Connor said, stepping around the counter, his arms loaded with bolts.

"I don't think today," she said, heading for the door.

"I'll come back later, too," Thomas said, holding the door for her.

She looked back. Connor had the strangest look on his face. She felt a little guilty, but his attention could be so annoying. He had no say over her. From that moment, she forgot about Connor and lived for the seasons when Thomas visited Claremorris, which he did frequently over the next three years.

She knew they would marry eventually, but since the famine, all young couples delayed marriage in the interest of survival. Some years, there was enough food; other years, the blight returned. In Catholic homes, getting married usually resulted in a baby nine months later; after that a family might grow to a baker's dozen in as many years.

Johanna was twenty-four and the eldest in a family of nine children. She took care of enough children already, and her parents needed her. Still, there was a limit, she thought, to how much her life could be sacrificed. She did not want children right away, but she did want Thomas. She knew the priest and the Church forbade it, but like Eve, she sought all there was to know. The drawn-out courtship had become intolerable. Although she hinted she was willing, Thomas held out.

Thank goodness for Kathleen. She had been betrothed to Michael for four years and was a veteran of nearly consummated relationships. Johanna asked enough questions that Kathleen, nearly tongue-tied with shame, had confirmed what Johanna suspected. She and Thomas were nearly having relations as it was. Forget that stodgy priest. They might not marry in the Church, but Johanna decided it was time to become one with Thomas in God's eyes.

On that wondrous day in April, they walked to the field behind the woods where they would be undisturbed. She carried a basket with roast chicken, bread, and blackcurrant jam, his favorite. Thomas brought two quilts. They walked past the winter wheat ready for harvest. The earth was renewed, the morning fog evaporating into a pearly mist. The light was magic. Johanna thought relations might happen, despite her priest's admonitions.

She could smell him: leather, castile soap, and some indescribable male scent. He shook out the quilt and spread it over the new plantings. They were pliant and made a soft bed underneath. The stalks around the edge formed a wall, sheltering them from the breeze.

"Here, love, climb under." Thomas pulled a second quilt over them.

"We're a sandwich," she said. He held her close and kissed her. She reveled in the tenderness and then his growing zeal. They stopped to smile at one another. She brushed the tips of her fingers across his beard, burnished red in the sun. His forearms were covered in downy fuzz. She trailed her hand from his wrist and under his rolled-up shirtsleeves.

"We must keep you pure, sweet love," he said, rolling away from her just when she most desired him. "The Church's teachings are clear, and you deserve to walk down the aisle untainted."

Johanna didn't truly see the difference between now and later, and even if God wanted her to be a pure bride, her body desired Thomas. Her resolve over the past winter was formidable, but Thomas seemed to have his own agenda, and it wasn't to seduce her.

"We've really got 'em now, the way we fought—those dirty Orangemen got what they deserved." Thomas sounded almost gleeful. It filled her with dread. He had been determined to prove himself, waiting for an invitation to the secret inner circle. She hoped he wasn't taking foolish risks, but this was not what she wanted to discuss. Not today. This was their opportunity to be alone. Their wedding day. What was taking him so long? She let her hand drop to his thigh.

He looked down, lifted her palm, and pressed it against him. She had his attention, and at last, the Mollies were forgotten. He lifted himself over her, put his weight on his elbows, his head directly above her.

"All I thought about was getting back to you, sweet one."

"How long can you stay?" she asked.

"I just came down to let my uncle know I can't help this spring. I have to go back in the morning," he said.

"No, Thomas, you just got here," Johanna said.

"You must keep it secret, that I got the call from the Mollies," Thomas said. "I have orders."

"You're a vigilante?"

"I wouldn't use that word. And you know I will take care of myself." He planted a kiss on her cheek.

"One day soon you'll come back to Ulster as my wife. And look at you." He nuzzled her. "They will all be so jealous."

He slipped his hand around her waist and cupped her breast. A flurry of energy traveled to a place between her legs that she couldn't name. She was ready for him to be her husband. The act would be the ceremony, this field their marriage bed.

She made him wait as she unbuttoned her blouse, sitting up to force his gaze on her half-naked body. Even with the sun's rays warming her skin, her nipples tightened. He took no time removing his shirt. Skin to skin, silky and intimate, it was glorious to feel nothing between them but the hair on his chest and the warmth of their bodies, his hands under her skirt. He touched her just as she remembered. She pushed his hand away and unbuckled his trousers. The rest of his body lay motionless, his breathing ragged.

"No more waiting," she said. "I take thee, Thomas, as my lawfully wedded husband."

He hesitated and then they gave in to each other.

Of course, she had conceived. How could she not have conceived a child when she was sheltered beneath him, cocooned between the quilts and his body?

Johanna was twenty-five years old. She had never worn a white wedding dress in a church or prepared a meal for Thomas in their own cottage. She had never had the chance to tell him she was expecting a child, nor was she told how he died. As the widow, she should have been informed. She soon learned how naive she'd been to think that a secret marriage in God's eyes was the same as one sanctioned by the Church. She was neither a wife nor a widow as far as anyone knew.

She guessed the Mollies had something to do with her lover's death. If she had understood the true danger, she would have begged Thomas not to go back to Ulster. He'd been so lighthearted, and she hadn't wanted to let those reckless troublemakers disturb their afternoon. How foolish. She felt guilty. She should have paid attention to stories about how each Molly Maguire was required to prove loyalty with action. She learned that what was usually demanded of the new Molly was to "take out" someone they named as an enemy. Something must have gone wrong. Maybe the man Thomas was to kill turned the tables and shot him? Maybe the Ulster police came after him.

There was no explanation, no facts, no reason, no peace. All she knew was one day the parish priest stopped by, just at teatime, as he often did. Johanna boiled water for tea, barely listening to the litany of parish news her mother so enjoyed.

"Oh, course, you've heard the worst of it," the priest said. "The O'Malley family has suffered a terrible loss up in Ulster. One of their eldest was murdered."

"Was it the lovely young man with the reddish beard?" Johanna's mother said.

Johanna held the edge of the table as the room spun around her.

She heard her sister's voice, faint and far away, "I hope not the one sweet on Johanna?"

Johanna couldn't breathe. She passed out, woke later in her own bed. Her mother was sitting next to her.

"You need more sleep. Stay in bed; I'll tell everyone you are ill."

Johanna lay, curled up in ball, trying to understand. The death made no sense and was never real to her. She did not attend a wake, see a body, or meet any of the miners from up north who would have known him or could tell her what happened. She got up the next morning and no one talked of the news or of Thomas. She asked her mother if she had learned more, and her mother simply said, "He's dead—to the world, to us, and to you. There is nothing to speak about."

For weeks, she saw Thomas everywhere: she was sure it was he on the path to town, plowing a field, two pews ahead of her at Sunday Mass. She once ran after a man she saw walking out of a pub because he'd had the same auburn beard and solid build. Reason told her it wasn't Thomas, but in desperation she reached out to touch the man's shoulder. He turned around, ready to pounce, and stopped short. He took one look at her crumpled face and left her alone.

Johanna walked through the first month in shock. She stopped eating, often feeling nauseous and dizzy. Her arms and legs were like sticks. One night, as she struggled into her nightdress, she noticed her round belly. Johanna lay down that night telling herself it wasn't possible, but she knew it was. She prayed Thomas was alive and would come back to her. Her child needed his father.

The next day, her mother sent her to pick up the weekly parcels and she found herself alone with Connor in the store.

"Johanna, it's none of my business," Connor said, loading their order into a box. "But I'm worried about you."

"What do you mean?"

"Since the news of Thomas's death, you haven't been yourself."

"We were … I can't …" Johanna could barely speak.

"Here, sit down." Connor helped her to a bench and sat down next to her.

"I've known you all your life, Johanna," he said. "Something is wrong."

"I just keep thinking, but what if he isn't dead? How do I know for sure?"

"He was in a dangerous place," Connor said. She realized Connor knew, had known.

"But there was no funeral, at least not here," she said. "I just want to know. Do you know anything more? How it happened? Oh, please, tell me anything."

"I don't, I'm sorry. But I can go north, see if I can find out more." And then he whispered, "If I find him, I can force Thomas to come home and do the right thing."

She stared at Connor.

"And if I don't find him, even if there is no proof of his death," Connor said, "will you marry me and give your baby a good name?"

She couldn't read Connor's face entirely, but there was something comforting, knowing he had guessed. She had an ally. She nodded.

Connor returned with a death certificate and the news that a body had washed up in the channel near Ulster the day after Thomas's disappearance. She cried for days. Her father asked if she was ill again; did she need to see the doctor? Johanna said no and managed to drag herself around. On the few occasions she vomited, Johanna made it to the privy and once barely made it behind the barn.

It had been three months since Thomas's death when Johanna woke to find her mother sitting at her bedside. She held a cup of tea and plate of toast.

"Johanna, sit up. Look at me."

Johanna knew what was coming; her mother had guessed. Her mother was more pragmatic than patient. And her daughter was running out of time.

"You must get a hold of yourself. This isn't good for you, or the babe," she said. "Now, drink your tea and eat something. I'll come back later to discuss what's to be done."

Johanna sipped the scalding tea and managed a few bites of toast. The bread scratched her throat as if she were swallowing wire. Her mother, who had long ago trained her to expect a harsh life, returned. She offered little sympathy and instead announced it was time for hardheaded action.

"Thomas's baby can't be born out of wedlock," her mother said. "Shall we send you to the nuns, and they can find a deserving family?"

Johanna could never give Thomas's child away. Connor was as dull as Thomas was charismatic. His brooding had always worn her down, but he had always been kind.

"Connor has asked me to marry him. I will accept the proposal."

She saw the dashed hope in her mother's eyes.

"I prayed you wouldn't have to marry as I did, that your life would be eased with a good match, someone who could take you to a bigger town or earn enough to feed you and the babies well," she said. "Connor may be that man; the family's store does well."

"But I don't love him," Johanna said.

"Johanna, it's the only thing to be done."

When the baby arrived, out of deference to her grief, Connor didn't object to her naming the infant Thomas. In fairness, she added Connor as a middle name on the parish records: Thomas Connor Kennedy. From the beginning, they called the baby TC, obscuring reality with initials.

Supporting a family in Claremorris was difficult. The store barely made enough for Connor's parents and siblings, and now he had to provide for three. Around the time TC started to walk, it was clear they couldn't afford to stay. Connor got a job as an iron worker in Liverpool. Johanna's second baby, Connor's son, came two years later. They named him Johnny after her father. He was born in the Liverpool tenement, far away from her family and friends.

The four of them slept in the same bed to stay warm. Johanna was in the middle next to Connor, the babies against the wall. Her husband, exhausted from iron work, drowned his sorrows in alcohol and passed out. When she wasn't pregnant, nursing a new baby, or taking care of household chores, Johanna lay between her husband and children, dreaming about the lavender smell of her mother's fresh sheets. She could still hear the strum of her father's fiddle; sometimes she hummed "The Wild Rover" and could almost see his dear face.

How she missed Ireland and wished she could share the joy of her beloved sons with her family.

She thought about her mother's soda bread, how the dough, raisins, and caraway seeds tasted so good. She could make her own soda bread when they had money for the raisins, but she could never recreate even one minute with those dearest to her back in County Cork.

Connor's shoulders and upper arms grew thick from his labor. His days next to a blast furnace melted the weight off his body. The longer they were together, the more exhausted and inward he became. They both were committed to the children and to making a better life. Connor worked double shifts. Johanna took in sewing and laundry. It was five years before they saved enough for passage to America.

**New York, New York, 1881**

On the third day of October in 1881, Johanna stood with her husband and sons on the deck as the *City of Rome* sailed into New York Harbor. The night before they docked, she didn't think she could endure the stuffy cabin one more minute. The trip had been harrowing, and she would likely never see her homeland again. When they set foot on American soil, their dream would become real, their decision to leave their home country—unless they came into great wealth—irreversible. Johnny had been deathly ill for most of the three-week voyage, and she still wasn't sure he would fully recover. Maybe they should have waited, not risked so much? Guilty, sad, grieving, she no longer remembered her dreams. Just let her family survive until they made it to dry land.

They packed up and gathered with others on deck to wait their turn to disembark. As the New York skyline took shape in the distance, she remembered the promise of America. She forced herself to banish her doubts. The ship hit the pilings hard, and everyone lost their balance, but it felt good to arrive. She stood close enough to the ship's railings that she could taste the salty drops of spray on her face. The sky was luminous; the sun reflected off the glass in the city's tall buildings. Her children, grandchildren, even great-grandchildren would have better lives.

Steerage passengers were the last to receive clearance. They were moved to a roped-off area closer to the ramp where others had lined up to exit. After more than an hour, an officer moved to their group and began checking off names on his clipboard.

"Connor Kennedy, aged forty, Johanna Kennedy, aged thirty-two, and sons: Thomas, seven, and John, five, free to disembark."

They descended the gangplank and were directed to the Castle Garden immigration center. It was a large stone building that Johanna guessed was a converted warehouse. They would be processed like packaged goods.

Despite the hundreds of people milling around, there was an eerie silence. Even the children were subdued, sensing their parents' apprehension. The chronic misery of frigid weather and rough seas was one thing. This was piercing fear. The inspection ahead could dash their hopes more completely than punishing waves had battered their ship.

Agents reviewed paperwork and doctors examined them: stamp, sign, stack. It took another hour for the family to inch their way toward the exit. In the final booth, a uniformed guard assembled their papers and scrutinized the family. At any moment they might be rejected for poor health or reasons that were never explained. The pitiful creatures not granted entry sat like ghosts on a bench. Johanna saw one woman coughing blood into her handkerchief; others stared vacantly ahead. Authorities would usher the group to a "coffin ship," thus named because many would arrive back home in a coffin. Johanna stifled a scream. They had survived so much. Please, God, don't let them be sent back to die now.

Then, suddenly they were outside. The sunshine gleamed on the masts and railings. Across from the dock were buildings with ornate stonework, like sandcastles in picture books. New construction blossomed beyond the fenced-in area. Throngs of people, horses, and carriages thrummed below the wooden scaffolds.

Johanna gave Connor a grateful smile. He had made this new world possible. He grinned sheepishly. Why couldn't she feel for Connor what had come so easily with the only man who had mattered? Still, she was grateful for Connor. She herded the boys together. In the fresh breeze the boys smelled worse than they had on board ship. She and the three men in her life walked across the wooden slats where the dock kissed land. She wanted to drop to her knees. Saints be praised: America.

## New York to Pennsylvania, 1882

The rooms the Kennedy family shared their first winter in New York were worse than any in Liverpool. Rats crawled through the ceilings. Lethargic children, weak from poor nutrition or illness, were housed in flats in the squalid buildings around them. One morning they woke to screams. The woman upstairs had found her week-old baby cold and stiff.

Johanna would never forget the stench that was worse than on board ship: corned beef, cabbage, and odors from the privy mingled with the smell of unwashed bodies. She washed their few clothes each night, and in the morning, their garments hung stiff from the frigid rafters above their bed.

At first, Connor had found odd jobs, and they had food. At Christmas, the aid society brought them a chicken dinner. But after the new year of 1882, Connor was unable to find work. Some nights, Johanna went to bed hungry so the boys would have enough to eat.

By February, Johanna was at her breaking point, trapped in the cold flat with small boys all day while Connor searched for a job.

Early in February, a letter arrived.

"It's from your Aunt Kathleen," she told the boys, ripping open the envelope and devouring the letter's contents.

"When your da returns we can tell him. We're moving to a new town."

The boys looked at her with empty expressions. How could she expect them to feel anything but dread after the last few months? She, however, was elated that they would leave this filthy tenement. Her dearest friend, someone she could speak honestly with over a cup of hot tea, would be close once again. They would raise their children together and laugh as they always had.

On their last day in New York, she splurged on ice cream for the boys from the hokey pokey man. Connor said, "We barely have enough for the trip."

She insisted. "I just want them to have something nice to remember."

They would take a train to Wilkes-Barre, Pennsylvania, and Kathleen and Michael would pick them up and drive them to their home in Nanticoke. In her letter, Kathleen said she was certain Michael could arrange a job in the coal mine for Connor and help them find somewhere to live.

The boys were wide-eyed as the train pulled out of Grand Central Station. It picked up speed over barren terrain. When they reached the first mountain, the tracks circled upward, and they descended to the valley. They saw farmhouses not much different from the ones they'd left behind in Ireland. Some were painted and well kept. Others had weathered boards, tarpaper roofs, and crumbling foundations.

"Are we there yet?" Johnny asked.

"I don't think so," TC said. "I think the houses get worser and worser."

"It will get better when we get closer to town," Connor said. "Look, lads, there's a slag heap. See it?"

"It looks like a huge pile of animal poop," TC said. "Like from lots of horses."

"Does coal make poop?" Johnny asked.

"Please, Johnny! That is not polite conversation," Johanna said. "Coal is what keeps people warm, and that heap is what is left over. The buildings are collieries, we had them in Ireland, and inside is the equipment they use to mine the coal. The pile is called a culm bank. Some of it is still burning. Your Uncle Michael digs it up inside those mountains. You never met Uncle Michael, or your Aunt Kathleen, but you will like them, and their girls."

"We don't like girls," TC said.

"Yeah, we don't like girls," echoed Johnny.

"You will like these girls," she said. "And have you ever seen twins before?"

"What are twins?" Johnny asked.

"That's when babies look exactly alike and are born on the same day."

"They're the same person?" Johnny asked.

"No, they are different people, but if they are identical twins, it's like one person is looking at their reflection in a mirror."

"Twins are spooky," TC said.

"Give them a chance," Connor said. He turned to Johanna. "I hope it's the right thing, picking up and leaving when we were just getting settled in New York."

"We weren't that settled, Connor. You could never find steady work."

## Wilkes-Barre, Pennsylvania, 1882

Kathleen and Michael Farrell and their daughters were waiting on the platform. Reunited after more than ten years, Kathleen and Johanna laughed, cried, and talked over one another. Michael had always reminded Johanna of a sweet giant, and she felt restored just watching his wide gait as he escorted them to the wagon. Kathleen and Johanna walked arm in arm, and the children followed. Kathleen's older girls jumped ahead, small cyclones of twirling energy.

Michael and Connor sat together in the front seat. The women and children climbed into the back, Johanna, Johnny, and TC across from Kathleen and her four daughters. Molly and Margaret were eleven and ten—"Irish twins," siblings less than one year apart. They were blond and fair. Mara and Maeve were three-year-old identical twins with dark curls like their mother's. They wore matching blue pinafores and pigtails tied in bows.

"It must be hard to not even know which one is which. How do you tell them apart?" TC asked.

"TC!" Johanna said. "That is not something you ask."

"I don't mind, Johanna. It's a good question," Kathleen said. "It takes time, but since none of my girls is sugar and spice and everything nice, you'll learn quickly when something memorable stands out."

"And why don't you girls talk and walk regular?" TC asked.

"TC! Really!" Johanna noticed the girls spoke without a brogue. She wondered if her sons would ever have enough energy to skip and dance the way the girls did. She needed to start teaching the boys manners, but the girls had not taken offense.

"We talk different because we were born here. And we leap because we're Irish dancers. It's practice. Plus, it's fun," Margaret said. "We'll teach you if you like."

"Boys don't dance," TC said.

"Some do, but we won't make you," Molly said. "What do you like to play?"

TC and Johnny did not have time to answer before the barrage of questions came.

"Did you like New York? How tall are the buildings?"

"What did you eat? I bet they have lots of candy."

"Did you get to swim in the ocean on your way from Liverpool?"

"Do they eat liver in Liverpool?"

When the boys did manage a response, the girls would repeat it and laugh.

"What did he say?" Margaret said.

"*Luv*-ly," Molly, the eldest, repeated. "I'm going to talk fancy like that, *luv*-ly."

They fell against one another, hooting. As the wagon bumped along, Margaret pulled a deck of cards, and within minutes, the boys were learning how to play a game called Spit.

TC leaned over to Johanna. "These girls are not like the ones back home. I'm waiting for one of them to start spitting for real."

They left the train station and drove through the bustling town of Wilkes-Barre and then on to open country scattered with farms. There were smaller homes, closer together, when they got to the outskirts of Nanticoke, and then more substantial ones in the city. They turned on Main Street and drove by the Catholic church. A brick Gothic Revival building with a bell tower, it was the largest structure in town. The front door came to a peak, like a pope's hat, with stained glass windows flanking either side.

"We only could afford stained glass in the front, but one day we'll have color on all of the windows," Kathleen said. "We have a building fund."

There was a low structure behind the church.

"Is that the school?" Johanna shifted so she could see it better.

"Right, and the convent is next door." Kathleen pointed to a large brick house.

Johanna imagined the sisters welcoming her boys to class and felt a flutter of optimism.

"We have a general store, a drug store, and see there?" Kathleen indicated a two-foot trench around an empty lot. "The town is hoping to attract bigger national stores. Maybe a company will come and build one of those new five-and-dimes."

Johanna had seen a five-and-dime store in New York but hadn't gone inside. Before she could ask more, Kathleen pointed in another direction.

"And there's the town's only hotel; there are rooming houses too."

"This town is growing. You and Michael picked a wonderful place," Johanna said. "Thank you for making it possible for us to come here."

"We couldn't wait for you to arrive," Kathleen said.

Johanna felt happy for the first time in years. Her boys would soon be as cheerful and bright as these girls and would grow up in a town with a church, a school, and a community.

## Nanticoke, Pennsylvania, 1882

Michael stopped the wagon in front of a yellow clapboard house.

"Welcome to Nanticoke, your new home," he shouted back to them. "The Sullivans have two rooms for you upstairs, and you can use the kitchen."

Johanna looked up a long flight of stairs to the yellow Victorian home with a wraparound porch. It would be lovely to sit on a rocking chair there when the weather got warm. Johnny was full of pent-up energy and already halfway up the stairs. She kept her eye on him. He wasn't used to such a steep rise. Midway, he stopped in his tracks and pointed. There was a boy at the top of the staircase. He looked exactly like TC, in different clothes. Johnny spun around to see if his brother had somehow gotten ahead of him, but TC was right next to Johanna.

"Ma, who is that kid?" Johnny said, gesturing to the boy.

"Hush, Johnny." Johanna turned to her husband with alarm. "Connor, do you see that child?"

"Johanna, a lot of Irish kids look alike," Connor said, but he didn't look as serene as he sounded.

"Is TC a twin, too?" Margaret asked.

"Hush, Margaret," Kathleen said.

There was a plump man waiting on the porch. The woman next to him was as thin as he was round. Her expression was grim, but the man smiled.

"What a fine family, just as Michael and Kathleen said you would be. Welcome to the Sullivan home." He shook Connor's hand. "Call me Fred. This is my wife, Fiona, and my grandson, Finn. His ma, Bridget, will be home soon."

"Morning," Connor said, putting his arm around Johanna. "This is my wife, Johanna, and these are our lads, Thomas Connor—we call him TC—and Johnny."

"Ah, Johanna," the man said, "I only just learned that you might know Finn's mother, Bridget. You're from Claremorris in County Mayo? We lived one town over, in Killeenfarna,"

"Of course, just east of us," Johanna forced herself to sound normal while her mind raced to clarify what was in front of her eyes. This boy looked as much like Thomas as did TC. She was distracted, watching TC from the corner of her eye. His eyes were locked on Finn, his hands clenched into fists so tight that his knuckles bulged. She knew he could throw a mean punch. The first few weeks in New York, TC had scuffled with some of the boys, especially when they teased Johnny. TC's body looked ready to spring right now.

"Indeed. Bridget's a widow, sad to say, here with this little lad. His father died, up in Ulster, right before our Finn was born. Johanna, you might have known him, Thomas Flaherty?" Mr. Sullivan looked expectantly at Johanna.

"I'm sorry. What did you say?" Johanna said, her heartbeat pulsing in her ears.

"Maybe not," Mr. Sullivan said. "Finn's da wasn't around much, worked north in the mines. But enough of the past—a bad business. How 'bout these two lads. Look at 'em, peas in the pod."

Johanna put her hand to her mouth, to stifle a sob, but then she let out a scream when she saw Finn sailing past her.

"Nobody gets to look like me but me!" Finn yelled. "You stole my face."

A dusty orb of fists and feet tumbled on the porch. TC landed on top of Finn, pulled his fist back, and drove his knuckles into Finn's face. Blood spurted from Finn's eye socket.

"Oh my God," Finn's scrawny grandmother screamed. "Do something, Fred."

Connor and Michael yanked the boys to their feet, pulling them apart. Mrs. Sullivan took off her sweater and pressed it over Finn's eye. "How could you let your ruffian light into my sweet grandson?"

"Calm down, Fiona," Mr. Sullivan said. "Take him inside, boy needs to toughen up."

Johanna watched his grandmother hustle Finn—blood dripping between fingers cupped over his eye—into the house. She went to TC, scolding him and checking for injury simultaneously. The Farrell girls were silent for the first time that afternoon.

"Apologies, folks. Boy bleeds like a pig," Mr. Sullivan said. "His grandmother will fix him up. Let's get you folks settled."

TC didn't appear to be injured. Johnny looked terrified. Connor was without expression. Johanna would sort this out when she was alone. For now, she just wanted to get her family upstairs.

Kathleen put her arm around Johanna. They followed Mr. Sullivan into the house and she whispered. "It's not possible. Could Thomas be that boy's father, too?"

"I can't think about it now." Johanna had to admit the boys were spitting images of one another.

"Right. Let's get you settled. I brought provisions." Kathleen handed her a basket.

"Thank you," Johanna said. "I'm not sure there will be a place for us at the Sullivan table tonight."

"Ah, Johanna, you're here. That's what matters," Kathleen said.

The Farrells left after a short tour of their two rooms. Johanna told the boys they would have an indoor picnic, silently thanking her friend for bringing them more than enough to eat. Later, when she tucked the boys in, Johnny said, "I like having an Aunt Kathleen. Do they get chicken, biscuits, jam, and pie all the time?"

"This was Kathleen's way of welcoming us, and it was special. There may not always be so much delicious food, but we won't be hungry here," she said, hoping she was right.

"And TC didn't mean to beat up on that kid, but he was making faces at us."

"I didn't realize," Johanna said. "But still, TC, it is always best to use words, not fists."

TC said, "Sorry, Ma. I just didn't like that kid sticking his tongue out at us."

"We'll talk more tomorrow," she said. "Get some sleep."

She left the door to the boy's room slightly ajar. Connor was staring out the window. It was dark outside, so Connor was actually feigning interest in a black rectangle.

She put her hand on his shoulder, "I didn't know that Bridget even had a child."

"I guess we won't be eating downstairs now that TC nearly took out Finn's eye," Connor said.

Johanna was barely able to make out his expression.

"How well did you know this Bridget?"

"Not well. She lived near, but we weren't at the same parish school."

"You may not have spent much time with her," Connor spoke with a throaty voice, "but Thomas certainly knew her well."

Johanna couldn't think. She needed time to consider.

"I'm not saying anything more than what's plain as day," he said. "You were his virgin, Bridget his whore. You know, the bad girl he visited late at night, after he took you home."

She remembered Thomas insisting she stay pure. She often wondered at his restraint. She now had a clue.

"Kathleen must have known about this," Connor said.

"But she'd never laid eyes on TC until today," Johanna said. "You can't blame her."

"There's somebody I can blame. He should have kept it buttoned up," Connor said. "Or you could have managed to hold your legs together."

Connor turned away from her. Johanna's entire body hurt.

She waited, and when he said nothing, she went to the wardrobe. She disrobed to her chemise. She doused water on her face, took a nightgown from their bags. She pulled the garment over her head and slid out of her undergarments. She decided to sleep in the boys' room. Before she pushed the door open, she heard their voices.

"Are Ma and Da mad or something?" Johnny said.

"I guess they don't like me looking like Finn."

So, her sons were trying to figure it out, too. What could she possibly tell them?

"Maybe Finn is my twin?" TC said.

"You mean Ma had two babies at the same time and they look exactly alike?" Johnny

said. "But then Finn would live with us."

"Ma always says we should share," TC said. "Maybe her friend wanted a baby, and Ma gave away the extra?"

"Ma would never do that," Johnny argued. "If Ma had only wanted one babe, why did she get me?"

"I have no idea," TC mumbled. "Go to sleep."

"Ma would never give away her own baby, TC," Johnny said. "Never."

Johanna rested her head against the doorjamb. She heard Connor lay down on their bed. A few minutes later, she listened as his snorts grew farther apart and then became the regular snores that came with sleep. The boys were sleeping too. She carefully climbed between them in bed. The moon was high, flooding the room with silver-white light. She gazed at TC's long fringe of eyelashes, at Johnny's mouth wrapped around his thumb. She pulled her legs up, stretching the nightgown over ice-cold feet. Even with her knees tight against her chest, nothing shielded her from the jagged sorrow lodged in her chest.

Johanna never got the opportunity to sit on the Sullivans' porch shelling peas in a summer breeze. The families avoided each other. When the boys did run into one another, they snarled. Finn provoked TC, she saw it, but TC should have ignored the taunts. Instead, there were pranks and name calling. It got uglier, and Johanna suspected that some of Finn's anger was fueled by Bridget, who clearly hated whatever the boy's identical appearance revealed.

Johanna was confident that Thomas had loved her but was puzzled over the paternity. It appeared Thomas had fathered Finn—what other explanation could there be? Perhaps a distant look-alike cousin had been with Bridget? Unlikely. The most obvious was that Thomas had slept with Bridget. But Johanna knew he loved her. Was Bridget the "fallen girl" he visited for release after time with Johanna?

She didn't want to confront Bridget and supposed Bridget felt the same way. She used the kitchen when it was likely to be vacant. If the Sullivan women did find her at the sink, they stood in irritated silence until she left the room. She often abandoned a task or left food uncooked rather than risk their displeasure. Two weeks into their stay, Johanna was up early, working fast to get last night's supper dishes washed before the household awoke. Mr. Sullivan walked in.

"Johanna, I've been looking to have a word."

She steeled herself.

"It's not working. Keeping these two boys apart is wearing us out. Bridget and my wife won't give me a minute's peace neither," he said. "You'll have to find another place. I'm sorry."

Johanna would be glad to leave but was terrified. They would be homeless.

In an odd twist of luck, that same day Connor—who had had only sporadic work—was offered a job in backup relief at the mine, making them eligible for a miner's shack at the edge of town.

Johanna tried to be grateful for a roof over their heads and means to put food on the table, but she was incensed that things had gotten so bad. Over the next few weeks, Connor was increasingly morose, and she stopped counting how many pints he drank. He passed out at night, and morning headaches kept him from getting up early enough to stand in the pool of men waiting for a backup position. Then the mine boss offered the boys jobs as breaker boys. Now her sons were tending a conveyor belt where coal, and their futures, bleakly rolled past them.

# CHAPTER THREE

# MAI LING

**Philadelphia, Pennsylvania, Winter 1880**

Since witnessing the railroad unite the country at Promontory, Utah, En had spent nearly a decade traveling the Western Territory. He collected odd jobs, and when he could, doctored destitute patients in need of his care. They usually had little ability to pay. He never found a town where a Chinese physician could earn enough to establish roots. Even places that had a significant Chinese population eventually drove the Railroad Chinese, as they were called, and their doctor, away. En heard that East Coast Chinatowns were growing, and early in 1880—a little over twenty years after he had taken his first steps on California soil—he stepped off the train to the wooden platform at Philadelphia's Broad Street Station.

Philadelphia could just be his land of opportunity, and if not, he might travel north to Nanticoke and find Michael. En was desperate for a job but reluctant to trust any white man—even Michael. Their correspondence had diminished to a few letters each year. In his last letter, Michael reported that he and Kathleen were expecting another child. En had lost track of how many babies they had, but he was certain it wasn't the best time for him to intrude. If he showed up at Michael's doorstep, even if Michael wanted to help En, how would his wife feel about it? En decided to look for work among the Chinese community and seek Michael's help only as a last resort.

The crowd outside of the station throbbed with the energy of the city. He walked down an alley lined with crates of whiskey, labeled barrels of molasses, burlap bags of grain, bales of hay, and boxes of oranges. On the next street he saw vendors, men pushing luggage carts. Groups of people hurried by—some well-dressed, others down on their luck. He walked down a block and spotted two Chinese men, who appeared to be father and son, sitting on their haunches and smoking cigarettes in an alley. En could hear enough of their conversation to judge their dialect to be similar enough to his own that he might speak with them.

En held up a hand. "Can you direct me to Chinatown, or perhaps suggest where I might inquire about a job?"

The men looked at one another, cigarettes dangling, and then eyed him critically. "What kind of job?"

"I was on the crew that built the railroad," En said, noting they remained disinterested. "And I know how to set up explosives."

The older one had a long black queue and said, "Ha, not much for Chinese coming from the railroad. Maybe some construction."

"He is too soft," the son said. "You sure you had a railroad job? Seems like you should do something with your brain."

"I am also an acupuncturist and bonesetter."

"Well," the younger man snuffed out his cigarette, "General might be interested."

"General is a tough bird, son," the father said.

"Working for the General is better than starving."

"Who is this General?" En asked.

"We call him Běnshuài."

En now understood; they were using the Chinese word for general.

"But take care. You do not want to cross the Běnshuài. He is powerful like a lion. He eats the heads of men who anger him."

"Thank you for the warning," En said. "You think he may have work for me?"

"You can go ask. He isn't far from here."

They made a crude map for En on the back of a newspaper. En followed their directions down an alley and through streets of row houses. As he got farther from the railroad station, the crowds thinned. He knew he was in Chinatown when he saw red lanterns and yellow silk banners waving in the gentle breeze. He could smell the ginger, garlic and five-spice of the Peking Duck, hanging in the restaurant windows.

En found his way to a brownstone where several Chinese men stood guard in front of huge mahogany doors. The double doors had opaque leaded glass and ornate brass fixtures that belonged on a castle. En stated his business and waited only a few minutes before they ushered him up the stairs and into the front parlor.

En was prepared for an imposing figure. Instead, the Běnshuài was a shrinking man with hollow cheeks and wispy hair. He sat in a thronelike chair, surrounded by lacquered furniture, vases, and terracotta pottery. He was dressed entirely in Chinese clothing, from his mandarin collar to the type of silk slippers that En had abandoned before leaving China. The Běnshuài's head was perched like an egg on his slight neck, and small hands rested on the chair's carved lion-head arms. He could have been a little boy playing grown-up except for his impressive facial hair: two tapered tendrils extended past his jawline in a drooping moustache.

"I understand your family name is Chang, and you are the eldest, En?"

"I am," En answered, wondering how the Běnshuài knew so much about him. He had not spoken in any detail to anyone since he'd entered the room.

"And how is your family? Ai, An, and Ji must be grown now," the Běnshuài said. "Are they living in California?"

How did this man know these things? Before En could answer, the Běnshuài bounded toward him.

"En, it's me. It's Woo. Do you not know me? It is wonderful that we have found each other in the land of gold, is it not?"

Woo's body was gaunt, although he had gained height since they'd parted. He squeezed En to him with such enthusiasm that En worried Woo might shatter.

"Clear the room," Woo said. The court of the Běnshuài scattered.

When they were alone, Woo gestured for En to sit beside him on one of the lacquered chairs.

"I am pleased to see that you are strong, my friend. Look at those shoulders," Woo said. "Have you worked as a laborer?"

"Yes, on the railroad."

"And what of the medicine your parents taught you?"

"I did treat the miners in the camp for a time."

"And since then? Have you found fortune?"

En was ashamed to say that he'd been living hand to mouth since the railroad.

Woo put his hand on En's. "You've had troubles, my brother?"

En described what led him to Philadelphia. Woo's lip trembled when he learned about the deaths of En's parents and siblings. He seemed delighted with tales from En's experience out West and his return to medicine because of the explosion that had injured Michael. Woo was outraged when En told him of the hatred he had encountered more recently.

"You have worked too hard to be cast off," Woo said.

En had not cried since the night his mother died. Now, Woo's compassion unlocked the grief En had carried with him since San Francisco. En's eyes burned, and he wiped tears away.

"Woo, you always told me we would meet again," En said, smiling into the wizened face. "And here we are."

"I know, my friend," Woo put his arm over En's shoulder. "Your mother and father were the closest I ever got to having parents. I am devastated about the little ones, too."

"The last time I spoke of them, I was with a friend at the railroad camp," En recalled the conversations he and Michael had had about the loss of their family members. En had known so much indifference and remembering Michael's compassion made him want to cry. He saw the same deep empathy in Woo's eyes.

"You have been alone too long, but we have found each other," Woo said, his smile spreading into the wide grin En remembered. "You once welcomed me when I was discarded, thrown in a ship's hold. Now I am honored, and our community is humbled, to welcome you."

"Thank you, Woo," En said, breathing deeply to regain his composure.

Woo called in a servant. "Please tell First Wife that we have a guest for dinner."

On the way to the dining room, Woo pulled En aside. "Of course, when we are alone, I am always Woo to you, my oldest and dearest friend, but please, once we are joined by others, you will call me Běnshuài." He took En's arm at the elbow. "Come. Let's eat."

The Běnshuài's wife, walking on hesitant feet, served each dim sum course personally. Over the best pork dumplings En had ever tasted, the Běnshuài told En of how he rose in the ranks of the Chinese community in Philadelphia. The same charismatic energy and grit that had drawn the orphan to En's family on board ship had connected him to the powerful in Chinatown. En had heard a lot about the criminal element in the city. Prostitution, opium, and bribery were all sensationalized in the newspapers. En recalled seeing two heavily made-up women wearing the checkered cotton head covering of fallen women, just a few blocks from the Běnshuài's home. He hoped Woo wasn't caught up in any of that. It was obvious that Woo was cunning, but immigrants needed shrewd leaders to protect them. Woo had too much integrity to be ruthless. His success was undoubtedly fueled by his charisma, not crimes.

After they ate, the Běnshuài lit his pipe and, through a billow of smoke, said, "You are my most revered friend. I am honored to have you among us and proud of your accomplishments, despite—or perhaps especially because of—your resilience. Wife, this man needs more rice wine."

"Yes, Běnshuài."

First Wife scuffled to fill En's glass. She was one of several people who jumped to anticipate the Běnshuài's every need. En could tell by the demeanor of each person in this house that his friend was both revered and feared. En doubted he would ever call him Woo again.

"Tell me, En, have you considered further developing the medical practices your parents taught you?"

"I have experience only with the illnesses and injuries of a work camp," En said. "As for treating disease, my parents were well-meaning, but acupuncture and bonesetting did nothing to prevent their deaths or those of my siblings."

"Ah, but your parents saved me, and what of your friend from the railroad explosion?" the Běnshuài said. "The man who now lives in the town Nanticoke?"

"The Western medicines at the camp did help," En said.

"En, think how formidable it could be to bring Eastern and Western ways together?"

"I did offer patients both acupuncture and bonesetting, and my parents brought me here to learn the ways of this country's medicine, but it was difficult, both to have access to Western treatments, and then to make a living. Most patients want one or the other."

"And I know work for Chinese laborers has dried up in these last years," Woo twisted his moustache. "There is no wife, no family?"

"No." En felt too defeated to explain, and then thought it was likely Woo knew exactly the problem that existed of too many Chinese men and very few Chinese women of marriageable age in America.

"Our community needs doctors. I will investigate training. There are a number of medical schools in the city. But you must be tired. We will talk again in the morning,"

The Běnshuài stood up and motioned to a servant. "Find my friend a place to sleep for tonight."

He put his hands on En's shoulders. "Our ancestors sent you to us, and I have not forgotten the kindness of the Chang family. I will have some answers by tomorrow."

En was escorted to a room on the third floor. Several young men who functioned as the Běnshuài's bodyguards were preparing bedrolls. They were silent, but not unfriendly, and gave En a mat and blanket.

En lay in the dark. Alone. En defined himself as a man who'd grown up in a clan, yet he'd had no family for years. Woo, without blood relatives, was now leading a tribe. En had no community and no longer practiced the religious rituals of his ancestors. He had celebrated Chinese festivals with other Chinese in the railroad camp, but that sense of belonging been fleeting.

There had never been enough money for professional mourners or funeral banquets when his parents and siblings died. He could not clear nonexistent graves or bring paper money, food, or other artifacts of worldly life his ancestors might need now. He had not maintained memorial tablets or altars to his ancestors. The spiritual ritual his mother practiced died with her. He wished he could take comfort in her faith but could not. He had learned on the railroad that exhaustion was the best way to numb his pain. Finding Woo, the grief he had pushed away invaded his soul. Talking about his parents and siblings made their deaths immediate.

En had not felt such visceral anguish since the day his grandmother, Nai Nai, died. He could still feel her, lying next to him on the ship's bunk. He had fallen asleep and was supposed to keep her warm. Instead, he woke to his grandmother's unyielding body. He remembered his father rolling her up in the blanket and putting her body with the other corpses in the corner of the hold. He did not see the sailors pitch her over the ship's gunwales, but he could imagine how cold she would be, plunged into the frigid ocean waters wrapped in only thin wool. He had sobbed for days. En wasn't sure if it was a memory or if his father's spirit was there in the room with him, but he heard Tan's stern voice, "Stop it. You loved Nai Nai. You were special to her. She believed you would grow up to be a man who did great things. She spoiled you, never scolding, always smiling. But she would not smile now. She would be ashamed of your tears. Your mother and I admonish you. Don't cry. It is over. Take this opportunity."

Hearing his father's voice, he willed self-control. It was bad enough Woo had recognized his weakness. He didn't want the men sleeping near him to suspect. He pulled his blanket around himself, grateful his journey today had been exhausting. Sleep came like a drug.

The bodyguards shared tea and biscuits with him the next morning.

"We have to work," one said. "You wait here until the Běnshuài sends for you."

A few minutes later, a young girl brought En a bright blue bowl, inside of which was what his mother used to call a "bird's nest" breakfast: an egg centered on a piece of toast. The dazzling yoke dripped bright yellow liquid, soaking the bread, and the richness of this simple meal felt like a good omen. En was overwhelmed with gratitude, and this time, he turned from the girl to brush away tears.

"Thank you," he said, "and is there anywhere I might wash clothes?"

Without comment, she gathered his dirty garments and left the room. She returned minutes later with a stack of fresh clothing, a razor, soap, and a bowl of water.

En took time savoring the egg, toast, and hot tea. Nothing had ever tasted so good. The razor was sharp, and the soap smelled of spice. The Western clothes she brought for him took some time to sort out, but he managed to put on the shirt, vest, and pants to the best of his ability.

He was just buckling the belt when one of the guards entered.

"The Běnshuài will see you now."

En was ushered ahead of petitioners waiting outside the Běnshuài's chamber.

"Good morning, my friend," the Běnshuài said. He looked less sallow this morning. "I hope you slept and ate well."

"I did. Thank you, Běnshuài," En said.

"You are to work at a nearby hospital under the direction of a Dr. Theodore Cobb. He will enroll you in the medical school as well. The school has graduated a few students from around the world, including a woman from India, her training justified because she would return to care for her own kind."

En was stunned with the speed of the Běnshuài's effectiveness, and like others, found himself under the Běnshuài's spell. He happily relinquished decision making; it would be a relief to be told what to do. As he left the residence with a young guard who had been instructed to make sure En found the hospital, En felt lighter, with a new sense of purpose.

They wove through the early morning crowd. A scrawny newspaper boy shouted, "Extra! Extra!"

En's escort walked fast and through puddles. He ducked through the crowds to avoid the mud but could not escape the sludge that splattered up from horses and carriage wheels. The animals urinated in the gutters and left steaming piles of excrement in their wake, just like out West.

At the hospital, brick pillars supported a massive portico, bell tower, and steeple. He climbed thirty steps into an immense lobby. There was a catwalk under a row of windows circling the domed ceiling. Pale gold light streamed through the glass, illuminating the waiting area below.

There was something hopeful about his first hours in the Philadelphia hospital. The giant reception hall inspired En. A large painting hung above the reception desk with a plaque that read, "Christ Healing the Sick in the Temple, by Benjamin West." The picture brought back fond memories of his childhood. When his family had settled in San Francisco, they had insisted En learn to read and write English. Nuns offered after-school classes to Chinese children to expose Celestials to the doctrine of Christianity. En had been an excellent student; his father believed in the Chinese tradition of scholarship, and the more praise En received from the sisters—who were delighted to save the heathen children—the harder he worked. He could read well and was fluent in English within a year of starting school. En had been especially attentive to the stories about Jesus healing the sick because his parents were healers too. En dreamed of doing the same when he grew up.

He gazed at the painting. It portrayed a bearded man who reminded him of the Irish laborers on the railroad. The Irish-looking Jesus was surrounded by a crowd. Several extended their arms, others knelt, and a few supported a figure too weak to walk. En had all day to examine the picture while a long-suffering receptionist studied him. Occasionally, she flashed him an embarrassed smile and said, "I have told Dr. Cobb you are here. I don't know what is keeping him."

In the late afternoon, she escorted En to an office. A hunched man, wearing a long white coat, sat behind a desk. He stared at En for a long minute, then motioned En forward, as if shooing a fly.

"Don't bother to sit."

En saw right away this doctor had no intention of offering him access to these hallowed halls.

"You are Asian? Chinese? Japanese?" Dr. Cobb put his hands in his pockets and scowled. "Doesn't matter. We can only teach just so many of your kind."

"I see," En said. "But the Běnshuài …"

"I don't want to hear about that criminal," Dr. Cobb said. "It's his kind who are ruining our town with drugs and luring our good white women to God knows what. I've treated some of those whores."

He shot a stream of tobacco into a copper pot under the desk. "Now, you get out and don't come back. And tell the Běnshuài we don't contaminate this hospital with the dregs of Philadelphia."

En got himself out of the room, down the corridor, through the reception area, and away from the building. He found his way back to the Běnshuài's brownstone. The guards seemed to expect him and pointed to the same parlor from yesterday, then pushed him through the threshold and shut the door behind him. The Běnshuài was alone in the room, in his chair, with his eyes closed. In repose, the exhausted face was no longer masked by a magnetic personality. He resembled the waif En had befriended years ago. En turned to leave. Through closed eyes, the Běnshuài said, "Tell me, En, how was your first day?"

En recounted his experience. When En finished the tale, the Běnshuài sat up. Above the moustache and clean-shaven upper lip, his eyes burned with rage.

"Go. Have a meal. Rest," the Běnshuài said. "We will speak again tomorrow."

"Perhaps there is somewhere else I can be of service?" En offered.

"No, just go, eat and rest. We'll talk in the morning."

En relished the steamed buns with meat, sharing a long table with the other servants in the kitchen. He declined a pipe.

"Not opium, tobacco," the man who held it out said, but En refused a second time. He was longing for sleep to spare him from reliving the day's humiliation. Only that morning, he'd felt so much hope. Now he would never walk the path that enabled him to continue his parents' legacy. What value did he bring to the world? Would anyone ever need him? Why go back to China, when there was nothing left for him there? If the Běnshuài couldn't help him, what other option did he have?

He was called to the Běnshuài's parlor early the next morning. The Běnshuài was surrounded by a circle of lieutenants and motioned En forward.

"We are in conference. I can't talk at length," the Běnshuài said. "My instructions are for you return to the hospital."

"But the doctor I met with yesterday was clear."

"Don't." The Běnshuài's face clouded with irritation. "Never contradict me, En. We have been friends, but now I am your Běnshuài, too. Do as I say."

En navigated the onslaught of rushing pedestrians, animals, carriages, and filth for a second day. He was by himself this time. When he entered the lobby, the same receptionist pointed to a man in a long white coat waiting for him. En looked up at the portrait of Jesus and wondered if this was some sort of miracle.

"You must be Mr. Chang." The doctor took En's elbow. He was younger than Dr. Cobb, with pockmarked skin and straight hair slicked back from an ample forehead. "I'm Dr. William Reynolds, the newly appointed director of the surgery training program."

"Good morning," En said.

"First, I hope you will give my best to the Běnshuài," Dr. Reynolds said. "He requested that I resolve yesterday's mix-up personally."

Dr. Reynolds escorted En down a corridor and opened the door to a cramped, windowless room. Small desks lined the perimeter.

Young men in short white coats were reading, a few stood together in a corner. One was clearing out a drawer. He tossed the last of his belongings in a box. He gave En a hard look and left the room.

"These are for you." Dr. Reynolds gestured toward a white coat, stethoscope, and textbooks that remained on the desk. "We have grand rounds, where physicians go to each patient's bed to discuss cases, at noon. Be there."

Dr. Reynolds then addressed the medical students.

"This is En Chang. He is a distinguished practitioner of Chinese medicine, here to learn about our medical practice so he can serve his fellow Chinese." Dr. Reynolds narrowed his eyes. "I expect you will make him welcome."

The doctors in training were silent.

"I will take a personal interest if Mr. Chang experiences any difficulties," he said. "He is under my protection. Pugh, show him the ropes."

The young man named Pugh looked relieved when he learned En could speak English. He handed En a short white coat and a stethoscope.

"Keep it in your pocket," Pugh told him. "It goes around your neck once you are approved to see patients."

He then explained the location of classrooms and laboratories and made sure En got to grand rounds. After that, Pugh and his colleagues didn't acknowledge En unless they were required to do so as part of a class assignment.

En's first week flew by: classes, observing surgeries, bedside conferences, and rounds morning and evening. En stood in the back and remained silent. On Friday, Dr. Reynolds pulled him out of rounds.

"En, you did well, and I hope no one gave you trouble."

En could answer truthfully that no one paid him any attention at all.

"We won't have you with patients right away. The hospital doesn't treat Chinese, but we'll find some for you to see. You may be excused from clinic on Friday afternoons while I sort out a clinic where we can get you into a practicum."

En nodded.

"Perhaps it's best that you let the Běnshuài know this is not part of formal curriculum until second year, so you will not fall behind. We might even set up a clinic in Chinatown." Dr. Reynolds seemed nervous and added, "Tell him I will stop by next week to ascertain his preference."

On his way home, En stopped by a market. He used the last of his money to purchase a large fish and a basket of vegetables and fruit for his benefactor. Had the Běnshuài enough power to put Dr. Reynolds in charge and reverse his fortune? And what of Dr. Cobb? En had not seen him all week. What kind of power did the Běnshuài wield? And at what price? En bought a newspaper from a boy on the corner and found a story on opium wars. It detailed the prostitution and murders linked to Chinatown. There was no mention of his old friend, either as Woo or the Běnshuài. En couldn't imagine him getting involved in anything that sordid or wrong. Perhaps this was just an occasion when Dr. Reynolds owed a favor, or perhaps Cobb's rapid exit was a coincidence.

En reassured himself that the Běnshuài was an honorable man. He had seen no evidence to the contrary. Of course, he did see homeless people—likely addicts—stumbling around near the market, but what city didn't have drugs or houses of ill repute? The Běnshuài had guards, but legitimate businesses required security.

He turned the corner. There was a line of Chinese men, women, and children snaking past the brownstone and around the block. Surely the Běnshuài was not all that influential in Philadelphia? But the crowd looked like half of Chinatown was waiting for an audience.

"Fridays are nights anyone can make a request," a lieutenant at the door said. "But Běnshuài left word that you are to go up immediately."

En argued with himself as he followed the guard. He had to admit the Běnshuài's influence and authority might be derived from more than charity work, but the man did care about these people. The

Běnshuài wanted En to be trained to serve the Chinese community. They might let a few select Celestials or Indians into the school—mostly young students with powerful and wealthy parents from these countries—but hospitals and physicians in America simply did not admit or treat people with brown skin. Too many died or suffered from injury or illness with no one to care for them and with nowhere to go. The community needed a physician, that had to be it.


The Běnshuài's moustache was freshly trimmed and waxed. His feet were propped up on two silk pillows, his small hands folded in his lap. He was surrounded by staff, family, and a flock of supplicants.

"Ah, it is Dr. Chang," the Běnshuài said, and his eyes brightened.

"Not quite a doctor yet, Běnshuài."

"Please, come in. I hear Dr. Reynolds has found a place for you. A shame about that other man. Cane? Corn? Cobb? Some kind of food name."

"Yes, Cobb, I believe, sir."

"Ah, Cobb, that's right. Run into him again?"

"I haven't seen Dr. Cobb since that first day."

The smile that flashed across the Běnshuài's face reminded En of occasions when his old friend bested him at games.

"That is as it should be. And are things going well?"

"Yes, they have been most welcoming, quite different from that first day, after your intervention." En placed the basket before him. "I am grateful for your hospitality."

"I did nothing. A simple mistake was corrected." The Běnshuài signaled a minion to remove the gift. "This was not necessary but appreciated. We do need to discuss your living arrangements, and then I must see to my people. The line is long today."

"I have intruded on your hospitality," En said. "Dr. Reynolds tells me I'll be receiving a stipend; I plan on renting a room."

The Běnshuài motioned to another servant. A set of keys was produced.

"Wise men think alike." The Běnshuài handed the keys to En. "This flat is near the hospital. I'm told it's small but comfortable."

"How much is the rent?"

"There is no rent. This is a gift."

"But I cannot accept any more from you."

"I insist, and remember, you are not to contradict me." The Běnshuài grinned.

"Then I hope to be of service in the future," En said.

"You can be of service now." The Běnshuài nodded to his wife. She was standing next to a reed-thin boy. En looked closely and realized the figure was a woman. Her head was bowed so he couldn't see her face. Her sleek black hair was twisted in a bun and covered with a beaded headdress that shimmered when she stepped forward. Thick eyelashes curved into black crescents on her flawless skin, her features so perfect she reminded him of a porcelain doll.

"En, meet Mai Ling," the Běnshuài said. "She, like you, has found herself with no one and no place to stay."

En was silent.

"Yes, you see my meaning," the Běnshuài said. "Mai Ling would make an excellent housekeeper and cook for now, and perhaps you would consider making her your wife at some time in the future?"

En was at a loss. There were few women available to a Chinese man, even in Chinatown. While he had wondered if he might find a woman in this community, medical school was his priority. He didn't wish to take a wife until he was secure, and this woman was practically a child, and a stranger. Still, the Běnshuài had made his future possible. Was refusing an option?

"Of course, my friend, you may do as you wish," the Běnshuài said. En was always amazed at his friend's capacity to read minds.

The Běnshuài gestured for Mai Ling to approach.

"Perhaps Mai Ling can help you move your things to the flat? She can assist you in the next few days, and then we'll see."

Speaking Chinese in a dialect that En did not understand, the Běnshuài gave Mai Ling instructions. En understood almost nothing that was said until she glided toward En. He felt a gentle pressure on his arm and understood he was to go with her.

"I am honored, but I am not prepared to take on …" En said.

"I understand completely. She will serve you only. That gives you more time for your studies. No obligation, but it does allow me a temporary solution for you both."

"I see," En said, feeling like he was a problem to be solved. "Thank you."

"And as to taking a wife, there are pleasures to be had with the female of our species." He smiled again. "This one is small breasted, and the narrow hips will make child-bearing strenuous." The Běnshuài took a minute to study Mai Ling's body. "She may not attract you now, but it is said that with time and patience, the mulberry leaf becomes a silk gown."

En allowed the woman-girl to lead him from the room. She knew her way around the streets of Chinatown and guided him to a first-floor apartment in another brownstone. It had a parlor, bedroom, bath, and kitchen. The larger room was furnished with a love seat, low tables, and two wooden chairs. To one side was a smaller room with a bed and a dresser, and to his left En could see the kitchen. Pots and pans hung beneath shelves of pottery bowls and mugs. On the counter was a covered dish next to a freshly roasted Peking duck. His mouth watered with the aroma of the five-spice. En could almost taste the crispy skin dripping with soy and brown sugar.

Mai Ling concerned herself with preparing the dish, spooning sauce over the duck. He wondered if she had spent the day here cooking, or perhaps other women in the community had contributed to the meal.

She motioned for him sit in the small living room. There were two black lacquered Chinese chairs with carvings that must have been from the Běnshuài's home, or possibly part of the collection of antiques he imported. The chair's hard seat mimicked En's discomfort. He was in debt to the Běnshuài for both his profession and his lodging, but he could no longer deny his growing sense that the source of the man's power was derived from illicit activities. As a beneficiary, he was complicit, and he considered whether he should refuse the medical training and Mai Ling. Even referring to her—a human being—as returnable upset him. He strongly desired the training, and he had no idea why he had agreed to house Mai Ling. He did not want her. Why had he not refused? Perhaps his decision was driven by his desire to please his friend, or maybe he had lost the will to fight back. He certainly was lonely, but they didn't even speak the same language. His friend had foisted his burden on En. How much payback was expected for his education?

After a few minutes, Mai Ling indicated he should join her in the kitchen. She brought a heaping plate of the duck to the table. She had prepared only one place setting. He sat down and took a bite. It was delicious. She continued to bring dishes: beef dumplings, fried rice, vegetables, spring rolls, and fried cabbage. Mai Ling would give him a sizable portion and then offer seconds.

He finally put his hand up and said, "No more."

She looked wounded.

He smiled and patted his stomach. "No, it was good. Thank you."

She flushed. She refused to let him clear his plate. She showed him the small room where she'd turned down the bed and gave him a carpetbag that someone had filled with his belongings. He unpacked while she did the dishes. He left two drawers in the dresser for her.

When he came back out to the parlor, a large metal tub filled with hot water was waiting. She indicated he should take a bath and then pointed to the bedroom. He noticed she was trembling and realized she thought he expected her to share the bed with him. He shook his head and mimed he would give the bed to her. After more pantomime, they finally settled on his taking the bedroom. She stayed in the kitchen while he bathed. He was uncertain what to do next. He put on the shirt and soft pants he wore at night and sat on the bed. She came to the door; he could see her body quaking. He once again put up his hand. "No." He saw her face relax with relief before she stumbled away. He didn't hear or see her for the rest of the night.

## Philadelphia, Pennsylvania, Spring 1880

They settled in. He thought about, but never got around to, taking Mai Ling back to the Běnshuài. He went to the hospital each day. She stayed in the flat, managing the meals and household tasks. She moved about silently. Perhaps because they couldn't use words, since they did not speak each other's dialect, she seemed to anticipate his every need and was attentive to the point of annoyance. After he ate dinner, he would go into his room, and once she realized he was not expecting her to join him at night, she was less on edge. She was clearly afraid of men, and he wondered about her past.

About a month after Mai Ling and he moved into the apartment, there was a knock on the door. One of the Běnshuài's guards handed Mai Ling a box. "Provisions. I guess the Běnshuài's ship came in," he said. "A gift from his wife."

Mai Ling exclaimed over the tins of Chinese water chestnuts and small containers of soy sauce. There were also large bottles of black beer. En invited the guard inside to share one. Mai Ling took the rest of the box to the kitchen. The guard sat with En in their one large room. He handed the man a beer, and they sat together. En enjoyed conversing with another Chinese, one who spoke his dialect. On the second beer, the guard remarked on how much happier Mai Ling appeared.

"Nice to see her here," he said. "I thought he might send her back."

"To China?"

"Yeah," the guard said. "It was a dicey situation."

He looked at En. "You don't know about it, do you?"

En knew if the Běnshuài had wanted him to know he would have told him, but his curiosity was so great he leaned forward and said, "She doesn't understand our dialect, but talk softly just in case."

The guard was only too happy to share. He told En that Mai Ling had come to America to serve in the home of a prominent Chinese family.

"I had night duty in their home and was checking the locks when the matriarch marched through the kitchen. Mai Ling slept in a room off the pantry." The man took a swig of beer.

"That woman opened the door, and there was Mai Ling, frozen like a statue, her head turned to the wall," the bodyguard said. "The husband had one hand underneath Mai Ling's nightdress. His robe was lifted high enough that I could see his rather large intentions. His wife could too."

En wanted to know more, but it was wrong to invade Mai Ling's privacy. Yet when the guard continued, En didn't interrupt.

"It wasn't the first time she'd found her husband helping himself to the tofu," the bodyguard recounted. "But it was the only time the man announced he would take a second wife. You should have heard the ruckus."

En shouldn't invite this gossip, but he now had to know.

"What happened?"

"She broke it up, and the next morning, the woman, who wanted to remain the *only* wife, invited her best friend to visit. Guess who showed up?"

"I have no idea," En said.

"Ha, the Běnshuài's wife," the man said. "Everyone in the house could hear the wronged wife screaming, 'Not enough Chinese women in America, one man should not have two wives.' Which is pretty much how it is for us. The only person who might have two wives here is the Běnshuài."

"Does he have more than one wife?"

"Not that I know of, but no one would object. Anyway, he calls her First Wife, and I've never seen him look at other women. In fact, if the Běnshuài's wife isn't happy, neither is he."

"So how did he appease her friend?"

"It was arranged to have Mai Ling removed," the guard said. "But none of the other wives would take her. That's when you got here."

Now En saw why the Běnshuài had housed them together. He also understood why Mai Ling was so frightened.

Although he had never seen Mai Ling put a mat the on floor, lie down, or fall asleep, after hearing the story, En hung a muslin curtain between his room and the parlor. He pulled it closed at night to give her more privacy. Each morning, he deliberately made noise before opening the curtain to warn her that he was entering the living area.

It was several weeks before she raised her eyes to meet his. Once she felt confident with the routine that kept them apart at night, she became more animated. She prepared delicious Chinese dishes. He had not eaten as well since the railroad mess hall. He soon added the pounds he'd lost when he was a nomad, possibly a few more. He came to anticipate the pleasure of a freshly made bed on Mondays and the warm bath she prepared for him on Saturdays.

Having another human being so near disrupted the private time he needed, but the Běnshuài was right: Mai Ling keeping house allowed him to focus on work. Their arrangement grew more comfortable, and as they grew easier with one another, Mai Ling started to make up amusing pantomimes. She would act something out, and he had to guess her meaning. He enjoyed the performance, she liked his attention, and it eased the isolation they both felt.

# CHAPTER FOUR

# NANTICOKE

**Nanticoke, Pennsylvania, Spring 1882**

Fending off the Coal and Iron Police was the final low point, but as Johanna reflected on it, the day she took charge and walked into town became the fulcrum for their new life.

She had told Mr. Walsh she would start the next day, and when she got back to the shack, Connor was still asleep. Thankfully, she didn't have to make excuses for her absence. The kitchen cupboard was nearly bare, but she had picked up some eggs and bread. When her sons came home from work, she watched as they scrubbed up. Johnny pulled his hands out of the wash basin and held them up.

"The dirt hides the slate cuts. I think the black is blood. Are your hands bleeding too, TC?"

"It's red top," TC said, "from the chemicals that blast the coal."

TC struggled to keep the smile on his face when he saw his baby brother's bruised and burning hands. Johanna had to look away. "I'll get some goose grease," she said.

TC said, "I sure don't want to grow up to be a miner."

"Me neither." Johnny took the towel. "Ma, today when the whistle blew, one guy came up and stuffed a sandwich in his mouth. The bread was black with coal dust."

"They get paid by the carload," TC said. "They gotta fill seven cars; it's the magic number. If they take time to eat, then they end up owing the money to the company store."

Connor was silent during dinner. She overheard Johnny tell TC that his back was sore. She tucked them in with a warm poultice.

Johnny said, "Thanks, Ma, this really helps."

TC said, "I love you, Ma."


The next day when Johanna got to the hotel, Mr. Walsh had a new apron waiting for her.

"Not sure what chambermaids do exactly," he said. "But I guess you could get started upstairs. First, make me a cup of tea."

She spent the day throwing out trash and cleaning. She scraped up disgusting, smelly, sometimes mysterious substances. She focused on the guest rooms and decided she would tackle the kitchen and laundry later in the week.

Walsh stayed in his office. In the late afternoon, when she was on her knees, polishing the hall floor, he appeared. Standing over her, he awkwardly put an envelope on the front table. "Your first week's pay in advance. Make a list of supplies you need, and tomorrow plan on cooking dinner," he said. "We'll get whatever you need delivered. That's how Mary used to do it."

"Thank you," she said, standing to face him. "I am so grateful, Mr. Walsh. I hope you are pleased with my work today."

He looked around, "Yep. Could use some help at the front desk, too. Can you read, tally sums?"

"Yes," she said.

"Clean in the morning, cook, and then the office at three o'clock from now on."

He squeezed up his owl face, and said, "You're like Mary, a good woman."

He walked away.

That evening, as she prepared dinner, Johanna felt a new sense of satisfaction that she was providing for her family. Connor wouldn't be happy about it, but he would come to accept her new job when he saw the money.

The kitchen in the miner's shack was small enough that she could reach the table without taking a step. She cut through the crust of a meat pie, spooned stew onto plates, and served Connor and the boys. They all looked tired and hungry. Her husband had worked in the mine that day. He didn't know she had been gone. She took her seat, and they held hands.

"Bless us, our Lord, for these, thy gifts, which we are about to receive, from thy bounty, through Christ our Lord, Amen," they said in unison. She watched them all take the first bite.

"Hey, there's meat in this pie," Johnny said. She smiled.

"Where'd you get meat?" Connor asked.

"I got an account at the company store," she said.

"God damn it, Johanna, a line of credit? Now the mine will own us forever," Connor said. He put his fork down.

"I didn't use the mining account. I have my own, and I paid cash," Johanna said. She had long ago stopped pointing out his blasphemy. He might still believe, but the more steadily he drank, the less regularly he attended Mass, made a confession, or took the sacrament.

"What?"

"I was about to tell you, about the hotel—you know, the one on Main Street? I went in yesterday to ask if Mr. Walsh—he's the owner—if he needed a chambermaid."

"What's that got to do with anything?"

"He hired me."

Connor raised bloodshot eyes and stared.

"I clean the rooms in the morning, cook and serve dinner midday, and then work at the front desk until evening."

"Who will take care of us?" Johnny asked, anxiety in his voice.

"Each of you has to pitch in." She glanced at her husband. "We'll save enough money soon, and we can get you lads away from that mine and off to school."

She wasn't sure what Connor would say. He wouldn't like his wife cleaning for other people, but he might not work again this month. How could he object? He was silent.

She and Connor didn't fight as much once she started her job, probably because she wasn't home. When the hotel was busy, she stayed late and left casseroles for the family on the stove. Thick cuts of meat were now part of their fare. The boys already looked healthier.

Over the summer, they worked long hours—the boys in the mines, Johanna six days with Mr. Walsh, Connor when work was available. It seemed the more Johanna worked, the less Connor did.

One day Mr. Walsh invited the family to Sunday tea. After Mass, they walked the two blocks from St. Francis Church to the hotel. Her sons were jumpy as they entered the lobby. She had become accustomed to the hotel, but compared to the miner's shack, the elegant furnishings, draperies, lamps—even the large silver tea service on the sideboard—was to her sons like visiting the Queen.

The men of her family stood uncomfortably next to the sofa.

"Hello, young men," Mr. Walsh said. In an uncharacteristic show of hospitality, Mr. Walsh offered his hand.

"Mr. Walsh, my lads are honored to meet you." Johanna nudged her sons forward.

They were speechless. Connor, hat in hand, said, "Pleased to meet you, sir."

TC and Johnny shook the hand Walsh offered. TC told her later that Mr. Walsh's fingers felt like a chicken foot.

"I see you don't wash under your fingernails," Mr. Walsh said.

"Coal dust is not easy to remove, Mr. Walsh," Johanna said with a smile. "Shall we sit here in the lobby?"

Walsh nodded.

Johanna had arranged for a new woman to help out on weekends. She brought the tea. The boys eagerly eyed the butter cookies and blueberry scones but had been warned not to eat until she gave them a nod. Unfortunately, the new maid was not well trained. When Mr. Walsh said the hot water wasn't at a rolling boil, it was Johanna who ran back to the kitchen. Then, because they waited for a new pot, he sent her to reheat his scones.

"He must be the devil, likes everything burning hot," she heard TC whisper to Johnny. She smiled to herself but gave them the evil eye.

"You boys read?" Walsh asked after tea.

"They are learning," Johanna said.

"Your mother reads well. And what about you, Connor, is it?" Mr. Walsh said. "You read?"

"Unfortunately, he never had an opportunity for schooling," Johanna said.

Connor clenched his jaw. She prayed he wouldn't be rude.

It was a long afternoon and evidently not as much about hospitality as it was a job interview. The next day Walsh asked Johanna if she thought Connor might like to tend bar.

Connor was pleased. Johanna worried that he would drink even more than he was drinking now, but at least he would bring in more money. It was also possible a less discouraged Connor might not turn to the bottle.

"I was thinking about offering to bartend myself. It'd be a lot better than getting down in that mine," Connor said, as if it had been his idea.

## Nanticoke, Pennsylvania, Summer 1882

Johanna worried that her husband and Walsh wouldn't get on and that it might jeopardize her employment. It turned out that Walsh was happy to allow Connor reign of the bar, especially after hours. Connor was happy, too. Between her morning cleaning and afternoon office work, she often found Connor at the bar, wiping the counter, clean shaven and whistling under his breath.

"Gotta keep it shipshape. Customers will think more of the place." He polished the wood like a priest shining the chalice before communion.

"But nothing is spilled," Johanna laughed.

She was glad Connor was getting on with the customers, and ironically, he was drinking less.

"More fellows coming in each day and I chat 'em up," he'd tell her.

One afternoon she ran into Connor carrying beer kegs and a tub of ice to the bar. She saw sweat dripping down his cheeks. She scolded herself; she really should be kinder to him.

"Having you at the bar has been good for the business," she said. "Thank you, Connor, for everything you've done for us." He peered down at the floor, embarrassed. "Do you think it's time we get the boys out of the mine and into school? The fall term starts next week," Johanna said.

"I'm not sure they need that much schooling, but there's no future for breaker boys—that's for sure." His eyes met hers. She knew he didn't want the boys in the mines; it was an admission of his failure as a provider.

"Maybe we should wait?" he said. "Pulling them out is a risk. And what if these jobs don't last? Then we'd have to take 'em out again."

"But they would have had some schooling." She tried not to let her exasperation show. He was so willing to accept their low station.

"Go ahead." He said. "Put them with the nuns. But don't blame me if it don't work."

She enrolled the boys at St. Francis Parish School for the fall term. TC was eight, and Johnny was six. They would start off behind the other students, but they were young enough to catch up. If they graduated, they would be the first in the family to finish school. There was only one problem: with Connor working evenings, she needed to leave work earlier. The boys couldn't stay alone after dark. Walsh insisted on her usual ten-hour day. She responded that, although she had complied with most of his demands, this was nonnegotiable. He could cut back on her pay, but she had to leave by six. Walsh fumed for days, and then one afternoon he walked up to where she stood at the front desk and threw a stack of papers on the blotter.

"Here's the plans," he said.

"Plans?"

"Sketches. The rooms in the attic don't rent well—empty most of the time. We'll build out the living quarters."

Johanna looked at the rough drawings for the entire attic floor. Walsh had crossed out walls to open living space. One room was labeled "parlor," and there was a bedroom on either side.

"So, we build out an apartment and rent that?"

"Of course not. It's still two flights of stairs. Guests won't like that."

She was baffled until she saw the notation "Boys" next to one of the bedrooms.

"You want us to move in?" She was touched. "Mr. Walsh, that is so generous."

"And don't go getting all sappy. It's smart business. Just don't let those boys run around like wild animals."

The rooms had low ceilings and would be hot in the summer. Connor resisted, saying they would have no privacy. Johanna agreed but argued they had only two options: displeasing the boss or leaving the boys alone. She pointed out that Walsh never came upstairs, and once they moved in, Connor's trip from the bar to bed would consist of a flight of stairs. Connor relented, and then her only challenge was keeping the boys quiet. She figured she would find ways to keep them busy upstairs or send them outside, even in the cold.

"This proves we are not shanty Irish," she told the boys on the August day they moved in. "We are lace-curtains Irish. See the curtains on our windows?"

"And now you boys will be learning the three R's," Walsh said.

"Reading is one," she said. "But what are the other two?"

"Writing and 'rithmetic." She laughed, but Connor and the boys didn't get the joke.

The boys started school in September. It was a dream to have them leave each morning as students, not laborers. Johnny had taken to his classroom right away. TC struggled. She told herself he just needed time. They walked to school with other children, and she could tell they were proud to come and go from the hotel. Even if they lived over the business, it was a lot better than the shack.

Each afternoon at three, she waited in front of the cubbyholes that held gold-tasseled room keys. Empty cubbies calmed her—it meant the hotel was full. She thrilled each day that TC and Johnny walked in the front door, book straps over their shoulders, hands and faces relatively clean. They looked like successful students, not exhausted miners. Sometimes she brushed tears of relief off her face. As busy as she was, she tried to stop whatever she was doing long enough to have them tell her one thing about their day before they went to the kitchen for a snack.

Johanna overheard Mr. Walsh tell the maid that the boys were "little squawkers," but in front of guests, Walsh would tousle their hair and say, "They're like sons to me, these young lads."

"Those boys are lucky to have you. You're the grandfather they left behind in Ireland," one woman told Walsh.

Since the family had moved in, guests seemed to be fonder of Mr. Walsh. More women traveled with their husbands now that the lodgings were improved. Johanna found Walsh's mock grandpa act cloying, but if it was good for business, he could keep it up. The boys avoided Walsh. When he was around, she instructed her sons to stop the sly comments and eye rolls.

For now, Walsh valued her enough to put up with the children. Still, his mood was unpredictable. He disappeared into his office most days, and Johanna kept track of his disposition. She tried to guess how he evaluated her work, worried a day would come when he might get tired of them. It was tricky to work for a man who never said thank you. She didn't mind for herself, but Connor was growing the receipts at the bar and bringing in more customers, who stayed longer. TC stacked wood, and Johnny carried boxes to the cellar, but there was no acknowledgment. Walsh should be pleased, but who really knew? He rarely checked her work or gave her direction any longer. Were these signs of trust or laziness? Finally, she gave up trying to figure it out. She continued to pick up more of the workload and improve profits, hoping to become invaluable.

The only time Walsh interfered was on Sundays. As they were leaving for Mass he would say, "Just one more thing, Johanna."

Her sons stood by the door, overheated in their coats, while she found Mr. Walsh's pipe or made him a cup of tea.

He also didn't like her to go out shopping; he said he preferred delivery. In fact, he got cranky anytime she was gone longer than an hour.

She didn't miss shopping, but Sunday Mass was a holy day of obligation. Connor skipped Mass, choosing to sleep in on Sundays. It was up to her that the boys got the proper religious training.

After Mass they ate dinner as a family, the only time the four of them sat down together. One Sunday dinner, they got to talking about Walsh.

"You won't believe what Mr. Walsh did last week," she said, passing the bowl of applesauce to Connor. "We had visitors who stayed just two nights. When I went to change the sheets, he told me that unless they stayed a week not to waste the soap and water."

Connor spooned applesauce over his peas. "I see his point. His sheets are so thin they won't last too many washings. Why not wait until they get crunchy?"

"They were like that when I got here." She smiled. "I thought I'd redeemed him."

"Ma, we're trying to eat," TC said. Connor laughed. It was nice to see him enjoying the boys more.

After dessert of bread pudding, she excused the boys, "And don't repeat what your father said about Mr. Walsh."

Once the boys left the table, she turned to Connor. "He's adding charges on the guest's bills for meals they didn't order. When they notice, he blames me, says I don't have a head for numbers, then scolds me right in front of them."

"I don't like that we're working for such a man," Connor said.

"I guess he's just trying to survive," Johanna said. "Maybe once your family has nearly starved to death, you can never make enough money."

## Nanticoke, Pennsylvania, Spring 1883

Almost a year after the Kennedys moved into the attic rooms, the hotel and houses were at capacity most nights. Johanna hired five employees to manage the growing business. Kathleen was the first official housekeeper. They both worked so hard that Johanna didn't see her friend often. Kathleen managed the chambermaids upstairs while Johanna spent more time in the front office.

On the first warm day in March, Johanna looked out the window and saw Kathleen hanging linens on the line. Johanna succumbed to the temptation for a chat and slipped away from the ledgers.

She walked around to the side yard path, where green triangles pushed their way through the earth, the yellow and purple crocuses announcing the ground was thawed. Johanna found Kathleen. Her friend had put on a few pounds and looked healthier for it.

"Down a maid today," Kathleen said. "Thought I'd use it as a chance to get outside."

"Let me help," Johanna said, picking up a wet pillowcase.

Kathleen grinned and handed her two clothespins. "I've been hoping to get a chance to talk. I have some news."

Johanna suddenly knew what Kathleen would say.

"Are you sure?" Johanna said. "It's been four years since the twins, and I thought you and Michael were going to …" She didn't know what she thought really, but she had hoped Kathleen would take a breather on babies. Johanna was well aware it was a sin to block conception. While women didn't have a choice, there were ways to delay.

"Johanna, it's a little late for advice," Kathleen said, patting her belly.

"I suppose it is." Johanna didn't want to criticize, but she feared for Kathleen. "The stork works overtime at your house."

"Yep, Molly came nearly nine months from the wedding night." Kathleen looked chagrined.

"What were you and Michael thinking?"

"Thinking had nothing to do with it," Kathleen said.

"That's not good," Johanna said.

"Oh, it was very good." Kathleen grinned.

"Michael could give it a rest occasionally," Johanna said. She should keep her mouth shut, but how many times had Johanna bit her tongue over Michael? He was a force of nature. And Johanna had to admit she was a hypocrite. At this very minute, she was benefiting from

Kathleen's generous nature and hard work. Even with the additional staff, Kathleen still did more than her share. Everyone loved her, too. Johanna sometimes wondered if she could develop the compassion that came naturally to Kathleen. Johanna knew people were wary of her. Maybe it came with the territory since she was the boss, but Johanna knew she would never have Kathleen's open heart.

"The sun goes behind the mountain in an hour. This last load might not dry," Kathleen said.

"It's the best we're going to do," Johanna said.

"I'll iron the damp out of them later. The dried lavender in the linen closet always makes them smell wonderful. Guests mention it all the time."

Johanna picked up the laundry basket and moved down the line. "When will the baby come?"

"Late summer." Kathleen put the clothespins into a bag.

"Will you consider slowing down, maybe cutting back hours?" Johanna hung the last sheet on the line.

"Not on your life," Kathleen said. "There are four children at home. My days at the hotel are when I relax."

"You can stop whenever," Johanna said. "But you must come back. You're the only friend I have in this town."

"That's not true," Kathleen said.

"The miner's wives listen for the accident bell. You do too. Connor and the boys aren't in the mine. I don't hear it anymore," Johanna said. "You may not resent that I'm exempt from mine tragedies, but others do."

"Just because your husband isn't in daily peril doesn't mean I can't see your troubles," Kathleen said, "Bridget and Finn among them. I think she's spreading rumors."

"I avoid her," Johanna said. "And she knows nothing about us; what kind of rumors can she spread?"

"She has it out for TC. My older girls tell me the kids are teasing him about the S word."

"What's the S word?"

"Stupid. One of the nuns sits him in a corner wearing a dunce cap," Kathleen said. "And Mrs. Sullivan is fanning the flames. Right in front me, she told another mother, 'I don't really want Finn going near that Kennedy boy. He's not right in the head.'"

Johanna felt sick.

"Remember TC's black eye that first week of school?" Kathleen said.

"I thought it was just the one time," Johanna said. "Oh, dear. I hate to say it, but he was happier as a breaker boy."

"I'm not sure there is much you can do. You have the burden of running a business."

"I have to think of something," Johanna said. "And I worry about you, too; five children will be a lot to manage."

"I wouldn't have it any other way. It's a sin to refuse the blessings of a child, and I love babies."

As frustrating as it was to see Kathleen seized by another pregnancy, Johanna gave up. Arguing didn't help. They carried the empty baskets inside, and Kathleen went off to bake bread. The new cook, Tilly, was not a baker, so Kathleen still made her light-as-air baked goods.

Johanna returned to her office. She tried to balance the check ledger, but she couldn't let go of her worry. What could she do to help TC? And why did Kathleen's pregnancy bother her so much? Kathleen and Michael made each other happy, and if a child of theirs had problems, they would work together to help that child. Connor wouldn't care about TC's school problems.

If she were honest, part of her envied Kathleen. Michael kept her pregnant, but he adored her. Kathleen was one of those women who blossomed in pregnancy. Johanna was bilious all nine months and felt inhabited by a creature that controlled her swollen body. Both deliveries had been a nightmare. After Johnny, the doctor, without much of an explanation, told her it was unlikely she would conceive again. She and Connor had relations often enough that the doctor was probably right. It was just as well. She didn't want to go through any of it again, and she didn't have enough time with the boys as it was.

Still, bringing a life into the world—raising her children—was the best thing she would ever do. She had always thought she would have a daughter and longed for a little girl. Her mother used to say, "A son is a son till he gets a wife; a daughter's a daughter for all of her life." She didn't know how to help a boy, but she could understand a girl—a daughter that would be with her all her life.

They had a small kitchen in the attic where Johanna could heat up food prepared earlier by the hotel's cook. Most nights she fed the boys at a drop-leaf table in their attic parlor. Connor ate later at the bar after the busy period. When they first moved into the hotel, despite tending bar, Connor stayed sober. Things gradually changed. Johanna noted it began after they saw TC and Finn on stage together in a Christmas play and then again on Palm Sunday when the school's students led the procession to lay palm fronds on the altar. Connor got drunk and hostile both times.

Johanna wasn't sure what made Connor so mercurial, especially with TC. Even though they had their own child, had built a life together, he somehow couldn't get over the past. Was it seeing the look-alike boys together that led to the drinking, or did the drinking reduce his inhibitions? One night, Connor came upstairs while the boys were eating dinner. He walked over to the table and cuffed TC.

"You didn't pick up the bar trash today," Connor barked.

TC jumped to his feet.

"I did so," TC said. Johanna knew TC tried hard to please both Walsh and Connor. His pride was as wounded as the cheek where Connor's handprint bloomed red.

"Don't lie to me, boy," Connor said.

"He did. I helped him," Johnny said.

Before she could stop him, Connor reached over and pushed Johnny's face onto the plate.

"Eat. What are you some kind of picky little bird?" Connor said. "Or is the food not good enough for you?"

Johnny stayed still for a long moment and then, too stunned to cry, slowly lifted his head. The mashed potatoes wedged inside his nostrils. Gravy dripped off his chin onto his shirt.

"TC," Johanna said, wiping Johnny's face with her napkin. "Why don't you take Johnny and help him wash up? I'll get a cold compress for your ear."

Johnny's face crumpled with hurt; TC's inflated with rage.

She thought of her mother's expression, "If looks could kill," and expected that when she stared at Connor, her dark thoughts might fell him. Instead, he looked at her defiantly.

She waited for the boys to leave. "You will never do anything like that again."

Connor sat down heavily on a chair. He pressed his fingers to his temples. He sounded truly pained. "I'm sorry. I don't know what got into me."

"Did you start drinking early? You may have to get back to the mines if you can't control it," Johanna said. "We have good boys. They don't deserve mistreatment."

"God, Johanna, I try. I looked the other way when that boy Finn turned out to be a dead ringer for TC," Connor said. "I thought after he died Thomas would fade, but he's with us every day. Reminds me of things I can't forget."

"I was always honest about Thomas. You knew from the first."

"It doesn't make it easier."

Connor stopped drinking after that incident, but within a fortnight, he started up again. She could hear him with customers at the bar, slurring his words, complaining about the mine bosses, as if he had spent years, not weeks, in a mine.

"It's their fookin' fault, those dirty Orangemen," he said. "We would have stayed back in the old sod, but they starved us."

The more he drank, the later he worked. She was glad to climb into bed early, luxuriating in her time alone. She stretched her body into an X across the cool sheets. Connor stumbled in a few hours before she got up to prepare breakfast. The room was cold, so it was nice to have a warm body next to her. Occasionally he slobbered over her, but usually he passed out, which was fine with her. No, a baby girl was improbable.

Mr. Walsh sat in his small office with the door closed. After he ate lunch at his desk, he took a nap. If she accidently interrupted, he denied he'd been asleep. Johanna wasn't sure exactly how old he was, possibly his late seventies? She didn't begrudge him his afternoon nap.

One day she waited until after two before she knocked on his office door. She heard his gravelly "Come in."

He was sitting up. One side of his face had a crease, an imprint from something on the desk. "What do you want?" He picked up his reading glasses and wiped them off.

"Sorry to disturb you. I brought you some apple cake," Johanna said. "And might I have a word?"

He took the fork and dug in. "Mmm, apples seem a little dry."

She didn't respond.

"Okay, what do you want?"

"We've been completely full for two months," she said.

"And you're going to tell me we need more help?" He smacked his lips. "Even with the new people just hired? That new chambermaid looks strong and speedy."

"I had to let her go yesterday. I thought it was bells in her apron pocket. I found a dozen spoons jangling."

"Riffraff," he said. "I said, it's up to you to let 'em go."

"It's not only staffing," Johanna said. "I've been thinking we could offer supper in addition to breakfast and lunch. No sense in having an empty dining room."

"Would we make money?"

"I think we'd do well, but we need a cook's helper and one more maid," she said.

"Don't bother me with details. Fire and hire them as you see fit," he said. "Got any more cake?"

"Of course," Johanna said. "Then you approve new hires and expanding our meal offerings?"

"Too many details," he said. "You handle it, but I'm holding you accountable if we lose a dime."

"I'll get you more cake," she said. "And the hotel is donating a dozen of these apple cakes to the Coal and Iron Police bake sale."

"Those bastards? Why?"

"They're much friendlier these days," she said.

"They're eating us out of house and home," he said. "But, yeah, if cake and whiskey keep them from dragging me in, do it. Now, that cake's a little dry, some cream and a spot of brandy over the next piece of cake, Mary, err, Johanna." He flustered. "Get on with you."

Perhaps it wasn't his age, but he called her Mary more often of late.


She hired a young girl to assist the grumbling Tilly, but she doubted it would defrost the woman's disposition or soften the permanent scowl on her face. Tilly was one of the reasons they could offer dinner. Her Irish stew was mouthwatering. Johanna didn't know how she kept her bangers and mash piping hot. Customers wolfed it down. The only problem was Tilly could never quite regulate her heavy hand when it came to scones and sponge cake. Thank goodness for Kathleen's talent with flour, butter, sugar, and spices. It was hard on her now, and she would be out for a few weeks. Hopefully, the new girl would take on the baking. Guests would miss Kathleen's baking; some asked if they could buy a slice or even take an entire cake home.

Walsh ate a lot of cake. He still pinched pennies. Johanna never told him the cake he loved was especially delicious because she bought the highest-grade eggs and cream. Nor did she mention the occasional free meal she offered an unhappy guest, or an extra night's stay to a regular customer when she sensed they were low on funds. It was a kindness, and to a point, generosity prompted loyalty.

While some guests didn't take meals, after about a month of adding dinner service, Johanna calculated that the majority of their customers were spending half again as much on dinner.

Johanna finished assessing the numbers and made a grocery list. Tilly came in with menus and Johanna made a few adjustments, which never pleased the cook. Tilly left for the market with her usual bad humor. She did not take the list. Johanna followed Tilly to the kitchen but had just missed her when Kathleen appeared.

"The second time in a month I get to see you," Johanna said.

"We're lucky." Kathleen smiled. "I thought I'd get started on tonight's dessert. I have a new recipe for bread pudding with whiskey."

"Sounds delicious. And I was about to go after Tilly—she forgot the list again—but I'd rather stay and chat with you."

Johanna was about to say more but realized that Mr. Walsh had walked in.

"All the two of you do is chatter," he said. "If you have that much time on your hands, Johanna, why don't you start managing the rooming houses, too?" He punctuated his words with a brisk head nod. "And bring me some more cake."

Once he was gone, Kathleen said, "I guess that was a promotion, without more money, of course. He can't manage the steep steps in the rooming houses but doesn't want to admit it—so he piles more work on you."

"You know him well," Johanna said. "Last week he wanted me to fix the plumbing in one of the bathrooms. I said we needed parts."

"What did he say?"

"He told me to fix it without parts."

They laughed.

"Soon he won't be able to check in a guest without your help," Kathleen said. "No wonder he gives you anything you ask for … you're running this business."

"He's been through a lot, and he's getting on."

"Maybe so, but the geezer takes advantage and pays you next to nothing," Kathleen said. "Have you asked for that raise?"

"I'm afraid to bring it up," Johanna said, as she put on the kettle. "What matters is that we have food and a roof over our heads. Plus, he's paying Connor now, too. As long as the Walsh Hotel and Rooming Houses are thriving, we're safe."

"You keep the books. Is the business doing okay?"

"More than okay. We're paying down the mortgages; soon the properties will be free and clear."

"What happens if Walsh dies, or his son returns?"

"I don't like to think about it. The son left after his mother died. I got the feeling he blamed Walsh or maybe they are estranged."

"Walsh alive might keep the boy away; Walsh's death could change the picture," Kathleen said, taking the mug of tea Johanna held out to her.

"You're right, but we can't fix it." Johanna went to the cupboard and took out three plates. "Sit down. He can wait on his cake. Let's give that baby of yours something to grow on."

"Okay, you don't want to talk about the future. We'll talk about something else for now," Kathleen said. "I bet you have ideas for the rooming houses."

"I've been hoping he would give me a chance. I was thinking: what about naming each house after flowers, like Rose, Butterwort, or Lily House?"

Kathleen took the plate of cake Johanna offered and said, "We could match things like color and wallpaper and find items with roses or lilies. I love it."

They began decorating over the next few weeks. The Rose and Lily houses were easy. There were lots of lamps and knickknacks covered in roses or lilies: stamped, painted, or sewn. The Butterwort house was not easily pleased. Butterworts were not an American flower. When they found the right magenta or violet accent to decorate a Butterwort room, it was a small victory.

Mostly, her life was better. Johanna was grateful. Her only sadness was thinking about Thomas. It had been ten years since she had seen him, but especially when she saw Michael and Kathleen together, she wondered what her life would be like if he had lived. Would she have gone to bed each night with a man who tantalized her, loved her body and soul? She gave it little thought during the busy days, but many nights she awakened. In the space between dreaming and consciousness, she could feel Thomas's body on top of her. She could even smell his scent and hear him calling her "sweet one."

"The Church's one foundation is Jesus Christ, her Lord. She is his new creation by water and the Word." Johanna's voice rose with the congregation. She would go to Mass every day if all they did was sing. The church wasn't particularly comfortable—hard wooden pews with kneelers covered in needlepoint cushions faced a raised altar platform. Above it, the life-size wooden Christ hung on a cross. On either side were alcoves with statues of Mary and Joseph spreading their hands in supplication. Today, the altar did look beautiful. A profusion of purple and white irises, the glorious flowers of June, were arrayed in containers on either side of the gold and white linen-covered altar.

The stunning flowers and strong voices lifted in song filled Johanna's heart with gladness, as encouraged in the Psalms. The problem was that soon the priest would begin his harangue. She didn't understand why Catholics kept showing up so priests could berate them. After a thorough dressing-down, the congregation was expected to toss hard-earned money into the collection plate, too. At least today the charismatic Father Ryan had come down from the big city parish in Wilkes-Barre. His sermons—in his sonorous bass voice—were delivered less with fire and brimstone and more with the polish of a politician running for office. She was glad for the change.

Johanna tried to pay attention. She knew her catechism, covered her head in church, and fed her family fish on Fridays. She put an envelope of money in every week because being part of her community was important for the business. She'd even joined the Society of St. Vincent de Paul, a women's auxiliary that met on Tuesday evenings and arranged charity projects.

It was her way of life, good and bad, but sometimes she questioned the dogma.

Just saying the words "Bless me Father, for I have sinned" could make Johanna anxious. The sound of a priest sliding the wooden panel along its track still brought shivers down her back. She kept her confessions all-purpose. She was too discerning to share her deepest thoughts or shortcomings with a priest who might not keep her confidence. She remembered Father James, a priest who would gossip at their kitchen table, perhaps only hinting at what he knew. Her mother had cautioned Johanna never to trust Father James. In America, Johanna's misgivings grew when she heard about priests who supported the mine owners during the strike. They were rumored to have leaked information that led to the apprehension of one man based on the confession of his own mother.

It wasn't that she didn't believe. And when the priests weren't shouting, she liked the quiet space of worship. Even if she didn't like the tone or substance of the priest's role, she did find a quiet hour with God could restore her soul.

The smell of the incense and receiving communion reminded her that there was something greater than herself. It brought her back to her childhood, standing outside the church with her parents after her First Holy Communion. The family had splurged to purchase lace for her dress and a delicate tulle veil. Their love for her and commitment to the Church melded so that one represented the other. Each of her four sisters wore the dress after her, and she supposed her youngest sister had worn it after she left for America. She would have loved to be there. Sharing the sacraments was one last bridge across the ocean to her family.

The Mass was long. She didn't bother to follow the Latin liturgy. Instead, as she did most Sundays, she let her mind wander across the ocean and back to her homeland. What did Claremorris look like now? Was the sea as blue, the grass truly emerald, or did her memory exaggerate the colors? Had her family gone to Mass earlier today? Would they laugh over a shared meal, as they had when she was growing up? Did they ever talk about her?

When they first left home for Liverpool, her sisters would write letters dictated from their mother. She and her siblings were the first in their family to read and write. The letters came with regularity—about once a month—and were full of funny stories. Then the intervals between letters grew longer. Counting their time in Liverpool, Johanna had been gone for over seven years. Her family ties, if not broken, were fraying. Her sisters were young women now. Two were married, one was expecting a baby. She supposed her mother would become deeply attached to the grandchildren who lived near her. Johanna felt deep sadness that TC and Johnny would not know the love of a grandparent. Her father was unwell.

Johanna wrote to ask questions about the nature of his illness, but there were no answers in return posts. In one of the last letters she'd received, her mother had said her four brothers were doing a fine job on the farm and that they could give their father the rest he deserved. Johanna expected she would one day get a letter telling her that her father had passed away. It didn't help to carry the worry around, so Johanna only allowed herself to think about her family this one time each week.

She did miss Connor when she sat alone in the pew. Connor attended only at Christmas and Easter. He wasn't going anywhere on his one day off. She wished he would at least come to see TC and Johnny as altar boys; they looked angelic kneeling next to the priests.

Most Sundays she got home in time to prepare dinner, but this morning there was a baptismal ceremony, and the family would provide lunch to the congregants after the service. Her day off was reduced to a short afternoon. She hoped they'd get home by two.

She closed her missal and, following the benediction, pushed the kneeler against the pew. She stepped into the aisle and genuflected, facing the altar. She dipped her finger in the holy water font by the door and saw Kathleen in the narthex.

"Ah, Kathleen, there you are, looking like a good Catholic woman—a babe in your arms and one on the way."

"We have to talk," Kathleen whispered. Johanna was mystified. Kathleen's expression was so serious. She'd only heard the somber tone once before, on the day Kathleen's father had died.

"What is it?"

"I can't tell you here," Kathleen said. "Come over tonight. What time do the boys go to bed?"

"It's Sunday. Connor won't be at the bar. I can come after supper," Johanna said. She tried to read more into Kathleen's expression and couldn't.

"Is the baby all right?"

"The baby is fine, but we can't talk here," Kathleen said. "There's no moon tonight. If you take the shortcut, you won't be able to see your hand in front of your face, so I'm glad you can come before dark."

There was never enough time in the day; there were always the demands of the hotel, the staff, the bills, and the children. The few hours she had on Sunday usually dissolved, but on this afternoon, waiting to talk to Kathleen, time turned to molasses. Johanna sat in the parlor, her sewing untouched on her lap. She made a mental list of terrible things. Was something wrong with one of the girls? Was Michael sick or about to lose his job? Were they in trouble with the mine boss? The wolf was always at the door—had it somehow gotten in?

After supper, Connor dozed on their bed, his legs propped up to ease his swelling ankles.

"I'm going to Kathleen's," she said. "I'll be back shortly."

Connor would be asleep in minutes. The boys would have to put themselves to bed. She instructed them to do it on time, but they would probably stay up until she returned.

There was still enough light to use the shortcut between their backyards. Michael had trimmed back the undergrowth, so they could avoid walking around the block. Johanna hurried though the arch of vine-covered branches.

Johanna let herself in through the kitchen door. A crucifix hung above the table where Kathleen sat in front of a pitcher filled with flowers. It was darker inside. As Johanna's eyes adjusted, she noticed her friend's pronounced cheekbones. Except for the protrusion around her middle, Kathleen was emaciated. This was not her usual glowing pregnancy. Johanna felt her throat close up. She couldn't bear to lose her friend to childbirth. How could she get Kathleen to eat more or slow down?

"Let me make you a cup of tea," Kathleen said.

"No, I've waited all afternoon." Johanna sat down. "Out with it."

Kathleen circled her palms around her belly, took a deep breath, and said, "Johanna, you know that no one here wants to see the Mollies rise up again."

"Of course not, but what does that have to do with me?"

Kathleen leaned forward. "You know nothing then?"

"What?"

"Michael thought Connor might have said something. I wondered if you noticed anything."

"I have no idea what you are talking about," Johanna said. Her heart was beating in her ears.

"Connor …" Kathleen hesitated. "Your husband is a ringleader."

"A ringleader—of what?"

"The Molly Maguires. They spend evenings at the bar on the night you and I go to the Society of Mary meetings. They're organizing, and not with any care. No telling who's listening."

Johanna exhaled. "Kathleen, you had me worried. Connor doesn't have enough energy to start up with the Mollies. I'm sure it's a mistake. I'll have that cup of tea now."

Kathleen did not move.

"It's not a rumor, Johanna. Michael told me. He's been asked to join. He's furious with Connor," Kathleen said. "And if Walsh finds out, he won't stand for it."

Johanna wondered if it was possible. Did Connor have the bravado to attempt something this dangerous? She felt strangely detached. One thought popped into her head: this is my ticket out of the marriage. She knew this was an egregious sin and decided not to reveal such hateful thoughts, even to Kathleen.

She was so anxious to speak with Connor that Johanna barely hugged Kathleen before taking leave through the kitchen door. The sun had set while she was inside. She didn't consider walking around the block. She wanted to hear Connor's explanation immediately.

When she got to the shortcut, the trees blocked out any remnants of remaining light. She extended her hands for guidance. The branches needed trimming where the path became a tunnel. A cobweb broke over her face. She used the back of her hand to wipe away the sticky threads. She gathered her skirts with one hand and guided herself along with the other. She had never been afraid taking this route before, but she stopped when she emerged from the shortcut. She could smell decomposing leaves, but there was something else. She heard a twig snap. The hair on the back of her neck prickled.

"Michael, is that you?" She couldn't think of who else would be there.

Suddenly there was a body—a man—behind her, pulling her. She struggled. When she tried to scream, he pressed a hand over her mouth. She twisted her body and managed to topple them. The man cursed under his breath. He rolled over, pinning her beneath him.

"Shhh, shhhh," he said. "I'm not going to hurt you."

Johanna clawed at his face. She attempted to lift her knee, to drive it into his crotch. He held her in a tight grip, but there was a gentleness, almost a caress.

"Johanna, it's me."

Someone had held her wrists before, exactly like this, but that had been pleasure, and this was the opposite, like a nightmare where she was too terrified to move.

"Shhh, Johanna, listen," he said. "It's me. It's Thomas."

How did this man know her name? Something was oddly familiar. It must be her Thomas dream. She even smelled his scent. If she cried out, she would wake up.

"Johanna, love, sweet one." The man used the same words of endearment.

"You can't be Thomas," she protested. "Thomas is dead."

"I'm very much alive." He relaxed the grip of his hand on her face. "No screaming, just listen."

It was a relief to take a breath.

"Good girl. Let me explain? Will we do that, sweet love?"

She nodded.

He shifted to rest next to her. She felt empty without his weight. She sat and pulled her knees to her chest. "Who are you?" she asked.

"I am your Thomas," he said. She knew it was his voice, his body.

"Not a day has gone by in these last years that I haven't thought of you, Johanna. I made a mistake going to Ulster. The Mollies did me wrong."

She heard him sob. She reached out to bring him close.

# CHAPTER FIVE

# THE MULBERRY LEAF

**Philadelphia, Pennsylvania, Summer 1880**

Several months into En's medical training, the Běnshuài sent word requesting a visit. En went immediately after work. He found his patron on his throne, surrounded by his usual assistants, except on this occasion there was a burly, middle-aged Chinese man standing behind the Běnshuài's chair next to First Wife. The man scowled at En.

"En, I hear you are a diligent student. Dr. Reynolds is much pleased, as am I." The Běnshuài did not waste time with pleasantries.

"Dr. Reynolds has been a most patient teacher."

"Good. Soon you will be caring for our sick," the Běnshuài said. "And how is Mai Ling?"

"She is fine, thank you." En had a premonition about where this conversation might lead. He'd taken too long to bring her back.

"And have you given thought to taking her as a wife?"

"I've been quite busy at the hospital." His stomach tightened.

"Yes, of course, your work is important, and I would not trouble you, but there is a new matter that requires our attention." The Běnshuài extended his arm to the portly man.

"This is my brother-in-law, Yin Niu."

En rarely saw obese Chinese men. He was fascinated by the rolls of fat. The man had no neck. Yin Niu crossed his arms defensively above his bulging stomach.

"Just before you arrived, Mai Ling was struggling to find her place in our community. She needed a good, safe place, and my wife thought that contacting her brother might help. Due to this unfortunate correspondence,"—the Běnshuài let his eyes rest on his wife—"Yin Niu is under the impression that Mai Ling is available for marriage. My wife no longer supports the match, as she believes Mai Ling is happy living with you."

His wife stared down at the silk-covered bundles that served as her feet.

"Yin Niu is planning to settle in the new frontier—Missouri, Kansas—some such place. He is willing to pay for a young woman who can push a plow and birth children. Mai Ling is petite. I'm not sure either will go well, but my brother-in-law is evidently swayed by a pretty face."

"She will birth me many sons," Yin Niu growled.

"Is this what Mai Ling wants?" En asked.

"She is here; you can ask her."

On this cue, the Běnshuài's wife retrieved Mai Ling from an adjacent room. En had never seen Mai Ling look anything but serene. Now he hardly recognized her. Her eyes were red, her face dissolved inward. Silent tears streamed down her face, spotting her tunic. The Běnshuài's wife kept an arm around the young woman's waist. Without the support, En thought Mai Ling might collapse.

"Mai Ling," the Běnshuài's said, "do you wish to marry Yin Niu, go with him?"

She shook her head violently side to side. Yin Niu snarled. His sister rebuked him with a glance.

"En, perhaps, for now, you could take Mai Ling home with you? She can gather her things and return in the morning, or if you so decide, we can arrange your marriage," the Běnshuài said. "This is entirely your decision."

En stood speechless.

"I will remind you that when you came to us you were a broken man, greatly in need of the connections our community offered. Although having a wife comes with certain challenges, as we see here today, I am certain you would benefit from the right marriage."

A nearly comatose Mai Ling was dragged across the room to where En stood. Ushering her home was like helping a patient take the first steps after surgery. When they entered the flat, she stumbled—nearly catatonic—and lay on the parlor floor.

"I'm going for a walk," he said, unable to bear her anguish.

The street noise pounded his shen, his spirit. En did not know this young woman. She annoyed him less these days, but he resented having to take responsibility for such a dependent soul. This woman was offered to him, practically forced on him. She had the body of a boy, although he had to admit that living in her proximity had stimulated vivid and pleasurable thoughts. Although he only saw her fully clothed, he occasionally woke from dreams where he had been caressing a naked Mai Ling.

But sexual desire was not a reason to marry. Was it fair to her that she would be part of an exchange? Her body for his career aspirations? He had made compromises when he accepted the Běnshuài's help. Did that make him complicit in the crimes he suspected the Běnshuài's operation aided or abetted? And what about this vulnerable girl? Wasn't this close to prostitution? What did that make him?

On the other hand, this would be an arranged marriage, not just an exchange of money for a sexual encounter. His parents had an arranged marriage. They had been a good team, treating patients, raising children together, more obligated than delighted with each other, but happy enough. And Mai Ling might not expect they would consummate the marriage. He had never made an advance toward her. Perhaps she would agree to marry him and count on their relationship remaining celibate? That meant no children. Did he want children? He had seen the torment when a parent lost a child. His father died after the death of Ai, so he lost only one of his children, but his mother was inconsolable when each of her daughters died, and the loss of Ji had finally killed her. Loving was dangerous.

His head throbbed. The fresh air didn't clear his thinking. He returned and found Mai Ling curled on her mat. He sat down next to her.

He stroked her hair, so soft, like holding strands of silk between his fingers. If he didn't marry her, would the Běnshuài give her to that barbarian? The man would work her to death. He thought of the brute taking Mai Ling. He would injure her, not only with the sex act, but likely with abuse. And would she survive childbirth on the prairie? If he didn't marry her, he might well be sending Mai Ling to her death.

"I will marry you, Mai Ling," he said. His voice sounded far away.

She lay still for a moment and then slowly got up onto her knees. In a child's pose, she kissed the ground in front of him. He pulled her to him in an awkward embrace. She was trembling.

He sent word. The Běnshuài had a large arrangement of chrysanthemums delivered with a note stating two elders would meet them at the courthouse the next day at three. He ended it with a small drawing of a leaf labeled "mulberry." En remembered the day the Běnshuài first suggested he take Mai Ling as a bride. The Běnshuài had said, "With time a mulberry leaf becomes a silk gown." This must be his way of reminding En that he'd known what was best, and his counsel had prevailed. En resented the smugness of the reference. He also wondered if the spin of marriage would bring them silk, gold, or misery.

They gathered the next afternoon, sitting in the courthouse hall among many couples. They were the first to be admitted into the judge's chambers.

"Those the Běnshuài sends are VIPs," the clerk said, ushering them past the others in the waiting area.

The judge stood with an open folder in front of him. En and Mai Ling walked forward, flanked by the Chinese elders. The judge yawned, and although it was a civil ceremony, he began, "Dearly beloved."

En rushed through his vows staring straight ahead. When it was Mai Ling's turn, the judge instructed En to take her hand. Her fingers were slender and ice cold. Did they share feelings of trepidation?

Some instinct made him want to warm her. He took her hand between his palms and pressed. Her hand was motionless in his. She did not meet his eyes, but he gazed at her, taking her in for the first time. He was surprised to note that she was pretty, her mouth delicate, her translucent skin almost luminous.

He repeated after the judge, barely able to manage an "I do."

Mai Ling looked directly at him as she spoke her vows. Only his little sisters had ever gazed at him with such trust. Her voice was soft with emotion, perhaps gratitude? Now he wished he had taken more time with his vows. She deserved more than perfunctory words. He had not seriously thought of marrying her, but the dread he'd felt only a day earlier had vanished. Why?

Perhaps it was the way she looked at him. Something about it unleashed the carnality he had long suppressed. He wanted her, and an overpowering yearning pulsed through his body. He desired more than a physical connection. He wanted a wife.

When the officiant said, "You may kiss your bride," En was unsure. She turned to face him with closed eyes. He bent toward her and brushed his lips across hers. He could smell her, clean like wind over a lake, the fragrance of peonies warmed in the sun. He wanted to linger, but fearing he was already taking advantage, he stopped. She had been subjected to unwanted advances, likely by more than the one man he knew about.

After the ceremony, they bid the elders farewell. One of the men pulled a bottle of Chang Bishi wine from his bag.

"A gift from the Běnshuài, with good wishes." The man pulled a red envelope from his coat pocket. "And here is the Lai See."

"Thank the Běnshuài." En took the bottle and pushed the Lai See envelope away. "I can't accept the wedding money."

"He told us you would refuse," the elder said. "And instructed us to say it is the least you can do for your bride. Mai Ling does not have the joy of a true Chinese wedding; she isn't wearing a qipao, the red dress, and the only double happiness symbol is on this envelope. You must accept these gifts to welcome happiness and prosperity."

En marveled his friend's ability to anticipate human reactions.

"Then I will accept with gratitude. Tell him we will come before the new moon."

En and Mai Ling walked back to their rooms. His mind raced. She slipped her hand in his. En's heart beat faster. He worried that his hand might be sweaty. Would that disgust her? He didn't want to let go. Holding her small hand in his made him feel powerful.

When they got to the flat, Mai Ling immediately went to the kitchen. She was behaving as if their lives were unchanged. En pulled out one of his textbooks to appear busy. He felt agitated. How could he concentrate? His unsettled thoughts turned gloomy. Of course, Mai Ling had only married him to get away from Yin Niu. What right had Woo to make him do this? He didn't have time for a woman. But perhaps she had wanted a husband, perhaps even in the fullest sense of the word. What did his new wife expect? What if he disappointed her?

The meal she prepared was more elaborate than usual. There were two place settings on the table for the first time. He sat down. She had poured them each a glass of wine. He drank rarely, and as the alcohol entered his bloodstream, he felt his tensions ease. They ate in silence; she glanced up at him from under hooded lashes. After dinner, she tidied up in the kitchen, and he retired to bed. Propping up pillows, he took out his notes to prepare for morning rounds, his body no longer as strained with want. The wine and food relaxed him enough that he could wait to see what, if anything, happened. Drained by the last two days, the tightness in his body lessened, the pages blurred. He decided to rise early to study and turned out the lamp.

He was sliding beneath the sheets when he saw her. She stood between the rooms, cocooned in a high-collared Chinese robe. He could make out faint patterns on the fabric; sweeping arcs of dragon's fire and swirling ocean waves glided in circles around her lithe body. He had never seen the silk robe before. She slowly untied the sash and the robe fell to her feet. Shapes warbled behind her in the dusky room, sea creatures dancing on the wall. She stood, ethereal among these shadowed beings. Her face was hidden. He could make out small breasts and the triangle where her legs came together.

"You are husband now," she said.

He stared.

"Please, En, you are husband."

Thinking what this display cost this young woman of exceeding modesty, he lifted the covers and shifted over on the bed. At least he could offer her some warmth. They lay together. Then she raised her leg over his thigh and sat up, straddling him. Almost involuntarily his hands traveled her taut skin, as smooth and cool as the silk robe. She was lovely. He considered resisting, although he had thought of little else since the ceremony, but this had to be her decision. He felt her trembling. His heart melted with tenderness for her. She began to touch him, his shoulders, his chest. Encouraged, he fought urgency, didn't wish to impose. At first, he moved uncertainly beneath her until she took him inside of her and rocked against him, slowly at first, and then faster. He grabbed her small buttocks and groaned with pleasure.

She lay with him that night and each following night. He recalled Michael's instruction about female anatomy. At first, he took only his own pleasure, but one night, after he had spent, he placed his hand on her. She clamped her legs together.

"Let me," he said, gradually sliding his fingers between her legs.

He had learned when examining patients that a confident touch helped calm them. He kept his caress gentle but firm as he explored Mai Ling's body, lingering in certain places, waiting on her breath. Soon he could elicit soft sighs, then gasps of pleasure. It took time for him to learn what gratified her. She was naive about her body, but she opened to the experience. Evoking her response was gratifying.

Michael's gift of information turned out to be truly, if not life-saving, life-affirming. One night, En rested his hand on her belly. His training prompted a diagnostic question, and almost reflexively he moved his hand to palpate a swelling breast. He waited for her to announce her condition. The next morning at breakfast she shyly mimed holding a bundle, swaying back and forth. She searched his face. When he smiled, she leapt up and kissed his cheek. Then she fell back into her chair, exhausted. It reminded him how much she depended on him, and for some reason, he now treasured the very thing he had most resisted. He had come of age in an America that challenged his humanity and manhood. But in her eyes, he was strong and capable. She assumed he had those qualities, and for her, he would do everything in his power to embody them. Surprised, he realized he adored her and that together they were weaving lives more beautiful than silk and richer than gold.

## Philadelphia, Pennsylvania, 1881

Mai Ling met him at the door of their flat. She was great with child, and her eyes flashed with exhilaration. He thought she had never looked more beautiful, and then it occurred to him that it might be her time.

"You are flushed." He felt a surge of apprehension. "Shall I get the midwife?"

She shook her head, laughed, and handed him a card. They were getting better at a shared language, incorporating both dialects, but the note, on heavy paper stock, was the fastest way for her to communicate. It was an invitation to dine at the Běnshuài's home, signed by the Běnshuài's wife. En had not read anything in his native language for years but gathered the Běnshuài wished to acknowledge their first wedding anniversary by hosting a dinner in their honor.

Mai Ling spent the days before the dinner in a flurry. He watched her try on clothes, but nothing adequately camouflaged her enormous belly. He often thought that if she toppled over, her legs and arms would never touch the ground. If he wasn't home, she would simply have to roll around until he returned to pull her back on her feet.

Once they had agreed to attend the dinner, En came home to a new assortment of clothing and hair accessories laid out on their bed. He didn't recognize the tunics, kimonos, or wraps, nor the elaborate sticks with jewels, beads, jade flowers, and other adornments. He assumed they were borrowed, but he had no idea from whom. Mai Ling apparently did not comprehend his question when he inquired, and she offered no explanation. She was happy, and that was all that mattered.

He got home early on the day of the dinner and discovered the source of the finery. There were two Chinese women adorning an elaborate coiled bun on Mai Ling's head. One was adjusting a pearl-encrusted stick. He entered and all three women froze in place, as if caught in some guilty act. Mai Ling was radiant, and he regretted disturbing them. He hoped to make the women comfortable, but they refused refreshment and left.

When the door closed behind them, En took Mai Ling in his arms.

"So lovely," he said, stroking her face and gently tracing the contours of her swelling breasts and abdomen. "I'm glad you have friends. They should come again."

Her English was improving, and even if she didn't know the words, she understood that he was encouraging her friendships. Mai Ling pushed him down on their bed and slowly lowered her body next to him. She covered his face with kisses and took his hand and placed it between her legs.

"No, dear, it's too close," he said. "It could bring on labor."

She nodded enthusiastically. The baby would be full term in a matter of days. Mai Ling would probably welcome labor. They had to be at dinner in an hour, but they knew the terrain of one another's bodies. The only thing that took time was repairing her ruined hairstyle.

Black tassels dangled from the red-and-yellow lanterns that hung over the Běnshuài's long table. The table was covered with a crimson cloth and set with gilded china plates. A dragon centerpiece of carved vegetables and chrysanthemums looked as if it floated in the air. In addition to the Běnshuài and his wife, there were two other couples. En recognized the men as senior advisors to the Běnshuài, both powerful and revered. They greeted En and Mai Ling with serious, almost forbidding expressions. Their wives were dressed in elegant fabrics and draped in expensive jewelry. Mai Ling was stunning in her less elaborate adornments. Most women would stay confined this late in a pregnancy, but the Běnshuài and his wife knew of her state when they issued the invitation. And Mai Ling, for all her modesty, would not have missed this evening. Her choice of elegance over embellishments drew attention to her regal bearing and beauty, minimizing her condition.

It was unusual for wives to join in at dinner. En wondered if the Běnshuài made the exception because his wife had always favored Mai Ling and wanted to recognize the union the Běnshuài had arranged. Given the guests, it dawned on En that the evening might be intended to vet him as a potential lieutenant. The Běnshuài would seek the opinions of the men in his command and possibly Mai Ling's, if not consent, acquiescence. Perhaps the Běnshuài needed him in the same opportunistic way that had led to his marriage to Mai Ling. Whatever had forced the timing of this dinner, En hoped he would not have to consider becoming a part of the Běnshuài's operation while he was still in school. He was now certain his friend's enterprise was far reaching and not always legal.

"I am so pleased you both could join us." The Běnshuài lifted his glass to En and Mai Ling. "We left you alone for your first year together. It's important for newlyweds to nurture tenderness and pleasure, but there is a matter of some urgency, and I couldn't delay. In any event, we can see that you have spent the time well, indeed."

Mai Ling blushed. The Běnshuài's wife, who sat to his right, said, "My husband is indelicate, but we are happy for the joy you and En bring to each other and our community."

"You have not had a fine meal until you sit at my wife's table," the Běnshuài said. "What is on our menu this evening?" En was touched to see his old friend smile at his wife with admiration and fondness. First Wife lowered her eyes at her husband's compliment.

"Please tell me we have spiced chicken," the Běnshuài said. "And lotus seeds with millet pudding?"

"Of course," she said. "And bird's nest soup, dumplings, and seaweed with bamboo shoots."

The Běnshuài swooned. En thought back to his childhood friend surviving on dumplings scavenged from garbage cans.

"But do not feel obliged to partake of the overly rich dishes my husband insists I serve." The Běnshuài's wife put her hand on Mai Ling's. "We do not have lamb or pineapple in any of the dishes. There is no risk to you or the baby with our meal this evening." En wondered if there was any evidence that lamb or pineapple was a serious health threat, but he was touched at the woman's consideration.

She continued, "And Mai Ling, I had our cook prepare a special soup for you tonight to balance the hot and cold required for good health. If you feel at all unwell, please speak up. We have a place where you can rest."

En thought it unlikely that Mai Ling would call attention to herself by requesting any special accommodations. He wondered if this dinner was too much for her, but once she had seen the invitation, there was no question she would attend unless she was in labor.

They started with wontons, hot and sour soup, and spring rolls. The main course included plates of sesame crab, orange chicken, Huang Men noodle, shrimp with garlic sauce, Buddha's delight, and steamed vegetables, followed by the house's signature pepper duck with plum sauce served with steamed bread. The Běnshuài announced that they were not to talk business while they ate, but midway through the meal, he violated his own rule and mentioned the need for medical care among the Chinese community.

"They made an exception to let En into the medical training program, no doubt because they expect him to treat Chinese," one of the lieutenants said.

"But the hospitals won't admit Chinese," the other said. "Will this give them an excuse?"

"We know it's early in your training yet, En, so no expectations," the Běnshuài said. "But we wanted to solicit your thinking. Many among us die due to the lack of emergency care. We also need skilled doctors to treat infectious disease. An epidemic could cost Chinese lives all over Philadelphia."

En was engrossed in the conversation. He only became aware of Mai Ling when she stood up and made a short grunt. One of the wives jumped to her side, and soon all of the women surrounded her. En stood to help, but the Běnshuài's wife intervened.

"Mai Ling may need the midwife," she said. As the women led her from the room, Mai Ling glanced back with a weak smile.

The men talked as if nothing significant had occurred. En could barely contain his anxiety. A few minutes later, the Běnshuài's wife returned and whispered in her husband's ear.

"Wonderful news," the Běnshuài said. "En, it is your wife's time. She is comfortably situated, and the midwife is already with her. It is auspicious that your first child, hopefully a boy, will be born under this roof."

"I must go to her." En put his napkin on the table.

"No, no, sit down," the Běnshuài said. "I assure you our women know how to assist at birth."

"But I have some experience. I delivered babies born to women in the railroad camp," En said. He had worried since the beginning about Mai Ling's youth and small pelvis. "She may need me."

"She would not wish it. No wife wants her husband at such a personal time," the Běnshuài's wife said. "You will stay here with my husband. I will keep you informed."

She spoke gently, but this was a command not to be challenged.

The dinner party continued well into the night, with En consuming far more alcohol than ever before. They were toasting one last round when the Běnshuài's wife came back and told En she had prepared a room for him. This time, instead of his usual room with the guards, she motioned for En to follow her to the second floor. He searched for a clue about Mai Ling's whereabouts, but she must have either been far from the central part of the house or perhaps suffering in silence.

The Běnshuài's wife opened the door to a large room. The walls were jade green, the rug a shade darker, and draperies, fringed in gold scallops, covered the windows. There was a carved poster bed, a chest of drawers, and a chair upholstered in ornate silk. The Běnshuài's wife showed him a washstand. A dressing gown was on the bed.

"When you wake, you will be a father." She smiled. "If it is sooner, I will come to you."

He lay on the bed, assuming he would barely rest, but the alcohol dragged him under. He woke in morning light, his head pounding.

He cleaned up as best he could. He had to find Mai Ling. He opened the door and saw a woman holding a stack of towels walking to the end of the long hall. Just as the woman opened the door, the Běnshuài's wife emerged. He thought he heard a faint animal cry as the door closed, but he might have imagined it.

"Ah, the doctor is awake. I am glad you slept in," the Běnshuài's wife said, taking his arm. "Mai Ling is doing well, but this is a first labor—it will be a little longer."

She insisted he get breakfast and go to the hospital. He took some tea and toast in the dining room. He was ashamed he had slept so late. Everyone had finished breakfast. How could he sleep while Mai Ling agonized to bring his child into the world?

He thought about going back to argue, or at least see her, but the women likely did have more experience than he did. He could wait in the house. Perhaps it would be easier for Mai Ling if she thought he was occupied.

He spent the day at the hospital, and every few minutes he would remember why he felt so unsettled. The thought that he might lose Mai Ling, or the baby, came in sickening waves. Messengers found him periodically, always with the same words, "All is well, be patient." Would this never end?

He left work at five, unusually early for him. When he returned to the brownstone, the Běnshuài's wife was waiting for him.

"She is making progress," she said. "It may be a few more hours. My husband is out this evening. I will have a tray brought to your room. Perhaps you will want to study or rest?"

En could do neither. He paced the floor until midnight when the updates came more regularly. He was told "within the hour" again and again. Finally, he could bear it no longer. Even if he destroyed the relationship with his benefactor or First Wife, or if it cost him the opportunity at the hospital, he had to see Mai Ling. He opened the door and marched down the hall with such determination he nearly collided with the Běnshuài's wife.

"En, I was coming for you," she said. "You have a beautiful baby daughter. Come and meet her."

En raced to enter the darkened room. It took him a moment to see Mai Ling, propped up in the bed, her face white as the pillowcase. No color meant loss of blood; he wondered how much. Even in the low light, he saw dark circles under her closed lids. Was she dying? He stepped closer. He eyelids fluttered open.

"En," she said. She smiled and looked down. He noticed the bundle for the first time. Mai Ling tried to lift the parcel but didn't have the strength.

He said, "May I?"

She nodded. He picked up the warm nest of blankets and brought it to his chest. Inside the swirl of cotton, a tiny red face with intense dark eyes stared at him. His heart was pierced with love.


En entrusted the care of his wife and baby to the women in the Běnshuài's home. Mai Ling would stay there for zuo yuezi, the sitting month of resting and eating enriching foods that would last for one lunar cycle after the birth. He knew there were many prohibitions on what his wife could eat and that the women would teach Mai Ling how to care for the baby, bathing mother and baby together because Mai Ling was susceptible to a chill.

En worked at the hospital each day and visited his wife and child in the evenings. One month after the birth, the women declared Mai Ling strong enough to return home. It was decided they would settle her and the baby in the flat while he was at work. En had spent enough time at his wife's bedside and holding his daughter that he thought the women could make Mai Ling comfortable and prepare the household for the baby better than he. He was able to focus on his work.

En stopped at the flower market on his way home and bought a large bouquet of red roses. He found Mai Ling already tucked into their bed. She wore a pink bed jacket that gave her cheeks some color. Her smile was radiant when he lay the roses across her lap. The women were delighted with such a demonstrative expression, especially as Mai Ling had not born him a son. They exclaimed how fortunate Mai Ling was to have such a loving husband.

The women bustled about the flat, and then finally, En and Mai Ling were alone with their new daughter. En, struck by the wonders of the human body, watched the infant suckling at Mai Ling's breast. His wife had nurtured every cell in this infant.

En made them each a plate from the prepared food the women had left and brought dinner to their bed. They put their daughter between them. They ate with their fingers and smiled at one another as the infant slept, her silky mouth working in and out, like a fish blowing bubbles.

They laughed and talked about the child. Mai Ling was clear that the baby must be given an American name. Although Mai Ling's English was still limited, they both knew a Chinese name might become an obstacle in their daughter's assimilation in their new country. Mai Ling liked some of the popular names of the time: Mary, Elizabeth, Martha, Ann, Hannah, Rebecca, Rachel, and Lydia, but they were Biblical, too far from the ancestors.

"Are we raising her as a Christian?" En asked, kissing Mai Ling playfully so she would know he wasn't criticizing. Growing up, any religious teaching had been secondary to his parent's faith in their medicine. He didn't practice any religion and had no desire to raise the child as a Buddhist. He had not seen Mai Ling invested in any religious tradition either and assumed she felt the same.

En took the plates to the kitchen. When he came back, Mai Ling's eyes were closed, their nameless daughter curled next to her. He could hear the soft breathing of his wife and child. One of the women must have put the flowers in a vase by the bed. The roses released a fragrance, like sweet almonds. The intricate petals were incandescent in the light. He had never seen anything more beautiful than the tableau before him.

"I'm not asleep," Mai Ling said. "Come, En, be with us."

He lay next to her. She was more asleep than awake, so he whispered, "I've been thinking. The name needs to cover the miles between America and China."

She didn't respond at first, so he closed his eyes. They could discuss it in the morning. Then she said, "We want her to be a part of new country," Mai Ling said. "Living here, but close to China."

"Yes," he said softly, glad that she agreed. "And the name needs to suit her. She is beautiful." Mai Ling nodded. "Why don't we call her Rose? Roses grow in both countries." He pointed to the flowers.

"Rose," May Ling repeated it under her breath, and then she picked up the baby and kissed her on the forehead. "Yes, Rose."

They were soon calling their little girl Rosie. They slept together, the three of them, that night, and in the following weeks. Mai Ling's recovery from the difficult birth was slow. En wanted her to sleep through the night, so he got up to change the baby and held her to her mother's breast. Mai Ling barely woke. Experienced parents assured him he would forget the exhaustion of these first weeks, but he was certain he would never forget the miracle of Mai Ling and

Rosie. He worried he was falling behind in his studies and he could not recollect what it felt like to have private time. But how could he regret the gift of this surprise family?

After a quiet three months, Rosie, who slept at night, started to erupt in crying jags during the day. The nurses at the hospital named it colic and said it would pass. En would return after a demanding day to find an exhausted Mai Ling with a howling infant and nappies flying like damp flags around the room. The infant raged when Mai Ling did not meet her every need. Where once Mai Ling had served him exclusively, now her attentions were divided. The baby came first.

En waited for life to get back to normal. By the time Rosie was four months old, it hit him: their lives would never be the same. The household was now centered on the needs of this helpless human being.

Even as he longed for a few quiet hours to gather himself, he was happier than he'd ever been. His work was meaningful; his wife was recovering; their daughter was blossoming. As Mai Ling's English improved, so did their communication. He found his wife more engaging. Although she'd endured a forty-eight-hour labor, and the demands that postpartum healing and nursing made on her body were substantial, Mai Ling never complained, and he admired her courage and forbearance.

His wife would always be timid and dependent, and between Mai Ling and Rosie, he sometimes he felt he had two children. He hadn't freely chosen to take on this responsibility, but he was grateful that his friend had pressed him into marriage. The gift of his daughter brought with it a deeper attachment to his wife. He loved her and was filled with a softness for the infant, too—a different kind of love, but just as profound.

## Philadelphia, Pennsylvania, 1882

En tried to call back his dream. A foggy curtain hung between him and the figures running in a dark passageway ahead. He was in bed and didn't recognize the room. He ran his tongue over his lips and tasted blood.

"Get the Běnshuài. He's awake." A woman's voice.

Someone tugged at his arm. He could not pull away. He floated underwater; it was translucent above him and he couldn't reach the surface.

"Get him a drink. Can't you see he's dehydrated?" It was the Běnshuài. "And lanolin. His lips are a mess. Who is in charge here?"

"He's been unconscious," the woman said. "We didn't want him to choke."

"For God's sake, give the man some water," the Běnshuài said, and in a softer voice, "My dear friend, return to us. You are safe, in my home."

En tried to speak. His tongue felt like rubber.

"You have been ill. Do you recall?"

En searched through the haze. He remembered the hospital, the lab. Then the profuse sweating, muscle aches, the dry cough. No, he didn't want to remember. He closed his eyes but couldn't repress the image. Looking down from above, he saw the beds in rows in the typhoid ward, the masked nurses, their hair tucked under caps, soundlessly moving from patient to patient. He saw himself with the doctors on rounds and then walking back to his microscope. He was walking fast. The research team was so close to isolating the bacteria—another piece in solving the typhoid puzzle. He was working quickly to prevent the specimens from drying out, staining slides, careful to avoid contamination—but then what?

"Home," he murmured. "Mai Ling and Rosie, in bed." He could see their flushed faces, inflamed eyes, distended bellies. He vaguely remembered lying down, the feverish bodies of his wife and child rolled against him, like molten weights.

"Sick, they are sick," En said.

"Yes, En," the Běnshuài said. "Typhoid."

He couldn't block the memories now and the stench of diarrhea. He forced himself to breathe, but his lungs barely expanded. He tried to sit up. The room churned around him.

"En, we'll talk when you are stronger." The Běnshuài gently patted En's shoulders.

Someone spooned a bitter liquid into En's mouth. He welcomed the oblivion it brought.

CHAPTER SIX

# IRISH NEED NOT APPLY

**Wilkes-Barre, Pennsylvania, 1883**

From where Father Ryan sat in the priest's cubicle, he could see Wilkes-Barre's most elegant sanctuary through the lattice screen. He'd started a successful building fund only a mere two years ago, so far raising enough to refurbish the pews, install a mosaic on the floor around the altar, and lay carpet on the steps. If he leaned to the right, he could see votive candles flickering under the statue of the Virgin and three of fourteen woodcuts depicting the Stations of the Cross. They were not simple plaques but rather works of art. He had personally cultivated the relationship with the wealthy art dealer, and Father Ryan anticipated this was only the first of many pieces that would adorn the house of the Lord that was entrusted to his care.

Most confessions were dull: routine disclosures, petty, venial sins. He supposed he should be grateful. Lies and lust were preferable to the more brutal revelations that made him sick at heart. How could a man beat his wife and children, offer a remorseful confession, and do it again the following week? He had to work at serenity and prayed to release the anger some confessions generated.

The sins, mortal and venial, were spread evenly among his congregants, but he spent more time in prayer for miners and their families. Their need was so great. Over the years, he had officiated at too many funerals. Accidents and lung disease claimed the men, childbirth took women, and malnourished children were vulnerable to a host of ailments that stole their lives. Sometimes the most vulnerable died of neglect. Mothers with so many children were overwhelmed. Fathers were drained of good health, toiling underground six days out of seven, then took sick and died young. Family needs exceeded capacity: hungry children in threadbare clothing and worn-out shoes overflowed in his parish schools—one teacher for sixty children with never enough pencils or books. It was essential he fill the coffers, one reason he preferred his educated and affluent parishioners. The more generosity he prompted from the wealthy, the greater assistance to his flock.

Father Ryan also worked with the mine bosses and politicians on behalf of his parishioners, believing he was called to bring God to the hearts of the powerful. When it all boiled over during the strike of '76, he was sympathetic to both sides. In the end, the miners lost. He'd tried to protect them, even the Mollies. He offered to act as a mediator, but the vigilantes had pushed too hard. The mine owners wouldn't tolerate violence, and he didn't blame them. At least the miners were back at work; half pay was better than nothing.

Someone entered the confessor's chamber. He was only one confession away from his glass of sherry, roast leg of lamb, and Mrs. D's potato and cheddar rolls. The thin wall in the cubicle shuddered as the supplicant dropped to the padded kneeler. Father Ryan gave petitioners a moment to gather their thoughts before he opened the mesh screen.

"Good afternoon," Father Ryan said.

"Bless me, Father, for I have sinned." The voice was deep, and Father Ryan detected an Irish brogue.

"How long has it been since your last confession?"

"I guess about ten or twelve years, maybe longer," the man said. Father Ryan placed the accent as County Mayo.

"I see." Not one of his regulars, but something about the voice was familiar. "And you are here to cleanse your soul?"

"I heard it was you, Joey. I thought maybe you could help me figure things out." The man's words came rapidly. "It's me, Thomas, from Derry."

"Tommy? From the old parish?" Father Ryan could barely make out the man's features, but he recognized the beard.

When they'd come of age together, Father Ryan had been enthralled by Tommy—his face, his body, and that reddish beard. During adolescence, Father Ryan observed Tommy's transformation from redheaded boy to breathtakingly handsome man. This was in stark contrast to his own development. He had always looked years younger than his peers, small boned with spindly legs. Puberty brought on a fuller nose, which shadowed his narrow chin, but he still couldn't grow a splotch of whisker.

Bullies sent Father Ryan limping home from his earliest school days, where he was called "Little Joey," and nobody at home seemed to notice. He was baptized Joseph Timothy Ryan, the youngest of five boys, but his father nicknamed him "the runt" and wanted nothing to do with him. His colorless mother was perpetually exhausted. She could barely keep a stew warm on the stove; the boys helped themselves from the pot when they were hungry. Some days, she didn't get out of bed; on other days, she simply sat and stared out the window.

His brothers were athletic and argumentative. Later, the family would joke about their favorite game, "Find the Baby." Some of his earliest memories were of waking up freezing in the woodbin or swinging from a rafter, stuffed in a sack.

He survived on cleverness; it took a certain cunning to play his brothers against one another. He escaped siblings and tormentors because, while he might never impress physically, he could rely on his intellect and fundamental desire to extend goodwill to others. Over the years, especially after he earned the respect afforded a priest, he cultivated a commanding dignity, and now, he was striking in his own way. The females of the parish certainly thought so, as did his male lovers.

"Father, you still there?"

Father Ryan realized he had been silent too long. Recovering himself, he said, "You go by Thomas now?"

"I do." The apprehension in Thomas's voice eased. "How are you, Joey?"

"I go by Father Ryan now," he said, reclaiming his professional demeanor. "I'm an ordained priest. Best if you call me Father."

"Sorry, Father. Just so glad I found you. I heard you were in Wilkes-Barre. Came all the way from Ireland but worth it."

"I am happy that I've been an instrument to bring you back to the true Church. Please continue with your confession."

"Jesus, Father Ryan, I can't do this. I was never any good at this stuff, and I forget how. I just need to talk to someone and …" Thomas sat back on the wooden seat.

"We are together in Christ. There is no rush," Father Ryan said, thinking he'd best pull back or Thomas would run, scared. "Is there a particular sin troubling you?"

"Well, Father …" He shifted his weight and moved closer to the screen. "A lot of them, more than one. Sin, I mean."

"Start wherever you would like. No sin is too great for God's forgiveness."

"Well, let's see. How about murder?"

"You committed a murder?" Father Ryan kept his tone even.

"One in Ireland and then maybe another here. I didn't want to do it—the one in Ireland—it was the mine boss. Got the kill order, and you can't refuse. I stabbed Buddy Green with a knife."

"Probably best that you not use names," Father Ryan said.

Thomas spoke rapidly, as if he could not contain words so long withheld.

"They said if I didn't murder him, they'd kill me and hurt my family. They sent someone with me, to make sure I did it, but directions got botched. The police were right around the corner. They nabbed my handler. I got away, ran to the safe house, and thought I'd be okay. Then the rest of the Mollies were there. They musta got scared. They put a bag over my head and beat me. Not sure if I blacked out from the beating or the bag. Next thing, I woke up in the hold of a ship."

"Although it was clearly a mistake to get involved with that lot, it sounds like you were coerced and then attacked," Father Ryan said.

"They didn't let me go either. Mollies met the ship, here in America. They said I owed them. They told me the only way I could keep their protection was to really kill somebody, to show I was with them. Ended up near here, with the group of Mollies, assigned to another contract killing."

Father Ryan shook his head. "And did you go?"

"Yeah, they were the only people I knew here. We took on a guy named Yost; he was lighting streetlamps out in Tamaqua."

Father Ryan put up his hand. "Please, no names."

"Sorry, but you know the rest. There was lots of talk. We killed him, plain and simple. I escaped back to Ireland. The others weren't so lucky."

"And none of this has caught up to you in almost a decade?"

"I hid on my cousin's farm. In the early years, if they knew, it would have meant death to me," Thomas said. "Then I guess everyone thought I was long dead and forgot about me.

"And I might not have been the one who killed him. I'm not sure which one of us—who took down the fellow. It was an ambush, and then a brawl. One died. The other one, he survived."

"I see. I recall the incident, in Pottsville, wasn't it? Some men were hanged for that murder, you know."

"I heard."

"Why were you not among the accused? The men who were hanged?"

"I was fresh off the boat. Never met the Pinkerton fellow, so they didn't know about me. Got back to New York—there was chaos at the docks. I paid a sailor to hide me. Snuck back and got word to my cousin. I was on that farm for nine years. Just me, my cousin, and his wife. Gloom and boredom. Everyone I loved, lost to me, no friends, nothing but fear."

"You didn't contact family or friends?" Father Ryan said.

"I wanted to … it was so lonely. But the Mollies thought I was dead. If they found out I was around—not sure what would've happened, to me or the people I loved. I had to stay low to keep everyone safe."

"And why have you returned now?"

"My parents died—never got to say goodbye. My sister moved to Galway with her husband. I couldn't stand that desolate farm one more season, so I decided that I'd risk it. Things had cooled off considerably too."

"Yes, we haven't had an incident here in the last few years," Father Ryan said.

"Also, I fathered a child. He's eight. I've never seen him. I wanted to get a look at him."

"And this child, is he in Wilkes-Barre?"

"No, Father, Nanticoke."

"And the child's mother?"

"Bridget, my wife. Boy's name is Finn."

"No names."

"Aye, Father, and, well, there are two lads."

"Your wife has been raising the children without you?"

"She's been raising Finn, with her parents' help. The other lad is … has … it's a different mother."

"And she is not your wife?"

"Yes, um, no, I …"

"And how old?"

"They're the same age, Father."

"So, you had two different women? Possibly more than one murder, and adultery? Is there more?"

"Hell, yes—oh, sorry, Father," Thomas said. "Will mind my language."

"I've heard it all," Father Ryan said, almost to himself.

"But that's pretty much the big stuff. Maybe the rest can wait for another day?"

"Yes, that might be good," Father Ryan said. Getting someone back into the Church was like holding an outstretched had to feed a deer: open palm, wait for the animal to come close, and don't move too close too quickly. "I can absolve you of these sins. And are you truly contrite and penitent?"

"Yes, Father, I am."

Father Ryan began the prayer of absolution. "God, the Father of mercies, through the death and resurrection of his Son …" He could recite these words without thought and put his attention on his voice. There was a reason he could hypnotize his flock. God had gifted him with a rich, resonant voice that was a comfort for tortured souls. He hoped Thomas received some of its calming advantage.

He ended with, "May our Lord Jesus Christ absolve you, and by His authority I absolve you from every bond of excommunication and interdict."

"Thank you, Father."

"And, Thomas, for your penance say fifty Our Fathers, fifty Hail Marys, and an Act of Contrition. And before you go, shall we arrange a time when I might provide additional guidance?"

There was an audible sigh from the other side of the wooden slat.

"I'd be grateful to see you face to face," Thomas said.

"Perhaps after your penance you could stop by the rectory? I should be in my study within the hour."

"I will, Father."

## Wilkes-Barre, Pennsylvania, 1883 and County Cork, Ireland, 1858

Father Ryan walked into his study, awash with flickering orange light. His housekeeper, Mrs. Donnelly, always made certain the fire was roaring when he returned from hearing confessions. She would call the room temperature "toasty," and he allowed the indulgence. He treasured this room where he wrote sermons and read. He had installed floor-to-ceiling bookshelves and an antique library staircase he'd found at an estate sale, and a book was always within an arm's reach.

He poured himself a sherry and sat in his favorite wing chair, upholstered in the same maroon velvet as the confessional curtains. Wine-red hues comforted him, like a womb. He considered Thomas. He'd thought his chance of ever seeing his friend again were remote. Thomas had traveled a long way to see his boys. Admirable. How many of these men disappear, leaving families in despair? Father Ryan was determined to help Thomas break the pattern and steer clear of the gallows.

On his way out of the church, Father Ryan had watched Thomas, kneeling in a pew. He'd given his old friend a long penance; it would do Thomas good to get on his knees. Thomas was hunched over, but Father Ryan could see through his ragged clothes that he still had a good build. Thomas's kerchief was tied around neck, probably to avoid being recognized. The spattering of gray at Thomas's temples made Father Ryan feel old. It had been over thirty years since they had been childhood friends. Two vivid incidents defined Father Ryan's adolescence and his decision to enter the priesthood. Thomas was central to both.

Back when they were altar boys, all his friends called him Little Joey. They played in the shadow of the Longtower in Derry before and after serving Mass. One day, after a sparsely attended morning service, Thomas chased him down the back stairs, trapping him in the vestment closet. Thomas pressed against him and Father Ryan could smell Tommy's sweet breath, could almost touch the stubble on his cheeks.

"Got ya," Tommy said.

Father Ryan had felt a rush of pleasure with his friend so close.

"I'd like to give you a licking," Tommy said.

He would happily submit to rough play and where it might lead. He was sure his friend didn't have the same inclination, so he responded, "Advent and wedding garments are white, and blood leaves stains."

Tommy laughed out loud. Entirely at Tommy's mercy, he lay crushed among the gilt and finery, but somehow held the upper hand, fighting back with cunning and bribes.

"Ah, Tommy," he said. "You'll not be bashing my brains today, not if you want me to do your sums. Sister Elizabeth is ready to skin your backside."

Father Ryan wasn't sure if it was his bribe to write an additional paper on the sacraments or the awkward moment where their faces were so close, but something caused Tommy to pull back. Father Ryan came away from the encounter thrilled and disturbed. He completed Tommy's homework, adding mistakes and poor handwriting to make it credible. He didn't understand why his body had flushed next to his friend, but the feeling had been delicious.

The second episode happened when they were skinny-dipping the next summer.

"Tally ho!" Tommy, stripped naked, swung on the rope over the black water. The other boys followed. He stood on the bank, fully clothed.

"Get on in here," a boy yelled from the quarry below.

Father Ryan could still remember the panic. If he disrobed, they would see.

"Give him a minute." Tommy plunged underneath the boy and pulled him under. Others joined legs and arms, splashing like a giant octopus made of boys.

He watched as Tommy disentangled himself from the sputtering mass and floated away. He could see the blur of Tommy's manhood under the water and felt that same heat.

"Come on. I can only keep them here for so long."

He removed his pants and gripped the rope. He trusted the cold water would solve his problem.

After that day, he grasped that he was different from his friends who felt this way around girls. When girls pursued him, alarm bells sounded. He avoided females and would simply describe a crush he had on another boy by attributing it to a girl. It required constant vigilance to not expose his urges. Uncovering those would mean annihilation.

He had it sorted out by the time he turned twenty. Another man was forbidden; Tommy was forbidden. The idea of touching a woman repulsed him. A vocation was his only option. Rather than becoming a pariah, he would be a revered member of society. All he had to do was keep his yearning under control.

He remained celibate until his first year in seminary. There were occasional lapses during those years, as was inevitable with so many men living together. After ordination, he had limited opportunities and more self-discipline. He had been with only one other man since becoming a priest: Father Neil. He tried not to, but he knew that he thought about his lover too frequently. After so many years of deprivation, he deserved affection and intimacy. What was the harm?

When he was with Father Neil, he could not fathom why what they shared was a sin, although he was conflicted afterward. The Church's teachings were clear. He decided it was a mystery why God had made him with the poles of attraction reversed. He took comfort in First Corinthians: "For now we see through a glass, darkly; but then face-to-face: now I know in part; but then shall I know even as also I am known." He would wait for answers and accept that Father Neil was his temptation, and when they were together, his deliverance.

Father Ryan helped himself to another sherry. The roaring flames turned the oak bookcases gold. The sherry eased his soul. There was a knock on the door. Mrs. Donnelly entered. He liked to eat alone in his study after hearing confessions. She placed the tray on the table in front of him.

"I'll come back with coffee and trifle," she said, flapping a napkin open and placing it on his lap.

"Thank you," he said. "The lamb smells delicious."


Father Ryan finished his meal and began to worry that Thomas might not come. Had he frightened him away? Mrs. Donnelly returned with tea.

"There is a man to see you. He looks rather down-at-heel. I made him wait so you could have your meal in peace. Shall I ask him to return in the morning?"

He hated the way Mrs. Donnelly made decisions without consulting him. Thomas should have been admitted right away, although he had enjoyed the respite. He said nothing to her; she didn't take criticism well.

"Do show my guest in," he said. "Perhaps afterward I can send him to the kitchen, and we can offer him some of that delicious lamb?"

She liked being his surrogate, and the word "we" would appease her enough that she would probably stay as late as needed.

When Thomas entered, Father Ryan stood and put an arm around him, gesturing toward the low sofa facing his wing chair. The wing chair was high, the sofa closer to the floor. They sat, and it occurred to him that he was literally looking down on his old friend: the prince and the pauper. He scolded himself. Just because this elegant office was his domain did not mean he should puff with pride. Still, how could he not savor this moment and the delicious awareness of how far he had come from the poverty he and Thomas had both known. It was a pleasant feeling—satisfying, like his full stomach.

The fire, crackling softly now, and the dark draperies and low-burning gas lights gave his study a womb-like quality. Father Ryan could barely detect the smell any longer, but when he had first arrived at the parish the strong scent of burning wax and incense floated like a vapor around the vestments of the priest then in residence. When Father Ryan was promoted as head priest and became the leaseholder of this study, he found comfort in the musty aroma. It also validated his ascent to power.

"Thomas, good of you to come," he said.

Thomas cleared his throat and bounced his knees up and down until Father Ryan looked pointedly at the jiggling legs. Thomas smoothed his palms down his thighs, as if willing his limbs still.

Father Ryan lifted the decanter from the table and poured them each a sherry. Life really was a mystery. Here he was with Thomas, sitting across from him in the flesh. Father Ryan suspected that Thomas had always understood his attraction, even if he didn't reciprocate. Perhaps that was why Thomas had gone out of his way to protect him and defend him when their crowd might have singled him out for derision, or worse. Now he had to do the same for Thomas: keep him out of the hands of the Mollies and the police.

"So, Thomas, what a fine mess you have here," Father Ryan said, handing him a glass.

"Aye, that is true," Thomas said. He sat back and gulped the sherry.

"I know you are in search of guidance, and I would like to give you God's perspective."

When Thomas didn't object, he continued.

"You can't fix the past. Thomas, you were forced not only to take a life, but to run under the threat of losing your life. Others, wicked men, controlled these terrible deeds. It's why I have always advocated that the Irish not take the law into their own hands. It has cost too much. You have paid a dear price, my friend: separation from your loved ones and banishment for all these years."

Father Ryan thought Thomas was blinking back tears. He wanted to cover his friend's hand with his own, but he'd seen empathy evoke emotional reactions from these stoic men. If Thomas cried openly it would embarrass them both.

He poured them both another sherry, giving Thomas time to collect himself.

"In truth, some innocent men went to the gallows. Some guilty men, from both sides, are walking down the streets in Ireland and here in Pottsville, Mauch Chunk, and Philadelphia. But enough killing and maiming. 'Vengeance is mine, saith the Lord.' You can't rescue the dead. You can only serve the living."

Thomas looked stunned. Father Ryan guessed that Thomas thought he would urge him to turn himself in. Father Ryan didn't trust the police, even though he occasionally spoke on their behalf. He had no intention of sending Thomas to prison, or worse. Besides, he also knew Thomas would never betray the brotherhood.

"Now, as to the living, I understand there are two young lads who could use your support and protection, and there are two different women?" he asked. He put his empty glass on the table and tented his hands, fingertips to his lips, the embodiment of a wise priest.

"You married one of these women in the Church?"

"Yes, I married Bridget before I came to America. She was with child, and I didn't know that Johanna was … sorry, Father, I shouldn't use names."

"So, you were working in Ulster. A wife up north and a second family in County Mayo?"

"No, no. The women lived in neighboring towns. I was just seeing them both, but, Johanna, she was going to be my wife. I wanted to keep her pure until we could marry. I couldn't offer much. She would have hated Ulster, and what if she got pregnant or if I died?"

"And the other woman?"

"I grew up in her village. Bridget was a family friend. Her mother always insisted I come for supper when I was down south. She made the best corned beef and cabbage. Bridget's father would pour fine Irish whiskey on the bread pudding."

"And was Bridget dessert as well?" The words popped out. He shouldn't speak so irreverently.

"She was that kind of girl," Thomas reddened. "Her parents said if I was tired, I should stay the night. They didn't say where and then went to bed. Bridget slept in the loft. I never made promises."

"I see. So how is it you came to marry her?"

"I got the kill orders from the Mollies. Went back to say goodbye to Johanna. We spent the afternoon together," Thomas grimaced. "It was the first, the only time, we—she said it was our wedding."

"I understand. And then?"

"I didn't want to stop by Bridget's, but what if I didn't come back? I owed them a goodbye, too." Thomas shook his head. "It was stupid. When I got there, Bridget, her parents, and a priest were waiting. Her mother and the priest, they glared daggers at me. Mr. Sullivan, he was nicer but said, real quiet like, that they didn't blame me, just wanted me to do right by Bridget."

"They assumed you were the father?"

"Yeah, I guess. The priest said something about unwanted pregnancies but no such thing as an unwanted child. We went into the parlor, and he married us. I don't remember much except that Bridget never stopped blubbering. Funny, Father Ryan, I had two wedding nights on the same day."

"Thomas, it sounds like it's been a difficult path for you, and I'm sorry." Father Ryan spoke slowly so Thomas would understand. "From what you have told me, I would say the woman you married is your wife in the true Church. It was a ceremony performed by a priest. Her child, your son, is undoubtedly registered as a legitimate birth in church records."

Thomas nodded.

"And this woman, your wife, where is she?"

"Living with her parents and the boy in Nanticoke."

"Do you think it is safe to live with her as man and wife in Nanticoke? Will the police or the Molly Maguires have reason to look for you here?"

"I got out quick. I don't think the police were ever looking for me. There are only a few men who knew I was here in '74. And the men who were with me during the attack are"—he gulped—"gone."

"Even if some of the Mollies know and carry a grudge, I don't think they'll act," Father Ryan said. "No one wants any more trouble. I think the Mollies would not begrudge you taking care of your family. That's what the strike was about."

"And the other woman and child?" Thomas asked. "I'd like to see her, do something for her."

"Ah, a different story, I'm afraid. The child is a bastard, conceived out of wedlock. I presume the woman was a full participant? If so, she owns the sin, too," the priest said. "Can she provide for the child?"

"Yes, she got married," Thomas said. "Her husband has raised my son as his own. I've heard they have a younger lad, too."

"Then she has no claim on you, and your son is better off in the family he knows," the priest said. "You understand it would be wrong to contact her again? It will be difficult, living in the same town, so you must be vigilant."

"How can that be, Father? I love her."

"Thomas, you are married; contact with another woman is adultery, plain and simple."

Father Ryan wished he could wipe the melancholy off Thomas's face.

"I know what it is to love someone, have it feel right, but that doesn't change the fact that it is sin," Father Ryan said.

"Why would God want something like that?" Thomas said.

"We must trust that God knows best," said the priest. "It isn't easy, but it's what God requires. Now, I will ring for Mrs. Donnelly. She will heat up some supper for you. Stay tonight. In the morning, we'll get you cleaned up and then reunited with your wife and son. You'll need work, but let's keep you out of the mines—no need to draw attention. Can you do simple carpentry, the work of our Lord?"

"Sure," Thomas said.

"I shall arrange a job in Nanticoke at St. Francis Parish."


After Mrs. Donnelly took Thomas to the kitchen, Father Ryan felt unsettled. He poured himself another sherry and considered his own hypocrisy. Was it perhaps a topic to discuss with his confessor? He'd told Thomas not to let his love for a woman lead him to sin, yet that was precisely what he and Father Neil faced. He wondered if the difference could be that some men—him included—were in the position to bend the rules because they kept it in bounds? Thomas was simply too impulsive.

He also knew he was fooling himself. He was as much a sinner as anyone.

Mrs. D had forgotten the trifle. He poured himself a splash more sherry and sat back to enjoy the dying fire. He would indulge himself for a few minutes with thoughts of a younger Thomas, his first crush, and then think about Father Neil, who was not unlike the young Tommy.

Father Neil's hair was blond, not red, but he had the same full beard, chiseled features, and magnetic charm. They had met in the dining hall at Pocono Mountain Monastery. They were in silence when Father Neil fixed his hazel eyes on Father Ryan at dinner. Father Ryan felt a charge, and of course, lust. Father Neil was good-looking, but there was something else. He knew that Father Neil would be important in his life. Father Neil followed him back through the monastery halls and into Father Ryan's chamber. He closed the door. Wordlessly, they disrobed and stood, both naked, facing each other in the small cell.

Father Neil's body was tight. He had worked the fields with farmers. They embraced with reverence, as if performing a ritual. Joining with Father Neil felt like a sacrament. They had both spent right away and would wait until they could go again. Instead of being guilt-ridden and rushed, as most of his encounters were, the act became a holy experience.

That first night Father Ryan's exhilaration made it impossible to sleep. His relationship with Father Neil was the most integral, authentic thing he'd ever done. And yet the Church said it was a sin. He was tormented but unable to stop. He gave himself to Father Neil every night that week. When the retreat was over, they parted and, without discussion, each scheduled the same retreat dates and engaged in the same indulgence the following year. Five years later, Father Ryan now felt a deep love for Father Neil. He was a good, honest priest. Father Ryan had never known a priest who gave more unselfishly to his flock. His lover had a beautiful face and physique, but Father Neil's true beauty was his core.

Early on, Father Ryan thought about asking Father Neil to relocate. They could live in the same parish, share meals, sleep in each other's arms. He knew other priests who lived together, as if they had been randomly assigned to the same location. They worked side by side during the day, careful not to reveal their intimacy. He assumed they made private arrangements at night.

He gazed around his study. He had everything he wanted: ordered files of journals and sermons, books, an amply stocked bar. He had the devoted services of Mrs. Donnelly. She supervised the parish cook, gardener, and houseboy on his behalf. If only he could have Father Neil here with him, too.

They had discussed it last time they were together. "The deception would get in the way of our ministry; our call mandates integrity," Father Neil told him. "Even if we're never caught, we'll know, and our daily intercessions on behalf of these beleaguered people would lose power. We can afford this one week, when we're not with our parishioners, but we would shortchange our ministry if we lived together."

They were of the same mind. Although Father Ryan might have risked it, Father Neil was right.

Sometimes after hearing a confession, especially if it stirred him, Father Ryan would daydream about Father Neil. When his fantasies of Father Neil caused him to behave in ways that weren't perfectly celibate, Father Ryan confessed. Self-pleasure was a frequent sin; he knew that from the burdens his more honest parishioners shared. After confession, Father Ryan attempted to pack his physical drives in a box, the one he and Father Neil unpacked once a year.

His life would be easier—perhaps his ministry would be more effective—if he kept his vows of celibacy. He often felt deep remorse, for both himself and his lover. God was not pleased, of course, when men fell short of His commandments, but that was precisely why the Church had the means to absolve sin. Once, following a confession, a fellow priest had urged him to truly repent and stop seeing Father

Neil. Instead, Father Ryan stopped confessing or would wait until he was in Philadelphia and didn't know the priest. He could never turn away from Father Neil's love. It sustained him. He hoped his love did the same for Father Brian Neil.

CHAPTER SEVEN

# A WORLD APART

**Nanticoke, Pennsylvania, Spring 1883**

T he ceiling in Johanna and Connor's bedroom peaked at the triangle over the dormer windows. An adult could only stand at full height in the center of the room. Johanna was in the corner, bent over and pulling clothing from a dresser drawer that was jammed against the short wall. On the opposite side of the attic, the boys were asleep in their room. With the kitchen and family room in between, she hoped they couldn't hear Connor.

"Please, you'll disturb the guests," she said. "You know sound carries through the floorboards. The man in 4A complained last week when the boys were playing tag."

"I don't give a goddamn who hears me," Connor said. "I married a banshee, not a woman. The people around here should know the truth." He had been lying on the bed but now was sitting, his chest puffed out like one of the roosters behind the miner's shack.

"I simply asked why you let the Molly Maguires under our roof."
She threw her undergarments into the valise she'd found in a closet.

"What do you mean?" he said.

"Kathleen told me last night about the meetings in the bar, that you invited Michael," she said.

"So what if I did? It's time I did more for our cause," he said. "I listen to these miners every night at the bar. What they say makes sense. They include me; they need my help."

"They are has-beens. There are no real Mollies now, just the pathetic lot that's left."

"You don't know what you are talking about," he said. The iron bed creaked under his weight.

She did know what she was talking about. The Mollies, though still around, were greatly diminished. Her conversation with Thomas had been brief. The Mollies had ruined him and taken their future. He told her that he could explain it all, even marrying Bridget. The vigilantes would have killed him if he hadn't disappeared. He admitted he'd been young and foolish. She was certain he had been ill-used. She couldn't stop thinking about one small choice that might have changed their fate: if she had asked more questions, persuaded him to stay an extra day … if, if, if.

They had been so close to happiness, to raising a child together. Why did he say he still loved her? Did she believe him? And what of Bridget? He said he married her because he thought he was going to his death. But he had cheated. She, Connor, Bridget, they had all suffered, and so had the children. There was so much to sort out, but she already knew that the Molly Maguires endangered anyone who associated with them.

She turned to Connor. "I know that the men who are in the Mollies are making foolish choices, especially the ones who are still at it. The strong ones got hanged. The smart ones realized they were being used."

She stopped hurling garments and looked at the man whom she had once trusted to bring them to America. "These men are cowards," she said. "They talk blarney about the Mollies. It's over, and they can't even admit they've lost."

"You want us to give up the fight—is that it?" He rolled his legs over to the floor. He needed a shave. His undershirt stretched taught over his fleshy gut.

"I want you to stay away from them—and stop allowing them to use Mr. Walsh's hotel as a watering hole," she said.

"They pay."

"Ha, I bet."

"Well, he owes me."

"I'm the one who has been working all hours, now with the office work on top of keeping track of the guests, the staff," Johanna said. "I started here on my hands and knees. You have no idea. It's disgusting what we clean up. You just drink and pour, in that order."

He put his head in his hands. If he didn't look so much like a hobo, she might feel some sympathy, but he had deliberately made them targets. His ignorance and passivity unleashed a rage so ferocious she had to get away. How could he be ineffective and arrogant at the same time? She forced herself to stay calm, to make it out of the room. Her husband repulsed her, especially when she thought of Thomas: his tenderness, the way his words excited her, his half smile when she teased him. She knew in her heart that he had come back for her; how could he have ever loved Bridget?

"You're running around like the Queen of Sheba," Connor said. "All you care about is another goddamn bloody dollar—ordering people around, firing good chambermaids, while toadying up to Walsh ... you hate the man. That's what's disgusting."

"Disgusted, are you? Well then, you find a job. You put food on the table and a roof over our heads. That'd be a change, a welcome one."

"You haven't done all of this by yourself, you know," he countered. "I'm standing at the bar until my feet swell."

"Let's not forget how you got behind that bar," she said.

Even as she said it, she wondered if at some level he resented her role. Was her success the reason behind his hostility? It didn't matter; he had to see the folly in assisting the Mollies.

She lowered her voice. "Stop helping them. They will make trouble, get arrested."

"Or you'll do what?"

"You know Walsh won't stand by while you ruin his business. He will throw us out. And what about the police? I don't want our boys to see their father hanged." Was it too much to ask that he not destroy the family? She would do the work and take the responsibility. She wasn't asking for much.

"Time I took a stand."

"Then stand up for your family, not a bunch of criminals," she said. He looked away.

There was no reasoning with him. She grabbed her nightgown and stuffed it in the bag. "I'm sleeping at Butterwort House tonight," she said, fastening the buckle on her bag. "Please, Connor, whatever you do,"—she put her hand on the doorknob—"keep the Mollies away from our home. Promise me you will stop."

"The Pennsylvania Cossacks are still after us, and it isn't right," he said, but his voice was subdued now.

"What's right is that our lads stay safe and get an education."

He glanced up at her, suddenly more helpless than defiant.

"Do you promise you'll stop?"

"I promise," Connor said, pulling his undershirt down. "I'm going downstairs. Sleep wherever you like."

Johanna almost felt sorry for him, sitting there half naked and defeated. Then she remembered how careless he had been with their lives, and she couldn't stand to look at him for one minute longer. She would go to Butterwort House and be back in the morning, before the boys woke up.

The St. Francis Parish School administrative office was cramped. Mrs. Heart's desk was at the center, surrounded by smaller tables for student helpers and parent volunteers. There were bookshelves next to a wall of teacher's mailboxes. Mrs. Heart was the school secretary and nurse. She kept a bowl of hard candy on her desk and first aid supplies in her right-hand drawer. She also managed access to the inner sanctum: the office of Mother Agnes, head of school.

Mrs. Heart, her gray ringlets shaking with displeasure, rapped on Mother Agnes's door.

"This young man has been sent to see you." Mrs. Heart stood in the doorway, holding TC by the shoulders. He cradled one hand in the curve of his arm.

"Skippy the two-inch ruler has struck again. That nun uses it like a weapon."

"Please, let's not give Skippy any credit. Sister is responsible for what happens in her classroom," Mother Agnes said. She came from behind her desk and gave Mrs. Heart a knowing look. Mrs. Heart embodied her name. She was all heart, and this boy's injury at the hands of a nun would upset her for days.

Mother Agnes put her arm around the boy's thin shoulders. He must be in a lot of pain and was clearly afraid of her. Mother Agnes knew the children saw her as ancient, although she was not yet sixty-five. When she looked in the mirror, which she rarely did, folds of skin pushed against her wimple like biscuit dough. Her face was covered in lines, the deepest around her mouth, the price of her smiles. Crow's feet, like tiny arrows, drew attention to eyes that could deliver an icy stare or compassion that magically calmed even the most troubled child.

"Sister Mary Catherine lost control this time," Mrs. Heart said, examining TC's finger. "She may have broken a bone."

TC looked away; tears streaked his cheeks.

Mother Agnes guided TC to one of the overstuffed chairs near the bay window.

"Sister Mary Catherine can be difficult." Mother Agnes gently angled him into the seat. She tucked her hands inside one of the many pockets in her habit and sat across from him. She wanted him to know that she believed Sister had been wrong to strike him, but she couldn't undermine one of her teachers by speaking too forcefully.

"You are no stranger to Skippy?"

"Yes, I mean, no, Mother Superior Agnes." TC winced when he spoke.

"Just Mother Agnes will do." She bent over and examined his finger. "I am very sorry you were hurt today. This shouldn't happen. There are so many children in our classes, far too many, and the nuns get overly tired. It's not hard to understand why they may sometimes lose patience?"

He nodded mechanically and turned to stare out the window. Mother Agnes liked the way her garden greeted guests: daffodils and red tulips bordered the garden now. She loved each season: sunflowers, blazing yellow-orange with heads bowed in the sunshine, the last bit of color fading in autumn, the frosty blue-gray of January. Spring captured rebirth and was her favorite. She wished she could send TC to the garden for recess and banish the troubles that had brought him here.

"Let's elevate it. Keep the swelling down." She placed a pillow on his lap, and he gingerly lowered his hand.

"I'll get some ice," Mrs. Heart said, adding, "That nun doesn't belong around children." Mother Agnes didn't respond, but Mrs. Heart was right. Last fall she had considered dividing the children among other teachers and relieving Sister Mary Catherine of her duties, but it would have made class sizes even larger. Next year she would find a way to recruit a new teacher and promote Sister to a job that kept her away from the children.

"It's possible that you and Sister Mary Catherine may not be well matched, and that does not make school a good place for you to learn."

"Am I to go home?" He sat up in alarm. The movement made him flinch.

"Oh, no, TC, please sit back. We'll have you feeling better soon. And we want you in school," she said. "But Sister's classroom isn't right for you. Can you tell me what happened today?"

"Yes, I mean, no, Mother Superior Sister Agnes." He shuddered. "I'm not sure." He clamped his good hand over his mouth.

She reached for a shawl. "Here, this will warm you up. How did it start?"

He mumbled under his breath, "I am not a crybaby."

"Who said you were?"

"Finn. I sat on the stool all morning, but I didn't know what those squiggles were, and I didn't know the answers, so Sister got mad," TC said. "I held out my hand, but I couldn't help crying when she cracked me. Finn made a face, and everyone laughed."

"How terrible for you," Mother Agnes said.

TC raised grateful eyes to her. Tears rimmed his eyelids.

"TC, you do not have to go back to that classroom," Mother Agnes said. "I promise you. I want you to be safe, and this won't happen again."

"Really?" His knotted brow eased.

"I have an idea. Let's see what you think." She spoke as Mrs. Heart came into the room with a towel filled with ice.

"I happen to know that Mrs. Heart is busy right now and could use a special student to help us in the office."

"I would like to help, but I'm not smart," TC said. "You probably should pick a different kid."

"I think we would like you. Isn't that right, Mrs. Heart?"

"Indeed." Mrs. Heart took a tin from one of the shelves and put out some cookies on a plate.

"And, TC, you might be surprised at how smart you really are. I have known many children who learn differently, but they do learn," Mother Agnes said. "Let's move you here to our office. You can sit at the special table next to Mrs. Heart and help her. And we will have schoolwork, not punishment, for you. That way you won't get behind."

"It's just that I can't learn," he said, eyes wide.

"TC, I have a secret gift. I can teach children to read, especially when they believe they cannot. I have special books. Would you like to learn how to read, TC?"

"I'm supposed to know how already," he said.

"That is not what I asked," Mother Agnes said. "If you will work hard, TC, and I believe you will, you will read. Would you like that?"

"Yes, Mother Agnes," TC said. She saw relief rush across his face, then worry return. "And what about Sister Mary Catherine?"

"Leave Sister Mary Catherine, and Skippy, to me."


The first night she packed her bag and slept at Butterwort House, Johanna thought it would be temporary. By late spring, she had been sleeping in the attic bedroom of Butterwort House for several months, essentially moving into the room on the third floor. This was the smallest room among the properties, and it was rarely rented. It had two tiny windows next to the chimney, and the wide iron bed barely fit. There was a straight-backed chair and a rag rug in the pinks and purples of the butterwort flower. Kathleen had appliquéd butterwort flowers on squares for the quilt. It was comforting to sleep beneath Kathleen's handiwork. Each time Johanna made the bed, her fingers touched the friendship and devotion of her friend. Guests stayed on the floors below, but this floor was hers alone. Only Kathleen, and now Thomas, visited.

At first, she'd wanted nothing to do with him. Thomas had abandoned her, disappeared for years, and then shown up, married to Bridget. But after their encounter, learning he had been a victim too, she'd found herself running into him in town or outside the hotel. It was more than a coincidence. Sometimes he asked if they could talk, and she brushed off the request. Finally, he started leaving unsigned notes—hidden in nosegays, under the mat at the kitchen door, or at the front desk. She was afraid someone would find one, so she agreed to meet him to tell him in person he had to stop.

She slipped away on an unseasonably warm spring afternoon to meet him at the agreed-upon location, past the field behind the hotel. The trees had just filled out with leaves, and she had to search to find him hidden in a cove.

Neither of them could hold back their wide smiles. He was sitting on a log, and she stooped to sit next to him. She lost her balance, and he caught her. She surprised herself by not moving away.

"I'm glad you came," Thomas said. "I want to know all about you, how you have been, about my son, how you managed—everything."

"What right do you have to ask?" She was aware that his arms were still on her waist. "We were married, that day in the field."

"I know, sweet love. I have always loved you, before that day, and especially after that afternoon," he said.

"I carried your child, too," Johanna protested. "Why didn't you contact me, let me know you were alive?"

"I had no choice. It might have brought trouble to your door. I had to leave Ireland with no warning, or I was a dead man. Then I got to America, but it went badly here, too," he said. "Then they were after me. If I tried to find you, it would have put you in danger."

"Why? Wait. You did it. You killed someone?"

"He deserved to die."

"Oh my God." Her body wanted to stay in his embrace, but another part of her wanted to run.

"That's all I can tell you," he said. "It's not what I wanted."

She pulled away but stayed seated next to him.

"I love you, Johanna." His hand caressed her shoulder. "I know it was terrible. I should have been the one to bring you to America. The boy is mine, and I haven't even met him."

He put his face close to hers. How long had it been since she'd wanted someone?

"But you married Bridget."

"Did it matter?" His lips were over hers. "I was a dead man."

"Of course it mattered," she said.

He was kissing her. Bridget was unfortunate and Thomas had been a man with a woman who made it easy for him. He had always held back with Johanna. She tried not to think about how Thomas took advantage.

"This is all we have, Johanna," he said. "Let's make it enough."

She felt his breath on her neck.

"I risked my life to come to you, sweet love."

She wanted to believe him. Connor didn't love her. If he ever had, now he was married to alcohol. He resented his job, the boys, and especially her. She hated his jeers of "boss lady." She was so lonely and too young to live like a nun.

The man she loved pulled her into an embrace. "Johanna, I have missed you," he said. His fingers reached under her bodice.

She could not live without this connection. Thomas was her husband. She was his wife. This was her true marriage.

"Tonight," she said. "I sleep alone in the attic of Butterwort House. I'll leave the door to the back stairs unlocked."


That night, a soft knock on her door marked the start of their secret existence. While she was still operating a hotel, pleasing customers, caring for children, and worrying about the future, when she let him into her room they created a world apart.

Thomas smelled of the outdoors, of her youth. She had not forgotten his scent. He had not forgotten her body. The years they had been apart dissolved without words.

Afterward, she lay with her head on his chest.

"Is this real?" she asked. "We have privacy, candlelight, and a warm bed?"

"You don't miss the breeze and the bugs?"

"If I have you, I miss nothing. Why are we so good together?"

"This is how grown-ups play," he said. "We're good playmates, and we trust each other."

"Why doesn't it feel wrong?"

"Because we are good people, doing the best we know how to do."

Thomas had done the priest's bidding and moved back in with Bridget. He didn't fully answer Johanna's questions, but Johanna gathered that Bridget and her parents also thought he'd been killed and were unaware of the years he had been in hiding. They evidently did not hold his disappearance against him and welcomed him to the same yellow house where Johanna and her family had first encountered Finn. Soon, Thomas was visiting at least once a week. Thanks to Father Ryan's arrangements, he worked as a handyman at the church on weekdays. The priest lined up a second job for him delivering ice in the early mornings, and the hotel was one of his stops. Connor was usually still asleep, so he never saw Thomas. She assumed Connor knew Thomas was back and with Bridget. It was something else they didn't discuss.

Thomas came to her in the middle of the night, sometimes closer to dawn. Johanna supposed he told Bridget that his work at the ice-house started then. Thomas used the cold surface of the ice block he delivered like a telegraph. A small flower on ice meant he could get away. Johanna felt a thrill when she saw a tiny violet or rosebud and would press the tip of her finger on the petals until it tingled with the cold. She would then warm her finger in her mouth, touching her tongue to where the ice had stung her flesh.

When he was with her, she didn't consider the consequences. His body delighted her. She knew he felt the same about hers, even her dimpled belly. His beard was fuller now, and she loved feeling it on her skin. He would tease her until she couldn't stand it. He sometimes would tempt her by refusing to get into the bed, prancing naked around the bed asking if she liked what she saw.

She could only laugh.

He never arrived without an arrangement. On nights she was alone, she reveled in undisturbed sleep. She left work early on days when she found the flower, had the chambermaid draw a bath, and pampered herself until he arrived.

When the first roses bloomed in early June, she filled her apron with petals. She carried them to her room and sprinkled them over the bed. When Thomas came that evening, she covered her body, too. He took one look at her and said, "Ah, Johanna, I'm coming in, and the water looks fine."

His desire was all she needed to respond.

After he left, always before dawn, she fell into a deep sleep. Running a hotel meant she was typically unable to sleep past six, but now she relished lying in bed, sometimes long enough that she had to rush to get to the kitchen before she was missed.

He never spoke of the past. Once she asked, "Are you sure the Mollies aren't looking for you?"

He was quiet and then said, "I've seen no signs that they are. The parish job is working out. I'm pretty good at oiling hinges and mopping floors."

He never spoke of his wife or how he saw the future. She knew it was impossible, but if he ever asked, would she run away with him? She could never leave her children—that would be impossible. And besides, would he ever leave Bridget and Finn? Occasionally she would hint about the time that lay ahead, if they might dream of being together. He gave non-answers, but within minutes he would mention Bridget, her parents, or Finn. She guessed he brought up his other family to prevent her from getting ideas, and it made her heart hurt.

When she wasn't with Thomas, she had more conflicted feelings. She was grateful he was alive and confused about what it meant. Did he love her, or was he the type of man who flew back and forth between two women? Fulfilled and abandoned, adoring and frustrated—the two things she knew—when she was in his orbit, he mesmerized her, and when she was away from him, she hated living a life of deceit.

Johanna woke to find Thomas gone. She lingered in bed, watching the sunshine ripple in bright waves across the ceiling. There was a sound on the stairs. She put on her wrap and opened the door. Kathleen was in the stairwell.

"Kathleen, what are you doing here? You're too far along to climb three flights." She ushered her friend inside. "Here, sit."

"It's nine o'clock." Kathleen sat on the bed. "I was worried you overslept."

"It looks like I may have." Johanna felt a pang self-reproach.

"I hoped it wasn't true." Kathleen ran her hand over rumpled sheets. "Johanna, do you think I'm the only one who knows?"

"I hope so," Johanna said.

"You hope so? That's pretty audacious."

"I wash the bedclothes myself."

"So, you aren't going to deny it. You and Thomas? One house away from where your husband and boys sleep?"

"Kathleen, he would have come back, but I married Connor."

"You married Connor because Thomas left you with child, and let's not forget: Thomas is a married man himself."

"He didn't know. He was certain he would be killed."

"My dear friend, there is a reason they recommend against lying down with dogs. The fleas are going to have a field day."

A few hours later, Johanna waited for Kathleen in the kitchen. Her friend usually mixed the bread dough and left it to rise overnight before going home. Johanna looked around. Unlike that first day, when she had stumbled into a filthy kitchen to feed the policemen, under Tilly's regime the kitchen was spotless. The room was more functional than cozy: neither haphazard, nor charming. Tilly didn't so much prepare recipes as engineer ingredients, and her kitchen reflected this no-nonsense approach. Pots were clean and stacked by size; jars of flour, sugar, and grains positioned in straight rows; tea towels folded in drawers. Any nuance of culinary invention was lost on Tilly, which was probably why her baked goods suffered. She beat any lightness from the batter with a militaristic spoon.

Kathleen showed up carrying a sack of flour.

"Here, let me help you," Johanna said. "We haven't spoken since the morning and I thought …"

"Is this a good time to continue with that particular topic?" Kathleen glanced around the kitchen.

"Tilly won't be back for at least an hour," Johanna said. "She went into town. She'll take her time at the butcher. Then she picks up Epsom salts for her aching feet and her weekly bag of penny candy."

"I hope it brings some sweetness to her life."

"Unlikely," Johanna said. "And I hope I haven't brought more difficulties to you."

"You mean since I found out what you are doing under the quilt I appliquéd for you?" Kathleen said. The words were harsh, but her eyes were kind.

"Do you want it back?" Johanna said.

"Absolutely not," Kathleen said.

Earlier in the day Kathleen had compared her to a dog, and Johanna wouldn't forget it, but in the last few hours, she'd softened when she thought of Kathleen's loyalty.

"I can see I've put you in a difficult position," Johanna said. "I'm sorry."

"You only confirmed what I already knew," Kathleen said. "I just want you to be safe."

"I didn't want to keep it from you, but …" Johanna said.

"I'm a big girl," Kathleen said.

"I love him; I always have," Johanna sighed. "How can I stop when he makes me feel so wonderful?"

"I'm not judging," Kathleen said. "I know you love him, and how hard it has been for you with Connor."

"It probably is a sin, but it's my salvation in some ways, too."

"Look, you deserve some happiness," Kathleen said. "Michael and I were lucky, but if we had been lost to each other and ended up in the same town, nothing would keep us apart." Kathleen reached over to hug Johanna but suddenly pulled away, holding her palm tight against her lower back.

"This baby is walking on my spine." Kathleen bent over. "It's worse than I remember."

"Did you have back pain with the others?" Johanna helped her friend into a chair.

"Not really." Kathleen let out a groan. "This pregnancy has been different. Maybe it's a boy this time, or perhaps I'm getting old?"

"I bet you can't wait until the baby gets here." Johanna stood behind Kathleen. "Show me where it hurts, and I'll rub."

Kathleen rested her hands against the counter. Johanna began kneading her friend's lower back.

"I love meeting my babies, but there's all that feeding and burping." Kathleen patted her growing abdomen. "Easier to take care of them this way."

"True," Johanna said. "You can stop work anytime, you know."

"I'd get bored." Kathleen pressed her back into Johanna's fist. "You're going to need more help while I'm out. Have you given any more thought to hiring that Chinese man, Michael's friend?"

"Of course, I will find some work for him." Johanna hoped Kathleen didn't sense her reluctance. She knew Kathleen would do anything for her. She and Michael were always helping someone. Johanna was so busy taking care of business she didn't look out for others, but then again, the business was why she was in a position to help with what really mattered—paying jobs. Johanna felt responsible. The Farrell family needed the extra money Kathleen earned. She had encouraged Kathleen and Michael to start a business, maybe a bakery, but Kathleen had shown no interest.

"You do enough for us, so take him on only if it makes sense for you," Kathleen said. "Michael thinks the world of him, says he's smart and a hard worker."

"How old is he?"

"Michael said he was in his mid-thirties, possibly a little older," Kathleen scrutinized Johanna. "You're thirty-four?"

Johanna nodded.

"Maybe your age but he looks much younger. Sort of ageless."

"What?"

"Irish skin just doesn't age well," Kathleen said and made a face.

"Oh, please," Johanna said. "Does he speak English?"

"He's fluent and knows Chinese medicine. They use needles or something."

"I doubt we will need Chinese medicine here, although we could ask him to stick needles into some of our guests?"

"Or Mr. Walsh," Kathleen said.

"Good luck. He's tough as shoe leather."

CHAPTER EIGHT

# THE CELESTIAL

**Nanticoke, Pennsylvania, Summer 1883**

The mirror behind the bar reflected double images, sparkling liquor bottles and upside-down glasses. En washed and dried the beer mugs and set them on the shelf. He had been at the hotel for a month, working with Kathleen in the mornings and handling carpentry jobs in the afternoons. Tonight, Connor had asked him to set up the bar and stay around in case he was needed while Kathleen and Johanna attended their church meeting. After Connor showed him how to tap a keg, he had nothing to do. Connor wouldn't let him behind the bar to serve guests. En hoped to get released soon.

Connor poured drinks for the miners as the bar filled. As on other Tuesday nights, he'd hung a "closed for private party" sign on the front door so only Mollies were allowed in. It seemed to En there were more men than on regular nights. And they were louder.

"It boils my blood. You see the signs everywhere, 'Irish Need Not Apply.'" Connor directed his voice toward the two tables the men had put together. Despite the cloud of defeat surrounding them, their conversation was animated. There was evidence that they had washed up since leaving the mine, but streaks of grit edged their faces.

"You're right, Connor," one man called back. "And don't forget the men they hung on Black Thursday have never been avenged."

Others chimed in, "We'll never forget … we'll get 'em one day."

Connor wiped his hands and left the bar to join the men. He gave each man the secret handshake and then sat down.

En felt uncomfortable. They didn't seem to notice him, but his instinct told him it could be dangerous to overhear this conversation.

"'Pinkerton never sleeps.' That's the damn bastard's motto." Connor poured from the pitcher and lifted his glass. "We'll make 'em sleep and never wake up."

"Hear! Hear!" The men raised their glasses. "Thanks for having us, Connor."

Connor put his hand up. "Wait. Don't thank me yet. I have bad news. We're gonna have to find another place."

"Are you going soft on us, Connor?" a man they called "Putty" said.

"Not at all; I'm more riled than ever, but Walsh lowered the boom, says he doesn't want trouble with the Coal and Iron constables."

"Can you still store the guns?" Putty said.

The room got quiet. En thought this might be a time he could respectfully ask if he was needed, but he couldn't catch Connor's attention.

"Walsh has no idea about the arsenal." Connor's voice was low. "And yeah, Putty, of course I can store them. Come in for a pint during the week and bring what you got."

En didn't know everyone's name, but Putty had a younger brother—for some reason named Paulie—who looked like a less used-up version of the same man.

Paulie said, "You sure? Walsh could be trouble."

"Walsh's just scared of the cops. They've roughed him up a few times. He didn't even tell Johanna, just took me aside."

"What about Johanna?" Putty said. "She suspicious?"

"I'll bet it's the wife, not the old man, putting her foot down."

The men jeered. "We know who wears the pants around here."

There was laughter. Connor frowned. He took a swig of beer. "I'm telling ya," Connor said. "She doesn't know."

"Connor likes 'em bossy. Johanna a suffragette yet?"

En felt perspiration on his lip. What would happen when they saw him?

"Johanna's too busy to worry about the Protestants or the suffragettes. She cares about her family, not the vote," he said. "And I keep her out of our business."

"Like this?" A man opened his coat and revealed a rifle. He grinned and handed it to Connor.

"Exactly like that, Hugh," Connor said. He put the gun under the table.

"What about that coolie?" A man pointed to En.

"I don't trust the Chinese."

En's heart galloped.

Connor picked up his fist and slapped it on the table.

En jerked as a loud *whack* reverberated in the room.

"See? He jumps at loud noises, too yellow to give us trouble," Connor said.

The men laughed.

"Maybe we'll recruit him. A slant-eyed Molly?" a gaunt old man croaked. The man was likely not yet forty but looked sixty. Miner's cough was slowly suffocating him. En wondered if acupuncture might help the man breathe more comfortably. Then he chastised himself. He just had to get by, not dream about medicine. That part of his life was over, and he did not want to look back or remember.

"There's a reason they're called yellow; he's harmless," Connor said, and turning to En he added, "Go ahead. Take off, En."

En took measured steps. They might come after him if he moved too fast. As he let himself out the kitchen door, he heard Connor say, "Look, are we doing this or not?"

"You bet," Putty said.

"Well, then, can any of you read or write?"

"Who cares?"

"We need a coffin notice," Connor said. "You know, a picture with an arrow pointing to the coffin, like you used to do. Someone draws the coffin and writes, 'This is you.'"

"Just once I'd like to see the face of a mine boss reading that."

En closed the door behind him. He could still hear the men hooting and cheering.


En was grateful to disappear in the cocoon of his shed. He had the ten-by-ten-foot room to himself. It was not insulated, but Johanna had provided a wool blanket and a thick quilt. He slept on a metal bed, usually wearing his clothes so they would be warm in the morning. The mattress was straw—much better than a bedroll on a dirt floor. He had a bedside table, a desk, and a chair. His soft gray tunic, trousers and other items he wasn't wearing hung on a nail. There was a small window, covered with a red-and-yellow dragon tapestry, one of a few things he'd kept from his former life. Mai Ling's silk robe from their wedding night was wrapped in tissue paper inside his desk drawer. His parent's medical bag was under the bed. He slept with one of Rosie's corn husk dolls, where Rosie's sweet scent lingered—or at least he let himself think so.

The loss of his second family was incomprehensible. It had been over a year; Rosie would be two years old if she had lived. His life was a haze of misery: sometimes he was numb; other times heartache impaled him with grief. Even more so than his birth family, these two people had been utterly dependent on him. His intimacy with Mai Ling had created their child, and he had failed them both. His last memory, lying with them in the sickbed, had been a moment when they were connected as one body. It was his fault they had been exposed to typhoid, and yet here he was, still alive. During his convalescence in Philadelphia, he had been in a daze. Now he was breathing, but he was not among the living. It was against his principles to take his own life. He and his parents had fought too hard to help other people survive, but his core was devoid of hopes, desires, and ambition.

He owed the Běnshuài and hoped one day to pay back his kindness. He knew he had disappointed his friend and patron. The Běnshuài, without any discussion, understood that En blamed himself and had nothing left to give to his studies or his people. He made no attempt to convince En to remain. His benefactor had wrapped his thin arms around En and held him against his skeletal body for a long minute. Finally pulling away, the Běnshuài said, "Go in peace, heal, and return to us. We are your community."

En almost changed his mind, but it would have been impossible to avoid painful reminders. He would be haunted every waking hour if he had remained in Philadelphia. Michael welcomed him to Nanticoke, and he and Kathleen had graciously invited him to dinner the night he arrived. En worried that breaking bread with an Irish family would rupture some rule of their society, but afraid to seem ungrateful, he accepted. Now he was glad for the job and the shed. If he lived with the Farrells, it might bring harm to the family. Michael was totally heedless as to how others might judge his friendship with a Celestial.

When En kept his focus on mindless tasks during the day, he could pretend Mai Ling and Rosie were waiting for him back in Philadelphia. It was after supper, in the quiet of his room, when the truth loomed over him like a warlord, wielding a sword dipped in poison. He wanted to fall to his knees and beg for a swift death. If only the warlord was merciful enough to release him. Some nights, the warlord complied, inflicting a mortal wound—En's soul bled like a butchered pig. He welcomed death's release, but then he woke. He had only the few precious seconds of relief each morning before he remembered where he was, and why.

As the earth warmed and the nights grew warmer, the depth of his sorrow diminished. Perhaps next winter he could add a stove. He worked hard and slept without nightmares or dreams. He accepted an anesthetized life. Someone here might decide he didn't belong, but so far, he was overlooked, unreal as he was undead.

Johanna was too busy to notice him, but she seemed to trust him. She would show him a task, provide supplies, and leave him to figure out how to get it done. He was assigned many "urgent" jobs before he started the porch floor in late June.

He spent a full day measuring and laying out the wood. Johanna asked to inspect it before he went further. He was surprised; she usually left him alone. Did she think he wouldn't install it with care or lay the varnish on a poorly finished surface?

He'd heard the staff complain she was exacting and that she often made changes or asked them to redo work. That had not happened for him, but this was his first big job. He was annoyed. Why was she was inspecting his work? Was she looking for an excuse to let him go? What if she was displeased? He had no idea what she required or how to impress her.

It put him in a bad mood, which was odd because he was not used to feeling any emotion at all.

The next morning, he was buoyed by the scent of newly cut timber and decided to approach the day with optimism. It wasn't unreasonable for Johanna to check on a new employee's work. Wood was expensive, and once stained and varnished, it would be hard to change if he got it wrong. These people had been good to him, and nothing in their behavior warranted defensiveness.

He waited on the porch for only a few minutes before he heard Johanna and Kathleen, their voices getting louder as they walked from the kitchen. Because of the path's curve, he could see them before they noticed him. Kathleen wore a blue dress, white smocking gathered in folds over the girth of the baby. He hadn't seen her since starting the porch and noted that she must be near the end of her term. Johanna wore a red dress, trimmed in lace that fit the contours of her body. He was aware of her figure for the first time and quickly looked away.

"I brought Kathleen with me," Johanna said, stepping up to the porch. "I told her to expect to find some beautiful carpentry." She stooped and ran the flat of her hand along the boards. En suddenly felt like a child at a bedside while his father judged his work.

"A nice job sanding, smooth finish, and in record time." She checked the fit between the joints. "This is excellent craftsmanship, too. You'll be done soon; I'd better check on what's next on the list."

He should have said thank you, but all he could do was let out a breath. He felt strange, elated and heavy, wishing her attention to be on anything but him.

"En," said Kathleen. "Fair warning, Lake Nuangola Day is coming up, and it means our dear boss will be giving orders nonstop."

En thought of something to say. "Is Lake Nuangola Day a town holiday?"

"It's Johanna's holiday, an all-day picnic," Kathleen said. "Walsh owns property at the lake, about an hour away. The party is Johanna's way to thank the employees and earn the goodwill of the town. It's also wonderful fun. The girls and I can't wait."

"Kathleen, you're surely not going this year?" Johanna said.

"I wouldn't miss it," Kathleen said. "I still can't believe you got Walsh to pay for a summer picnic—two years in a row."

"I caught him in a weak moment."

"Two weak moments—a record." They laughed. "The girls are already talking nonstop about the food and canoe races."

"Indeed, but are you really going to take an hour-long wagon ride now?" En heard the displeasure in Johanna's voice. She sounds like a boss, he thought.

"The worst that can happen is it will bounce this baby right out of me," Kathleen said. "Plus, I like watching you charm the town."

"I think you should stay here," Johanna said. "Why risk trouble with you or the baby?"

Kathleen got quiet. She looked more like a chastised schoolgirl than a woman about to become a mother for the fifth time.

This was not a conversation that two Chinese women would have in front of a man. As a doctor, he would tend to agree with Johanna. A wagon ride was a risk he wouldn't recommend. But why did Johanna have to be so abrupt? She was tough-minded and blunt, but surely she could understand why Kathleen wanted to relax with family and friends? He knew from his days practicing medicine that the best thing he could offer a patient was stern advice. Too much empathy confuses the message; reassurance sometimes made a patient less vigilant.

Johanna put her arm around Kathleen. "It's worth the effort if we all come together and have fun, and either way, the wait to meet this baby is nearly over."

En felt better. Johanna's tone had been conciliatory. He thought about endorsing her opinion and suggesting Kathleen stay back, but Kathleen spoke up first, and he gathered that she was neither offended by Johanna nor ready to take her advice.

"I'll be careful," Kathleen said. "Most important is helping you make Lake Nuangola Day a success because it's good for business."

Johanna smiled. "It doesn't hurt to make people feel important."

After they left, En wondered why he felt easy around Kathleen but tense when Johanna showed up. He could see Kathleen had a comfortable give and take with Johanna. Why was he so awkward with her? He knew Michael from earlier, and the Farrells had done so much for him, and Johanna hadn't been cold. Still, he got the feeling she had not been entirely happy about making him a hotel employee. Perhaps it was just that she was always in a hurry, driven. He would understand if she resented him, or perhaps it was his race? If she did wish him gone, he wasn't sure which reason would be the more troubling.

Boxes filled with provisions—tablecloths, utensils, napkins, tins of cookies and nonperishable food—were stacked along the walls in the hotel dining room.

TC was on the floor, twisting a yellow tea towel into a ball. "The canoe had too many flowers last year," TC said. "It needs jungle animals and scary things."

"Yeah, TC, that looks great, like a tiger, right?" Johnny said. There was nothing his older brother did that Johnny would not find praiseworthy. "Need any help?"

"Nope," TC said. "Just getting some straw for whiskers."

Johnny ran to where Johanna was putting the items into large boxes. He grabbed a handful of paper lanterns.

"Here, Johnny, fold them so they don't take up so much room," Johanna said. She was grateful whenever she could create normalcy in their lives. The magic of making pretend animals or hanging paper lanterns was how children should spend their days.

"Will we stay all day and all night?" Johnny balled up some streamers.

"We have an early start, to arrive when the lake is like glass," Johanna said. "We will stay for a full day of canoeing and swimming, until after dark. But bed now."

"Can my new friend come to the lake?" Johnny asked.

"Who is your new friend?" She took the streamers from him.

"I call him Mr. En, to be polite like you told me," Johnny said. "But he says just call him En."

Johnny could use a friend, but Johanna wasn't sure she wanted it to be the Celestial handyman.

"He's only been at the hotel a few short weeks. It's too soon for him to have a day off," Johanna said. "Did you remember wire to hang the lanterns?"

"But I like him, and everybody should get a holiday."

"He will after a time." She found the roll of picture wire and put it in the box. Johnny was probably afraid no one would play with him. If only TC would include him more.

"Why don't we bring En a piece of Auntie Kathleen's pie?"

"I don't think he likes pie, Ma. He eats rice. Not like ours from the store, but from a big burlap bag. He boils it—the rice, not the bag—and he cooks it until it's sticky and makes it like a ball. He gave me a bite. It tastes like porridge."

"Johnny, En has to stay here to watch over things." She kissed him and hugged TC, who no longer allowed kisses. "I love you, my littles."

"It's not fair that En has to miss Lake Nuangola Day," Johnny said. "And I'm seven so don't call me little."


En worked late to lay the first coat of varnish. It would dry overnight, and then tomorrow, when the children were gone, he would finish it without fear of footprints. The odor stung his nostrils and took him back to the smell of shipyard docks. He was living an entirely different life, perhaps even on another planet: no Chinese people or traditions, both of his families wiped off the face of the Earth. His parents' medical bag and his dream of becoming a doctor were gathering dust under his cot.

The last rays of the sun glinted against the woodgrain. The beautiful summer evening made him think of Mai Ling and Rosie, how they would have enjoyed sharing the sunset together. He forced the images of his wife and daughter away, focusing on smoothing the final brushstrokes.

It was dusk when he finished. He sealed up the can of varnish and opened the porch door as Johanna walked up.

"Still working?" she asked.

"I thought I'd get the first coat done." He could never get a full sentence out around her. He took a breath. "It can dry while everyone is gone."

"Yes, smart," she said. "When you're done here, could you load up the wagon? The boxes in the dining room are ready to go."

"Yes, Miss Johanna," he said. "I'm almost cleaned up."

"I was going to ask Connor to add a keg, but since the bar is busy, why don't I give you my key to the cellar? Bring one, no, better make it two kegs." She handed him the key. "I'm going over to Kathleen's for a few minutes. Just hang on to the key until I get back."

"Yes, madam," En said. He saw her stifle a smile at his formality. En was pleased for any response other than a command. "I'll go now."

By the time he got to the cellar stairwell, it was in shadows. He popped the lock, spread the metal doors open on either side, and descended the cement stairs into a pitch-black cellar. He struck a match.

The flickering light was uneven. As his eyes adjusted, he could see kegs and, stacked behind them, boxes too large to hold wine or liquor. He smelled another familiar scent. This one took him back—not to the ship, but to memories of Chinatown festivals and the smell of fireworks. It also took him back to the Sierra Mountains. The scent of black powder was unmistakable. He found his way to the boxes stacked next to barrels, put his hands on the lid of one barrel, tugged, and removed it. He reached in and pulled out a heavy object wrapped in terry cloth. His fingers grazed the cold metal. He felt the handle, the long nose of a pistol. He was certain this was the arsenal the men had been talking about.

Should he find Johanna and tell her, or should he get out of town? Johanna possibly already knew about this, but he doubted it. He had been in the bar when Connor was collecting guns. Did Connor think he could harbor a cache of weapons and not get caught?

Johanna and the boys would get hurt, and this could reverberate to Michael and Kathleen. En had nothing to live for, so why not help the people who had received him so hospitably? He had to find and tell Johanna. He climbed the steps, closed and locked the cellar doors, and set off for Kathleen's.

Johanna decided to walk the long way around to Kathleen's, feeling content in the summer evening. She was planning a party, a happy day. Because of the hotel's success, her sons would have a summer picnic and canoe races on a lake, just like other children.

Kathleen sat in a rocker on the Farrells' porch. The younger girls were on the front lawn, cutting and linking paper chains, the older girls folding tissue paper into flowers.

"Finish up, girls. The wagon for Lake Nuangola leaves ear—" Kathleen said, but stopped on the last word. Johanna heard Kathleen's voice catch.

"Is anything wrong?" Johanna climbed the stoop.

"No, nothing, I'm fine." Kathleen looked pale. Johanna wasn't convinced.

"The paper decorations look lovely," Johanna said.

Kathleen stayed seated. She wasn't even sewing. Maybe she was finally taking it easy these last few days? Johanna felt uneasy. Kathleen's face was drawn, waxen.

"Girls, I'll finish up collecting these lovely flowers," Johanna said. "It must be near your bedtime. Go wash up."

When the screen door slammed shut, Kathleen tried to get up, groaned, and fell back. There was a puddle of liquid at her feet. Johanna raced to her side.

"I think your water broke." She didn't mention that the fluid was streaked with blood.

"It's never happened this way before," Kathleen said.

"How long have you had pains?"

"All day, starting, then stopping, not ever this bad." She buckled over.

It was her fifth baby. Johanna guessed Kathleen had not even told Michael she might be in labor. Why was Kathleen so aware of everyone's needs but her own?

"Where's Michael?" Johanna asked.

"He's out back, in the garden," Kathleen said.

"Hang on. I'll be right back."

Johanna started to the backyard but hesitated—should she leave Kathleen? She pivoted and practically knocked over an approaching En. Although she had given him clear instructions, she had never been happier to have an employee not follow her directions.

"Is something wrong, Miss Johanna?"

Johanna noticed En was perspiring. He must have run over. How had he known?

"Oh, En, yes, please," she said. "It's Kathleen."

She heard a gagging sound and turned back. En followed her. They reached Kathleen just as her head fell backward.

"Oh my God, Kathleen! En, her eyes are rolling back."

"She is convulsing," En said. "Do you have a handkerchief?"

She reached into her pocket but found nothing.

"What can I do?" Johanna asked.

He tugged at the hem of Kathleen's apron.

"Here, put this between her teeth. She might bite her tongue," he said.

Johanna did as she was told while En tilted her head back further.

"En, you used to be some kind of doctor. Do you know what this is? How we can help?"

"I've only seen this once before. As soon as the baby arrived, the mother recovered. Kathleen's in labor, right?"

"I think so," Johanna said. "Please, can you do something?"

Kathleen's body had stiffened with the seizure, and then suddenly slackened. She was limp in the chair.

En took Kathleen's wrist between his thumb and two fingers. He counted silently, his other hand on her abdomen. After a minute, he said, "Another contraction. We need to get her in the house. Where's Michael?"

"I'll get him." Johanna ran to the backyard, yelling Michael's name.

Michael, hands covered in dirt, came running. Together, they lifted Kathleen and carried her into the parlor, positioning her on pillows resting against the sofa.

"I'll get the doctor," Michael said. "Take care of her, En."

"Johanna, find some towels, a knife or scissors," En said, "and a basin of hot water."

He spoke softly to the barely conscious Kathleen. "Relax, take slow breaths," En said. "I worked in a camp, mostly men, but there were women. I've delivered some Celestial babies, and one or two Irish ones. We'll be fine."

Johanna found towels in the kitchen. When she returned, she found En on his knees in front of Kathleen. "May I examine her?" he said.

"Yes, oh yes, you have done this before. I haven't." Johanna was silently pleading for help—from God, the doctor, En, anyone.

"I should have asked her husband's permission, but we may not have time."

"He said take care of her. That's permission," Johanna said.

"This baby is nearly here, Miss Johanna, but Miss Kathleen is barely conscious," he said. "I need your help. Move behind her and get ready. On my say, place your hands there, on top of her abdomen. Yes, like that."

Johanna braced Kathleen's shoulders with her body.

"On my signal, lift her toward me and press," En instructed.

"Now," he said.

Johanna did as she was told. Each time Kathleen tensed with a contraction, En told her to push, and again Johanna exerted pressure. Nothing happened. Johanna started reciting the rosary: the Our Father, then a Hail Mary. There was no change.

"She's too exhausted, En," Johanna finally said. "She can't do it."

"Okay, Kathleen, you just be quiet now, no pushing," En said. "I will help your baby arrive."

Johanna couldn't see over Kathleen's belly. She continued reciting her Hail Marys until she heard Kathleen gasp. Johanna felt Kathleen's too-tight abdomen release. Kathleen's head flopped back against Johanna. En was cradling a tiny human.

"Take the baby," he said. Johanna slipped from behind Kathleen and held the infant as En cut the cord. He grabbed some of the towels she'd brought and packed them against Kathleen.

Kathleen was shaking violently. Michael and the doctor arrived just as Kathleen slid sideways, lifeless.

The white-haired Dr. Murphy stooped down next to En. "The baby has arrived?" he said.

"Yes," En said.

"Is the child in good health?"

"The baby seems fine," Johanna said. "But Kathleen …" She felt her heart in her throat.

"Kathleen?" Michael slipped next to his wife and took her hand. "En, is she breathing?"

"She's been seizing. I need my herbs, my leather medicine bag," En said. "It's under my bed."

"No, I don't think herbs are the right approach," Dr. Murphy said, taking out his stethoscope. "It's one thing to help out in an emergency, but …"

"It will help control the seizures," En said.

Johanna clutched the baby and said, "Michael, can you get the bag?"

"Sounds like Chinese voodoo," the doctor said.

"They are safe," En said simply. "I've used them before."

"Michael, I have seen women seizing like this recover," the doctor advised.

"I'm getting your bag." Michael ran for the door.

"You are making a mistake," Dr. Murphy called after him.

Johanna just wanted someone to help Kathleen. If En thought he could do it, let him, for goodness' sake.

"Dr. Murphy, if she bleeds to death, it won't matter about the herbs," Johanna said.

The doctor scowled at Johanna, but he stooped down next to En and said, "I'll hold the towels in place so you can be ready with your mumbo jumbo when Michael gets back."

Kathleen's breathing was irregular. Johanna could barely breathe herself. It seemed like an eternity before Michael returned.

Michael burst into the room and just as he handed the bag to Johanna, Kathleen went into another convulsion.

En moved next to Kathleen's head.

"Johanna, search for a bag labeled schizonepeta."

She found it and gave him the mortar and pestle. He ground the herb into a fine powder.

"The spasm has locked her jaw," En said. "Johanna, there is a glass straw—it would be wrapped in cardboard."

Johanna found the cardboard case, unwrapped it, and handed the straw to En. He gave her the bowl, which she held as he sucked the powder into the glass cylinder. With the straw between his lips, En positioned his mouth below Kathleen's and gently blew the powder into her nasal passages. Kathleen's eyes fluttered open.

"She's back with us," Michael whispered. He moved to her side and held his wife's hand against his lips.

"Well, I never!" Dr. Murphy swore. His voice brought the girls to the top of the stairs.

"Can we come down? Is Ma all right?" they yelled.

"Stay where you are," Johanna called. She looked at her friend. She was breathing. Johanna climbed the steps, cradling the baby, and went to the girls.

"Girls, look," she said to the four sets of eyes waiting on the landing.

"Is it a girl?" Molly said.

"I don't know." Despite the turmoil in the pit of her stomach, Johanna felt a bubble of laughter. "I forgot to check. Let's look together."

She took the baby into a bedroom and placed the bundle on a bed. She let the girls unwrap the towel.

"He has a wee-wee," Maeve and Mara said together.

Johanna hoped the baby had a mother.


En sat at the Farrells' kitchen table. The room swarmed with women preparing food and discussing the removal of bloodstains from carpet. Someone gave him a glass of brandy. En left it untouched on the table. If he lifted it, they might see his hands tremble. It was not just that he had delivered a baby. For the first time since he'd lost his own child and his wife, he felt a tenderness threatening to crack open the shell around his heart. He wanted to weep, but beneath the sadness was a sliver of joy. If he moved, he might lose the moment.

"You did it." Dr. Murphy walked over to En. "How did you bring the babe so quickly, and what's in that brew?"

"I'm sorry. I couldn't wait for a proper doctor." En hoped he conveyed a sense of deference. It wouldn't help if his actions made him seem arrogant. He had to show he knew his place, especially to the town's physician.

"You did what was right. I regret doubting you." The doctor patted him on the arm. "Now where did you get that brandy?"

En was relieved when the doctor went in search of a drink. The more the kitchen filled with people, the more removed he was from the fray. No one saw him sitting alone, which was better than getting tossed out. Then he remembered the reason he had come to find Johanna. How would he tell her about the cellar?

Michael burst into the kitchen and put his hand out. "My friend, you saved me, and now you've saved my wife and son."

They shook hands, and En said, "May I see Miss Johanna before I leave?"

"She's with Kathleen." Michael looked down at En's blood-soaked shirt. "You might want to change before you visit, my friend."

"Of course," En said. "I hadn't noticed."

"A lot going on today," Michael said. "Come back later?"

En could think of no excuse that would allow him to see Johanna now. She rightfully belonged with Kathleen, but En had to tell her. If he found the guns, others would too. He decided to take a swig of the brandy to play for time just as Johanna appeared.

"Kathleen insisted I come down to thank you," she said.

"How is she?" En stood up.

"Drowsy, but she can smile at the baby. Thank you, En." Johanna embraced him. He should pull back—a servant should refuse contact, especially with his female employer—but he had no choice. He leaned into the hug and whispered, "Miss Johanna, we must talk. It's serious."

She pulled back, questioning him with her eyes.

"I think I'll ask En to walk me home," Johanna said to Michael. "We both need to clean up."

"Of course," Michael said. "En, you keep this up, saving every one of us in the Farrell family, for the love of Jesus, at this rate I'll never make it up to you."

Away from the others Johanna said, "What is it? En, is Kathleen still in danger?"

En didn't know where to begin. The last hour had been harrowing. The timing was not good. She had been kind to him, given him a job and a place to stay. Together, they had ushered a new life into the world. His news would blot out the relief and the joy of the day. Perhaps he should have just left? How could he go? It had been a long while since he cared about anything, but these people were starting to matter.

"Johanna, I have some bad news."

"En, that's impossible," she said.

They were getting near the hotel, and she was exasperated with him. Johanna had just started to respect this man's intelligence, but really, where did these Celestials get their sense of drama? Perhaps the fright of delivering Kathleen's baby had disoriented him.

"You're new to Pennsylvania, but this isn't the Wild West. Most people here don't even own guns."

"I'm sure about it, guns and ammunition," he said.

The sun had gone down. She stepped carefully on the stones leading to the cellar.

"I don't know what you saw, but I can assure you it's not an arsenal."

She willed herself to stay calm, but an undercurrent of alarm registered against her disbelief. Connor had been reluctant to give her the cellar key. He was unaware that the original lock came with two keys and she had kept one for herself. Even then she did not entirely trust her husband.

"Good, no one is around," she said when they stepped down the staircase.

"What about your husband?" En said. "Should we get him?"

"No, he's at the bar. Listen, you can hear him holding forth about something or other," Johanna said. Connor's outrage droned above their heads. Even at a distance, she could hear his ain't-it-awful condescension.

En removed the lock and pulled the metal flaps open. Johanna held on to the concrete walls as she made her way inside. She heard En yank the canvas tarp off the containers.

As her eyes adjusted, she saw only boxes, no kegs nor cases of wine. She smelled gunpowder. En lit a match.

"En, did it occur to you that lighting a match might be a bad idea?"

She heard him chuckle. It was absurd, but his amusement was contagious.

"It's a strange evening we are having," Johanna said. She laughed too. This was silly. Then they were both guffawing, probably a release of pent-up emotion. She put her hand on his arm and had the strangest sensation. Here was someone who she had not even wanted in her household, and she was suddenly grateful he was standing next to her. He had just saved her friend's life and was now risking his own by showing her whatever this was. They looked around at the guns and ammunition surrounding them and stopped laughing.

They each spoke. En deferred to Johanna, who said, "We should go somewhere else to talk about this."

"Exactly my thinking."

They exited the cellar and, as if by mutual agreement, walked to his shed. She followed him inside, ducking under the doorframe. She was surprised by the pleasantness of the space, which had been essentially an outbuilding for storage. Bright silks, with red-and-yellow dragon patterns, were draped artfully on the bed and window. There were newly constructed shelves, packed with neatly arranged books. A teapot and a small candle sat on the bed stand. She smelled the perfume of a rose that stood in a glass of water on the desk.

"That's one of the tea roses from Rose House," she said.

"Yes, the stem had broken," En said. "I apologize for taking it without your permission."

"Oh, nonsense. I plant the roses for everyone's enjoyment. I'm delighted you like them, too. It looks like you read, En," she said. "What are you studying?"

"Before coming here, I studied medicine," he said. "Western medicine. I thought it might work better than the medicine of my country, but I was wrong."

"Yes, I remember now. Michael told me. Whatever medicine you practiced worked well today."

She noted a book on anatomy and a pamphlet: *The Practitioner's Reference Book: Adapted to the Use of the Physician, the Pharmacist, and the Student.*

"The talk of my studies might be for another time, Miss Johanna. About the cellar…"

"Of course," she said. "I can't really believe it. How many barrels and boxes do you think?"

"At least twelve, maybe more."

"What shall we do?" she said. At first, it felt hopeless, but as she spoke, the answer came to her. "First, we need to get out of these bloody garments. Then I want you to run an errand for me." She reached over to the rose and pulled off a handful of petals. She picked up a pencil and paper from his desk. "May I?" she asked.

He nodded.

She wrote a note and, rather than signing it, put a few petals inside. She folded the paper and gave it to En. "Do you know where the Sullivan family lives?"

En nodded.

"Take this to Thomas—only him—and don't let Bridget or anyone else see it. I've asked him to come at midnight and to bring the ice wagon with the reinforced bed."

"You're going to move the guns?" En said.

"Not just move—they are going to disappear."

"What about your husband? Can he help?"

"En, I believe my husband is the reason these boxes are here," Johanna said.

"What about Michael, or the police?"

"Michael needs to be with Kathleen," she said. "And if this is Connor's doing, the police will arrest him. It's evidence they are vigilantes. They will hang."

"And what will we do with the wagon?" he said.

"Tomorrow is Lake Nuangola Day; we'll get the boxes there and dump them in the lake. There is an old Indian trail on the opposite side of the lake. It's heavily wooded and hard to find. We just need to get the weapons into the wagon before sunrise."

She could feel his skepticism.

"En, I am not presuming you will help," she said. "I have no choice. If you can take this note to Thomas, he will know how to get these weapons out of here."

En was silent. She wondered if he knew about Thomas.

"It's a bad plan," En said. "Too much could go wrong. But I will help."

She started to laugh. "So why are you willing to help?"

"I don't have a better idea," En said. "I'll clean up and go to Thomas."

Johanna looked directly at En, "Thank you." He held the shed's door open for her.

"I'll see you at midnight."

She ran to her bedroom and stripped off her clothes. She pulled a black blouse and skirt from the wardrobe—better for the darkness—and dressed quickly so as not to run into Connor. He was accustomed to her leaving at night, so he wouldn't miss her, but he might wonder why she was changing clothing at this time of day.

A surge of anguish threatened what little composure she had. Tomorrow was a day she had anticipated all summer. She should have been celebrating; instead every muscle in her body contracted with dread. Connor—his guns, his foolishness—mocked her. She had so little to offer her sons, and he put it in jeopardy.

"Well, En, what a pleasant surprise, you popping in on the Sullivan clan." Mr. Sullivan sat on the porch swing, smoking a cigar, and motioned En up the long staircase. "You'll be wanting to speak with Thomas. He is right here at hearth and home, like a good husband. Nice to have a son-in-law fixing up the place. Like the new paint job? What do you think of the color?"

It was a moonless night. En couldn't begin to guess the new color, possibly gray. He was relieved that Mr. Sullivan didn't expect an answer. The rotund man shuffled past En and opened the screen door.

"Wait here. I'll get him."

The screen door banged shut. En stood there, wondering again if he was *feng*, crazy, not to get out of town. He knew the rumors; Tilly never let a thought go unsaid and often made comments about what Johanna was "up to with that redheaded Irishman"—once he heard her joke that they needed an ice delivery since Johanna "always seemed overheated." Since Tilly often saw wrongdoing where none existed, he had given the gossip little credence. Still, if there was some truth, En didn't want to know. Yet here he was summoning Thomas.

"Why didn't you tell that coolie to come around to the back door?" En recognized the spoiled child cadence in Bridget's voice.

"Daughter, your husband delivers to the hotel. That's Walsh and Johanna," En heard the father answer. "I know that makes him suspect in your book, but he has business with Thomas, probably needs more ice for Lake Nuangola Day."

"She calls, and my husband comes running. For God's sake, why can't my own father stand up for me?"

"Bridget, it's my job," Thomas sounded tired.

"And Lake Nuangola Day, what a hoax," Bridget said. "A few canoe races, some chicken, and pie. It's just Walsh and Johanna drumming up more business. I could skip the whole thing."

"You'll not be stopping Finn from good fun with his friends," her father said. "You don't have to go tomorrow, but I'm taking the lad."

"She thinks she is so high and mighty," Bridget said. "We'll be entertaining soon as the house is fixed up, and not because we want people's money."

"Bridget, Finn is going," Mr. Sullivan said. "Now, let your husband find out what the Celestial needs."

Thomas pushed open the screen door and closed the front door behind him. He looked En over, "I would guess this isn't a social call."

En pressed the note into Thomas's palm. "She'd like you to come at midnight."

Thomas unfolded the paper. Rose petals fell through his fingers. He stepped next to the window so light from inside would illuminate Johanna's note.

"Tell her I'll be there."

# CHAPTER NINE

# BLOOD IS THICKER THAN WATER

**Nanticoke, Pennsylvania, Summer 1883**

Johanna rested against the railing of the back stairs at Butterwort House, waiting for En and Thomas and trying to think of another way out. Lake Nuangola Day would serve as a distraction, but was this the right thing to do? And what right did she have to endanger Thomas and En? Michael had learned about Connor hosting Molly meetings at the bar, but if either Michael or Walsh suspected that Connor had been stashing munitions, they would have insisted he get rid of them. Walsh might also have thrown her family out as well. And if the police discovered the weapons, the boys would lose a father to prison, or worse. There was no wait-and-see scenario. She felt woozy. The horror of what Connor had done was a black hole that they could fall into at any moment.

En arrived a little before midnight and stood with her in the shadows. Thomas came a few minutes later. He almost kissed her but saw En just in time. Johanna explained about the weapons and her plan to dump them in the lake. Thomas didn't seem particularly surprised. It suddenly occurred to her that she had never stopped to consider if he was also in on it. Yet during their evenings together, he spoke bitterly of the Mollies. Since he'd been in Nanticoke, he had clearly distanced himself from the organization that nearly cost him his life. Unless she truly didn't know the man, Thomas was done with the Mollies, just as Connor was enamored of them.

It was reassuring that Thomas's first words were, "Goddamn Mollies, putting you and your family in danger."

She exhaled. He was with her and not about to run to the Mollies. He was ready to help. "Do you think this will work?"

"I expect the boxes will be heavy enough that they will sink. Silt at the bottom of that lake will cover them within minutes," he said, raking his fingers through his hairline, a gesture she found endearing.

"It is still dangerous, getting the guns out of the cellar, driving them to the lake," she added. "Thomas and En, you don't have to help."

Neither man moved.

"I'll get the wagon," Thomas said. "If you two carry boxes up from the cellar will the hotel guests see you?"

"We only have a few guests tonight, all staying in front rooms," Johanna said. "En and I will see you shortly."

Thomas returned an hour later with the wagon, and the three of them carried crates to the wagon bed. When it was filled, they fit a piece of plywood on top and covered it with quilts. The children could sit above the cargo. En had the foresight to open each box and douse the contents with water, but it was unnerving to think of children riding over rifles, ammunition, and powder. The police were already looking at an Irish celebration with a wary eye. Would they search a wagonload of children?

At dawn, Thomas had to leave for his regular ice runs. "You two should try to get some sleep. I'll see you at the lake, near the Indian trail."

Johanna barely slept. She got up before the boys to check on the wagon. Returning to the kitchen, she found the boys downstairs, buzzing with excitement. Johanna had invited several neighbor children and the staff to ride with them. They arrived and helped carry the perishable food out to be loaded. The Farrells arrived just as the group was climbing into the wagon. The four little girls bounded toward her. Like TC and Johnny, they were unaccustomed to vacation or picnic days and could barely manage their exhilaration. Johanna clenched her teeth. Couldn't these children have just one day happily swimming and canoeing?

Johanna saw Molly running ahead of her sisters. She bounded in front of Johanna. "Auntie Johanna, Mama says I'm to tell you to have a grand time without her and that our baby boy is already giving trouble."

Johanna looked alarmed, and Molly added, "In a good way; he cries loud."

"And when he's really mad, then his face turns purple," added Mara.

"Do you girls like having a baby brother?" Johanna asked.

"Everyone but Maeve; she's mad because she wanted a sister littler than her," Margaret said, "but Da says he needed some company and that we can still dress him up until he gets big. Then, when he goes to school, he gets to wear what he wants."

"That seems fair," Johanna said.

Michael kissed Johanna on the cheek.

"So, does the baby have a name?" Johanna asked Michael.

"We can't make up our minds. Kathleen wants to call him En Chang, but that presents problems for an Irish lad, don't you think?" Michael grinned. "We'll have one or two names to run by his Auntie Johanna soon."

Michael helped his girls into the wagon. Johanna cringed—children, potato salad, and explosives were all jumbled together. She cursed Connor again.

"The rear of that wagon bed has more picnic than children," Michael said.

"I may have packed too much, but the picnic is for guests from out of town, too, and with staff and neighbors, we could get about thirty families."

"It's becoming the social event of Nanticoke."

"I'm not sure what that says, if this is the highlight of the season," Johanna said, concerned he might detect false levity. "Kathleen's pies will be the hit, as usual."

Johanna desperately wished she could think of a reason to curtail the unfolding plan, but it was in motion. Instead, she accepted Michael's hand. He hoisted her up to the front seat. En hopped up next to her.

"En, so you are going after all," Michael said. "Johnny must be pleased."

They started up. As they got farther away from Main Street, the wagon jerked over some rough roads. Johanna leaned close to En. "Do you think this is safe?"

"Probably, I didn't see any stick dynamite, but even if there are explosives, I doubt we'll generate enough sparks to set it off," En asked. "Does the roadbed get any worse?"

"It's not bad until we get near the lake, mostly large rocks we can avoid," she said. "We could let the children out early. There's a path to the dock."

The ride took over an hour. Johanna kept her hands tight on the railing, glancing back to monitor the children whenever they turned a corner. She told En to stop at the hill before the picnic site.

"Children, get out here," she said. She and En climbed down to help supervise and gather the younger children until the older ones could claim them.

"En and I are going to the picnic site. You may go down to the lake, but mind Molly and Margaret. And, girls, don't let the little ones near the water until I get there."

They drove on and stopped again near the picnic site. They unloaded supplies along the path.

"I told the staff we'd leave the picnic things here. They can carry them down to the dock," she said. "Now we have to find the path leading to the Indian trail."

Her heart pulsed each time a wheel rolled over a tree root or pothole. About a quarter of a mile in, En found a dense grove of trees.

"Let's put the wagon here. There's a lot of overgrowth," En said. He tied the reins to a tree trunk. The horses nibbled grass along the trail.

"En, I think it's best to dump the weapons during the picnic, but that means you and Thomas will have to do it without me. I'm the hostess. It would be strange if I wasn't there."

"It took us over an hour to move the boxes to the wagon last night, and that was with three of us. Will we have time?"

"I didn't think of that," Johanna said. Disoriented from lack of sleep, she was at a loss.

"We need at least one more set of hands," he said. "Is there anyone coming today that you can trust?"

Connor was out the question. She couldn't send back for Michael.

"En, honestly, there is not another man in this town I trust right now."

"Then I don't see how we'll get it done in time."

"We'll have to ask the boys."

"TC, maybe, but these are too heavy for Johnny," En said.

"Then TC can do it, and Thomas will have to ask Finn."

"Johanna, TC and Finn might be strong enough, but I'm not sure they are old enough to keep quiet."

"It's time they learn blood is thicker than water," she said.


En stayed with the wagon, and Johanna walked back to the picnic site. As she got close to the oval of green water, she marveled at the grace of marsh grasses waving in the breeze. Would she ever feel that serene and peaceful? But she wasn't withstanding a breeze; gale force winds were knocking her over.

She walked down the hill to where her staff were setting boards on sawhorses, covering them with red-and-white-checkered tablecloths. She helped them set out platters covered with cheesecloth to protect against insects.

When most of the picnic was in order, she left them and joined the children who were decorating canoes on the grass by the water.

"Looks great, doesn't it, Ma?" Johnny shouted.

She thought she'd never seen either of her sons more captivated, or happier.

"They look wonderful," she shouted back.

She turned and saw Thomas heading toward her.

"Got that second wagon load of ice, Miss Johanna," he called, publicly enacting their business transaction if anyone was listening.

"The extra ice is welcome, thank you."

She shielded her eyes from the sun and moved closer to whisper, "En's waiting in the cove, but there is a problem."

"Just one?" He smiled.

"Seriously, we don't have enough hands," Johanna said. "I can't leave. We have to enlist TC and Finn, or it will take too long."

He started to protest, considered, and then nodded.

"They're nine—so young—but then again, I wasn't much older when I took off for Ulster."

"You were," she said. "And smart enough to have known better."

He lifted his eyebrows and gave her his bad boy smile.

"Sorry, poor timing," she said. "Oh, to have a problem as trivial as a broken heart."

"I'll ask Finn," he said. "And you'll send TC?"

"Yes. About thirty minutes sound okay?"

"It may take that long to get Bridget settled and make up an excuse to pull Finn away."

"The path is after the fallen oak, just past the turn off."

"Good, the water is deepest on that side of the lake. I'll invite Finn to take a look at the old Indian trail."

"Won't Bridget want to go?"

"No, I'm certain of that."

He tipped his hat like a good deliveryman. She watched him walk past the picnic tables and to where Bridget was laying out containers of food on a blanket far away from the crowd. Seeing Bridget made her more real. Johanna had never wanted to hurt or betray her. The nagging worry about Thomas returned. Was he an honorable man caught up in a terrible time? She had built him up in her mind, overlooking some terrible things he'd done. She was proud of his sense of justice and his courage, but his choices had hurt so many.

Thomas was speaking to Bridget, and even from a distance, Johanna could tell the conversation was strained. Bridget's hopes must have soared when Thomas returned, but she looked unhappy now. Johanna had purposely not thought about Bridget, but her heart went out to the woman. Thomas just wasn't good at playing the part of doting father and husband. Johanna, for the first time, also admitted he likely wouldn't be any different if they were together.

She had to face the fact that he had been seeing Bridget while he was seeing her. Despite his excuse—that it had allowed him to keep her pure, on a pedestal—it was wrong. And could Johanna justify seeing him now because of the so-called vows they took alone in a field? She made a commitment that afternoon, but he had then gone on to marry the other woman. If he was not a cad, he certainly had been a coward. No matter how passionately she loved him, what she was doing now was not who she wanted to be.

She saw Bridget gesture to Finn, who was lying on a blanket. Thomas leaned over and offered a hand to the boy. At first, it looked like Finn wouldn't move, but Johanna knew how persuasive Thomas could be. Finn wouldn't turn down an invitation from his newfound father. Johanna didn't want Bridget to notice her interest and joined in on an animated conversation with some of the guests, but not before she saw the look on Bridget's face as Thomas and Finn tramped up the hill. Bridget interrupted her parents to point. All three watched Thomas and Finn with pride.

Johanna walked back to the water. She found TC dangling his legs over the dock. He was sopping wet, a result of an impromptu contest to see who could make the biggest splash. She didn't think he would leave the party willingly. She called him, and he doggedly ran across the grass, Johnny at his heels.

"TC, I need you to run an errand to help En," Johanna said.

"I get to go too, right?" Johnny asked.

"Not this time, Johnny."

"What? I'm En's buddy, not TC."

"Johnny, I need your help here with the picnic," she said. "Some of our family should stay as hosts, okay? You get the next turn to help En." Johnny deflated for a second, but one of the girls called to him and he was easily enticed back to the water.

She put her arm around TC's shoulders and steered him toward the woods.

"Do I hafta do this right now?" TC said.

"TC, I've asked En for help with a serious job," she said. "Johnny is too little, but it's important for our family. Our safety depends on it."

"What do you mean?"

"En will explain, but I am trusting you, and what you are about to do is a secret. Do you understand?"

TC's eyes grew wide.

"Now, I will tell you how to find En and what is expected."

TC nodded. He looked eager and terrified.

En sat on the front seat of the wagon. He heard TC before he saw him, and he hopped down to greet the boy.

"Ma said I should come help you," TC said.

"Did she tell you how important this is?" En asked.

"Yeah, for her and our family," TC said. "Moving some dangerous stuff, right?"

"Follow me. I'll show you." En and TC climbed into the wagon bed. En lifted the quilts. "These are weapons, collected by bad men who want to do harm. Have you heard of the Molly Maguires?"

"Ma says we mustn't speak of them."

"Yes, that's right. I won't say the name again, but some of these men are planning to hurt people with these weapons. Our job is to get rid of them."

TC nodded. "Like we're the sheriff, protecting the town from outlaws."

"Exactly," En said, relieved that TC appeared to trust him. He had worried that Connor may have taken the boy into his confidence, possibly bragged about the Mollies. But TC seemed eager to help. He supposed that he and Woo would have jumped on a chance to fight villains on the ship. It isn't always easy to define the bad guy, and En wondered if he should explain that the Molly Maguires existed because of injustice inflicted on the Irish.

"So how are we going to do this?" TC said.

En turned in the direction of the lake and pointed just as a blood-curdling yell came from behind them. It sounded so much like the rebels taking their village that En nearly ducked for cover. He pivoted and saw Thomas in the woods and Finn rushing the wagon. The boy leapt up and took TC to the ground.

"You and that Chink are steeling my da's wagon," Finn yelled.

"Stop it," TC wailed.

Finn pounded until TC rolled over and straddled his attacker. Grabbing Finn's shirt in his fists, TC slammed Finn's head against the ground.

Thomas and En ran toward the boys and yanked them apart.

"What in the hell is wrong with you? Bloody cut it *out*," Thomas shouted.

En pulled TC to his feet and took the boy by the arms. Thomas lifted Finn.

The boys were dusty, but the altercation had been so brief that neither of them looked seriously injured.

"It's time you grew up. I'm ashamed of you," Thomas said, shaking Finn. "I told you we had a job to do."

"But it's your wagon," Finn said. "They aren't supposed to be here."

"Yes, they are," Thomas said. "They are here to help."

Finn wiped his mouth with the back of his hand and said, "I didn't know."

"Well, apologize," Thomas said.

Finn mumbled, "Sorry."

"He was just doing what he thought was right," En said.

"Listen boys, I know you haven't always gotten on, but this is serious," Thomas moved so he was in front of both boys. "You're not kids on a playground anymore. No more fighting, or I will beat the living tar out of you."

The boys stood, heads down.

"Now, they'll be coming after all of us if we don't empty this wagon," Thomas said. "TC and En, get up there and start unloading boxes down to us."

En and TC climbed back into the wagon, lifted the first crate and lowered it to where Thomas and Finn then carried it down to the water's edge.

"On three," Thomas said. Holding the barrel aloft, they hoisted it out into the water. It was airborne for a few seconds and then made a whopping splash. A crater punched through the still surface of the lake, and the box disappeared into concentric ripples that fanned out across the water. A minute later, the surface was smooth.

They repeated the process until the wagon was empty. Near the end, the boys could barely raise the barrels.

"Let's rest before going back." En's face was shiny with sweat. He pulled a bucket of water from the wagon. "And remember, this is forever a secret. Don't talk about this with anyone, not even with each other or Johnny," En said, filling a dipper with water. "Now, come. Take a drink."

"Proud of you, son." Thomas patted Finn on the back. "And, TC, you are a strong and willing lad. Let me say, I could not be prouder of you if you were my son."

En watched Finn's indignance as TC stood taller.


Johanna allowed herself an extra minute in the outhouse. One day, she would get Walsh to build a cottage with indoor plumbing, but for now, the privy was the only structure. The men could use the woods, but the ladies needed shelter. Inside, the wooden slats were warm to the touch. Rarely used, the outhouse smelled like the mint growing under the floorboards. The clean smell refreshed her. She looked up and saw a canopy of trees, the sunlight-dappled leaves silvery green. She remembered other summer days at the lake, back when life was normal.

It had been less than twenty-four hours, but her world would never be the same. She might make sense of it when she wasn't terrified or exhausted. In a few minutes she would have to cheerfully welcome guests, offer refreshment, and host a canoe race. And Connor hadn't arrived. He must have slept in and was probably just leaving the hotel to join them for the afternoon, but what if he checked the cellar? And En, Thomas, and the boys were still gone; had they been caught?

Ever since that first day in America, she had been optimistic, even when they'd arrived in Nanticoke and their stay at the Sullivans' had soured. She'd always believed they would make it—find some measure of financial security. The wolf might always be at the door, but over these last few years, she'd reinforced the building and added locks and bolts. What else could she do to make them safe?

"Ma, everyone is waiting. Hurry up." Johnny banged on the wooden slats. She straightened her skirt and pushed the door open.

Johnny took her hand, and they walked back to join the others. "TC got lost in the woods, but he just got back," Johnny said.

"That's good. We can't delay the canoe race," Johanna said.

"Ma, guess what?" Johnny said. "TC is getting on with Finn. Isn't that the strangest thing? He and En are on a rowing boat team with Finn and his father. See them?"

Johnny ran ahead, jumping like a jackrabbit. A crowd formed around the dock. Thomas and En were getting into a canoe with Finn and TC, their nearly identical faces streaked with dirt. Kathleen's girls called to Johnny, "We saved you a seat. Come on."

She watched her youngest boy joyfully climb into the Farrells' canoe. Sparkling ripples of light made diagonal stripes across the lake. She walked to the where a captain's bell was fastened on the dock.

"Okay, Mrs. Kennedy." One of the older boys lined up the racers. "They're all set. Everyone, hush up so's Mrs. Kennedy can talk."

The crowd quieted and looked expectantly at Johanna.

"Thank you for coming to our second annual Lake Nuangola Day," she said as her voice faltered. A few men hooted, and everyone clapped. She took a breath and continued, willing her voice steady. "Before we begin, I have a message from Mr. Walsh. Unfortunately, he wasn't up to being here today. I speak for both of us when I extend our gratitude to the families of our hardworking staff and those who support the hotel as customers and suppliers. We can never thank you enough and hope you have a wonderful time today."

Everyone cheered. The children and adults waited, paddles across their laps. "Now, are the racers ready?"

They yelled, "Yeah!"

"Paddles up: take your mark … ready … go!"

She rang the bell.

Johnny was in the front of a canoe with Kathleen's girls, laughing as he struggled to get his paddle in rhythm with theirs. TC and Finn were flanked by En and Thomas, the men paddling hard and the boys barely lifting their oars.

"Where have you been?" Connor slurped his tea at the kitchen table, surrounded by picnic supplies. They had returned too late to unpack the night before.

"We were visiting Kathleen and the baby," Johanna said, setting down a basket that had contained leftovers. The boys had been full of chatter about the day before but fell silent when they saw their father.

Breakfast was long over, and most of the hotel's guests had checked out. The staff was upstairs, turning over the rooms. Tilly had left a note that she had gone to visit her daughter but would be back before dinner. There was no one else around. She hoped Connor wouldn't use the opportunity to start an argument. He might be too hung over.

"Boys, time to get started on your chores," she said.

TC and Johnny left without acknowledging Connor.

"You'd better not start in on me for missing the race," he said. "I deserved a bartender's day off, and there was lot to do before I rode all the way out to that godforsaken lake."

She took the empty containers out of the picnic basket and didn't reply. There was no indication he knew about the missing arsenal.

"So, how about some conversation?" he said.

She stopped and considered him. His face was covered with stubble. How long since he had shaved?

"Is Kathleen okay?" he asked.

She watched as he buttered a piece of toast, and instead of eating it, he tossed it on the table.

"Kathleen is weak, but she'll recover," she said. "And the baby is tiny but doing well."

"Good."

She started to sort through the picnic items.

"And the boys won the canoe race yesterday?" Connor said.

"That's right."

"You could have waited," Connor said. "You knew I'd get there."

"We did wait, just not long enough I guess," she said.

"So instead, I show up and there's our boy in the canoe with Finn, Thomas, and that Chinaman. TC seems buddy-buddy with Thomas too."

"They were getting along. It was a competition, nothing more."

"I thought Finn and TC were like oil and water?"

"It seems TC and Finn are no longer enemies," Johanna said. She wanted to ask him how he dared to criticize the very people who had risked so much due to his foolishness. But she couldn't give him any reason to suspect. He would go to the cellar soon enough, and then what?

"TC should watch himself around that boy," Connor said. "Finn is a lazy no-good. He's not going to turn out well."

Johanna almost pointed out that although Connor had been an industrious boy, it wasn't going well for him as a man.

The door to the dining room swung open and Walsh, leaning heavily on his cane, hobbled toward them.

Johanna stepped forward to take his arm.

"I'll be out at the bar shortly, sir," Connor said.

"It's the Coal and Iron Police," Walsh panted.

"Here, sit down, Mr. Walsh," Johanna said. "Catch your breath."

"They want to see …" Walsh plunked down and pointed at Connor.

"Yeah, take it easy," Connor said. "I'll handle it."

Johanna made sure Walsh was seated and followed Connor to the lobby. She knew one of the policemen. He looked past Connor and said, "Mrs. Kennedy, we're here to inspect the hotel, starting with the cellar."

"We can't be letting anyone—" Connor said.

"It's fine." Johanna stepped around him. "I'll take them."

"They need a search warrant." Connor reached to pull her back, but she walked ahead.

"Officer, this way," Johanna said.

"Johanna, I have the only key," Connor called after her.

"I have one," she said to the policemen. "The locksmith made us several, so I kept this one."

The policemen exchanged a look. She guessed everyone in Nanticoke knew about Connor's drinking. She thought it might help to hint that Connor was not always responsible.

"Wives have to help husbands find things all the time," she said, noting the fury on Connor's face. He'd complain later that she made him sound like a drunken Mick. She probably shouldn't have said anything, but it was the best she could think of, and it was too late to take it back.

The policemen followed her through the kitchen and down to the cellar. She took out the key and opened the lock. The police officers pulled up the metal doors, and they descended the steps. Sunlight poured down through the doors and particles floated in the dusty light. There was new straw on the floor, several kegs of beer, and a few crates of whiskey. She looked back at Connor, sweat beaded on his upper lip. He should have stayed in the kitchen.

"Why fresh straw in midsummer?" one of the policemen asked.

"We've been sprucing up," Johanna said.

The other policeman used his Billy club to push the straw away. "Just dirt."

"If there's nothing else, Connor will open the bar when you're finished," Johanna said.

"Well, ma'am, we can't drink on the job."

"Come on," Connor said. He gave them an uncertain grin. "You never turn down a free one."

"Are you suggesting we accept bribes, sir?" The officer reached for his belt.

"I'm sure that is not what my husband was trying to say." Johanna smiled. "I assure you there is nothing—"

"Ma'am, it doesn't matter," the policeman said, pulling out handcuffs. "We have some serious allegations. Your husband needs to come with us."

"Handcuffs?" she asked. "Are they necessary? You found nothing."

The officer unhooked the cuffs.

"Quiet, Johanna," Connor said. His skin had a greenish tinge in the sunlight.

The policeman pulled Connor's arms behind his back and fitted the metal links around his wrists.

She followed the police, up the cellar stairs and across the lawn. Her heart was pounding, but another part of her felt detached from the oddity of the last twenty-four hours. She almost laughed at the number of terrible scenarios she'd agonized over these last months: not having enough to feed the boys, one of them getting sick, the priest coming to the door with news of an accident. She could never have worried about this unimaginable picture.

"I'll be back before supper," Connor said.


Father Ryan was annoyed when he received word that he was needed immediately. He had a sermon to prepare. His demanding schedule was now interrupted because of the Nanticoke men taken in for questioning. He had insisted the Nanticoke parish summon him for serious matters that might trigger underlying tensions, but so far nothing had required his presence. He didn't want to see the Mollies start up again, but he didn't want to go to Nanticoke either. He wished he'd never offered.

After a long, hot ride, he got to the jail just before sunset. They allowed him ten minutes with a dazed Connor, who barely spoke. Since he was already in town, he decided he'd better check on Johanna and then go over to see Thomas. He ate the overly warm sandwich Mrs. Donnelly had packed for him while his driver took him to the hotel. His visit was brief, merely to assure Johanna it would be cleared up soon. The sun was setting as his driver went through town to the darkened Sullivan house. He knocked. No one answered after his second knock, and he was turning to leave when the door opened.

"Father Ryan? Come in. Come in," Thomas said. He dangled a bottle of beer in his hand. "You're about the only person I'd want to see tonight."

"You know, most people are alarmed when a priest shows up," Father Ryan said, crossing the threshold.

"Give me a minute to get more beer," Thomas said. "Then you can worry me. I know sherry is your drink, but beer's all we got."

"A beer sounds good." Father Ryan looked around the front parlor. "Where is your family?"

"Clan Sullivan is having supper at the neighbor's," Thomas called from the kitchen.

"Aren't you part of the family, Thomas?" Father Ryan took the bottle and they sat down.

"Don't get started on me. I'm a working man, got an early delivery." Thomas lifted the beer to his mouth. Father Ryan watched his friend's Adam's apple rise and fall as he swallowed.

"So, why are you here?" Thomas asked. "Should I be worried?"

"I assume you haven't heard about Connor?" Father Ryan tasted the beer. It was sour. He didn't like homemade brews.

"So, not a social visit?" Thomas said. "What about Connor?"

"Sounds like they have him implicated with the Molly Maguires. Something about weapons stashed in the hotel cellar."

"Jesus, did the police raid the place?" Thomas asked.

"They didn't find anything." Father Ryan stared at Thomas. Sometimes he could bore into a soul and see the lie.

"Well, good," Thomas said. "Then there's nothing to worry about."

"I'm not so sure. The police have him in custody."

"That means Johanna is alone?" Thomas said.

Father Ryan considered Thomas's peculiar reaction. Did he know something about Connor, or did his expression change when Johanna's name came up? It might be nothing; the police could just be flexing muscle—but what an inconvenience for him. How could he get this troublesome parish out from under his control, maybe pass it along to the King of Prussia parish to the south?

"Johanna should not be the first thing that enters your mind," Father Ryan said. "I'll remind you she is Connor's wife."

"But if he didn't do anything?" Thomas sounded as he once did when a nun caught him cheating in primary school—a good offense is always the best defense.

"I don't know what he did or didn't do," Father Ryan said. "And what do you know about these shenanigans?"

"I have a clear conscience, Father."

The priest held Thomas's eyes. "Are you involved with the Mollies again? Are you seeing that woman? She's married. Both of you are."

Thomas had the same teasing attitude as when he was a guilty child. Father Ryan would place odds he was indeed involved with Johanna.

"You didn't deny it," Father Ryan said. "You don't have many friends among the miners or the Coal and Iron Police. If they come after you, I can't protect you."

"Father, Johanna needs me," Thomas said softly.

"So, it is Johanna," Father Ryan said. "You are married to Bridget. Finn is your son."

Why did he bother to come over? He should have gone back to Wilkes-Barre and let these people tangle themselves in knots.

"TC is my son, too," Thomas said.

"This is dangerous," Father Ryan said. He shuddered. He couldn't stand by while another man was hanged, especially Thomas. He didn't know what was going on, but whatever muddle was unfolding, the best he could do was to get Thomas out of the line of fire.

"Thomas, the police and the Mollies can be vindictive. Either way, it may be time you leave town."

"Why would I do that?"

"If you don't leave by choice, it might be by paddy wagon … or coffin." Father Ryan was now convinced Thomas was hiding something.

"How do you figure that?"

"If you know why Connor was picked up, it's only a matter of time before they bring you in," Father Ryan said. "They may not have much, but Connor knows about your past and has plenty of reason to want you out of the picture. He could make it up, and they'd be happy to pin it on you."

"He doesn't know anything," Thomas said. "And he's been friendly enough."

"That was before he was looking through bars. You could end up sharing a cell with him, or worse." Father Ryan finished his beer in one gulp. "Don't be a fool, Thomas. I have little power these days with the authorities."

"I appreciate everything, but I don't think we see eye to eye. I'm confessing nothing," Thomas said. "It's possible I'm a sinner for loving two women, but I want to do well by them both."

Father Ryan pursed his lips and sighed. "Then I'll take my leave, please give some thought to getting your family to safety."

Thomas nodded.

"God bless you, my dear friend," Father Ryan put his hand on Thomas's shoulder. "Let me know if you want help relocating."

Several guests checked out early, probably to avoid further trouble. They were kind enough to make up excuses rather than mention they watched the police carting off the bartender. The few who had nowhere to go remained, but Johanna expected they would spend the evening hiding in their rooms. She couldn't think about what this might mean for the business; the events of the day had already put Mr. Walsh in bed.

She decided to sort out the ledger. It would occupy her mind, and she hadn't filed the billings since Lake Nuangola Day. The boys were upstairs, and En was with Mr. Walsh. She was bent over the books when the front door opened and Thomas walked in.

"Father Ryan just stopped by. I've heard the terrible news," he said as he came around the desk. She stood, and they embraced. His hands felt solid and warm on her back. He bent down to kiss her. She tasted beer on his breath.

"Never let me go." She could breathe in his arms, but a doubt bubbled up: Thomas never came to the hotel. Why was he here?

"Did Father Ryan stop by?" Thomas asked.

"Yes, and mentioned he was going to see you next."

She felt wary. Father Ryan was not always a friend of the Irish.

"He came over about an hour ago. And I want to talk to you about something." Thomas's lips were on the top of her head.

She had wondered why Father Ryan had done so much to help Thomas get established. She knew about their childhood friendship, but Father Ryan was almost too protective of Thomas. He wouldn't want Thomas to get in trouble because of her. She felt her body go cold—Father Ryan wanted Thomas to leave town. And Thomas probably should, for his own safety.

"You're here to tell me you are leaving Nanticoke," she said.

"Ah, my sweet, you know me too well," he said.

She grew cold. He was going.

"I can't lose you, not right now." She put her hands on his chest and lifted her head to look into his eyes. "Please, don't leave me."

"I don't want to, but Father Ryan says my staying could make it worse for you, and Bridget's been harping on me to leave Nanticoke."

He was bringing up his wife, separating from her already.

"Bridget's been collecting maps and train timetables. Father Ryan, he just gave me his opinion."

"Is it because of Connor? Did he say anything?" It had just occurred to her to ask about her husband. She hadn't done well by Connor, likely one of the reasons Connor had been taking such risks. She'd made him feel small, and she felt terrible about what was happening to him. No one would wish the Coal and Iron jail on anyone.

"Did Father think Connor would be released?"

"No one knows," Thomas said.

"You think they will charge him, convict him, what?"

"They have nothing, no evidence, thanks to you." Thomas stroked her back. "You can take heart in that."

"Yes, that's true." Johanna felt less apprehensive. Even if Thomas was offering her false reassurance, Johanna wanted to believe that their lives would return to normal soon—perhaps even tomorrow—if the police had no evidence.

She realized Thomas was speaking, but she only heard his last few words, something about TC.

"What should TC know?" she said.

"Yesterday, at the lake, I was proud to be his father," Thomas said. "Johanna, I don't want to go to my grave without his knowing that I'm his father."

So, this was not a discussion. Thomas had decided to leave.

"You can't tell him, surely, not now." Her world was falling apart. Was Thomas going to make things harder?

"You're right. It's not time to tell him. But when the time is right." Thomas reached into his pocket. "I have this for him. It's a hunting knife that folds into the handle."

"He's only nine. He's not old enough to own a knife."

"But I want to give him something, so he remembers me." Thomas looked so eager. "Even if he doesn't know right away, having a family friend give him a gift, what's the harm?"

He held out the leather pouch. "Finn picked it out, told him I would give it to him when he turned fifteen, but I can get another for Finn. You could keep it until TC is that age or older. You decide. Just hang on to it."

She wanted to say no, but perhaps she was wrong. What if Thomas left town and someday TC discovered his father's true identity? Perhaps a gift would help him make sense of his father's abandonment. She would keep it until later. Maybe she could still convince him not to leave right away.

"Can you come tonight?" she said, the first time she had ever asked him to visit her. "We can talk further?"

"I wish I could," he said. "Bridget's in a state."

Thomas lifted her chin with his knuckle, tilting her face to his. She lost herself in the lingering kiss.

There was a clatter. Thomas stepped back, and Johanna saw a metal dustpan had hit the floor.

Tilly stood in the doorframe, holding a broom, "Excuse me. Didn't think anyone was in here."

"Tilly, you should announce yourself." Johanna dropped her arms, realizing the abrupt gesture only made it worse.

"I was just coming to turn out the lamps. Don't want to tempt fire." Tilly nodded toward one of the gas lamps. "Don't mind me, you two. I'll come back."

"I was just taking my leave," Thomas said. "Mrs. Kennedy is not feeling well. Perhaps you could help your mistress to bed?"

Johanna felt a visceral loss as Thomas moved to the door. She could think of no way to hold him back. They would have to finish the conversation later. Tilly wouldn't keep what she had seen to herself either, but she would bide her time so Johanna just would worry about stopping Tilly's gossip later.

He was gone before she could say goodbye.

Father Ryan would get to Walsh's sickbed by midafternoon if his wagon driver would speed up. Now, for the second time in a week, he had to make the trip to Nanticoke, and it would likely come to naught. He scolded himself for not having spent more time cultivating a relationship with Walsh. He'd never expected the old man's health to go downhill so rapidly. Father Ryan had envisioned ministering to an infirm but grateful gentleman on his deathbed. It was maddening that the old guy could die without a period of suffering to bring him back to the true Church. Father Ryan decided to make this trip on the off chance he could wedge even a small bequest to the Church into the will.

He sighed. It was probably a good idea to check in on Connor, too. At least he would appear diligent in offering pastoral care, and who knew whether that would pay off? He would make sure the mine bosses knew how closely he was monitoring the situation. He'd heard only that Connor was still in jail and that an investigation was underway. Father Ryan frowned, thinking about what they might discover. There was more to the story; there always was. The priest eventually gets all the gory details: impure thoughts, wicked deeds. The mess in the Kennedy household was revolting: a fool of an Irishman in prison, yet another loser abandoning his family and languishing in jail. This would take all day, and Saturday afternoon was his time to prepare his Sunday sermon. He might not make it back to Wilkes-Barre in time for Mass tomorrow.

He visited the jail first, in case there was news. He found Connor in the cell, unshaven and grubby. The only change was the man's growing lethargy. Drying out from alcohol was probably contributing to his deepening depression. He stood up when Father Ryan entered the room but then sank back on the bed and gave monosyllabic answers. The priest was there only five minutes. Before Father Ryan even exited the cubicle, Connor had laid back on his cot, eyes closed.

Tilly was in the lobby when Father Ryan arrived at the hotel. She led him to the darkened room where Walsh lay, his breathing nearly a death rattle. Johanna and En were on opposite sides of the bed. He tried to remember how long Walsh had worked in the mines before he started managing the hotel full-time—likely long enough that the man's lungs were clay. Judging from the labored breaths, the old guy didn't have much time left. Damn Connor. No wonder Walsh's chest seized up after the police raid on his hotel.

The Celestial with the ridiculous pigtail was more civilized than he would have expected and appeared to be skilled at administering medication. Father Ryan watched as En felt the old man's pulse and pressed a compress to Walsh's forehead. Despite En's skill, the patient was agitated. Suffocating is a terrible way to die. Father Ryan could see it was unlikely Walsh would carry on a conversation. He was nearly gone.

"Father, thank you for coming," Johanna said. She gave the basin she was holding to En and stepped away from the bedside.

"I'm so sorry, my dear." Father Ryan took her hand. "How is he?"

"En just gave him more medication. The sedative was wearing off," she said.

"Has he been conscious?" Father Ryan asked. The priest had no problem if this Chinese doctor gave Walsh enough to knock him out, as long as it didn't kill the man before he could receive the Last Rites.

"Earlier he was asking for George, his son, but not any longer."

"Perhaps it is time for Last Rites? Then you and I can speak further about my visit with Connor. I'm afraid there hasn't been any change in his situation."

"Thank you for checking," she said. "And I'm not sure Mr. Walsh would want Last Rites, Father. You know he was not a practicing Catholic."

"True that he rarely attended Mass since his wife's death," he said, thinking back to the man's disdain when Father Ryan had suggested he donate to the building fund, "but a man often has a change of heart as he faces eternity. It can't hurt to offer him the sacrament."

Father Ryan placed his valise at the foot of the bed and took out his stole, a cue for Johanna and En to leave.

She hesitated and then signaled to En for them to go. Once they did, he took the old man's hand. "Mr. Walsh, can you hear me?" he said.

The man's eyes shot open. His voice was a hiss, but the words were clear. "Get out." Despite the medicine, Walsh was not asleep. "It's my time. I know it." As if to prove his point, Mr. Walsh gasped for air. "The price ... for my ... release from ... this Earth."

"We can never know what God intends, but perhaps you would like to make the Act of Contrition?"

"I loathe the cruelty of a god I don't believe in ... you ... get out."

"I do understand, but perhaps this day you will be in eternity, and a confession would allow you to see your loved ones—"

Panting, the old man forced his next words. "My Mary ... she believed, not so with George ... shot himself ... there's likely no heaven, but anyway, George won't be there."

Father Ryan couldn't force a man to confess. "Very well," he said. He said a short prayer for Walsh's soul and laid out the items needed to administer Last Rites.

Walsh made a choking sound, and then as if he were being pulled from above, he stretched out his arms.

"I see her and …" He opened his hands. "And, George, is that you?" Father Ryan watched Walsh lift his arms toward the ceiling. "The light," he said. "Beautiful light." Then Walsh fell back, lifeless.

Father Ryan was stunned. What had he just witnessed? He watched a tear slowly move down the withered cheek. Perhaps the man was imagining his loved ones. He'd seen it before, but a part of him truly hoped that Walsh had walked into welcoming arms. Either way, Walsh was out of pain. Father Ryan put his fingers on the man's eyelids and closed them. Then the priest put on his stole. Walsh might still benefit from the rite of Extreme Unction.

He was in prayer when there was a light knock at the door. He got up, holding the bottle of oil he'd used to anoint the body.

Johanna stepped into the room. "How is he?"

"He is with the angels."

"Oh," she said. "I had hoped to be here, with him."

"He may have wanted to spare you, my dear. Sometimes people choose to escape when those with whom they are close are not present," he said. "It was a peaceful death. He reached out to his wife, and a son. They came to him in the last minute. I've seen that before."

"Really?" she said. "I didn't think he was a man of faith, but he did love his wife and son deeply."

"He called out to a Mary and then a George."

She gripped the bed railing. "Of course, his family. Mr. Walsh could be cranky, but he was a kind and generous employer." She put her hand over the man's grizzled hand. "I relied on him more than I knew. I loved him."

There was something about this woman that rubbed Father Ryan the wrong way. Who did she think she was? First of all, she showed a real lack of deference to him. Even now, she acted like she was family, like she owned the room. And the few times he'd heard her confession, which were not many, they were milquetoast. She was secretive. And poor Connor—wives were supposed to submit to their husbands as the Church does to Christ, yet she seemed to run things around here, and she had barely asked after her husband.

"I'm sure you will miss him, my dear," he said.

He watched her fold Walsh's hands on his chest and pull the sheet up over his body. There was something devious about her, too, a conniving woman.

"I will miss him very much," she said. "I wish I could have done more to ease his suffering."

"You did what you could," he said. "He was like a father to you, and there is this difficult business with your husband. Did he make any arrangements in the event of his passing?"

"I don't know. He had been a little under the weather, but this last serious illness has only been the last few days. You said that his son, George, came to him," Johanna said. "I think George is somewhere out West, but I don't know how to reach him. I've never seen any correspondence."

"The Lord will provide," Father Ryan said in the tone he'd mastered to signal the end of a conversation. He was glad she didn't assume Walsh's seeing George meant the son was dead. He didn't want her to suspect there was no heir, although George could be alive; Walsh may have been hallucinating.

"I would like to sit with him," Johanna said. "Perhaps you would like some refreshment?" she offered. "Kathleen is just outside in the hall. She can help you with anything."

"If you are sure you want to be alone, my dear," he said, suspicious of what game she was playing but anxious to get away from the deathbed.

Johanna nodded. He cupped his hand above her head and recited a brief benediction.

He exited the room and found Kathleen sitting on a bench, Johanna's two boys on either side of her. The one, did they call him TJ, TP—he couldn't remember the two initials—looked exactly like Thomas, the hair color, the eyes.

Kathleen peeled away from the boys and stood.

"Mr. Walsh is gone," he said.

"I'm sorry. We expected this. Oh dear, Johanna is—was—fond of him," Kathleen said. "As crazy as the old coot was, now she's without her husband and her benefactor."

"And perhaps her home," Father Ryan said absently. When he saw Kathleen's expression he continued. "But let's not worry yet, Kathleen. That son, George, will get here, and he may ask Johanna to run the place." Why not just let the myth of George remain? Perhaps he could find a way that Mr. Walsh would yet contribute to the Church.

"But that could be weeks," Kathleen said.

"Then life will remain unchanged for the time being. Right now, the most important thing is to help Connor," he said. "Ah, here's the Chinaman. Perhaps you could prepare something to calm your mistress? And, Kathleen, why don't you take the lads with you until tomorrow?"

"And what are your plans, Father?"

Father Ryan removed the stole from around his neck. "It's probably too late to get back to Wilkes-Barre. I must stay at the rectory."

"We don't have a rectory," she said. "Only a building fund."

"Well, I can't stay in a building fund," he said. These people couldn't raise two pennies to build a mud hut. "Sister Mary Catherine is resourceful," he said. "I trust she will come up with something."

"You are welcome to stay with us," Kathleen said.

He adjusted his cassock. A button was missing, one of thirty-three, each representing a year of the life of Christ. Damn, it was probably on top of the corpse. He'd have to get one of his parish widows to replace it.

"A kind offer, but I would much prefer Mother Agnes arrange a small, quiet room," he said. Saints bless us and keep us—all he needed now was the cacophony of a large family. "No, no, it would be an imposition for you. I'm sure Mother Agnes will make arrangements. I'll go to the convent now."

Johanna emerged from the bedroom and TC and Johnny embraced her.

"I'll take the boys home with me tonight," Kathleen said. "They can play with the girls, and you need some sleep."

Johanna nodded and kissed them, "Be good and I'll see you in the morning."

"I must be going, too. I'll have the nuns let you know where I'll be staying," Father Ryan said. He needed a sherry. "We can discuss the funeral tomorrow."

"Thank you, Father Ryan," Johanna said. "You've been so kind."

"Get some rest," Father Ryan suggested. He watched En take Johanna's arm and guide her down the hall. Father Ryan felt a distant alarm, as if he should pay attention to an unseen threat.

# CHAPTER TEN

# THE QUEUE

**Nanticoke, Pennsylvania, Summer 1883**

The convent at St. Francis was a two-story brick building. Mother Agnes's outrageous landscaping—almost an obscenity of color—bedecked the front. The interior of most convents were shabby, but Father Ryan wasn't surprised when the young novitiate let him into a foyer with an enormous flower arrangement on a round pedestal table, the wood polished to a sheen. The chintz fabrics on the walls and furniture featured cabbage roses floating on ivy, and there was a floral motif on the carpet that circled up to a landing with floor-to-ceiling windows. Only Mother Agnes could have managed such welcoming and elegant living quarters for nuns. Where did she get the money?

"Ah, Sister Mary Catherine." Father Ryan held out his hand to one of the teachers who worked with Mother Agnes. She would have been attractive if not for her holier-than-thou countenance. Still, unlike Mother Agnes, the sister gave him some respect due his position.

"Mr. Walsh is dead, I suppose?" Sister said.

He nodded. His eyes rested on the sophisticated bureau in the corner. He would like one with the same carved inlay for his rectory.

"Such a pity," Sister said. "Mother Agnes is not back from the school yet, but I will inform her immediately."

"Yes." He cleared his throat. "Perhaps you are aware of my need for accommodations this evening? And that I require solitude for prayer."

"We thought you might come to us," Sister Mary Catherine said. Father Ryan would watch her walk a fine line here. It was an imposition, and she liked to grumble. Still, he was a senior priest from the wealthier Wilkes-Barre parish. She and her wimpled compatriots would want to win his favor for it was rumored he would be named monsignor within the year, possibly to a post opening in Philadelphia where he could do them some real good.

"Although it is quite irregular for a priest to stay in the convent," Sister said, "Mother Superior has found a solution."

Good, his power reached to Nanticoke. He'd made them scurry. He could likely count on a dinner invitation, and it would be a delicious meal, too. It was rumored Mother Agnes had come from wealth, and however she managed it, her cuisine and wine standards were high.

"We have a room at the school," Sister said. "I'm sure you won't mind sharing with our visiting priest?"

Share? He had specifically said he wanted solitude. "Sister, I need seclusion."

"I'm sorry, Father. Unless you want to stay with one of our families?" she said. "I'm sure you would agree that it is most unsuitable to house a priest in the same building as nuns."

He was trapped, as well she knew. She opened a cabinet and took out a key ring. "I'll take you over." They walked across a courtyard to the upper school. He followed her downstairs to the basement.

"Here we go. This used to be the janitor's room. Mother Superior believes in utilizing space," Sister said.

Near the furnace room? Janitor? Father Ryan could not believe the indignity.

"It's wonderfully warm, especially in winter months. Of course, it's underground so even in summer it's comfortable. You will sleep well."

When they reached the bottom of the stairs, she stood aside. "Here is the reading lounge." There were bookshelves on all four walls, a long table, and several overstuffed chairs. "Mother Agnes designed this for our older students. They can read what they like, when they complete their studies, of course. The bedroom is through this door."

Father Ryan followed her. He would have been happy to have this room to himself, read his catechism and take his dinner on a tray. Sharing such a small space—barely room for the two single beds—would not do.

"We eat dinner at six. Mother Superior would like you to join us. Perhaps you would care to wash up now?" She opened a drawer and pulled out a towel. "Can you find your way back to the convent?"

"Yes, thank you, Sister," Father Ryan spoke through tight lips.

"Oh, and Father Neil will join us. He should be finished with the five o'clock Mass about now."

"And here I am, Sister."

Even before Father Ryan heard the voice, the name stirred him. He turned to see the flaxen blond head and bearded face of his lover.

"Father Ryan, allow me to introduce Father Neil," Sister said. "He is willing to share his room. It will only be the one night."

Father Ryan yearned to embrace Father Neil but instead stood immobile, his limbs heavy. Fortunately, Father Neil, completely composed, had the presence of mind to extend his hand.

"So good to meet you," he said. "I hope you don't snore."

"Auntie Kathleen let us catch fireflies," Johnny reported. "Maeve caught the most. I caught second most, seventeen."

Johanna sat in bed, a breakfast tray across her lap. TC helped himself to a muffin, layering it with peach preserves. How wonderful that her lads had the luxury of eating well, but for how much longer?

"See, boys—your mother is fine," Kathleen said. "Now, go change. Ask Tilly if you need clean clothes."

"I'll be downstairs soon," Johanna told them.

"And is Mr. Walsh laid out yet?" Johanna asked Kathleen.

"No, we thought you would want to have a say about where," Kathleen said. "He's on ice."

"On ice?" They both started to laugh.

"He liked a cold one every once in a while, eh?" Kathleen said. "Perhaps we can pour a whiskey and join him?"

"He would have wanted us to have a stiff one," Johanna said, "in his honor."

"If he ever had a stiff one himself," Kathleen could barely get the words out. Johanna laughed too, until tears came down her face. Then, suddenly, she was crying.

"What's to become of me now, Kathleen?" she said. "They won't even let me visit Connor."

"They never let the Irish visit their kin in prison. Only the priests get in."

"And if George comes back—if we become homeless?"

"We'll fit you in at our house."

Johanna wiped tears off her cheeks.

"You warned me about Connor. Oh, what has he done to our life? I tried to stop him."

"I don't want to add fuel to the fire, but he's made terrible choices for years." Kathleen handed Johanna a napkin.

"Thanks, but I'm too exhausted to sustain a good cry." Johanna blew her nose. "How's the baby?"

"Sweet, you must come see him."

"I'm looking forward to a formal introduction. And how are you feeling?"

"Better. It was such a fast labor; En did most of the work." Kathleen sat next Johanna on the bed. "And some good news: Michael has asked around, and he says they have no evidence against Connor. Unless a witness comes forward, they likely won't charge him."

"Good, although I wouldn't put it past them to make up charges."

"I've thought of that. And if Connor was with the Mollies—and if something he did angered them—the real problem could come from the men who will want their contributions back," Kathleen said. "I understand they were collecting weapons."

Johanna always marveled at how Kathleen seemed to know, or intuit, things before she was told.

"Do you know where they are, Johanna?"

"You don't want to ask me that question."

"Then Connor might be safer in prison," Kathleen said. "I guess that doesn't cheer you."

"No."

"But here is something that may. I found this in Mr. Walsh's desk." Kathleen handed Johanna a thick envelope. Scrawled on the flap were the words "For Johanna Kennedy in the event of my death."

"You found this, accidently?" Johanna said.

"Okay, I picked the lock on his desk drawer." Kathleen half smiled. "But we would have gotten around to it eventually."

The edges of the seal were puckered. Kathleen had undoubtedly steamed it open.

"And you have read the contents as well?" Johanna smiled. "I wouldn't think you had this much extra time in your life, to spend so much of your future in the confessional."

Kathleen gave Johanna a blank look.

"I'm not buying that false innocence," Johanna said. She pulled out the papers and read from the sheet on top:

*To Whom It May Concern.*

*Having lost my dear wife, Mary, and my son, George, as a consequence of the Long Strike, and having no other earthly kin, I leave my hotel and houses, along with all of my worldly goods, to Johanna Kennedy in gratitude for her diligent service. Enclosed with the formal will are the deeds, which are free and clear of mortgages.*

*William Walsh*

Under his signature was a seal and a witness.

"Is this possible?" Johanna sat up.

"I think it might be. That signature belongs to the priest visiting the Nanticoke parish now," Kathleen said. "Father Brian Neil."

"But why didn't Mr. Walsh ever tell us his son was dead?"

"I always suspected it," Kathleen said. "He talked about his son and his wife in the same faraway voice. Never got even one letter. Perhaps he couldn't admit he'd lost them both."

"I suppose." Johanna looked through the stack of documents, hoping to unearth a clue.

"And why wouldn't Mr. Walsh leave you the hotel and the houses? It's your cleverness and hard work that turned his business around. These properties have been yours for a long time; you just didn't know you owned them."

Kathleen walked to the wardrobe and pulled out a petticoat. She handed Johanna the undergarment. "You're a wealthy woman."

"We'll see," Johanna said. "But take this and the deeds to Michael. Maybe he can find out what we do next?"

Kathleen took the package. "It's a red-letter day, but I suppose you should wear black."

Johanna chose a black dress made of heavy cotton, consistent with the grief she felt. Mr. Walsh had been a dichotomy: critical, demanding, and a bully, but also a loyal protector. She also felt giddy with relief. Each time her eyes met Kathleen's as they prepared the body for the funeral, they couldn't help but exchange smiles over the discovery of the will and what it meant for the future.

That night, Johanna lay in bed, and thinking that perhaps Walsh's spirit still lingered near Earth, she whispered, "Thank you, dear man. I wish I had known how much you cared about me when I could have thanked you in person. It would have made you uncomfortable, but if only I had just five minutes more with you, I would hold your hands in mine and speak my gratitude. I was dear to you and that means more than you can know. I will never forget you."

She fell asleep quickly, her heart less troubled because she had loved, and been loved by, Mr. Walsh.

En gathered his sisters in his arms. They were light as air. He could see the flames lapping the window frames of their adobe home. Smoke filled his nostrils. He woke, choking—another dream where he couldn't save Ai and An, but this one felt real. He opened his eyes to fog. No, fog wouldn't burn. And the odor. This wasn't a dream. He bolted up and opened the shed's door. Red-orange flames were leaping from the half-circle windows in the hotel attic.

En raced to the kitchen and kicked in the back door. Adrenaline pumping, he climbed the stairs two at a time. It was dark except for an orange glow throbbing around the doorframe of the boys' room. He crawled on his hands and knees to stay low. How long had it taken him to cross the yard? Two minutes? Three?

He reached the bedroom door and hesitated. Opening it would draw air into the room, possibly feed the fire. If he got in, he could drop the children from the window. Would the window open? He thought he'd heard Johnny's cries. He had to open the door.

The doorknob was hot to the touch, but he forced his fingertips on the red-hot metal. He rotated the handle and pushed.

"Johnny, TC," he said. "Are you in here?"

The fire snapped and popped. Flames engulfed one of the beds. Was he too late?

"Here," TC choked.

He extended his arms and moved forward. Suddenly he felt something soft. A garment? An arm? He wrapped his hand around what might be a wrist and tugged. As if he had yanked on the right string, both boys tumbled on top of him. He flipped them beneath his body.

"Keep going, that way," he said. They didn't move so he wrapped an arm around each midriff and dragged. "Keep still." He could feel his lungs singe with smoke.

They cleared the door, and En pulled them toward the stairs. Just as he thought he could go no further, he felt something heavy, a blanket, thrown over them.

"This way," a man said.

He managed to keep the blanket over the three of them. A piece of furniture toppled inches away from his legs, disintegrating into a burst of sparks that showered hot embers on his exposed arms. Someone tugged him down the stairs.


He regained consciousness lying on the grass. He hurt everywhere. Waves of pain throbbed from his shoulders to his fingertips. His scorched throat resisted taking a breath until his body forced a violent gasp. His lungs filled as if still on fire.

He heard a voice shouting above the fire-alarm bells.

"The wind ain't gonna help."

There was clanging far away.

En squeezed his eyes shut. When he opened them, soot dangled in his line of sight. A deep voice yelled commands through a speaking trumpet. Two firemen walked in, holding a ladder sideways. Several firemen worked the hand-pump engine. A bucket brigade lined up and tossed pails of water down the line.

"Why isn't there more water?" someone shouted.

"Sorry. The central water distributor isn't in place yet," a fireman said. "We're doing the best we can, ma'am."

The blanket was still on his shoulders, draped so it stuck to his arms. He should examine them, but the thought of ripping the fabric from his scorched skin made him weak. He was fully present to agony and yet strangely detached. He watched the fireworks and explosions and ceilings and floors collapsing, A chimney tumbled and pieces of burning shingles sailed down from the roof. At one point, a hose caught fire, and some of the men stamped it out with boots and sand.

The street in front of the hotel was melting red-orange. He tried to shift farther back on the grass, but any movement was excruciating. Flames whirled around the building, gave out, and flared up like an ocean squall. He was mesmerized at the horror and beauty. Finally, there was only a blackened mound. A few items charred beyond recognition rested in steam and ashes. The fire had consumed the hotel; trees hung over the remains like skeletons.

He gazed through the haze of cinders and saw Johanna rushing toward him.


Father Ryan appreciated the thickness of the oriental rug. The bed linens had been ironed. The room did not feel like a basement. He turned his attention to unbuttoning Father Neil's cassock.

"It was torture, sitting through that dinner with the nuns again," he said. "All I could think about was undressing you."

He tugged at Father Neil's undershirt.

"And those nuns, so confused when you told them you might stay a few more days."

"I'd not been too gracious about sharing a room, but it seems clear that the work of the Lord demands I remain: Connor in prison, Walsh's funeral," Father Ryan said. "And I have others who require my ministrations." He pushed Father Neil's tunic aside.

"Where are those nuns now?" Father Neil said. "There's no lock on the door."

"The nuns are in a separate building. We are the only two people in this entire school, and we're in the basement for the love of Jesus, more privacy than the monastery. Relax."

Father Neil surveyed the room. "Let's push the beds together."

"What if we try them horizontally?"

They rearranged the room and lay down crosswise.

"That's better," Father Ryan said, slipping out of his remaining underclothes.

They lay naked. They would have a predictable first round. First one, then the other, would spend. In between, they would hold each other and talk. The next time, they would add tenderness and creativity. Father Ryan wondered if married couples had similar habits.

"Ahh, the first time with you, it's always just like the first time," Father Neil said, lying in the crook of Father Ryan's arm.

"You have a real way with words. 'The first time is like the first time,' ha. Have you considered preaching?"

"But it's true that we always make each other happy right away, don't we?"

"Indeed. Still, the best is yet to come." He pushed his leg between Father Neil's.

"No, not quite yet," Father Neil said. "I want to talk."

"About what?"

"Oh, I don't know. I want to ask you about life. What do you think of this parish?"

"I think it's two-bit," Father Ryan said. "You can do better."

"But I like it here, the people, Mother Agnes."

"Have you noticed that there is no love lost between Mother Agnes and Sister Mary Catherine?" Father Ryan kissed Father Neil's neck.

"I can't figure it out," Father Neil said.

"Mother Superior has the power," Father Ryan said. "Sister hates it. She lashes back in ways that Mother Superior can't confront directly."

"Sister Mary Catherine is mean," Father Neil said. "I've seen her with the students. She picks favorites and can be cruel, especially to the vulnerable ones."

"Ah, she's an amateur," Father Ryan said. "The one to watch is Mother Agnes. She is wise as a serpent and gentle as a dove. She'll sink her teeth into you, and you won't figure it out until the venom hits your bloodstream."

"She strikes me as a deeply loving person," Father Neil said. "Mary Catherine is the sadist."

"You are so naive. Sister Mary Catherine can't control her temper; Mother Superior doesn't let hers show."

"But Mother Superior has empathy for people. She cares."

"Maybe so, but if I'm getting ambushed and had only one rifle, I'd give it to Sister Mary Catherine," Father Ryan said. "Give a gun to Mother Superior and she might shoot you."

"That's a ridiculous analogy," Father Neil protested.

"Let's agree to disagree. You are wrong about which nun is more trouble, as it appears you were also wrong about how ready you are."

Father Ryan gazed down at their naked bodies, slick in the candlelight. Both men were well-endowed, both fully stimulated. "We look glorious," Father Ryan said. He was about to suggest that Father Neil roll over when they heard a noise. Before either could move, the door opened. Sister Mary Catherine, holding a lantern, said, "Father Neil, Father Ryan, we need—"

Father Ryan saw the nun stop in her tracks, "Mother of *God*!"

"Oh, for goodness sake, Sister Mary Catherine, just get them up." Mother Agnes shouldered her way around the sister and into the room. She saw the reason for her colleague's blasphemy.

"Gentlemen," she said, focusing her eyes on the ceiling and with a tone that Father Ryan thought was remarkably calm, "there is a fire at the hotel. Please get dressed and meet us there. We need to offer comfort to those afflicted."

Dragging the still sputtering Sister Mary Catherine away, Mother Agnes closed the door.

Behind the haze of smoke, a wash of pink slashed the sky. Johanna's nostrils burned. Ash coated her throat. She wondered if anything would ever take away the taste. She looked at the remains of the hotel. The chimney stood, a pillar of blackened stone. The office safe stood like a tombstone amid the ruins.

"We kept it from jumping to the other buildings, but the hotel was too far gone," the fire chief said. He removed his helmet. Above the line of soot below his hairline, his skin was stark white. "I'm sorry, Mrs. Kennedy."

"You saved my boys. That is all that matters."

"We'll stay here with shovels to make sure it's out," he said. "I suspect it was arson."

"Why?"

"It started up too fast to be anything else, but we'll know more after we can inspect."

She walked back across the lawn to where Kathleen had bundled TC and Johnny in quilts. "Let's get the boys back to my house," Kathleen said. Johanna nodded and steered the sleepwalking boys along.

They had taken only a few steps when she saw a man, knees up and head bent between them, hands dangling from his blackened arms. Then she noticed the queue going down his back.

"Oh, En, my God." She started running.

Johnny yelled to her, "Ma, where are you going?"

She was on the ground next to En. His hands were like raw meat, nearly twice their normal size. "We need a doctor," she shouted. "Kathleen, take the lads," Johanna spoke over her shoulder, "and have Michael get Dr. Murphy."

"But, Ma?" Johnny cried. She yearned to turn to Johnny and carry him to Kathleen's. She hesitated just as En looked up. She saw such pain in his eyes. His need was greater. Without her, he might be ignored, left here to die. There was no question: she had to stay with him.

"Johnny, I'll be there soon," she said.

She watched Johnny walking away, his sad little body dutifully following his aunt Kathleen. Johanna would have to make it up to him. Right now, En needed a doctor and fluids. How is it that no one had noticed him? Where was that fire chief? Who could help get En inside? She knew Dr. Murphy was with the fire company. Where was he?

Johanna's head jerked up, her neck stiff. She had been asleep, sitting next to En's bed. The shed had been leeward of the fire, and the room barely smelled of smoke. En lay in the bed, his eyes closed, and he was breathing without difficulty. The doctor had been there and said there was little they could do except wait for En's arms to heal and hope infection didn't set in. Before he left, and now of the mind that Chinese medicine couldn't hurt, he had told Johanna if En wanted any of his herbs, she was free to give them to him.

It must have been a few hours since Dr. Murphy left. Immediately after, Johanna had found En's medicine bag and brought it to his bedside. She opened it and said, "Show me what to do; what can I do to help?"

"We need to apply alternating applications of medicine," he spoke with some effort. If only she had asked earlier, learned some of what he knew.

"Look for …" En whispered, "sumac gallnut, centipede, and borneol—mash them."

Thankfully, the bags of powder were labeled in both Chinese and English. She picked up the mortar and pestle and mixed the herbs together.

"Find … honey," he said. "On the shelf."

She followed his instructions, fighting panic that she might cause more harm than good.

"Now, on the burns," he managed to say.

She could tell he was stifling moans as she dabbed the ointment on his burns. After all, he was in agony.

"There must be something more?" she said. "For the pain?" She scanned the box and held up a large packet of a white substance.

He nodded, "Add water."

She cleaned out the mortar and pestle, and using the scoop in the bag, placed a generous amount in the bowl and added water. She spooned the liquid into his mouth. He fell asleep almost immediately. She must have drifted off soon after.

She shifted in her chair, unable to determine how long the sun had been up. The room was airless and hot. En's face glistened. Did all Celestials have such ageless skin? His thick black hair had worked free from the queue. There were burn marks on his face, but his arms and hands had taken the brunt of the fire.

She decided he might be cooler without the sheet and carefully pulled it off his upper body. He was more muscular than she would have thought, his chest smooth like polished amber.

"Miss Johanna," he mumbled. "Go to the boys."

"I will stay for a while longer," she said. She took a towel from the nightstand. The glass that held the rose just a few days ago was gone. She dipped the cloth into a basin of cool water and bathed his forehead. "Would you like a sip of water?" she asked.

He nodded. She found a cup and filled it with water. She lifted him gently and held the cup to his lips. He drained it, and his head dropped back on the pillow just as Dr. Murphy returned.

"How is the patient?" he asked.

"I didn't think you would come back," Johanna said. She was tired, or she would not have been so candid. She half expected the doctor would resent treating a Celestial, or at least not provide treatment after the initial emergency.

"You mean I don't treat Celestials? Well, that's true in most cases, but what we have here is not an ordinary Chinaman," Dr. Murphy said. "He's saving more lives in this town than I am."

He picked up En's wrist to take a pulse. "Lots of your kin, now that I think of it."

"Are the injuries bad?" she asked.

"Something fell on his shoulder, but nothing's broken. The ribs are probably just bruised. So far, his airway and lungs seem fine."

"And the burns on his hands and arms?"

"They look worse than they are. If we can keep them from getting infected, he should recover. May not have full use of his hands, though."

Johanna wondered if En could practice medicine without his hands.

"I'm going to examine him. There could be some injuries I missed—I need to palpate his abdomen, not appropriate for you to be here."

"But he might need me."

"My wife is on her way," Dr. Murphy said. "She can sit with him today."

"I see. Well, please have your wife give him plenty of water."

"Johanna, my wife is an experienced nurse. And she is also an abolitionist. She will be only too happy to care for someone of another race." He took out his stethoscope.

A desire to protect En made it difficult to leave. Her sore muscles protested movement, but she should see TC and Johnny.

"Someone's waiting outside for you," Dr. Murphy said.

The glare was bright when Johanna emerged from the shed. "You are safe." Thomas was there. "How are the boys?" As her eyes adjusted, she saw that the man looked as if he had not slept in days.

"Fine, they're at Kathleen's."

The rhyme "*Ladybug, ladybug, fly away home; your house is on fire; your children will burn*" bounded into her head. She used to read it to the boys. She had been so concerned about En, but it suddenly felt urgent that she see her sons.

"How's En?" Thomas asked.

"Uncomfortable, but he should recover if his burns don't get infected."

Thomas moved to embrace her. "No, Thomas," she felt nauseous, "don't. You know this is our fault."

"Johanna, no. The boys are safe, and En will recover," he said.

She was speechless. She felt nothing for this coward of a man. He was going to run again; she knew it.

He cleared his throat. "And, it's not the best time, but I have news."

"When have we ever had good timing?"

He smiled sheepishly. She did not return the smile.

"I'll get right to the point," he said. "Finn's hands have been injured, and he refuses to tell us where he was last night."

"Finn has burns on his hands?" The fire chief had mentioned arson. At the time, she thought it highly unlikely. She was so naive. "Are you telling me Finn had something to do with the fire?"

"I don't know for sure."

"You don't *know* for sure? And what about En, who may never use his hands again?"

"Don't jump to conclusions," he said, shuffling back and forth. "But we have decided we're going to follow Father Ryan's advice and leave town."

"So now you're taking off, teaching Finn how to run away, too?"

"He's young. I don't want to accuse him. Maybe he was a bystander? And if he did have anything to do with the fire … well, I don't want to see him hang."

"You are going to leave, even if he's an arsonist?" she said.

Thomas was silent.

"I see." And she saw more than she wanted to accept. Thomas was stuck in the life he had created. He took the easy road. He had the same helpless look on his face that she despised in Connor. She really could pick them. Another coward. How could she have been so misled? This man was a child—no, a con man. Where once she had found him irresistible, now he repulsed her. Kathleen had been absolutely right. It was wrong to let him back in her life. Anger would come, but at this moment, she was too tired. She just wanted him to go away.

"At least this time you're telling me before you go."

"Johanna," he said. "Please. You have to understand." She turned and started walking, but he grabbed her arm. She just wanted her children. She ran past the smoldering remains of the hotel where men were still tossing sand over the embers.

"Mrs. Kennedy?" The fire chief walked toward her, flanked by two firemen. She barely managed to stop, but these men had saved her sons and deserved her attention.

"What is it?"

"Ma'am, just wanted to let you know we're sorry, but we were unable to save the coffin."

"I see."

"And do you want us to take the safe somewhere?"

"Take it to Butterwort House. That's the best place for a temporary office."

"Yes, ma'am," he said. "And we'll check with the undertaker about moving Mr. Walsh's remains."

"Thank you, all of you, for saving my sons," she said.

She shook each man's hand. Then she ran all the way to her sons. *Your house is on fire; your children will burn.*


Father Ryan watched the bucket brigade pack up. He and Father Neil had prayed with the displaced guests and helped guide them to shelter at the school. They waved to the firemen still monitoring the scene on the way to the convent.

"What are we going to do now?" Father Neil asked.

"We could be defrocked or worse," Father Ryan said. "I can only imagine what those nuns think of us."

Father Neil said. "I want you to know you are dear to me, no matter what happens."

"I should not have allowed it. I'm senior to you, and I led you astray."

"We have each broken our vows. I was a full participant. If I remember our first night together, I pursued you." Father Neil shook his head. "Funny, I thought we might get caught on retreat. Never imagined we'd shock nuns out of their habits."

"You're trying to make me laugh, but this is too tragic, for us both," Father Ryan said. "The best thing is to confront it. I'll go to the convent to speak with Mother Superior."

"I will go with you," Father Neil said.

"No, seeing us together—even fully clothed—could make it worse. She hasn't had time to contact anyone yet. I will beg for mercy."

"No matter how persuasive you are, there is no escape from consequences."

"Indeed. But let me go alone. I know her. She will be more offended if we show up together. Go back to the room."

"I can't go back there. I'll be praying in the sanctuary." Father Neil gave Father Ryan a faint smile. "Come find me when you're done."

Father Ryan walked up the convent steps. A novitiate opened the door on his first knock. "Mother Superior said she was expecting you. Please, come this way." She led him down a corridor. There was a comforting aroma of coffee and bacon. He swallowed tears. If only he were back at his home parish, one last breakfast of shirred eggs with a rash of bacon before the guillotine.

"Father Ryan for you, Mother." The novitiate spoke through the closed door.

"Please, bring him in."

Mother Superior was sitting at her desk, framed by the bay window. She might have been a portrait. She looked composed. Father Ryan fixed his eyes on the garden behind her. There were trellised rosebushes, heavy with blooms. Deep-purple morning glories saluted along the stone wall next to riots of spiky orange flowers.

"Please, Father, take a seat," Mother said. "We should talk about how to help with the healing."

"Mother, I'm here to beg your forgiveness."

"I'm not sure what you mean," she said.

"For what transpired last night."

"It's true: what happened last night was a tragedy for this town," she said. "But it wasn't your fault. Still, lives have been disrupted. We must help them get back on their feet."

"Oh, yes, of course. Only—"

"I suggest we hold a special Mass today, perhaps vespers? You and Father Neil might serve together. Your joining our parish priest as senior pastor from a larger parish would send a message of unity and support."

"A good idea," he said. "And may I also—"

"Father Ryan, I trust you and Father Neil will work together in all ways to bring healing."

"But I want to explain. Last night? What you saw?"

"Father, I have prayed over that matter. It is just as I said: I trust you and Father Neil will find your own path to redemption. For now, you must lead your congregants to take comfort in their abiding faith." Mother Agnes stood up. "We can all become truly healed people as a result of this hardship."

"But, Mother—" Father Ryan said.

"I assure you," Mother Superior said, "and I speak for Sister Mary Catherine, there is nothing else for us to discuss, now or ever."

Father Ryan had not thought it possible to feel worse than he had before the meeting, but this was a new low. This woman, who had never really shown him the right amount of deference, could finish him off. Instead she was releasing him? It was as if she were acting as the priest and he the supplicant. He was grateful, also humiliated. At a loss for words, he breathed out, "Thank you, Mother Agnes."

"No need at all." She walked him to the door. "I will pray for you."

Taking what was left of his dignity, he exited her study and somehow made it out of the convent. He ducked behind the building and found the back door of the church, which was, thankfully, unlocked. He saw no one on his way to the vestment room. He sat on the same bench he used when dressing for Mass. He gripped the wooden seat, steadied his breathing, and waited for the trembling to subside. In a minute he would find Father Neil.


Johanna arrived at the Farrells' house out of breath. She heard Michael's fiddle and laughter and relaxed; her boys were safe. She peeked through the screen door. Kathleen's four girls were dancing. The older two had mastered the complicated steps of a slip jig. Their slender legs snapped at the knees in precision, upper bodies stiff, arms held at their sides. When Johanna learned Irish dancing, her father had told her that the unmoving arms were the way the defiant Irish made accommodations after the English banned dancing. In her opinion, tapping, skipping, and twirling to high-spirited Irish music—but with straight arms—was marching, not dancing.

Molly and Margaret knew exactly when to dance away from one another and when to glide close, grab hands, and circle. The movement was pure joy, made sweeter when Maeve and Mara, the two little ones, hopped along, imitating their older sisters. The four finished with a flourish as the older girls picked up their baby sisters, spun them around, and bowed to the audience. TC, Johnny, and Kathleen, holding the new baby, cheered.

"They're real good at dancing, Auntie Kathleen," TC said, clapping.

Johanna was so proud of her sons. In the last few days, they had watched police lead their father to jail, held vigil for Walsh, woken up with their bedroom on fire, escaped, and watched their home burn to the ground, after which their mother had disappeared. And TC remembered his manners. She hurried into the kitchen and joined in the applause.

"You're here!" Johnny dashed to her. TC followed. She wrapped her arms around them.

"Ma, enough," TC said, pulling away with a grin.

"So," Kathleen said, "how are things—anything new or burnt to a crisp since we've seen you last?"

Johanna smiled sadly and reached over to touch the baby's cheek.

Johnny tugged at her sleeve. "Is En dead, Ma?"

"Oh, no, my darling," she said. "En is getting better. He has some burns on his hands, but they'll heal. He told me that your shouting is what helped him find you." She hugged the boys again. "You were both so brave."

"We'll help En get better, right, Ma?"

"Of course, we will."

"But we lost the hotel," TC said.

"Yes, but don't worry." Michael put the fiddle in the case. "I expect there was insurance."

"What's that?" TC asked.

"It's a way to get money to fix the hotel. Let the grown-ups take care of it. You did your job last night and saved your brother and yourself. That's enough taking care for one lad."

"Kathleen, time to feed this bunch. They look hungry." He put the fiddle on a shelf. "Is En in a lot of pain, Johanna?"

"He's sleeping, but I think he may be uncomfortable when he wakes. The doctor said healing will be slow. It's not clear whether he will ever use his hands again."

"Let's talk about that later," Kathleen said, tipping her head at the children. She passed the baby to Johanna. "How about a good Irish breakfast?"

Johanna nestled her face into the bundle. "Isn't a baby's head the most wonderful smell?" She kissed the feathery hair. "Next to your delicious bread."

"And there are barmbracks fresh from the oven," Michael said.

The children sat on benches around the table, chatting happily, while Kathleen dispensed bread and butter, apples, and cheese. Johanna felt relieved and grateful to have these two wonderful friends.

"Auntie Johanna, can the lads stay with us tonight?" Molly asked, her cheeks stuffed like a chipmunk.

"Molly, don't talk with your mouth full."

"Please, Ma, can we?"

Both boys seemed recovered. Perhaps it was best they spend the afternoon distracted with other children.

"How about this—you can stay until dark, but we move to Butterwort House tonight? I want you sleeping near me."

Kathleen put a platter of scrambled eggs on the table.

"I thought we'd move the hotel operations to Butterwort House, too," Johanna addressed Kathleen and Michael. "We can make a small office in the parlor and build out two guest rooms in the attic. The boys and I are used to sleeping in the attic."

"No dining room, but it's better than nothing. I'll come by later and help you," Michael said. Lowering his voice, he added, "We can also talk about the will and those deeds. I have them in a safe place."

"The safe made it. I told them to take it to Butterwort but not to open it," Johanna said. "Is it my safe, or does it belong to Mr. Walsh?"

"We should open it in the presence of the executer of Walsh's estate," Michael said. "Did he have an attorney here in Nanticoke?"

"Maybe in Wilkes-Barre? I'll see if anyone knows. I also want to speak with the hotel staff. They must be worried about their jobs."

"Will you keep them on?"

"As long as we can. I guess it depends on insurance and the will."

"And what about En?"

"I need to make arrangements for his care. I left him with Dr. Murphy and his wife. I thought I'd get Tilly to sit with him this afternoon."

"Bad idea. Tilly might kill him," Kathleen said. "Don't you see the way she looks daggers at him when he enters a room? I'll come by."

"You're probably right about Tilly, but you just had a baby."

"Send a chambermaid here to watch the baby. I'll go to En. You need to get some sleep. I made up a bed in the girls' room."

"Thank you. Sleep sounds wonderful."

"The priests are saying a special Mass later. Michael will take the older girls, but maybe you want the boys to stay here with you?"

"I do. The lads won't mind missing a Mass," Johanna said.

"And shall we tell Johanna the news about our baby boy?" Michael said, leaning over to kiss his wife.

"Yes, but she must keep it a secret until we can tell En," Kathleen said.

Johanna looked at them expectantly. "Well?"

"We have decided to name our boy after En Chang."

"A Chinese name for an Irish baby?" Johanna said. She was too exhausted to talk Kathleen out of it.

"We thought we'd modify it slightly by dropping the 'En' and just use the 'Cha.'"

"His name is Cha?"

"Close. It's Charlie."

"Oh, that's a wonderful name. En will be pleased."


He dreamed he was back in the hold of a ship, his arms raised to steady the boiling pot of rice threatening to spill over on the girls and baby Ji. Starving passengers crowded around him, bowls in hand, hungry eyes threatening to devour him.

He tried to hold the cauldron steady, but its bubbling contents rolled down over his shoulders in torrents of pain. He woke with a start, his hands throbbing from his wrists to his shoulders. He recalled the scream, the boys, scalding flames, passing them into open arms. He felt thankful. The boys were alive.

His next recollection was Johanna holding a cup of water to his lips. There had been a doctor, Kathleen, and that gentle chambermaid. He saw his arms were swathed in white. He was suddenly fully conscious. He had survived the fire and had burns up and down his arms, the source of his agony.

He'd had experience with burn victims in the camps. When the burned tissue healed, it grew thick. He would get strictures between his fingers, inhibiting movement. If he let scar tissue form, his hands would be useless. As soon as possible, and daily, he would need to peel away the damaged tissue until the skin underneath healed.

Anxiety about treating his arms and hands cleared his head. If his recollection of the blaze was right, the hotel was gone. Butterwort House was likely serving as the main hotel. He knew Johanna would be working. He had to see her. The sweet chambermaid was soft. He would have to convince Johanna that he needed someone else to help with treatment—someone tough and with a strong stomach.

It occurred to him that a short time ago he wouldn't have cared whether he lived or died. Something was different, from the time he decided to stay and help Johanna eliminate the guns or perhaps the moment when he pulled the boys from the flames. He wanted to live. He had connected himself to this Irish family's lot. Once again, he was a survivor. And he had saved lives. He must make his life worth something now, and that meant getting the right care for his burns. He had never tried to fit into Western culture. He'd thought Chinese who kowtowed in that way lost something of themselves, but now he was willing to do whatever it took.

He sat up. Lightheaded at first, he waited for the room to settle. He looked down and saw he was naked above the waist. Someone had put him in soft pants. He hoped it hadn't been Johanna. The idea of her dressing him like a child was embarrassing. He heaved his legs off the bed.

It was early, so he hoped not many people would be about. He shuffled to the door. His hands were useless. It took several minutes for him to get on the floor and twist the door handle with his feet. He got back up and wobbled outside and down the path. The screen door of Butterwort House was propped open.

En slipped into the kitchen and walked to the small room behind the parlor. He had guessed correctly that Johanna would use that room as an office. She was sitting at the desk, sipping a cup of tea and reading the ledger.

"Miss Johanna."

"Oh, my God, En, what are you doing up?"

She jumped up and half carried him into the parlor, seating him on a chair. She closed the pocket doors. "What possessed you to get out of bed?"

"I need to speak with you," he said. Just the concern on her face made him hopeful. Still, she might not want to harbor a Celestial who couldn't earn his keep. He would have to appear less obtrusive and, when he was better, prove his worth.

"I was coming to see you today. I thought we'd move you as soon as I relocated guests. I didn't think you'd be up this soon."

"Move me?"

"Yes, to better quarters, inside one of the houses. You can't recover in that shed."

"I am your humble servant. You should not be concerned with me," En said. "I'm sorry I cannot be more help."

"En, you are not my servant," Johanna said. "I'm the one indebted to you."

"No." He always found it difficult to speak to her, but now he couldn't even understand her. Was she offering him somewhere to live—even if he couldn't work?

"En, I want to do anything I can to help," she said.

"I am grateful. And I may stay, even if I can't work right away?"

"Of course, En," Johanna said, "and do you have any methods, in your Chinese medicine, that will help you recover? Can I get anything for you to help?"

"Yes, it is why I sought you out. I have requests. Miss Johanna, lying in bed is my enemy. My arms and hands … need treatment." He lifted his bandaged arms and grimaced. "I also need dried earthworms, more than I have in my medicine box. They must be cleaned and ground up with honey; it will protect the skin, move blood, and reduce pain. Later I would like to add lonicera flower to clear heat and reduce inflammation during the evening, and sesame oil to stop pain at night."

"We'll get anything you need."

"I will need help preparing these treatments. I also need my wounds to be scrubbed," he said.

"Oh, that sounds so painful," she said. "Dr. Murphy says you must lie still to let them heal."

"I have seen burns in miner's camps, from explosions and campfires—terrible burns. Once the skin knits together, scar tissue forms."

"Isn't that good?"

He had to get her to see. "Not if movement is inhibited."

"Sounds awful, but washing?"

"Scrubbing. I've done it and had remarkable results. New tissue grows. It is the only way to get my hands useful again," he said.

"The doctor might not agree."

"Most physicians, here and in China, would not agree, but I have seen it work," he said, adding, "The doctor could not save baby Charlie."

"Kathleen and Michael told you his name when they visited yesterday? He's named after you."

"Yes, an honor," he said. "But, please, Miss Johanna, Dr. Murphy and Western medicine could not help baby Charlie. He's wrong about burn treatment."

"Your ancient medicines do seem better than ours. Can Annie help?"

"She is too softhearted. I need someone stronger."

"Then not Annie." She looked thoughtful. "I don't think it can be me. I couldn't bear to see you in pain. I hope you understand." She was looking directly at him. Something in his gut got tight. "We'll find someone, I promise. You said you had two requests. What is the second?"

"I want you to cut off my queue."

"You do? Why?"

"It's too hard for me to reach and too much to ask others to braid."

"No one minds helping."

"I've given this thought. It would help me belong here. People are calling us the 'yellow menace.' There is hostility against Railroad Chinese all over the country. It might be why the fire was started."

"First, I'm certain you are not the reason the fire was started. I can't prove it, but I may know who did," she said. "Let's not worry about that today. We need to get you back to bed."

"You said you would do anything. I want you to cut the queue off now."

"Why don't we wait until you are feeling better?"

"I will be grateful if you cut it at this moment, as a promise that you will honor treating my burns as well." He hoped this did not offend her, but he had to take charge of his future. Severing the final ties to his homeland might make him, and all of them, safer.

"Wait here," she said. "The good scissors are in the kitchen."

He thought about standing up but was afraid he was too unsteady. He sat on the chair, arms stiff, ears buzzing.

She returned with a sheet, hand mirror, scissors, and a comb in a glass of water. "Tell me how you want it cut."

"One cut, across the back, then trimmed short."

En bowed his head. He'd seen Johanna cut her sons' hair. He trusted her barbering skills. Johanna put the sheet on his shoulders. A chill ran down his spine when he felt the cool blade resting against his neck. She had to make several cuts through the thickness. When the braid was free, she held it up for him.

When she saw that he could not take it in his bandaged hands, she put it on the table. "Now, a bit more, so I look like a Westerner," he said.

In a few minutes, he would be a Celestial with an American haircut. The sound of snipping was liberating and appalling. She kept snipping, put her fingers in the glass of water, and shook drops of water on the sides and top of his head. She trimmed his neck. Then she held up a mirror.

"If you allow the shaved part in the front to grow back, you will look like an American."

"Yes." He gazed at himself, something he didn't do often. His head looked much larger without the queue pulling it taught. It would take some getting used to, and he'd have to learn how to use a comb.

"This will be good for the hotel and you, madam. I thank you."

"It was not necessary, but if it makes you happy," Johanna said. "And En, you just saved the lives of my children. Please call me Johanna; drop the missus and madam."

"Yes, madam."

"I will be patient." She smiled at him.

Holding her gaze, En said, "Maybe I could change my name, too, to one with a more American sound than En Chang?"

"Really, you want to do that too?"

"Yes, I think it would be good, but what?"

She furrowed her brow. "Hmm, let's see. We're used to calling you En, so we should keep that as your first name. What about a twist on Michael and Kathleen's idea? Instead of En Chang you could be En Charlie?"

En looked doubtful.

"Maybe that's too informal. Let's use the formal name, Charles. En Charles."

"I like it, Miss Jo—I mean, Johanna."

She dipped her fingers in the water again, then raised her hand and sprinkled his forehead. "I baptize you En Charles."

"I will call you Johanna, and you call me En Charles," he said just as the room shifted. His head pulsed; space around him blurred.

He swayed forward. He felt her prop her body against his to keep him upright, but she didn't have the strength to stop his solidness from slipping through her arms. Losing consciousness, he slid off the chair and into a heap at her feet.

CHAPTER ELEVEN

# THE BRAID

**Nanticoke, Pennsylvania, late Summer 1883**

Butterwort House was serving as the main building, so Johanna decided it should look better than a rooming house. Together, she and Kathleen sewed velvet pillows and matching draperies. Johanna splurged on gold tassels. They found a pair of old brass candlesticks in the attic and arranged them on the mantel.

"It is a much smaller room, but it resembles a hotel lobby a little." Kathleen came in from the garden with an armload of gladiolas.

"We're lucky Mr. Walsh never got rid of anything," Johanna said. "This huge vase we found is chipped, but it looks okay if we turn it sideways."

"And the tablecloth hides the warped top," Kathleen said. "In the fall, we can display pumpkins and gourds, maybe garlands for the holidays."

"If we're still open," Johanna said.

"It's been three months since the fire." Kathleen plucked off the shriveled blossoms at the end of the tall stalks. "Still no word from that highfalutin' lawyer in Wilkes-Barre? You're going to run out of money by Christmas."

"I got two requests in the mail this morning to reserve rooms in September," Johanna said, grateful that Kathleen joined the pretense that three rooming houses would make up for the business of the lost hotel.

Johanna didn't want to worry Kathleen—or admit it to herself—but the hotel was nearly out of money now. She would have to let some of the staff go. If she didn't cut back, no one would have work or food. She'd always thought her husband would make the difficult choices, but he was gone. So was Thomas. She could have used a man—weren't women supposed to nurture, not make impossible decisions?

"What if you stop paying me? We still have Michael's income," Kathleen offered, snapping stems and stuffing them in the vase.

"That wouldn't help. Plus, you're the one I want to pay." Johanna glanced at her friend. "You realize you're hopeless at arranging flowers? Use the pruning shears. The stems take up more water that way."

"How many rooms total now?" Kathleen continued to break the stems, leaving them stringy and uneven.

"We squeezed in four extra rooms at Rose and Lily houses, so up to twenty-eight total, down from thirty-six. Overall, our occupancy is down by half. Plus, the bar's closed, and we only have a makeshift dining room. I'll have to let two maids and the kitchen help go at the end of this week, at least until bookings improve or ownership and insurance are sorted out."

"You can't let Emily and Mary go; those sisters support their entire family," Kathleen said. "At least let me cut back."

"You are only one of twelve people. It won't make a difference."

"But they need the jobs more than I do."

Johanna appreciated that Kathleen wanted to help, but her friend didn't understand simple business: she couldn't pay people if customers weren't paying her.

"What if you asked for more credit?"

"Kathleen, I'm going to need more credit anyway, but I have to stop hemorrhaging cash," Johanna said, unable to hide her impatience. "It isn't about charity. It's about survival."

Kathleen didn't understand that the hotel's reputation, and her own, were at stake. She needed the trust of the business community, and she couldn't allow accounts to go unpaid.

"There must be something you can do," Kathleen said, her eyes misty. "What is taking so long?"

"I'm told probate can take a year and the insurance depends on the court," Johanna said. "I don't know what to do, Kathleen. I'm an ogre if I fire people, but if the hotel goes under, the town will say a woman ruined Walsh's business."

Kathleen pulled in her lower lip. "I know, Johanna. I'm not criticizing. If only you could find a way to keep some of them on just a few more weeks."

Johanna noted Kathleen didn't use the word "we." Kathleen indulged in her tender sympathies—a beloved, empathetic angel—as Johanna and Michael faced reality on her behalf. But as Johanna looked at Kathleen's hands—raw skin, chapped from the hours she spent peeling potatoes and wiping down sinks and toilets—she knew Kathleen was only trying to help. Johanna felt guilty for taking out her fear on this guileless woman.

"I am already looking for loans. I could ask loyal customers, those who could benefit from our business staying afloat," Johanna said. "Maybe Sam Kress? He's opening the five-and-dime on Main Street."

"Tall, moustache?"

"That's him, and he's doing well. His people will stay here once he starts construction."

"He's not afraid of the scandal with Connor in jail?"

"I gave him the opportunity to go somewhere else and he wouldn't hear of it."

"He's a smart businessman. He might say yes because you will soon steer guests to his new store," Kathleen said.

"I can only send our customers to him if we have customers." Johanna tossed the debris from the gladiolas into a bucket. She touched her friend on the shoulder. "I'm not sure what to do, but you'll be the last person I let go, even if your flowers look like the devil himself jammed into that container."


After Johanna cut off his queue, En felt hollow. He had asked her to do it without anticipating the sense of loss he would feel.

It had actually been easier to maintain the queue. If he didn't wear a hat to bed, he woke up with porcupine hair that stuck straight out from his scalp. Worse, without the thick braid of hair warming the back of his neck, he felt exposed. He was acutely aware of breezes and felt anxious when people behind him stood too close. There was also the symbolism: his queue connected him to his country, his ancestors, his tribe. Now he was literally cut off. Unkempt and vulnerable, he lost confidence. He hoped that he looked less foreign. Guests didn't seem to stare at him as often, and maybe that could help the business and secure his future.

After En collapsed in Johanna's study, she wanted to move him to one of the rooming houses to stay in bed. He refused. He knew she was having financial difficulties and didn't want to take up a room, adding to her burden. They compromised: he would rest for an additional week if he could remain in the shed for an undetermined period.

The morning he returned to work, he wrapped gauze around his hands and covered them with thick gloves. If he worked slowly, using his upper arms, he could clean and stoke the fireplaces. The gloves protected him from infection but not the pain of a heavy log held against his wounds.

Each night he soaked his hands in a medicinal bath and then peeled off scar tissue. Johanna found a tough-minded young man, a former war medic, to help. The pain was searing, as if his hands were still on fire. Afterward, he applied scar ointment made of sumac gallnut, centipede, and borneol, and slathered his fingers in lanolin. He slept with his arms above the covers, open to the air, at night. The flesh was growing back healthy, but he wasn't sure how much improvement to expect. He attempted demanding work, but the regenerating nerves still limited him. What if he was unable to return to manual labor? He still dreamed of caring for patients, but without sensitivity in his fingertips it might not be possible.

For the time being, he tried to bring value where he could. No one paid attention to a servant sweeping or laying a fire. Working unseen, he could observe and learn about the operation of the hotel. He had listened in on Johanna's conversation with Kathleen about letting staff go and was impressed with her grasp of reality. He was raking the fireplace when he overhead another conversation between Johanna and a banker.

"Just checking in, Mrs. Kennedy," the banker's cordiality was threatening at the core.

"Mr. Walsh's will is in probate," Johanna said. "Just as it was last week when you inquired."

"And what about your husband? Any news?"

"Unfortunately, no," Johanna said. "We do appreciate your patience."

"Whether he gets charged with conspiracy or not, I remind you that we won't extend credit to a woman once this loan expires at year's end," the banker said. "We're not in the business of giving money away, even to ladies as pretty as you."

En felt helpless when he saw the man slither too close to Johanna. Because their paths crossed several times a day, En observed the steady stream of complaints, demands, and decisions she shouldered. When he thought of himself as her employee, he worried about keeping his job. When he thought of her as the woman who had sheltered him as he recovered, he grew concerned for her business. When he thought of himself as her physician, he saw himself as a healer again, and he wanted to protect her from harm.

He agreed with Johanna that she couldn't keep everyone on the payroll. It wasn't his place. She also might not heed the view of a servant, but it couldn't hurt to add his voice. There was no one else validating her reality.

After the banker left, En occupied himself in the hall outside Johanna's office, waiting to intercept Tilly when she brought tea. Tilly lumbered down the hall, and he stepped forward to take the tray, "I will serve madam today," he said.

"Madam, indeed. Your new haircut doesn't win me over." Tilly gave a little harrumph. "Still, don't mind if I put my feet up."

En winced when Tilly dropped the tray on his forearms. Balancing the heavy burden, he knocked on the door with his foot.

"En, you're bringing tea?" Johanna opened the door. "Thank you. Please, set it on the table."

He put the tray down, "I will pour."

He wasn't wearing his gloves, and he grasped the handle of the metal teapot without thinking, nearly dropping it.

"Let's not add boiling water to your troubles," Johanna said, grabbing the handle. She filled the strainer and drizzled the water over the loose tea. She took the cup and saucer, moving the Mass cards that were spread out on her desk to make room, and sat down.

"Father Ryan did a fine job with Walsh's funeral Mass," Johanna said, stacking the cards. "He managed to say some nice things about

Mr. Walsh, which wasn't easy. I'm so behind—just getting around to writing the thank you notes that should have gone out weeks ago."

"Yes, madam."

"Madam, again? I've managed the switch to En Charles," she said, shaking her head. "Honestly, how hard is to call me Johanna?"

"May I speak with you about that … and …" He let his words trail off.

"What is it, En?" She looked directly at him. Her eyes were the palest blue. Maybe he was adjusting, but Johanna looked better than most of the big-nosed women in America.

"I take up resources," he said, wishing he'd thought to wear a cap. Was his hair pointing at the ceiling? If he looked silly would she listen?

"En, you have recovered quickly, but you have to be patient."

"I must do more."

"Can you fill the rooms with paying customers or figure out how to get that Wilkes-Barre lawyer to respond to my inquires? How about getting Connor out of prison? Or maybe they'll finally come up with charges—maybe stupidity."

"Perhaps he was trying to protect you, to fight injustice?" En disliked Connor, but he pitied him, too. Sometimes men with nothing left to lose made desperate decisions.

"Don't give me that 'he was trying' poppycock. Connor was playacting, pretending to be a big shot," she said. "His foolishness put many people, including you, in danger." She gestured to the chair across from her desk. He sat. She leaned closer to him and lowered her voice. "Do you think they will find the weapons?"

"It rained hard that night," En whispered. "Those boxes are buried in mud, even if they knew where to look."

"And what if there were witnesses, or the boys talk?"

"No one saw, I'm sure of that. The woods are thick with undergrowth," En said. "And Finn and TC are terrified. They won't say anything. Besides, Thomas …" He hesitated. He knew Johanna and her husband slept separately, and Tilly's hints implied the rose petals had meaning.

"En, it's okay to mention Thomas. I know he's gone, and it's the least of my worries."

"What is your greatest worry?"

"Hard to pick just one." She half smiled.

He hoped she trusted him enough to speak honestly. It had been his decision to show her the cellar. Maybe the weapons would have been secretly stashed for years, and he had caused her to take needless risk. Now her situation was worse, and without Connor and Walsh, she had no one. He felt most alive when people needed him. Death had extinguished everyone he loved and numbed his soul. His decision to stay here had restored him. Fate had brought him here, to this woman, this time and place. There must be a way he could assist her.

"I believe you are worried about money? Possibly you may have to close the business?"

"You heard my conversation with Kathleen?"

He nodded.

"It's a good thing I trust you," Johanna said. "Yes, we are losing money. And I have another big concern." Johanna tilted her head to the corner of the room. "See those boxes stacked there? I found them in the basement of Rose House—old files; they're a mess, like all the junk in the attic. It's difficult to predict expenses and renegotiate terms with suppliers without written contracts or bank statements. Plus, there could be insurance documents or bank accounts that still contain cash."

She paused. "En, you speak well, but can you read English?"

"Yes."

"I have an idea. How about you help me search for some answers? There must be something in these old files, but there are too many for me to review by myself."

"I was just about to offer my services," he said.

"Good." She swept her arm in the direction of the stacks. "Where would you like to start?"

Johanna and En worked in the cramped Butterwort office, sorting through boxes and arranging papers. They spread them out on the desk, coffee table, and finally on the floor.

Several hours later Tilly knocked on the door, "Miss Johanna, collecting the tea tray?"

"Oh, Tilly, come in."

Johanna and En were sitting side by side on the love seat, surrounded by piles of paper.

"En and I lost track of time. We still have work to do. Could you bring more tea? And, En, you must be hungry. Tilly, bring more biscuits and an extra cup?"

Tilly puffed out her checks, "May I speak with you in the hall, Miss Johanna?"

"We are quite busy," Johanna said, reluctant to lose track midway through sorting.

Tilly was practically tapping her foot.

"If I must," Johanna sighed. "Excuse us, En." She left En, closing the office door as she suspected Tilly might be unpleasant. "What's the trouble, Tilly?"

"Ma'am, my days are long and hard—making beds in rooms the size of a broom closet with guests stuffed in the houses, managing without the big kitchen. My feet, my knees, my back. You know me; I offer it up to Jesus. But, ma'am, it's beneath my station to serve a coolie."

Johanna glared at Tilly.

"If he's one of my chores,"—she shuddered—"I'd just as soon go live with my daughter or find other employment."

Johanna didn't have time or patience. She supposed she should feel sorry for the old woman, but Johanna wouldn't mind being rid of her. As the cook, she should be one of the last to go; the money their few guests spent on meals was precious. But Tilly's effect on staff morale was costly, too. If Johanna heard about Tilly's bad back one more time, she thought she might level the woman with a swift kick slightly lower down.

Johanna once had mentioned Tilly's threats to live with her daughter in Pittston, and Kathleen had scoffed, "The daughter wants a free cook and babysitter. Tilly wants a quiet room, and all she can eat. She's not going anywhere."

Even so, Kathleen went out of her way for Tilly, filling tubs with hot water and pouring in Tilly's favorite Epsom salts for her "aching feet."

"And you're not helping by pampering her," Johanna had said and then felt bad.

Johanna shook off her thoughts and returned to the stare-down contest with Tilly. "Tilly," Johanna sighed. "I wouldn't wish to lose your services, but it is your choice. Why don't you take the rest of the day off? I'll get our tea."

"Yes, ma'am, and thank you for understanding."

Johanna watched the woman rearrange her smug expression. Tilly thought she'd won. "And, Tilly, to be clear," Johanna said, "I'll get the tea today, but En is a member of our hotel staff, about to take on broader responsibilities. If you choose to come back to work tomorrow, you will not refuse my requests, or his, from now on."

Tilly's body jolted upright.

"Come back only if you are prepared to accept these conditions. Otherwise, I shall offer you two weeks' pay and a reference."

Johanna strode past Tilly, who was frozen like a statue. She worried she'd made a terrible mistake. Who would take Tilly's job in a nearly empty hotel? And Tilly was influential with the staff, who might follow her lead and go. Still, she could not have her refuse direction or treat En with disdain. She trusted En, and she needed his help. She would be careful—there were likely unforeseen challenges giving him more responsibility—but she had no choice, and neither did Tilly.

When Johanna returned to her office with a second pot of tea and scones, En was standing. "Madam, is there trouble?" he said.

"En, I have no idea what you're talking about, but you *are* to call me Johanna," she said. "I brought scones, butter, and marmalade, too. Let's take a break. I'm starving."

"Jo-Johanna," he stumbled. "You must not bring me tea. Tilly is offended, and others will be too. If I take tea with you, or call you by name, it will cause trouble."

"But we've just started, and I have hope for the first time in weeks that we'll find something."

En raised his eyebrows and shook his head. "We've found nothing so far."

"An extra set of eyes, even skeptical ones like yours, could make a difference." She held up the sugar bowl. "I don't know how you take tea. Sugar or cream?"

"Nothing, plain, please."

"And I thought of something else while I was in the kitchen." Johanna opened the jar of marmalade. "First, please don't mind Tilly. She is a small-minded woman. Sometimes I wonder why I keep her around."

"It's not for her tender scones," En said. He split one in two and it snapped like a hard cracker. He gave Johanna a mischievous look.

"Indeed, they could sink a ship." She dipped the stone-like scone in her tea. Their eyes met, amused. "While you eat, I will tell you something that only Kathleen and Michael know," she said.

En nodded.

"Walsh did leave a will, leaving the properties to me."

En grinned. "That is good, good."

"There could be another will—one written after. We won't know until the safe is opened, or perhaps we'll find one here. I need your help, En."

"Very well," he said. "But I can't call you Johanna, not when others can hear."

"When we are alone then?" She handed him the cup and saucer. When she let go, it nearly tipped over. She saw his hands were trembling. She guessed it was more than his burns.

She spread butter and marmalade on a scone and held it out to him. After a long pause, he accepted it, lifted it to his mouth, and took a bite. Had she gone too far in breaching employer and employee, Irish and Chinese? And there was perceptibly another tension between them: one between a man and a woman.

A smear of marmalade lingered on his upper lip. Johanna thought about wiping it with her finger as she might with the boys. That would certainly send him flying back to Philadelphia, or perhaps all the way to China.

## Nanticoke, Pennsylvania, Fall 1883

"The lark is up to meet the sun. The bee is on the wing. The ant its labor has begun. The woods with music ... rrr-iing? Is that right, Mother?" TC asked her. "Does an R sound and an 'ing' make ring?"

"It does. My goodness, how you can read." Mother Agnes sat across from TC in her office. She reached over and patted his hand. The McGuffey Reader was their ally. A Protestant text taught in public schools, the book was considered heresy for Catholics. Unlike most school texts that relied on rote memory and dull lists of hundreds of words, McGuffey used vocabulary in stories, adding new words and repeating familiar ones. Especially for boys like TC, the McGuffey

Reader held a child's interest and provided a secret arrow in her magical reading quiver.

"I can read, Mother," TC said, "and I didn't think I ever could."

TC's smile spanned beyond his face, one of the many endearing things about the boy. If only he smiled more often. She tried not to have favorites, but TC was special. There was nothing she liked better than taking a creature—whether a stray cat or bewildered boy—and offering a second chance: a bowl of milk, a warm place to sleep, or the nourishment of a book.

And she had ensured that TC would be the last child in her school to suffer under Sister Mary Catherine. She had to admit it: the woman was cruel. Thank God she had found funds to build a new library. Sister was doing well with planning, purchasing and cataloging books. Mother Agnes explained to the teachers, in Sister Mary Catherine's presence, that the nun had been promoted to a new role and must focus entirely on the library. In the future, only classroom teachers were responsible for the behavior of children during library visits. Privately, she warned that if Sister Mary Catherine berated or punished any child, Mother Agnes would consider it insubordination and unpleasant consequences would thus result.

TC had withstood Sister Mary Catherine's abuse better than most. It was a travesty, but he was a survivor. He reminded her of herself, full of contradictions: confident and fragile, brilliant and dark, loving and angry. He had developed some confidence during their months together, but it had diminished after what had happened to the family over the summer.

"Do you like your new teacher?"

"Yes, Sister Elizabeth is sure nicer than—" TC stopped.

Mother Agnes half smiled. "No need to speak ill of another human being."

TC gazed at the bookshelves around them. "Might I never come back as your special helper?"

"We spent some lovely hours together, didn't we? But I want to see you learn even more, and it's good to have new friends and teachers."

"You are the best teacher I ever had."

"Thank you. And I miss you. I asked you to visit me today to see if you would be willing to visit me one afternoon a week? We could chat and read," she said. "Would you like that?"

"Oh, Mother, yes, I would," TC said. He flashed his wide smile, and then quickly tucked it away.

"Now, tell me, what does your mother think of your reading?"

"I haven't told her."

"She doesn't know?"

"Nope, she's kinda busy."

"TC, school is over in just a few minutes. Will your mother be home this afternoon?" she said.

"Ma is always home; we live in the rooming house."

"Perhaps I could stop by? We could tell her together?"

The color drained from his face.


Mother Agnes picked up the parcel on the foyer table, headed outside, and took the path to the rooming house. Rather than disturb the paying guests, she decided to use the kitchen door, more like a friend than a paying customer.

"I'll get you boys a snack. How's brown bread?" she heard Tilly's voice. "But stay there, you imps. I've just mopped the floor."

God bless that woman, even her voice was aggravating.

When Tilly opened the door, she sounded like a different person. "Oh, Mother Agnes Gertrude, do come in. What an honor for the likes of this family."

Mother Agnes saw TC and his brother sitting at the kitchen table next to the Celestial man. He was nodding as Johnny displayed his school notebook.

TC looked miserable. She guessed he'd been upset ever since she'd told him she would visit. His usual experience was that any conversation with his mother was liable to be an unhappy one.

"Now, Mother, why did you come to the back door?" Tilly said. "Let's get you to the parlor where you belong."

"Good afternoon, En," Mother Agnes said. "You look in better health each time I see you."

En nodded, "Yes, Mother. Thank you, I'm doing well."

She stepped closer to the boys, "Good to see you again so soon, TC. And, Johnny, how do you like school this year?"

"I like it fine." Johnny alternated between staring at the nun and his brother, his eyes pleading for mercy.

Tilly said, "One of you, go fetch your ma."

"I'll get her." Johnny ran down a hall. "Ma, TC's in trouble."

"Oh, TC, we know you are not in trouble, don't we?" Mother Agnes patted his shoulder. "I'm here to tell your mother what a fine job you're doing."

His jaw slackened, but he was still wary. At least he was recovered enough to lead her to the parlor.

Mother Agnes sat on the sofa. Johnny bounced into the room like a puppy chasing a ball, Johanna following him. Mother Agnes was gratified to see that Johanna was keeping the family and business together.

"I'm glad to see you," Mother Agnes said, opening her bag. "You know that TC helped me in the office last semester? With the busy new school year, I realized just today that there has been an oversight." TC looked at his lap. "TC, this is for you." Mother Agnes handed him a brown paper package.

"Thank you," TC mumbled. He tore it open and pulled out a book, *The Original McGuffey's Eclectic First Reader.* The cover was caramel-colored leather; the front panel depicted a woodcarving of a boy and a girl petting a dog.

"Thank you, Mother," he whispered. He ran his palm over the raised imprint. "It's fine looking."

"TC, now if only you can learn to read it," Johnny said.

"Johnny! That is not a nice thing to say," Johanna gently pushed him down on a bench and sat next to him.

"I have another gift, but this one is for you, Johanna," Mother Agnes said. "TC, come sit by me and bring your reader." She patted the cushion next to her, opened the book to a marked page, and gave it back to him. "Go ahead," she said.

He looked down at the page and slowly started, "The lark … is … up … ta … meet … the sun." He read straight through to the word "ring." When he finished, the room was quiet, and then everyone was talking at once.

"TC can read!" Johnny shouted.

Tilly was standing in the doorway and shouted, "Saints be praised."

En was near the hearth and clapped his maimed hands together. Johanna crossed the room, wiping tears from her cheeks.

"Oh, TC, what a wonderful present!" She hugged her son and looked at Mother Agnes. "This is a great day! I can't thank you enough."

"It was TC who did the work," Mother Agnes said. "As Sir Francis Bacon said, 'Reading maketh a full man.' Fill TC's life with books, and his imagination will have no bounds. Now, I must take my leave." She stood up. "Perhaps you would walk me out, Johanna?"

"Do you have time for tea?" Johanna said.

"Not today. I pray with postulates each afternoon, but let's do have tea soon." Johanna walked Mother Agnes to front hall. "So nice to see the boys doing well. They get along with one another and are so helpful to En. His hands and arms are healing well?"

"It's been difficult, but yes, he can do more every day."

"I haven't known any Celestials, but he is certainly good with children, and it appears he can read?"

"He's quite educated," Johanna said.

"Well, Johnny seems devoted," Mother Agnes said.

"I'm so busy. It's been nice for Johnny to have En's attention, and with his father …"

"And how is your husband faring?"

"I think well enough," Johanna said. "So far it's been just waiting."

"It's a lot to manage, my dear."

"I hope our troubles are not a problem for the school," Johanna said.

"There is no one at the school who thinks the circumstances reflect poorly on you or the boys."

"I've heard there was one parent who wanted the boys expelled," Johanna said.

"The very idea—I won't comment, but you know I would never entertain anything of the sort," Mother Agnes said. "What is most important is this: if there is ever *anything* I can do to help, you must come to me directly. Will you promise you will ask?"

"I promise," Johanna said, "and thank you for the book. It means the world to him."

"I expect there will be many more. He is a smart lad. I hope we can keep him in school and out of the mines."

"I do too. My husband doesn't read, but educating the boys is why we came to America," Johanna said. "One of the reasons, anyway."

"You are all in my prayers," Mother Agnes said. "Do come and see me at the convent."

As she walked back home, Mother Agnes prayed for the family. She always made a point of saying at least one quick prayer immediately after she pledged to do so.

**Nanticoke, Pennsylvania, Thanksgiving 1883**

Butterwort House was festive with harvest-themed decorations: the cornucopia on the front table overflowed with small pumpkins. They were hosting a Thanksgiving dinner for guests. Johanna borrowed enough tables to seat thirty people, placing them in the living room and foyer. The tables were draped in gold fabric, and dried flowers arranged in hollowed-out pumpkins served as centerpieces. Johanna kept her religious themes low key. Kathleen and the other Catholics in town mounted holy water fonts by their front doors. They hung pictures of Jesus or the saints on walls or over mantels. Johanna didn't display statues, crosses, or fonts. Mr. Kress and his associates were non-Catholics. She didn't care what religion her customers practiced, only that they ordered meals, whiskey, and beer.

Johanna walked among the tables, greeting her guests as the waitstaff served, receiving compliments on the meal. She hoped the dinner served up enough hospitality that the conversations would remain civil. Just as she avoided religion, Johanna discouraged debate of the divisive politics of the day. The hardship of the Civil War and the pain of losses reverberated for many. She wanted guests to feel at home, no matter their views.

She decided to check on the kitchen staff. Tilly, up to her elbows in soapy water, was shouting, "The high-and-mighty Lincoln declares Thanksgiving back in '63, and that what gets us all the drudgery,"

"Tilly, you speak the God's truth," one of the chambermaids said. "Not that I don't think well of the man. We haven't had a decent president since. But God knows, that war made a mess outta this country."

"I supported Blaine this last election, mother's a good Irish Catholic woman," Tilly said. "But that Chester A. Arthur sneaked himself into office."

"The man is corrupt and not fit, a new low for our country," the chambermaid replied.

Tilly glanced at Johanna. She didn't make eye contact, but she did change the subject. "Now where is that bum we hired to wash dishes?"

Johanna knew Tilly complained and sowed discord where she could, but she was still at work—a relief. She was cool to En but didn't refuse to serve him. Now if only Tilly would keep her opinions to herself.

"Tilly, the holiday is popular with Americans, and remember I asked you not bring up politics," Johanna said. "We want a festive atmosphere today. Same for the caroling parties."

"I'm against those caroling parties, I don't mind telling you. We just finished serving Thanksgiving dinner," Tilly said. "Don't know why poor Kathleen now has to bake Christmas cookies for days."

"You've probably noticed a lot of rooms are empty," Johanna said. "We got a good turnout for this dinner. When we carol, we will hand out flyers, inviting people for a Christmas supper, and offering discounted rooms for out-of-town visitors."

"It won't work," Tilly said. "Families around here keep kin under their own roof."

"We'll make a few stragglers welcome, and it will help until business customers are back in January," Johanna said. "I hope we can earn enough to give everyone a year-end bonus."

"Bonus? Well, then, I guess some might unload nasty aunts or lecherous uncles," Tilly said. "Time to serve up the pies. I'll be taking off for Pittston to see my grandbabies once the kitchen is clean."

"We're going over to Kathleen's in about an hour," Johanna said. "Please see the pies are served. I'll be in my office. If I don't see you before you go, have a nice holiday."

She was barely in her office when Johnny appeared. "Ma." He bit his lower lip.

"What is it, honey?" She took the handkerchief from inside her sleeve but hesitated before she gave it to him. Johnny was nearly eight years old and wouldn't want her to notice he was near tears. "Oh, Ma, En says he won't come to Thanksgiving dinner at Auntie Kathleen's. We talked about it lots of times, but now he says no, he won't. He is my best friend. You said Thanksgiving is for family and friends."

"I did say that," Johanna said. "But he might not feel comfortable."

"Maybe he doesn't want to have goose and colcannon? Or he is pretending to be my friend? TC has friends. No one likes me."

"Johnny, En likes you but …"

En stood in the doorway. "Miss Johanna—oh, Johnny is with you."

"Ma, tell him to go away," Johnny said.

Johanna and En looked at each other. She tried to not to laugh. He wasn't smiling. She put her arm around Johnny. "We must make En know how welcome he is."

En's feet were planted, his arms crossed over his chest. Perhaps the Chinese were inscrutable, but En's thoughts were transparent to her. It would be tough to get him to change his mind.

"En," she said, "our gratitude on this day of Thanksgiving starts with what you have done for us."

"It is not right for a servant to sit with the family."

"En, we are *your* servants, and besides, you've had dinner at Michael and Kathleen's before."

Johnny raised his head, the eagerness on his face would be hard to resist.

"En, Johnny will not be happy unless you try the colcannon. Did he tell you the secret's in the melted butter?"

"He did, ma'am," En said.

"Then we shall expect you," Johanna said.

Johnny raced across the room. "You'll be so glad, En, really."

The boy put his arms around En's legs. En accepted the embrace; his body was stiff, but he put his hands on the boy's shoulders. Johanna thought En was possibly cross with her but perhaps a bit pleased too.


Serving a Thanksgiving meal was nothing compared to anticipating a dinner prepared by Kathleen. Guests were lingering as Johanna, En, and the boys put on coats, hats, and mittens. They walked around the block together rather than go through the shortcut. Fighting a strong wind was refreshing; leaves swirled around them in cyclones of orange and brown. She watched En and Johnny together and was touched to see how close they had become. En was talkative and laughed easily at the boy's stunts.

"Watch my cartwheels; they are faster in the wind," Johnny shouted.

TC seemed happy too, and not to be outdone by his younger brother, challenged him to a race. As the boys ran ahead, En and Johanna walked side by side. Johanna had forgotten what it felt like to be quietly content with another human being.

"I hope you weren't offended that I hesitated to join you," En said. "I am most grateful for all you have done for me. And I wouldn't ever hurt Johnny's feelings."

"Of course you wouldn't, En," Johanna said. "Even after all that has happened, he is growing into a confident and joyful little boy. Your friendship and counsel, well, you have been there for him in ways he needed. He's so much more relaxed too, a changed child."

"He has changed me too," En said. "He lives with such an open heart. Mine was closed, but he managed to find a way in."

"That's Johnny," she said. "I have so little time. He's needed a man to give him attention and guidance. Thank you."

"An honor," En said. "I see how much responsibility you have, and I am glad I can be of service."

"Me too," Johanna said. She felt she had more to say, but they had arrived at their destination. The four of them floated in on the aroma of roast goose, onions, nutmeg, and cinnamon.

"So good to have all of you with us," Michael took their coats. "En, is this your first Thanksgiving?"

"Celebrating with a family, yes, it is," En said.

"It's good to have you. Kathleen's outdone herself on the goose, and you know how good her pies are." He put his arm around En and walked him into the parlor. "Now, what can I get you to drink?"

Kathleen, holding baby Charlie, kissed Johanna and each of the boys. "They're getting so tall," she said, "and handsome."

"They are," Johanna said. She was so proud of her sons. "I do miss the days when I could hold them on my hip. Charlie seems to like the view with his arms around his mama. It's wonderful we have a baby among us again. Where are the girls?"

"Upstairs, primping," Kathleen said.

"I brought some ribbons for them. I'll run up." Johanna patted the baby.

At the landing, she could see into the bedroom where Molly and Margaret were spinning around in circles. They were too excited to notice her, so she had a moment to watch. It was like looking back on a time she and Kathleen were together back home, giddy with anticipation. The girls shared a hand mirror, trying different hairstyles. Maeve and Mara hovered, and when their sisters were distracted, the twins grabbed the mirror.

"I *need* it!" Mara insisted, doubling over to cradle her treasure. Maeve pounded on her sister's back.

"Give it to me. It's mine."

Molly, the only sister the twins would occasionally obey, tried to cajole her younger sisters. "Here, let me make your hair pretty for Thanksgiving."

"*Me* do it." Johanna remembered when TC had been about this age and was just as insistent. She decided it was a good time to share the ribbons.

"Girls, I have something for you," she said. The twins were distracted and soon exclaiming over the colors. The older girls wove them into their braids. The twins demanded Johanna tie a ribbon on their dark curls and a bow on their aprons. Johanna led the parade of bedazzled lasses down the steps.

"Those two look more like Christmas ornaments than little girls," Michael said, pointing at the twins.

Thanksgiving dinner got underway. Kathleen had singed the goose a bit. When her husband tasted the crispy skin, he said, "I like it, nice smoky flavor."

Mara picked up the expression, and pronounced each bite she took as having, "nice 'moky flavor," which Maeve repeated until they both were taken with giggles.

Johanna watched En try to swallow the goose and could tell he didn't like it. Michael noticed. Laughing he said, "En, just spit it out!"

"Spit out my cooking?" Kathleen said, feigning anger.

"No, not at all." En looked anguished.

"I told you, En would prefer duck to goose; he and his compatriots on the railroad just don't like our white meat," Michael said.

"Good thing Michael told me to put water chestnuts in the dressing and add ginger to the pumpkin pie," Kathleen grinned. "Something for everyone."

Johanna watched En flush, unable to hide how much this kindness meant to him.

"Thank you," he said softly. "I do like the dressing, and the pie smells wonderful."

They all declared the ginger made the pie better than ever. After they finished dessert, Michael took out his fiddle, and the girls performed a treble reel. The acclaim among the audience prompted an encore. After they took their final bows, Johanna lifted her glass. "What amazing dancers! And to my dear friends," Johanna said. "En, we are so glad you joined us tonight."

"'Specially me," Johnny said.

"And to my beautiful boys, to Kathleen, Michael, and your lovely children and baby Charlie, of course. Everyone around this table is why I'm thankful this holiday."

"And we thank you right back, for our livelihood, and most important, your friendship," Michael said. "And, En, you fit right in."

En's eyes glistened. He cleared his throat, lifted his glass and said, "And you, my friends, have restored my faith in … in living."

They each took a sip of wine and smiled at one another. Whatever happened with her life, Johanna felt richly blessed among the people she loved most in the world.

"Let's have more pie," TC shouted. "I want all the kinds."

They lingered over pumpkin and mincemeat pie until Johanna realized it was getting late. "Kathleen, you have outdone yourself; everything was delicious," Johanna said. "Boys, help me clear the table."

"You have already served a houseful of people," Kathleen said. "Let us do it."

"Ma, it's snowing outside." Johnny was at the window. The children ran to join him.

"I want to build a fort," TC yelled.

"I guess we should get home," Johanna said. She looked over at En. He nodded. Together they found matched mittens and hats and divided the task of getting the boys dressed.

"I'll wrap up some pie and rolls," Kathleen said. "Michael, come with me and carve up some meat for them."

"At least we don't have to force the children to go," En said.

"Can we have a snowball fight, En?" Johnny asked.

En pulled a cap over the boy's ears. "Ask your mother."

"Yes, a short one," Johanna said. "Go outside. I'll get the leftovers."

Johanna watched En and the boys descend the snow-dusted steps, hanging on to one another to keep their footing. She walked toward the kitchen. Michael and Kathleen had their backs to her, and for the second time that night, she found herself unseen, this time observing the adult Farrells.

"It's one big happy family," Michael said.

"What do you mean?" Kathleen said.

"Johanna has been so alone, having to raise those youngsters by herself, Connor such a lout. I'm glad she has someone looking out for her, that's all."

"You're right. They have become close." Kathleen sounded distressed.

"Kathleen, you want them to be happy, right?"

"Michael, don't you see? Johanna is happy. En gets TC's hat while she finds Johnny's mittens."

"So?"

"Michael, it's not fine. En is an oddity in this town. The people are used to having him around, like a pet, but they don't see a man," she said. "And if they did, there are some in Nanticoke who would shoot him dead, especially if they thought he was anything but Johanna's servant."

"Oh, wife, you do carry on. The town's been good to En."

"What? He steps aside to let people pass. He still lives in that shed."

"Johanna tried to move him; he won't go."

"He's much more realistic about how people are than she is. Just because they haven't run him out on a rail—only the children greet him."

"I say hello every time I see him," Michael said.

"Oh, Michael, really. What about the Chinese Exclusion Act?" Kathleen said. "If En leaves the country, he can't even come back."

"But he's already here."

"Maybe, but I hope he doesn't push his luck with Johanna."

"I hope he gives it a shot—there's nothing sweeter than an Irish lass with a nice 'moky flavor." Michael nuzzled her hair. "You smell like a goose."

"Oh, Michael, if anyone's a goose, it's you."

They turned and saw Johanna. She smiled, pretending she'd just arrived.


The snowflakes turned the coal-dusted world into a pristine snow globe. Johanna wanted to suspend her distress over what she'd heard and enjoy the walk home with En and the boys. She looked forward to the next three days—a few precious days alone—and she wanted to relax and stop worrying. But Kathleen's words were a groove in her head that wouldn't fade away.

She saw En leap behind a fence. He pawed together snowball ammunition. He had become adept at using his forearms, but she worried that he was not protecting his new skin. En lobbed what amounted to armloads of snow at the boys, hoisting an arch of snowflakes over them all. Johnny ran through the flurry of powder and piled on top of En, laughing. This would be something Kathleen might take for granted, since Michael played with their children constantly, but Johanna feasted on the moment. She wanted to treasure tonight, even if it was an illusion that she was raising the boys with someone who cared as deeply as she about their welfare. Kathleen's words had snatched the sweet interlude away. Couldn't her friend have granted her just this one evening to enjoy what she took for granted?

It was impossible to quell her unease, and Johanna gave herself up to her dark thoughts. She worried about En. It hadn't occurred to her that other people might be treating him with disregard, possibly contempt. Except for warding off Tilly's hostility, things seemed to be going a little better; still her heart broke for him.

Kathleen, with her gift of insight, had stated the obvious. Johanna had little experience finding strength in a man, and yet this man was protecting her. En listened and offered wise guidance. Johanna trusted him, looked forward to their time together. But she was married; she should not let these feelings grow. True, she had not honored her vows to Connor, but that was because in her heart she was already married to Thomas, or at least that's what she told herself. As she looked back, she wondered how she could have been so taken by Thomas. At least Connor had married her. Thomas had no honor. She had been gullible and as guilty as he was. Even so, she didn't want to hear, or heed, Kathleen's admonition.

Johanna had to admit she was jealous, too—and ashamed. How thoughtless she'd been to En, thinking only of herself and possibly putting him in jeopardy. She had crossed the line. She smiled too much when he was around, feeling proud that she cheered him, sharing too much, relying on him more than she should. No wonder he had been reluctant to take tea with her or to call her Johanna. She had put him in a terrible position. She had to admit: the more he resisted her, the more determined she had been to make him take notice, come out of his shell. Had she been playing a game that made her feel better at his expense? But, no, she had enjoyed their closeness. Was that wrong?

En's voice called her back to the present. The boys were trudging along the snow-covered path, and he had circled back for her.

"Are you coming? Best get inside. It's really coming down."

En put his arm around her. "Watch—it's slippery."

When they got back home, En offered to start a fire, his signal they could spend the evening together. She froze. She wanted to talk by the fire, plan, laugh, even make a late-night snack together as they sometimes did. But it wouldn't be a good idea to spend another evening with him, especially with no one around.

"It's been a long day, En. Take the evening off," she said.

He gave her a quizzical look, recovered quickly, and said, "Of course, sleep well."

The boys required minimal supervision, a good thing because she was rattled. "Yes, Johnny, you had the biggest snowball," she said. "No, TC, you may not stay up one minute later, even if you do have a new book."

When the boys were finally in their beds, she came downstairs and walked in the kitchen. Before she could get to the stove, she heard a door creaking open. She was startled and almost screamed, but before he spoke, she knew who it was.

"It's me, Thomas." A shadowy figure stepped from the pantry.

"When are you going to stop accosting me in dark places?" She backed away from him.

"Sorry, may I light the lamp?" he asked.

"No," she said. "Leave the light off." She didn't want to look at him. "What are you doing here? I thought you went west, to save Finn?"

"We only made it as far as Maryland."

"That's south, not west. Just barely to the Mason-Dixon Line."

"I found some part-time work, but not enough money for us to move further. We're safe enough in Ellicott City. There is a railroad there, and we can get out fast if we need to." He was walking toward her. She moved away. Eventually he backed her into the butcher block.

"So why aren't you in Ellicott City now?"

"Bridget was homesick. I brought her back to see her parents for the holiday. We were careful, came in before light, kept the shades down."

He stood too close. His hips touched hers. "Ah, Johanna you look beautiful, what I can see of you."

"And did you bring Finn with you?" She pulled her body away from him.

"Aye," Thomas said. "He misses his grandparents. And I had to see you, sweet one. It's been terrible. Me not getting work, Bridget moaning about leaving home, Finn's burns—for a time they were bad," he said. "And how are you? Have you missed me?"

"En can't use his hands either. Hard to muster much sympathy for Finn," she said. "And I can't imagine why you are here."

"I love you, lass," he said. He raised his arms, about to encircle her. She ducked before he could pin her.

"Thomas, stay where you are," she said. "Give me a minute."

She moved quickly so he couldn't block her. She made her way to the office and unlocked the desk drawer now functioning as the hotel safe. She found the envelope with the proceeds from Thanksgiving dinner. She started back but stopped, took half of the money out and returned it to the drawer. She came back to the kitchen with the envelope.

"I was hoping you'd return wearing your shift?" he said.

"Thomas, here is the money we made tonight." She held out the envelope. "It was going toward a fund to rebuild the hotel, but I realize now it could be put to better use."

"I don't know what you mean?" Thomas said. At least he was staying put.

"There is enough cash here for you to take your family west, but"—she held the envelope back—"if you take this, you must never return. Bridget or Finn either."

"What?"

"Finn tried to murder my sons, one of them his half-brother," she said. "Johnny saw Finn—did you know that? And he told TC. I have forbidden them to speak of it, so they now carry the burden of another secret on their young shoulders—and I want to make certain they will not be terrorized by Finn ever again. If you, Finn, or his mother set foot within fifty miles of Nanticoke, I promise you, I will go to the sheriff and turn Finn in myself."

"Johanna, please." He rounded the table. "You know you want to surrender, even when you are angry. Lucky, I like a woman with an Irish temper."

She recoiled just as Thomas cried out in pain. He wrenched backward and fell.

En stood over Thomas, who was lying face down on the kitchen floor. En pressed his boot against Thomas's spine. "Johanna gives you money," En said. "Take it and time to leave."

"En, that you? Jesus, I just want to talk," Thomas said. He attempted to turn sideways, but En pushed down harder.

"Johanna, do you want to talk?" En said.

"No, En, I don't."

"You owe me, guy," Thomas said. "We dumped those weapons together. I don't deserve this. Get off."

"Thomas, I will lift my foot once you agree to leave," En said.

"Okay, okay," Thomas said. "Ouch, stop, you're gonna break my back."

"Get up, slowly, slowly. Take the money and leave." En lifted his boot about an inch. Thomas crawled to where Johanna had dropped the envelope.

"I will repay this, I swear," he said, pocketing the money.

En followed Thomas back to the Sullivans'. When he returned to Butterwort House, he found Johanna in the parlor. She sat with her skirts bunched around her, as if she had simply run out of energy and collapsed. She didn't appear hurt.

"Johanna, can I help you up?"

"No, En, I want to sit right here, but you can get me a whiskey, over on the sideboard," she said. "Do you need some light?"

"I can see well enough."

"And pour one for yourself, En."

He had not had whiskey since the mining camp, but he did as she asked.

"Join me," she said.

He sat cross-legged next to her.

"Where's your hand, so it doesn't spill?" He reached out and curled his hand around her fingers. He felt a tube of cold metal. "Johanna, is this a gun?"

"Yes, but it's not loaded. It was Walsh's. I couldn't find any bullets. They may be in the safe," Johanna said. "Isn't that funny, En? Everything I need is in that safe. And I gave it away to the lawyer who won't acknowledge me."

He replaced the gun with the glass of whiskey.

"Let's toast to your saving yet another one of us," she said. "This time it's me." She clinked his glass.

"How did you happen to be here?"

"Sometimes I check on the house. You don't always remember to lock doors."

"I'm sorry you had to hear that. I assumed you might know about Thomas and me, but I've tried to keep my suspicions about Finn to myself."

"I had them, too, Johanna," he said. "Johnny said he saw a boy ghost that looked like Finn start the fire."

"He did?" she said. "What did you say?

"I told him that it didn't matter, that Finn was gone, and he shouldn't worry."

"I don't understand how Thomas could think I would even want to be in the same room with him." She took another gulp.

"Johanna, I don't know Thomas well, but I think if a man lies to himself for a long time, he can no longer find the truth," En said. "Thomas might be such a man, the kind who pretends all is well until his life ends up in shambles."

"And you aren't like that, En," she said. "You are careful, truthful, even as some here treat you so horribly."

"I'm not that honorable myself. I once sought recognition without regard for those I cared about," En said. "It cost other people dearly."

"Not since you've been here. Your judgment is good," she said. "Unlike mine. Even tonight, I probably made a mistake giving Thomas the money."

"If it means he won't come back, it was money well spent."

"Of course, I'm less gullible than I was—I didn't give him all of it." He couldn't quite make it out, but he sensed her smile.

"The right decision," En said. His eyes had adjusted to the dim light, and he could see her profile. Her hair, usually pinned on her head, was loose, the glossy braid hung thick against her shoulder. He reached up and traced his fingers along the plait.

She put her hand on top of his. Her face in shadows, she leaned toward him. She held her lips a breath away from his. He moved so his mouth grazed hers.

He could taste the whiskey. He tried not to respond, but he couldn't pull away. They were silent, lips pressed together. His free hand cradled her head. She melted into him.

She moved closer. His body was insistent, but he felt sick inside. He forced himself away. This was wrong. She was in no condition, even without the difference in their stations. She was frightened: that was all.

"Finish your drink, Johanna," he said. "Then I will walk you to the stairs. You need sleep."

She placed her cool palm on top of his scarred hand. The tenderness of her touch seemed more intimate than the kiss. "I'll stop, but please, En," she said, "I can't be alone just yet. Stay and talk to me."

"Of course, but I must apologize for …" His face burned.

"En, let's not talk of it, not now. I didn't think, but I should have. You are concerned I am not in my right mind, and perhaps that is true, but I wanted to kiss you," she said. "I think some part of me has wanted this for a while."

He wished to tell her he felt the same way, but she was slurring her words. She might not even remember this conversation in the morning.

She reached up, grabbed two pillows from the sofa, and positioned them against the wall. She moved over and rested her back against the wall. "Ah, this is comfortable," she said. "More whiskey?"

En got up and brought the bottle over. He sat next to her, filled her glass, then his own.

"I don't think I've ever looked at the parlor from this angle before. The sofa looks ready to pounce, like an angry bull," she said. "And the dowels on the back of that rocking chair are picket fences holding the sofa from attack."

"They remind me of the enclosure that my family lived in during our voyage to America," En said. "We spent weeks looking at slats like that."

"Sounds like a jail."

"I guess it was. As a child, I was too small to make the comparison."

"We had a small cabin, with two bunks. My strongest memory is willing Johnny to live. He got sick right after we left Liverpool," she said. "I'll never forget that first breath of air when we came up on deck."

"Yes, wonderful to finally see daylight," En said. "The clean sea air, and then your feet are on dry land, and the elation of reaching a long-anticipated destination."

"And all of that, for what? I'm grateful we haven't starved, but it's not been what I expected either. I may lose everything. Even tonight, we worked so hard to put on a Thanksgiving dinner, and Thomas takes off with half the profits," she said. "It's beyond me to know what to do next."

"From here, the rocker looks like bars, but tomorrow, in the daylight, it will be only a rocking chair," En said.

"Perhaps." She reached for the bottle.

He held it back. "Listen to me. You can't stay in the hold of the ship forever. Why do you let them keep you penned in? Why not fight back?"

He heard her take a quick breath.

"A forward question, I'm sorry," En said. "It is not for me to ask."

"En, no, you're right. I'm used to having answers, but I have none," she said. "I'm afraid to make the wrong move."

"You will always have your boys, so deciding not to move is making a decision, too." Worried he sounded preachy, he added, "There are worse things than a wrong choice."

They were silent. Then he added, "You know I lost my family?"

"Yes, Michael told me," she said. "Your parents and all of your siblings? I'm so sorry."

"That was my first family," En said. "I also lost my wife and infant daughter."

"You did?" she said. "Michael never said anything about that."

"He doesn't know," he said. "Other than the people in Philadelphia who were there, you are the first person I've told."

"How terrible for you," she said. "I'm so sorry."

"Yes, indeed, tragic," En said.

"Thank you for telling me, for trusting me, En."

"It was typhoid … and I caused it."

"Surely no, it's a disease, and you did all you could …"

"I was working in a research lab. I was in medical school, and more concerned about my work and reputation than my family's safety," he said. "I thought if I could isolate the bacteria, they would know I was a good scientist, as good as the other doctors."

"I'm sure you were, but I'm surprised. They let you go to work in a medical school?"

"Not easily. I had friends—a friend. I wanted to please him, too, and I thought, with such a grand discovery, things might work out," he said. "But I wasn't careful." En didn't know why he felt compelled to tell her that it had been his fault. "I brought the disease home. It killed my wife, Mai Ling, and our daughter, Rosie. My pride killed them." En pulled his knees to his chest.

"No, En," she said. "They could have contracted the disease from anyone."

"It doesn't matter. They are gone," he said. "Your boys are still alive. You must fight."

$$\infty$$

# CHAPTER TWELVE

# A GLASS OF WATER

**Nanticoke, Pennsylvania, December 1883**

"This could be our Christmas miracle," Johanna said. She sat between Michael and En on the front seat of the wagon. Johanna was happy to see that En could hold the reins without difficulty. They rested their feet on warm bricks. The canvas top did little to block the wet flakes that stung their cheeks. Halfway between Nanticoke and Wilkes-Barre, the bricks turned stone cold.

"I can't feel my toes, but it will be worth it," she said. "Father Ryan did it. He got a meeting with Judge Doyle."

"Don't get too excited. It just shows Father Ryan's got clout with crooked judges," Michael said. "I don't trust the lot of them."

En pulled up in front of the two-story office building on the square in downtown Wilkes-Barre.

"I'll be over at the livery," En said.

"Thanks." Michael helped Johanna down. "Want me to check to make sure they'll let you stay inside? Looks like it's gonna snow hard."

"I'll be okay," En said. "I hear some Celestials are working there."

"Come get me if you have any problems," Michael said. He escorted Johanna around shards of ice edging a slushy puddle where someone's boot had plunged though the crust. "Whoa, this is the high-price district." Michael held the door for her.

"I'm getting ideas for the hotel," she said, scanning the two-story foyer. "How about a paneled lobby and crystal light fixtures mounted on mirrors?"

"It's all about power," Michael said. "They want to make you feel small."

"It's working." Johanna shook off her coat and stamped her feet as feeling tingled back in her toes.

"Don't let them get away with it."

An older woman with an oblong face presided over the reception desk. She wore a high-collared black dress, her hair pinned in a severe topknot.

"Mrs. Johanna Kennedy for Mr. Doyle," Michael said.

"You are her attorney?" The receptionist pursed her lips.

"Michael Farrell," Michael said, "her friend."

"May I take your coats?" The secretary accepted their garments with obvious distaste.

"Judge will see you now," she said. "Father Ryan has already arrived."

They walked through the double doors. Judge Doyle sat at a carved mahogany desk. The surface was bare except for a shining wooden gavel resting on a brass strip engraved with the words *The Honorable Judge Justin Hayes Doyle*, to clarify in case anyone in his office was unsure. Father Ryan was seated in one of the three chairs opposite the judge's desk.

Judge Doyle attempted to raise himself from his padded leather chair, wincing when he put weight on his knees. "Please, sit down." He dropped back in his seat. "Father Ryan has briefed me already."

"Thank you for meeting with us," Johanna said.

"Yes, yes. My time is short. Let's get to it," Judge Doyle's voice was ragged. "We have opened the safe."

"You did?" Michael said.

"Standard practice. I review everything ahead of time," Doyle replied. "Now, if there are no further impediments … the will."

"I brought it with me," Johanna said.

Judge Doyle paused. "What?"

"I have the will," she said. "Mr. Walsh left it in his top desk drawer."

"There's another will?" Doyle said. "Let me see that."

"Yes, it's the original," she said, placing it on his desk. "It gives the properties to me and assigns the insurance money as well."

The judge took his time reading through the papers. Johanna fidgeted with the straps on her bag. The priest rested his hand over hers and whispered, "Be still, child."

"Just making you feel small." Michael spoke so only Johanna could hear him.

"Mrs. Kennedy, this is quite irregular," Judge Doyle said. "This document is likely a forgery, but in any case, it predates the will from the safe."

"I do not forge documents," Johanna said. Michael leaned forward, ready to tackle. Johanna shook her head "no," and he sat back. "The will in my possession names me the new owner and further states the owner is the beneficiary of the insurance payment."

"I wasn't implying you had forged the document, not at all, my dear. But we must consider the possibility that you have been duped. Putting this bogus issue aside for a moment," the judge said, "the good news is that there is documentation of insurance here. The new owner can rebuild."

"That is a relief," Johanna said.

"However, due to the death of his son and only heir, the will, as I expect you know,"—Judge Doyle cleared his throat—"leaves the hotel and other properties to the Church. Father Ryan is named executor."

"That can't be." Michael stood up. "Father Ryan, tell him that this is nonsense. Walsh hated the Church."

Johanna felt dizzy. Mr. Walsh would never do such a thing. She had been a fool to rely on a truthful or fair system. She was getting better at knowing when she was swimming in the river of betrayal. She was about midstream, and the tide was rising. She was certain that her will was authentic and that Judge Doyle's was the forgery. Mr. Walsh was difficult, but nothing these two men were proposing was something he ever would do.

The judge's meaty hand rested on her documents.

"I feel unwell." She raised her hand to her forehead. "Father Ryan, might I have a glass of water?"

"Of course." The priest stepped around Johanna. "I'll find the receptionist. Michael, lower her head, have her rest on her knees so she doesn't faint."

Johanna bent at the waist, and Michael leaned over her; both were below the judge's line of sight. "When I get up," she whispered, "grab the papers."

She stood and reached out her hand, "Thank you so much, Judge."

Judge Doyle was taken aback at her quick recovery. He automatically lifted his hand to shake. Michael grabbed the will. The judge banged his palm down but was too late.

"I should like to study that," Doyle said.

"This belongs to Johanna," Michael said, tucking the papers in his pocket. Johanna propped herself against Michael, blocking access to his jacket.

"I really do need air," Johanna said, "Michael?"

The priest returned with a glass of water, and Michael shoved him out of the way.

"Thank you for your help, Judge, but I believe I shall retain my own lawyer." Johanna turned by the door. "And don't break ground on a new rectory just yet."

"What the goddamn hell was that?" Judge Doyle huffed, his turkey neck quivering.

Father Ryan ignored the profanity. "She's just upset. We have her, and she knows it."

"Father," Doyle said, "we have nothing of the kind. First, the insurance documents do not name the Church as the beneficiary, but they do name her as estate representative and hotel manager. Second, need I remind you that we fabricated the new will? It's a lot fancier than hers, and we hope it will stand up better in court, but it's a fake."

"You drafted it. I'm sure it's stronger, and it won't come to that anyway."

"Ryan, hope is not a strategy."

"I understand," Father Ryan said. He could feel the semicircle of sweat spreading stains under his arms.

"Let's review the bidding here," Judge Doyle said. "Our plan was Walsh's estate goes to the Church, and then you sell it at a good price to my investors."

"The proceeds are for a worthy cause: improvements to the sanctuary and a new school hall in Wilkes-Barre, and with what remains, a rectory in Nanticoke," Father Ryan said.

"You can buy all the stained glass you want. I don't give a damn. I care about getting caught."

Father Ryan looked at Doyle's puffed-out cheeks and saw a fish he had once pulled from the Susquehanna. "We left her Butterwort House. She has every reason to accept this arrangement," he said. "I'll talk to her."

"Yeah, well, I didn't see her listening today," Doyle said. "You said it was a gold mine down in Wilkes-Barre. I've already got three committed investors, and now it's going to hell. Why did I ever agree to partner with a priest?"

"Wait. I have an idea."

"I've been unimpressed so far," Judge Doyle said. "But let's hear it."

"We probably can't budge her; the more I think on it, you are absolutely right about that. She's a stubborn woman. But we do have some leverage," Father Ryan said. "We need another witness, someone who will testify to seeing Walsh sign our will."

"But there are no other witnesses," Judge Doyle said. "Must I keep reminding you it's bogus?"

"What about her husband? As a witness, I mean?" Father Ryan said. "He's in prison, but there are no charges. You pull strings to get him released. I'll make arrangements for some compensation and get him to stand witness?"

"What's his incentive?"

"Besides getting out of prison?"

"I see your point, but they may not believe him. And how do you know he will stick to the story once he's free?"

"First, he's already running scared. He's always been weak, but after a few months behind bars, he'll be an easy target. Plus, he's sick of his wife ruling the roost. Maybe we offer him a job. If she had to depend on his income instead of the other way around, he'd go for it. He blames her for getting locked up in the first place and suspects that she had something to do with the weapons disappearing."

"It's risky," Judge Doyle said, mopping his face. "If anything goes wrong, you'll take the fall."

Father Ryan had spent his life building up credentials to make sure he would never take any kind of fall. He would make it work: simple, but not easy. He considered his options. They could give up the forgery, but why should she get the spoils? He was the one who had worked: building up his authority in the Church, winning the approbation of his community. He was on his way to becoming Monsignor Ryan—possibly even Bishop Ryan. It was up to him to save Johanna from herself; she could never make a business work. God had put this treasure right in front of him and intended for him to be a good steward for the good of all.

"I'll take care of it," Father Ryan said. "Just get the husband released."

Johanna gazed out the dining room window. It was a miserable December day. There were no guests at the Rose or Lily houses, and the Butterwort house was nearly empty. She hated the endless gray this time of year; the gloom reminded her of Liverpool. Kathleen held a sleeping Charlie. Michael sat next to her on the sofa. En leaned against the door, as if on guard.

"Walsh wouldn't leave a wooden nickel to the Church," Kathleen said. "If he'd had the strength, he would have tossed Father Ryan out in the streets."

"But Walsh is dead," Johanna said. The familiar pit of fear drilled into her. She and the boys would be homeless; her best hope was that she might still have a job, if Father Ryan didn't sell the property out from under them. And what of Kathleen and Michael, the other staff—and especially En? Where would a Celestial, without the full use of his hands, find work? She had seen cartoons of Chinese with murderous features, reptilian eyes and fangs, or depicted lying in a stupor of opium. Americans were raising the same objections to Chinese as they had the Irish: they were dirty, destitute, and drunk. She'd heard about demonstrations, not locally, but in larger cities, where crowds chanted, "We will not give up our country to the Chinese." People blaming unemployment on immigrants, just as they had with the Irish. There was nothing she could do.

Lost in images of a throng closing in around En, she startled when Michael spoke. "We just have to get this will into the court record."

Johanna looked over to En. He was safe here but for how long?

She heard the baby stir and saw him open his eyes and squirm against Kathleen. "Ah, excuse me. Charlie is not a patient young man," Kathleen said. In the next second, a fully awake Charlie pounded fists on her breast. As Kathleen exited the room, they could hear him wailing.

"Charlie's good at asking for what he wants," En said. "We can learn from him."

"Not too subtle, En," Johanna said.

"You have to find someone to help."

"I agree, but Father Ryan turned out to be a traitor. Is it worth taking another chance?"

"Not everyone is a scoundrel. There are good people," En said. "What about Mother Agnes?"

"We need someone with political power," Michael said. "I'm not sure how a nun could help."

They were silent.

"What about Sam Kress? He's a successful businessman and knows influential people," Johanna said. "He seems interested in the hotel, too."

"Maybe he's interested in you?" Kathleen entered the room with a blanket draped over her shoulder, the nursing baby underneath. "He's not married. Is he fresh with you?"

"Not at all. He's only interested in business."

"Do you think he might know a lawyer?" En asked.

"They can't all be owned by the mine bosses, can they?" Michael said.


Peeling paint flaked off twenty-foot plaster walls surrounding the dusty prison courtyard. Inside, run-down buildings stood at odd angles, linking a maze of corridors, each housing endless rows of narrow cells. A small square window, crisscrossed with iron bars, was an inmate's only view. Often three men squeezed into a cell designed for two. Father Ryan served communion to the men in common rooms but had often walked the corridors of locked doors, lined up like dominoes, to tend to men too ill to stand, sometimes placing the wafer in the mouth of a nearly unconscious soul. After serving, he would rinse the chalice in the prison yard sink. Even after the long drive back to the rectory, the odor of despair clung to his vestments and his spirit.

He walked through the building's main doors. He hated the prison, but he had to handle this matter in person. Getting Judge Doyle to release Connor was the easy part. It was his job to persuade Connor to go along with the plan. It wouldn't take long. Father Ryan held all the cards. Then he'd drop Connor at Johanna's and leave for a retreat: a week with Father Neil. His reward.

"Do you have the release authorization?" the guard asked.

"Yes." Father Ryan slid the papers under the slot below the window. "Am I required to go inside?"

"No, someone will bring him up. Just wait here."

Five minutes later, the guard opened an inner gate. Connor, already dressed in civilian clothes, waved at the priest. The guard handed Connor a brown envelope. He shook out his wallet and wedding ring.

"Will I be needing this, Father?" he asked, holding up the ring.

"Let's get outside," Father Ryan said.

As soon as they were in the courtyard Connor said, "So, tell me, about my wife and sons. Why aren't they here?"

"They are safe back at Butterwort House," Father Ryan said. "I'm here to take you to them."

"Hard to believe I'm sprung," Connor said, climbing next to Father Ryan. "Nearly six months, but not too much snow and ice out here."

"Sorry it took this long; it wasn't easy," Father Ryan shouted over the crunch of wheels grinding against patches of ice on the gravel. "But I'm glad it could be arranged. And I offered to pick you up because there is something I want to discuss."

"If it's money, forget it," Connor said. "I'm broke. I doubt Johanna would give me a loan."

"No, not money. I'm your priest," Father Ryan said. "I'm concerned for you."

"That's nice of you, Father."

"I wanted to warn you that this might not be over."

"But I'm out, right?"

"Indeed, but you're not out of the woods."

"What do you mean?"

"I know about the weapons." Father Ryan flicked the reins. "Get on, you old nag."

Connor gripped the wooden seat with both hands as the wagon picked up speed. Father Ryan glanced over at the man. Connor's brow was knit with uncertainty—unsure whether to admit or deny. Points of dried blood spotted Connor's chin; likely today was the first Connor had shaved in weeks. The blades given to newly released men were dull as a kitchen knife.

"I can see you are surprised. Don't be," Father Ryan said. "And I heard about it, not from the police or in the confessional, but from men who are loyal to you."

"How so?" Connor said.

"They don't want retribution, but they're afraid others do. They had a lot of hard-earned money invested in that arsenal and hold you responsible for whatever happened," the priest said. "And you heard about the fire?"

"I did."

"Arson—possible retribution. Anyway, the hotel is gone."

Connor opened his mouth, making a soundless cry.

"You're going to need protection," Father Ryan said. "Your life may be in danger."

"It's that bleak?"

"Not necessarily. I have ways of keeping your family safe."

"I've had months to think about it, Father." Connor searched the barren trees along the road. "I brought violence under my roof … my sons asleep there every night."

"You weren't smart, but I'll not be hearing more about your crime until we're in a proper confessional." Father Ryan took one hand off the reins and gave Connor's shoulder a reassuring thump. "I have a proposition for you."

"I'm listening."

"You could, of course, leave town and start fresh."

"Fresh, without my sons, without my wife?" Connor said. "That is nothing short of a long death. Jesus. Take me to a bar. I need a drink."

"You need a lot of things, but a drink isn't one of them," the priest said.

"And who are you to be telling me what I need?" Connor hawked spit into the wind. "I can taste prison still. Father, it's been months."

"Under the seat," Father said. A calmer Connor would help move his agenda. "Inside the carpetbag. Help yourself."

Father Ryan watched Connor scramble for the bottle like a starving animal and take a long slog. "God, that's like breathing fresh air after suffocating down a mine shaft. Swig?"

"No, thanks, you go ahead. We'll talk when we get closer to town."

Connor nursed the bottle during the two-hour drive.

When they reached the outskirts of Nanticoke, the priest pulled into a grove of pine trees. Ahead, a stone bridge arched over the swollen Susquehanna River. "Why don't you put the bottle away?" Father Ryan said. Connor scowled. The priest used his sermon voice. "Put it away, now."

"Father, sounds like you want me to leave," Connor said. "But you've never been much on standing by the Irish."

"What do you mean?"

"I was in Liverpool back in '76, but people talk. Everybody knows you betrayed those men sent to the gallows on Black Thursday—you might as well have been working for Pinkerton yourself, and now you're gonna force me to get on a train?"

"Don't be going on about things that happened long before you got to the valley," Father Ryan said. "Leaving town is an option, but I believe I can offer you a better one." He moved closer to Connor and reached for the bottle.

"Ah, so you're propositioning me?" Connor pulled away. "I know about those goings-on. You think the men here don't see you've always been a bit off, Father Ryan?"

Connor threw the empty bottle over his shoulder. It landed with a thud. "You and Thomas," Connor said. "I've seen how you look at him. Unnatural is what it is."

Not once in Father Ryan's experience, going all the way back to his altar boy days, had anyone ever mentioned his proclivities—at least not to his face. He had sometimes wondered if they even knew. Now Connor was not only accusing him; he was naming Thomas. Father Ryan would not allow this pathetic jailbird to sully Thomas.

"Connor, this has nothing to do with Thomas," Father Ryan said. "Just listen." He explained that he was not asking Connor to leave, but merely to testify. "You may not have seen them actually sign, but if you say you did, it will help Johanna. She can back away from her claim, acknowledge that her will is not authentic."

Connor looked at the priest with bleary eyes.

"Women are easily fooled, Connor. That is why your wife needs you to take control," Father Ryan said. "If you agree, this can be good for you and your family."

"You must really want this bad," Connor said. "God damn you to hell, Father, and I mean that."

Connor's outburst and his accusations about Thomas were unsettling. For the first time, Father Ryan worried this might not work—time to sweeten the deal. "And there is cash, of course," Father Ryan said, "small bills, in a big envelope."

"I never witnessed anyone signing a will." Connor was drunk but understood more than Father Ryan had intended.

"That's true, but think of the greater purpose here," Father Ryan said.

"You disgust me. You always have, Ryan," Connor said. "Asking me to call my wife a liar? Have you no shame?"

"I'm trying to help Johanna."

"No, you just think I'm such a lowlife that I'd do anything to save my own skin." Connor jumped off the footboard, landed unsteadily, and lurched up the embankment.

"Come back here." Father Ryan scrambled down to the slippery ground, running to reach Connor, who had started to climb the stone wall above the bridge. "Get off," he said. "It's slippery."

Connor balanced himself on the narrow ledge. "You fookin' excuse for a priest, get away from me."

"Don't be stupid." Father Ryan could barely hear his own voice over the roar of the waterfall below.

"You think I'll let you steal from Johanna—that I'll let you and that goddamned church raise my boys?"

Connor hoisted himself up on the wall. Father Ryan stood below him. Without warning, Connor spun around and leapt into the air. His body landed right in front of Father Ryan, and he slammed his fist into the priest's jaw. Father Ryan put his hands to his face and Connor took advantage of the opening. He punched a hard left hook into the priest's belly. Father Ryan fell to the ground.

"It's a sad day when a sorry excuse for a man has to beat up a priest, but nobody would believe me if I told them what you suggested," Connor shouted. He leapt back to the ledge and stood over the rushing water. "Yes, a sorry day when the best thing I can do for my wife is not come home."

Father Ryan got to his feet. He was covered in dirt and wiped the blood from his mouth. "Connor, please," he said.

Connor was swaying and nearly stumbling backward. "You are the devil himself tempting me. Because, Lord knows, I could use a fistful of cash," he said.

"Get down," Father Ryan said. He reached for Connor's legs.

"And I'll go to hell for sure if I take it," Connor said.

He stepped back to avoid the priest's grasp and fell soundlessly off the edge.


It was past midnight when Father Ryan finally fell asleep. They were in Father Neil's room at the monastery. Father Ryan was awake, trying to make sense of the last hour. He always happily anticipated their encounters. Usually with Father Neil, it was easy. Sometimes Father Neil would tease him by pretending to resist. His reluctance elicited slight aggression in Father Ryan, tinged with the delicious threat of pain, but Father Ryan never hurt Father Neil. But tonight, there had been something alien.

Father Ryan said, "Please forgive me. I didn't mean to hurt you."

"You were not as you usually are with me," Father Neil said, "but I am unharmed."

Father Ryan had thought Father Neil was asleep, but he felt Father Neil stroke his arm.

"What is it?" Father Neil said. "You are not yourself. What's happened?"

"Bless me, Father, for I have sinned," Father Ryan said. "I *am* a hypocrite and a cheat. Terrible things happen to men in my care."

"You mean during the strike? Those men who went to the gallows?" Father Neil said. "You have to forgive yourself."

"I'm not talking about that. I sent a man to hell earlier today."

Father Neil's hand lay flat on Father Ryan's back.

"I provoked him," Father Ryan said. "I wanted to lead him to sin."

"Are you telling me you have been with another man?"

"Not that kind of sin. I wanted him to betray someone in a business deal. The goal was noble, to help others, but my methods were wrong."

"I'm sure you had your reasons, and as you say, you had good intentions," Father Neil said. "That's not the same as committing murder."

"But I made him want to die," Father Ryan said.

"But it was his choice, right?"

"We were standing on a bridge. He fell."

"It sounds like an accident," Father Neil said. "There are no sins, nothing so impure, that Jesus cannot forgive, regardless. I absolve you in the name of the Father, and of the Son, and of the Holy Ghost, Amen."

Father Ryan wept.


Sam Kress was studying a set of blueprints laid out on a coffee table in the hotel lobby. Johanna cleared her throat to get his attention. He rolled the papers up and said, "You wanted to see me?"

"Yes, if you have a minute?"

He nodded, and she took a breath. There was no one else around. She sat down next to him. It took some time to explain, but she ended up asking if he might refer her to a good lawyer.

"A difficult scenario," he said. "Let me think."

He took off his glasses. His sober expression gave her confidence he was taking her seriously. "I'll be blunt, Mrs. Kennedy. I don't know any lawyers who would represent an Irish woman, especially if the Molly Maguires are involved."

"They're not. Walsh's estate and my husband's situation are entirely separate," Johanna said.

She and En had practiced how she would approach Kress, but now, face to face, she had trouble formulating answers.

"Do you know where your husband is?" Kress asked.

"We're all mystified. He was never charged, and then they released him to the care of our priest, Father Ryan. Father says he took Connor as far as Main Street in Nanticoke, that Connor wanted to walk the rest of the way home."

"And no one saw Connor in town?"

"No."

"Did the priest have any idea what could have happened?"

"Father Ryan speculated that Connor was worried his coming back might endanger us. Evidently, Connor had asked about work down south, implied that he might go there, make some money, and then return."

"And what do the police say?" Kress said. "Have they investigated?"

"They claim they released him, and unless there are signs of foul play, they won't do anything."

"My dear, I'm so sorry," Kress said. "I see why you're anxious to resolve the estate."

"I don't wish to impose," Johanna said. "Thank you for speaking with me. You have always been kind."

"And I have admired how you walk with grace through these difficulties," Kress said.

"I'm glad that it appears that way," Johanna said. "A friend tells me I must continue to fight, but I'm not sure how."

"Well, now that I think," Kress said. "There is one man, Kevin Bruce, who lives with his wife live in Hazelton. He's kept a few of your countrymen from the gallows, and he has a reputation for going up against magistrates who have no use for the Irish. He even wins a case every so often. I'll see what I can do."


A week later Mr. Kress had secured an appointment with the lawyer. Johanna, Michael, and En got in the buggy once again—this time on a warmer December day—headed for Hazelton. None of them could predict how the new lawyer might react to a Celestial, so En stayed outside.

"Is the brick still warm, En?" Johanna said as she stepped off the wagon.

"I'm fine," En said. "I have a good feeling about this man. You persist, and it will pay off."

Michael and Johanna followed a curving stone walkway to an unassuming cottage. Michael knocked on the door and it was opened by a woman with a pleasant smile. Her gossamer hair, the color of flax, framed her face like a halo.

"I'm Alice Bruce," she said. "You've traveled such a long way."

Something about Mrs. Bruce's manner, her sympathetic eyes, felt like sanctuary. She ushered them into a book-lined room and introduced her husband, who bounded up from his chair with such amiable energy that Johanna felt strangely reassured.

The couple listened as Johanna and Michael explained the situation. Mr. Bruce glanced through the will. "On first appearances, I would say this is valid. Based on what you have told me, it likely represents the wishes of the man who wrote it," Mr. Bruce said.

Johanna felt a shred of hope. "Oh, thank you, you are an answer to our prayers."

"Well," Mr. Bruce shook his head, "we are going to need a lot more than prayers. I would say that if there is another will, chances are it is flawlessly executed. It may be a forgery, but that will be nearly impossible to prove. And, regardless of the facts, most judges rule against the Irish if the Catholic Church or business interests are the opposing party."

"But things are getting better for the Irish," Michael interjected. "Labor just helped elect Terence Powderly mayor up in Scranton ... and on the Molly Maguire ticket."

"Yes, but he doesn't appoint the judges," Mr. Bruce said. "For us, it will be an uphill battle."

Johanna noted he was using words like "us" and "we."

"This is also going to cost you money. Mr. Kress has kindly offered to cover my time, but there will be court costs and possibly some detective work."

"I still have money," Johanna said, touched at Mr. Kress's generosity.

"Before you spend it, let me warn you: it's not only the potential expense. If this becomes a high-profile case, as it may, it could hurt your business. I don't know how many of your current customers are non-Catholics, but I assume if Sam Kress is staying with you that some of your paying clients are businessmen. It's one thing to stay in your hotel, quite another if you go up against the system that keeps them wealthy."

"I understand, but what do I have to lose?"

"Living rent-free in a house for the rest of your life is better than living in the poorhouse. If you want my advice, I wouldn't challenge the will." Mr. Bruce folded the documents. "Take what you can get."

Johanna felt queasy.

"She can't do that," Michael said. "It's her business. Before she came along it was a few cheap rooming houses. She's the one who made it successful. It's not fair."

Mrs. Bruce cleared her throat. "Kevin, couldn't we offer to study this matter before making a final decision? Perhaps there are some facts that could put the situation in a more favorable light?"

Mr. and Mrs. Bruce locked eyes. "She's in charge." Mr. Bruce inclined his head toward his wife. "All right, give me a week to see if I can learn any more about the insurance and obtain a copy of the other will. I'll send word about what I find."

"You must have faith," Mrs. Bruce said, touching Johanna's arm. She stood up and called to a young woman who brought in a tea tray. "I will pour." She handed Johanna a cup and said, "The difference between success and failure is the number of times you dust yourself off."

"I have a close employee, a friend, who says something close to that," Johanna said. She felt that she never wanted to leave the comfort of this parlor. Johanna could be tough against adversaries, but Mrs. Bruce's empathy brought tears to her eyes.

"I just made some shortbread, and there's cake, too," Mrs. Bruce said. "Cake and prayer, always a good combination."

"Mrs. Kennedy, you have built a valuable property," Mr. Bruce said, a forkful of cake poised in the air. "There are people who will go to great lengths to take it away. I'm not optimistic, but despite my skepticism, my wife's methodology may offer the most effective strategy for now."

"Cake and prayer, depending on the situation, can be just the thing." Mrs. Bruce smiled.

Mr. Bruce put the fork in his mouth. "Mmm, lemon sponge."


En and Johanna began spending evenings in her small office. It was a game of make-believe. Still, he thought that planning the new hotel might help her keep a positive frame of mind. Mr. Bruce had told them not to expect a court date anytime soon. They would have to endure Christmas, not knowing whether they would have a roof over their heads in the new year. Imagining the hotel and garden layouts became a welcome diversion.

"Do you think Rose House could use a new roof?" she asked.

"It can wait a season, and wouldn't it be more fun to hang wallpaper?"

"It would," she said. "How about some of that flocked style, maybe in red?"

"Johanna, everything can't be red."

"What?" she said. "But you have red silk all over the shed … you know, the shack outside that I can't get you to abandon?"

"I like it there."

"We won't argue about it again," she said. "At least tell me: is the stove heating properly now?"

"It's very warm."

"Good, but speak up if it goes out," she said. "Now, let's think about colors. We have yellow and pink at Rose House, purple at Butterwort House, and white at Lily House—although it shows dirt."

"Oh, that reminds me," En said, "Johnny and I divided the bulbs from the Lily house walkway. We replanted, but we could use several dozen more iris bulbs."

"You two are quite a team," she said. "Do you think next spring we might plant a flowerbed that is only green and white? I was thinking hostas for the border, and plants with white blooms: peonies, clematis, carnations, gladiolas, and baby's breath."

"We could also use lily of the valley, daisies, irises, Sweet William," En said. "And dogwood or white cherry trees, for height."

"It would be lovely," Johanna said. "Something will always be in bloom."

Companionship after sunset was a luxury for En, having had so little time over the years with family. He spent his days anticipating what to ask her, what he could say to make her laugh. Each night he waited anxiously through supper. He was glad she seemed to find it easier to spend time with the boys, but he often grew impatient when she didn't come directly to the study after tucking them in.

One night he intended to show her designs for the green-and-white garden. He heard her say goodnight to the boys, but instead of coming to join him, she walked down the back staircase and talked with Tilly about napkin rings and nonsense.

The conversation went on and on. His irritation grew to indignation. When she finally came, he decided not to share the layout.

"And what do you have for me tonight, my favorite physician and coolie?"

Michael called him Doc Coolie, but she named him En Charles. Coolie was a slur, especially under the circumstances. "Johanna, I am not a coolie." His jaw tightened.

"Why, En, I was just—"

"I am not a coolie, to you or anyone."

"Oh, En, I've wounded you," Johanna said. "I was just teasing. Now I realize it wasn't funny. I'm sorry. Did you get the green-and-white garden done?"

"Not yet," En said. "I will take my leave for this evening. Goodnight, Miss Johanna."

When he got to the shed, he was vibrating with anger. Back in the mining camp, having an Irishman call him Doc Coolie was flattering; it singled him out for recognition and appreciation. But Johanna's use of the word had a different meaning and was inexcusable. The first months here, he had been faceless and nameless, which suited him then. He had done better alone, believing he would never again have feelings for anyone. Then he got sucked in and lost his sense of the divide between them—giving too much, being too available. He thought she related to him as, if not an equal, at least someone who was not a servant. Yet she kept him waiting, and then the indignity of that word. He had misjudged, forgotten that white women saw only what they had been taught to see.

Johanna decided to surprise the boys with a puppy for Christmas. TC would be ten and Johnny eight in the coming year; they were old enough to take care of an animal. The puppy could distract them from the harrowing past and be at their side for the uncertain future.

The puppy stayed with Michael and Kathleen for the few days before Christmas. The Farrell family brought him over as a Christmas morning surprise. Johanna heard the girls downstairs.

"Walk on tiptoe," she heard one of them whisper and then laughter. She left her bedroom and found the boys at the top of the stairs.

"Someone's there. Can we go downstairs now?" Johnny asked.

"Wait here until I light the candles."

She found Molly and Margaret in the parlor, trying to fit the wriggling puppy into a stocking.

"It's not working, Auntie Johanna," Molly said.

"Maybe just hold him?"

Margaret gave one more push, and suddenly the puppy was swallowed inside the red fabric. The girls turned him face up.

"Ready?" Johanna asked.

The girls nodded.

"Boys, it looks like Santa has been here. You can come down now."

TC and Johnny flew to the bottom of the stairs, where the girls huddled around the stocking. Johnny was immediately suspicious. "What do you have there?"

TC ran ahead. The girls put the wriggling stocking into his arms. A black cocker spaniel puppy swam his way up and out. He bounced on the floor and ran in circles, licking the children's hands and yipping.

"Is the puppy for us?" Johnny picked up the wriggling animal.

"He is," Johanna said.

The puppy jumped out of Johnny's arms and squatted.

"No," Johanna called. "Take him outside. Fast!"

TC moved to scoop up the puppy, but it was too late.

"Well, I guess that's working," Michael said. "I'll get a rag."

The boys took him outside. When they returned a few minutes later the puppy's fur was covered in snow.

"He looks like a snowball," Johnny said. "Can that be his name?"

"Snowball? For a black dog?" TC nuzzled the puppy. "It's perfect."

After they exchanged gifts, they sat down for Christmas breakfast. There was no question whether En would join this holiday. Despite his reticence lately, he had agreed to make the children his sticky rice and dumplings for Christmas breakfast. They ate En's delicious dish along with the eggs, pancakes, and scrapple.

The Farrells packed up and were gone soon after the meal. With the puppy and seven children, it had been a frenetic few hours. Johanna was glad they'd left early. She was exhausted from the demands of the season and, more so, the relentless anxiety.

The boys had new things to occupy them: books and a set of marbles. They took turns going outside with the puppy. En did not join them for supper, and the boys played quietly until bedtime.

After tucking them in, Johanna sat on her bedroom rocker, too weary to go downstairs for a cup of tea. Although she liked an evening to herself, the eerie quiet at Butterwort unsettled her. None of the rooming houses was ever silent: there were always low tones of conversation and late at night guests would cough or slide a suitcase across the floor. She should enjoy the peace and be grateful for the shelter.

She hoped the boys would have good memories of this Christmas. She had wonderful recollections of the holiday when she was growing up—especially of the years they'd had money for sugar, yarn, and fabric to make gifts. One of her favorite memories—she must have been about ten—was of coming home after the last day of school before the holiday recess. The parlor smelled of fresh pine. Her mother made cookies in the kitchen and gave her paper to cut snowflakes for the tree. As she and her sister hung their lacy ornaments, the holiday stretched before her: school was a distance too far to contemplate and her family was so close. She hoped her boys would reminisce someday, even about the Christmas their father was missing. Perhaps the puppy would be the memory they kept in their hearts.

But this would not be a Christmas she would recall with fondness. She had to work hard to keep her sadness at bay, to live in the present when all she could think about was what the future held.

Everything was off this year, except the numbers for the business. The caroling parties generated more guests than they'd expected. They managed to accommodate them and turn a profit. The Christmas party hosted at Rose House was successful, too. Even though the space limited them to a buffet, rather than a sit-down dinner, it turned out that the guests preferred mingling. The eager salesmen flooding the town to make connections had a great time.

Everyone who attended the parties knew the court date was set for January and that a judge hearing the case might signal her ability to keep the property. Vendors and business owners stopped demanding upfront payment and extended credit. She doubted it was because of holiday goodwill. If she prevailed, so would her commerce. She hinted that she was well positioned to win as often as she could.

Privately, Mr. Bruce's opinion had modified only slightly. He said she would get her day in court, and the insurance policy naming her as administrator strengthened her position, but as he suspected, the copy of Judge Doyle's will that he reviewed was airtight. The court would favor giving the estate to the Church, especially if—as Bruce suspected—whoever was behind this challenge was getting a kickback.

The oddest part of Christmas hadn't been the shadow cast when Connor disappeared, but how little he was missed. No one mentioned his absence. She wondered if Connor had decided to go off on his own, and whether he would return with fistfuls of cash, ready to become a committed partner in business and life. He had not shown initiative since they'd left Liverpool, except perhaps at the bar, and in retrospect, that had been less about supporting the family and more about looking good in the eyes of the men. It was hard to imagine he had the fortitude to seek a fortune. But where else could he be?

She got up and poured herself a small whiskey from a bottle she kept at the top of her wardrobe. The taste reminded her of the night with En. She had to admit that part of her melancholy was because he was so distant. She missed their conversations and the way his head nodded up and down with enthusiasm, offering good advice on everything from running the hotel to playing marbles. She wondered if her thoughtless use of the word "coolie" was the reason. She had apologized again, and although he had said it was fine, she sensed he had neither forgiven nor forgotten. True, they had been busy with holiday events, but she also noted that he was around less. He worked on projects well past the time he might have stopped for the day and spent more time on repairs in the rooming houses or outside. He was avoiding her. She didn't miss Connor or Thomas, but she did miss En, especially knowing he was so near.

She wanted to cry thinking about how rude he'd been this past week. Even this morning, he had gifts for the children, and a lovely wooden bowl for Kathleen and Michael, but nothing for her. She hoped that in the jumble of gift exchange no one had noticed her disappointment. When she saw he wasn't going to give her anything, she nudged the gift she had for him beneath the sofa. She wasn't sure how much he had told others about his desire to learn Western medicine, but she suspected it was one reason he'd endured the painful stretching of his hands and fingers. She had found a book on Western pharmacology that she thought he would like. After everyone left, she retrieved it from the hiding place.

She was tired of him ignoring her. Even if he behaved as a thoughtless friend, she was a bigger person. She would show him; she would give him her gift. It was still early, and she was certain he would still be awake.

She looked outside, saw light snow blanketing the front lawn, and draped a shawl around her shoulders. She had covered the book in lavender paper and slipped it underneath the wool to keep it dry. The cardboard soles of her slippers crunched through the snow accumulating on the path. If they were ruined, it was too late to turn back. She hesitated at En's door. Red light shone through the curtained window. Should she disturb him? The last time she had been in his shed was following the fire. Once she had arranged for his burn care, she had not returned. They never discussed it, but she thought he appreciated her decision to give him privacy.

She stood, unsure, when En opened the door, standing naked from the waist up, holding a struggling puppy.

"Oh, so the boys gave you the first night with the puppy?"

"They did." He didn't look unhappy about it.

"That isn't why they got a puppy; they will take him from now on."

"I offered."

"Still, it's their dog."

"Miss Johanna, excuse me, I opened the door because Snowball needs to go out." En placed the puppy on the snow. Snowball ducked between En's legs and ran back to the warmth of the shed.

"Snowball prefers being warm tonight."

"Ah, yes," he said. "And I think Black Bunny would have been a better name."

"Probably," she said. A gust of wind blew through her. "En, I have something for you, a Christmas gift. Perhaps you would be kind enough to extend the warmth of your shed?"

"Please, yes." He stood aside. He took a shirt off the bed and lifted his arms to put it on. She stared at his broad chest and the hair under his arms. She was sorry when the shirt covered his golden skin. Her eyes wandered down to where the drawstring held his pajama pants closed.

"I have a gift also," En said. "I had it with me this morning, but then I thought it unwise, with everyone there."

She felt a beat of happiness. The stove glowed warm. They were together, inside the coziness of his shed. It was Christmas; no one would disturb them. Heat poured from the grate, flames bathing them in peach-colored light. En pulled out a chair for her and she sat. When he reached over her to retrieve a small box from the shelf above her, his body so close, she ached to touch him.

He sat across from her on the bed, the only other seat available.

"Me first," she said. She handed En the book. He unwrapped it, and when he saw the subject matter, she could tell he was pleased.

"But this is too expensive."

"It is what you need to learn. Is it the right book?"

"Yes, it is exactly what I am looking for. I know my herbs, but not the medicines of this country. Thank you. I am honored by the gift. It will help me to practice medicine again." He smiled at her. She couldn't look away. "And for you." He gave her the small box.

She lifted the lid. Wrapped inside a square of silk was a pearl necklace. "Oh, En, how beautiful." She held it up to her neck.

"Here, let me," En said. He stepped behind her, pulled her braid to one side, and fastened the necklace. She reached up to finger the rope of pearls and felt his hands gently pressing on her shoulders. He bent his head and brushed his lips against the nape of her neck.

Johanna didn't move. She felt his breath and then his palm rotating her torso toward him. He kissed her, this time fully on the lips. She embraced him, and still kissing her, he lifted her to his bed. She fell back against the silk coverlet. He was next to her, lifting her skirts. He wedged his fingers under her garter. His touch was like sandpaper against her thigh. He made little progress with her undergarments. She reached up, pushed his hands aside, and undid the garters. He raised himself off her for the few seconds it took for him to open the drawstring on his pajamas. He did not enter her right away. His knowledge of the female far surpassed anything in her experience. For the first time, she understood what Kathleen had alluded to when she spoke about Michael's skill as a lover. No wonder they had so many babies.

Johanna did not think and simply responded. When she finally said, "Have mercy," she could see En grin. Then she delighted in his full weight on top of her.

Afterward, they stayed entwined, listening to the puppy's shallow panting. Warm currents of air wafted around the room.

"Did you ever think, when you first came here, that one day we would find ourselves together, like this?" she asked.

"Not at all. It can be dangerous for a man like me to look at a woman like you. I would not have entertained so much as kissing you, except perhaps in my dreams."

"You weren't attracted to me?"

"I tried not to think about it."

"Can you guess when I was first attracted to you?"

"Ha, not at all. I can't even believe you are now."

"How could you doubt it?"

"Indeed. So, when was it?"

"We were in the cellar, surrounded by the guns. You had just delivered baby Charlie. I thought you were so kind and capable. Then you struck a match, and I looked at your arms." She ran her hand over his bicep. "I thought, I'm in this basement scared out of my mind, but I'm with such a strong man."

"But could you see me as a lover then?"

"We both had other things on our minds, but I remember I did feel something. I take it you didn't?"

"I was just trying to survive."

"Of course, you had just lost your wife and child," she said.

"I truly never thought …" He stopped.

"That you would be close to anyone again?"

"Yes. Plus, you were worlds away from me. I did think you were lovely. I found it hard to look at you or speak. Don't you remember I was tongue-tied?"

"I thought it was the language barrier, or that you hadn't spent much time around women."

"I was nervous for many reasons, but you took my breath away, long before I could admit it, even to myself."

"I'm sure those first few months you were grieving. I'm astounded at how you got through each day. You had more strength than I even knew."

"I've felt that way about you, especially after the fire and leading up to the hearing. I watched you get good at fighting."

"Thanks to you. You cheered me on, believed in me."

"I still do." He kissed her.

"You know, it was the same for me, that night, after you threw Thomas out. I'd always thought men should have that kind of response, but you were the first man in my life who acted."

"I was drawn to you for much the same reason. My grandmother was strong like that. She used to tell me that women are like willow trees."

"Are there many willow trees in China?"

"Yes, by the rivers. They are elegant, even in a powerful wind. Their movement is dignified."

"Is that why they are like women?"

"Yes—strength with a supple grace—Nai Nai, my grandmother, called it feminine beauty. Willows look fragile; they bow but never break. They kiss the earth, like the hem of nature's garment, but they rise again, no matter how much they have been battered. Their roots are strong enough to crack walls and drain rice paddies, too."

"I would have liked your grandmother."

"And she would have liked you." He pulled her closer.

The flame on the candle flickered. Outside, the snow turned to icy hail. They lay together, cocooned in their frozen castle shed.

"Merry Christmas, En."

Pellets of ice danced above their heads, celebrating all that was good in the world. She held her breath, listening to his heart beat.

# CHAPTER THIRTEEN

# NEW YEAR

**Nanticoke, Pennsylvania, January 1884**

Mother Agnes waited for TC in her office. The overstuffed sofa hit her at just the wrong spot, pinching her back. She placed a rolled-up blanket at the base of her spine and tried to shift to a comfortable position. She lay back and closed her eyes. The discomfort subsided for a few seconds, but the twinge would intensify if she didn't move again. She didn't think a pulled muscle took weeks to heal, but what else could it be? Was it her imagination, or was it getting worse?

She hoped school was now a refuge rather than a trauma for TC. Today would be their first time together since before Christmas. As they did each Wednesday, she and TC would spend an hour reading and then share lunch, just the two of them. One of the best parts of working with boys like TC was the pleasure of reading together, as entertaining for her as it was for her pupil. She wondered how he'd fared over the holiday.

Removing TC from Sister Mary Catherine's classroom the previous school year had been a turning point for him. He was thriving in his new classroom, his reading level now well past the McGuffey Readers. He was not only an exceptional young man; he was also a resilient one. When children succeed at reading, the recognition from teachers and families reinforces their efforts in all subjects.

She heard the door open, and Mrs. Heart said, "Don't get up, Mother. I'll bring TC to you."

"Good day, Mother," TC said, standing in front of her, a good inch taller but still a beanpole. He gave her one of his beatific smiles; the devotion in his eyes brought back her lifelong desire to have a child of her own. She would have wanted a son exactly like TC: handsome and kind. She resisted the temptation of regret; she had many blessings in her life. If her beloved husband hadn't fallen down a mineshaft at the age of twenty-four, she might have had a child. Instead, the Lord had called her and bestowed on her the privilege of raising many sons and daughters. She was grateful for what God had bestowed.

"Did you have a nice Christmas?" She adjusted the blanket, relaxing into the few moments of respite.

"We got a puppy," TC said. He sat down and handed her a book. "And I read the Hans Christian Andersen stories you lent me."

"A puppy, how wonderful," Mother Agnes said. "And how did you like Hans Christian Andersen?"

"Pretty good. *The Emperor's New Clothes* was funny, but I still pick *Arabian Nights* as my favorite."

"Let's see what you think of *The Strange Case of Dr. Jekyll and Mr. Hyde*," she said, removing the book from a stack on the table. "You are such a good reader by now, I'll just listen."

"But I like it when you do voices," TC said.

"Then I'll read too. Before we start, how are things at home?"

"Okay, I guess." He twisted his hands. "Ma is really busy—proba-bly not a good time for another visit, what with the court case and all."

"Of course." She smiled. "I won't need to come back any time soon, but it was fun to share your success with your mother. She's so proud of you."

TC squirmed, lowering his head to hide his smile.

"But do tell me, this court case? I haven't heard much."

"I'm not supposed to talk about it," TC said, "but Father Ryan wants all the houses and the hotel, too, so he can give them to the Church. He told Ma that Mr. Walsh said so."

"Really?" Mother Agnes worried Father Ryan's self-proclaimed role as defender of the Irish—when he was furthering his own ambi-tions—might be getting out of hand. "I didn't think Mr. Walsh was close to Father Ryan, or the Church."

"Me neither. Mr. Walsh said priests were pathetic mongrels, always begging for scraps from people too poor to have any to throw away," TC said. "Beg pardon, talking about a priest like that." He took a gulp of milk.

"It's best not to repeat that kind of talk," Mother Agnes said. "And what do you think will happen?"

"We might have to move to the poorhouse," TC said. He scrubbed at a dribble of milk soaking into his shirt.

"Well, the Lord has his ways," Mother Agnes said. "Even with priests."

## Nanticoke, Pennsylvania, February 1884

Father Ryan had attended some of the Molly Maguire trials, held in larger and more imposing courtrooms, where Lady Justice seldom smiled on the Irish. This county court was a dressed-up square box with cheap oak wainscoting nailed on the walls. The desk where the judge would preside was mounted on a plywood riser. Father Ryan sat next to Judge Doyle at a table. Johanna and her lawyer—a man radiating with vitality not generally associated with defenders of the Irish—sat at a similar one to their left. Spectators were crammed into five rows of benches behind a rail. Father Ryan recognized some of Johanna's employees and a few of her business associates.

"All rise." The bailiff stood guard by the judge's chambers. "This court is now in session, Honorable Judge Stephen Tippet presiding."

Judge Tippet took his place, scrutinizing the assembly. He took off his glasses and polished them on his robe. "Doyle, that you?" he said. "My God, it is. Good to see an old friend."

"Nice to see you too, Steve," Judge Doyle said.

"Not quite the same without your sparkling wit around here," Judge Tippet said.

"Did my best to make a tough job easier," Doyle said. "You have my admiration for your good work, despite the thankless task of managing criminals."

"Thanks, that means a lot from one of our own. And is that Father Ryan? Another outstanding member of our community," Judge Tippet said, returning his glasses to the tip of his long nose.

Father Ryan suppressed a self-satisfied smile. Johanna looked nervous, and there was no need to signal how the judge's greeting gratified him. This was going to be too easy.

"Now, let's see what we have here." Tippet shuffled through his papers. "Disputed will? This shouldn't take too long. Bailiff, call the first witness."

"The court calls Mrs. Tilly O'Brian."

Father Ryan turned to watch Tilly, wearing a voluminous yellow dress, struggle forward. Father Ryan hoped she would remember his admonition to stick only to the subject matter of the will.

"Please raise your right hand," the bailiff said, holding a Bible. Tilly rested her palm on top.

"Do you solemnly swear that the testimony you are about to give is the truth, the whole truth, and nothing but the truth?"

"I do." Tilly sat, perched in the witness box like a plump canary, her ample bosom spilling over a wide sash, the neckline highlighting her décolletage. A large cross, suspended from a gold chain, dangled between her breasts.

Father Ryan recalled the day Tilly had come to the rectory, a few months after Mr. Walsh's death. She had been tentative at first, but once she got started, there was no stopping her rant about how poorly treated she had been. He'd had no interest in any of her absurd stories. She spoke of how Johanna had forced her to serve a yellow man, implying there was something unsavory going on between the Celestial and Johanna. How absurd. When she added, "And he wasn't the first man—" Father Ryan interrupted to ask about the hotel and rooming houses. What was her understanding of the ownership since Mr. Walsh's passing?

As he listened, he gauged how easily Tilly might take direction, especially if he offered the vindication she needed. Had the Lord sent her as an instrument to further his plan?

The donation of Walsh's estate would build his empire. With the sale of the hotel and properties, Father Ryan could make improvements in Wilkes-Barre and Nanticoke that had been a long-held dream. He could expand the charity gifts of food and medicine to the destitute. He might set up a home for the fallen young girls—perhaps even an orphanage. They could make money on adoptions and find good Catholic homes for the children, too. Then he would develop his masterpiece: he already had some preliminary drawings to spruce up the rectory, perhaps with a tasteful addition of a small art gallery. Of course, he wanted what was in Johanna's best interest, too. She couldn't possibly run that hotel and the rooming houses. The level of acumen was beyond any woman. The business community would roll right over her.

He was impatient to get this resolved. If the property eventually went to the Church, he had the responsibility to preserve the current value, not let her destroy the business before he could find a buyer. Because Doyle was managing the Walsh estate, it was easy to copy the man's signature. The important thing was not how this happened but that it was done for the good of all.

The notion of having Tilly testify that she'd witnessed the signing came to him during her visit. Her lack of sophistication made her believable. Her testimony would be icing on the cake.

When he'd first approached her, Tilly had no idea what he was talking about. He took his time, reassuring and praising. Soon, she was volunteering her own recollections, Doyle asking for more pudding, the sound of pen on paper. Of course, she had been there. And now here she was, testifying.

"And so, Tilly," Judge Doyle said. "May I call you Tilly?"

"Yes, sir."

Each time Doyle spoke, he baptized Tilly with a spray of saliva. Father Ryan applauded the woman's ability to resist taking out a handkerchief.

"How long did you work for Mr. Walsh?"

"Almost a year."

"And you were close to Mr. Walsh?"

"I was, sir." She fingered her necklace. Gold had been a good choice, as well as the large cross. When Father Ryan gave it to her, he told her it was the least he could do to thank her for doing the right thing and suggested she wear the cross as a demonstration of her piety. She had been overcome with gratitude.

"Mr. Walsh was a fine employer." She released her fingers, and the cross swayed between the mounds. It was possibly having a positive effect on Judge Tippet. The necklace had been an inspiration.

She was deferential at first, explaining how hard she'd worked and about the difficult conditions after the hotel fire, but soon indignation took over, and she recounted the indignity of serving the Chinese man and the rumors about Johanna.

"To the matter before the court, can you tell us your understanding of the hotel's ownership?" Doyle interrupted her.

Father Ryan chuckled to himself. Even Doyle couldn't control where this woman went with her fanciful stories. Doyle limped over to the witness box, probably to see if his physical presence would reel her in. The ten steps winded him. Doyle caught his breath and assumed the posture of a predator. Father Ryan wanted to shout, "Don't stare at her cleavage," but there was nothing he could do about the man's lechery.

"Was there a time—an evening last year—when Father Ryan visited Mr. Walsh?"

"There was," Tilly said. "I served them dinner in Mr. Walsh's office."

"And did you know why they were meeting?" Doyle rested his hands on the railing. Father Ryan hoped Doyle had enough stamina to remain upright.

"It was to sign Mr. Walsh's will," she said. "He was getting tired of her goings-on with the men." She gave a meaningful look to Judge Tippet.

Father Ryan had been clear: nothing but the will. He felt the heat rise under his collar. He did not intend to sully Johanna. There was no need to ruin her reputation or draw attention to Thomas. And the fantasy about En was ridiculous; it hurt Tilly's credibility.

Mr. Bruce stood. "Objection. Hearsay."

"This is a preliminary hearing," Judge Tippet said. "We'll dispense with formality. Just get on with it."

"You believed Mrs. Kennedy had fallen out of favor with Mr. Walsh?" Judge Doyle asked.

"Objection." Mr. Bruce stood up again.

"Mr. Bruce, we are just presenting facts today. I don't have time for this up-and-down nonsense," Judge Tippet said. "You'll get your turn soon enough. Judge Doyle, proceed."

Bruce sat down.

"During the time you knew Mr. Walsh—" Judge Doyle was overtaken by a fit of coughing. He held a hand up and returned to the table. Father Ryan poured Doyle a glass of water. Doyle drained the glass. "My apologies to the court," he said, clearing phlegm.

"Tilly, were you aware of any reason why his opinion of Mrs. Kennedy might have changed?"

"I never knew what he saw in her. She was a hussy from day one. But to answer your question," she said, nodding to the judge, "before her husband was thrown in jail—suspected of being a ringleader of the Mollies, he was—Miss Johanna would entertain a certain gentleman caller."

Father Ryan flashed her a stern look, and Tilly averted her eyes. She was deliberately defying him. "But when she started carrying on with the Chinaman"—Tilly rolled her eyes—"that was when Mr. Walsh got suspicious." There was a buzz in the courtroom.

"But to be clear, it is your conviction today that Mr. Walsh intended to leave his property to the Church, and you further certify to the court that you witnessed the signature of documents formally enshrining that intention?" Doyle said.

"Yes," said Tilly. Father Ryan thought she looked a little sheepish, but then she added, "So help me God."

"Thank you, Tilly," Doyle said. "No more questions."

Father Ryan supposed Tilly had served her purpose, but he was irritated she had not followed his directions. He had not intended to publicly humiliate Johanna, but he could see the shame on her face. He had offered her a way out; going to court had been her choice.

Mr. Bruce stood and took several steps toward Tilly. "Good afternoon, Tilly," he said, smiling. "Thank you for being here today."

Bruce was acting like her best friend. Father Ryan hoped she'd see through the man's hypocrisy. "Did Mr. Walsh ever discuss with you

Johanna's relationship with either of the men you have mentioned?" Mr. Bruce said. "I remind you that you are under oath."

"No, of course not. He wasn't that kind of person."

"And you say that you personally witnessed Mr. Walsh signing documents the night in question?" Mr. Bruce said.

"I did." Father Ryan felt a bubble of satisfaction.

"And how do you know what they were signing?"

"It was Mr. Walsh's will."

"You saw the papers?" Mr. Bruce said.

"Yes."

"Then perhaps you could read a little from this document now?" he said.

Tilly flushed. "I did not—I mean—I wouldn't read something on my employer's desk."

"Can you read, Tilly?" Mr. Bruce asked. She stared at him.

Jesus, Mary, and Joseph—had it never occurred to Doyle to find out if Tilly could read? Father Ryan's heart drummed in his chest.

"Shall I repeat the question?"

Tilly looked at Judge Tippet.

"Tilly, you are required to answer," Tippet said.

"I can read some," she said.

Mr. Bruce held the document out to her. She did not take it. "Not anything fancy like that."

"You can't say with certainty that you witnessed Mr. Walsh signing a will because you can't read the will," Mr. Bruce said.

"No," she said. "But what else could it have been?"

"No further questions."

Father Ryan watched Tilly step down. She looked like a schoolgirl who'd just lost the spelling bee. As Father Ryan observed her walk past the railing and take a seat, he noticed the doors at the back of the courtroom swing open and Mother Agnes enter. Tilly slid over to make room for the nun, but Mother Agnes walked toward the group of supporters sitting behind Johanna.

"Your Honor, I would like to add two names to our witness list," Mr. Bruce said.

Father Ryan stared at Mother Agnes. She met his gaze. He looked away first, but then it hit him—two names? Behind Mother Agnes was his lover. Father Neil looked directly ahead. Father Ryan could barely breathe. He leaned over and whispered to Doyle, "This is trouble. Can we stop those two?"

"Jesus," Judge Doyle said. "What now?"

"Don't let this happen. They can't testify," Father Ryan said to Doyle. "We'll lose."

Judge Doyle scowled and reluctantly hauled his balloon-like body out of the chair. "Judge Tippet, it's entirely too late in these proceedings to add witnesses," Doyle said.

"New information has just come to our attention," Bruce said. "I would be happy to share it with the permission of the court, or in your chambers if Judge Doyle and Father Ryan prefer."

Doyle rotated toward Father Ryan. Father Ryan shook his head. "No?" Doyle rolled his eyes. "Jesus." He stood to address Judge Tippet. "My apologies, might we have a short recess?"

"I'll allow you the lunch hour, Justin, for old time's sake. Use my private conference room if you'd like," Judge Tippet said. "I expect both parties will be ready when we return."


"Jesus Christ, what just happened?" Doyle said. His spittle dotted the table in Judge Tippet's private conference room.

"I am a priest. There are things told to me in the confessional that I can't reveal." Father Ryan hoped this excuse would buy him time to come up with something better.

"In the last two minutes, something happened that prevents you from testifying?" Judge Doyle said. "That priest and nun, did they jog your memory?"

"Something like that," Father Ryan.

"I line up investors, arrange for this woman's idiot husband to get released from prison, take her to court—which has not exactly made me popular with the Irish"—Judge Doyle hawked into his handkerchief—"and now you tell me to drop it?"

"It's my moral obligation. I'm sorry."

"You're growing a conscience *now*?" Doyle spat. "I'll tell you what my conscience is telling me: it's time to go over your head. I'm pretty cozy with Bishop McCarthy, the one who has his position in Philly, thanks to me."

"Then I have no choice," Father Ryan said. "I will tell the truth."

"You would admit to perpetrating a fraud?" Doyle said. "Whatever they have on you must be big."

"Yes, Doyle, it is," Father Ryan said. He raised his eyes to the ceiling as if listening to the voice of God. "I may be late in doing what is right, but it's time."

"What the hell does that mean?" Judge Doyle made a series of guttural sounds.

"Honestly, Judge? I have nothing to lose," Father Ryan said. "And if you challenge me, I will be forced to disclose other business transactions."

"You can't prove anything."

"Possibly not, but the notoriety will sink you. You have a less-than-sterling reputation."

Doyle steadied himself through another spasm of coughing and said, "I'll be goddamned if you'll get away with this." He stood up and limped toward the door. "You can say goodbye to becoming a monsignor anywhere in the Pope's Pennsylvania." He stormed out.

Father Ryan rested his forehead on a stack of file folders. The cardboard felt smooth and cool. He was ready to surrender, was tired of all the lies. He would confess. He would serve only the poor. He felt relief flood into his soul until he thought, if he were to follow God's commandments, he would have to give up Father Neil. The love he had for Father Neil—even if he never acted on it again—was not something he could forsake. He searched his mind to think how he might at least save Father Neil. If today revealed the truth, he would insist he had forced the encounter. Perhaps that would allow Father Neil to keep his position and his reputation.

Mother Agnes gripped the rosary in her pocket, the wooden beads worn smooth. She had been praying this day would never come, and now here she was, in the lobby of the courthouse. Father Neil stood next to her in the group surrounding Johanna, who was pale and holding back tears. Mother Agnes hoped she had made the right decision and that the outcome would help keep Johanna and her boys secure. She could think of no other way but through the valley of the shadow.

Once TC told her about Johanna's dire situation, she immediately suspected Father Ryan's duplicity. He had always been hard to love, yet his role as senior priest demanded her obedience. She would not judge Father Ryan, or Father Neil, but she was not prepared to permit a miscarriage of justice. She also believed that forgiveness created a path that allowed miracles. She hoped one day at least all would be forgiven—if not forgotten.

After she had prayed on the matter, she made the trip to Hazelton. The meeting with Mr. and Mrs. Bruce had been disconcerting. Unlike many nuns, because she had been married and widowed before joining the convent, she knew exactly what she and the sister had stumbled upon that night with the two men. Talking about it was another matter.

It was raining the day she had the convent caretaker drive her to the Bruces' home. Mrs. Bruce had welcomed her to the snug parlor, tea laid out on a table next to a plate of scones, Devonshire cream, and lemon curd.

After the formalities, Mr. Bruce balanced his teacup on his knee and looked up at her. "You mentioned in your note that you had some information that might shed light on the validity of Mr. Walsh's will?"

"Yes," she said. She felt the color rush to her face. It took several starts, but finally she managed, "About these two priests, and their relationship, I have reason to believe ..."

Mr. Bruce sat with a pen poised over his notebook. "Yes, go on."

Mother Agnes made several more attempts. "It's about those two," she said again.

Finally, Mrs. Bruce, her cheeks bright pink, said, "Kevin, could you join me in the hall?"

When they returned, Mr. Bruce moved his chair closer to Mother Agnes. "I'm certain this is difficult for you, Mother. My wife has suggested what you are struggling to describe. You witnessed Father Ryan and Father Neil—please excuse my indelicacy—engaged in unnatural acts?"

"Yes, Mr. Bruce," Mother Agnes said, letting out a breath of relief.

"And you have seen evidence of this with your own eyes?"

"Yes, I have."

"And are they aware that you witnessed them together?"

"They are."

She had hoped to feel better—the truth shall set you free—but instead she was awash with guilt. She had never intended to expose these men. They were good priests, and their private torment was none of her business. The older she got, and the more people confided in her, the more compassion she had for the heavy burdens so many carried. Men were encumbered with sexual urges. Regardless of what attracted them, they did their best to resist. Everyone gave in to lust, especially when young.

"I see," Mr. Bruce pushed his chair back from her. "Well, let's think about how this might come to light."

"I would prefer it never does," Mother Agnes said. "Can that be avoided?"

"I don't know," Mr. Bruce said. "But, if necessary, are you prepared to speak publicly?"

She felt sick, but she had made a prayerful decision—not a happy one, but in her heart, the right one. "I am," she said.

Although Kathleen offered her bread and fruit, Johanna was in a state of panic—eating during the recess was not possible. She was prepared for the court to rule against her, but hearing Tilly describe her behavior was mortifying. The fact that much of what Tilly recounted was also true was something she couldn't accept about herself. She had taken not one, but two lovers. By the time Mother Agnes and Father Neil arrived, she could only think of how stupid she had been. She should have accepted the offer for a life tenancy in Butterwort. Now all would be lost.

And she was horrified to think that Michael and Kathleen—who had looked the other way with Thomas and likely guessed about En—were still defending her. Their association with her would cost them acceptance in the community and would damage the future they were hoping to build for their children. Her stomach roiled. Her ears were buzzing, and she was unable to conduct an ordinary conversation with the people around her. The bailiff announced court was reconvening and she walked, comatose with misery, back to her seat next to Mr. Bruce. She looked over and saw that the table to her right was vacant.

"Can we start up again if Father Ryan and Judge Doyle aren't present?" she asked Mr. Bruce.

He raised his eyebrows and said, "Let's see what the judge has to say."

They stood when Judge Tippet was announced. A document fluttered in his hand as he stepped on the platform and impatiently motioned for everyone to be seated. "The court has been informed that the petition of Judge Doyle and Father Ryan is withdrawn."

He consulted the paper in front of him, paused, sighed, and said, "Considering the disavowal, this court declares the documents presented by Mr. Bruce on behalf of the Walsh estate valid."

He took off his spectacles and looked directly Johanna. She sat up, her limbs trembling. "Mrs. Kennedy, once the papers are filed with the court, you will become the rightful owner of the land where Mr. Walsh's hotel once stood, along with his three rooming houses, and the land at Lake Nuangola. In addition, you will receive the proceeds of Mr. Walsh's bank accounts and his worldly goods."

There was a stunned hush, and then a cheer went up in the courtroom.

"Please,"—the judge rapped his gavel—"order." Johanna couldn't move. "Mrs. Kennedy, I hereby name you the beneficiary of the Walsh estate, and consistent with the stipulations in the insurance documents, the court names you as representative of the hotel and beneficiary of all insurance policies. Mr. Bruce, will you file the appropriate documents with the court?"

"I will, Your Honor," Mr. Bruce stood. "And on behalf of my client, we appreciate the attention of the court and your ruling today."

Judge Tippet glowered, started to speak, but then shook his head and rapped the gavel. "Court dismissed."

Johanna sat stunned. Mr. Bruce was smiling at her, and soon his wife was at their side, hugging Johanna. "My dear, this is wonderful news." She leaned close to Johanna and said, "And don't let Tilly's lies mar this wonderful gift. You are safe, and I'm certain this is exactly what Mr. Walsh wanted."

Mrs. Bruce was still hugging her when Mother Agnes and Kathleen joined in. Johanna relaxed into the women's embrace. She didn't yet feel truly safe, but she did feel some relief. Michael pushed his way between the women and nearly lifted her off her feet. Johanna saw En, standing near the back doors. Their eyes met above the crowd. For a moment, it was just the two of them. She mouthed, "Thank you."

He held his hand over his heart and then gave her a thumbs-up.

They made their way out of the building, where Johanna was surrounded by well-wishers. Some of the hotel staff were wiping their eyes. Several salesmen, who previously had harassed her for payment, shook her hand and said they would be calling. The properties were hers; the business would move forward. She wondered if, for that reason alone, this community would look past Tilly's salacious testimony.

As if she knew Johanna's mind, Kathleen whispered, "Don't worry. They might have believed gossip about you and Thomas, but the idea of En was so far-fetched that they don't trust anything Tilly says."

"But—" Johanna said.

"I know. Only love is blind, but the prospect of filling their coffers keeps other things out of focus." She gave Johanna one of her mischievous grins.

Johanna was still reeling, but Kathleen was right: no one was shunning her. In fact, it appeared to be quite the opposite. It took several minutes for her to greet the throng. They seemed intent on making sure she knew their loyalty, that they had been there—perhaps only at the moment her luck changed, but they wanted credit for that at least.

After the crowd dispersed, Mother Agnes said, "I am so happy for you and what this means for your family. Father Neil and I must be going, but we will get together soon to celebrate."

"I can't thank you or Father Neil enough. Just for being there," Johanna said.

"Apparently, that's all it took," Kathleen said.

## Mountain Top, Pennsylvania, March 1884

A winding road, nestled between two mountains, led down to a valley where the city of Wilkes-Barre was expanding. No matter how exhausting the trip, whenever Father Ryan returned to his affluent parish, he felt rejuvenated. Each time he had descended the mountain, there were more city lights. The town was glowing with enterprise, bright beneath the star of his leadership—until that day in court two weeks ago.

Recently, Judge Doyle made good on his threat of revenge. Now, instead of traveling the mountain road to a golden future, Father Ryan was headed in the opposite direction, in all manner of speaking. He was assigned to St. Jude's Parish in the town of Mountain Top. His new parish didn't send a carriage, because they could ill afford one, and Father Ryan borrowed a small wagon and a nearly lame horse from the nuns. Alone on the nearly impassable road, he gave up trying to get the horse to trot. Other travelers passed him by: a metaphor for his future in this backwater community. He would be passed over again and again—the junior priest for years to come.

The tears he shed over Father Neil had long dried. Instead, with each plodding step, Father Ryan felt a helplessness that blackened to fury. Alone on the road with the sun setting behind him, he bellowed, "Why? Why, God? Why is this happening to me?"

The horse froze. Father Ryan, enraged, grabbed the whip and lashed it across the horse's flank. With each slap of the whip, he yelled, "Why, why, why?"

The horse wobbled another mile. Father Ryan finally saw signs for the church. After climbing two more steep hills, he got to the rectory, his legs and back stiff. He tied the poor horse to a pole behind the rectory and walked up to the entrance.

"You must be the new one." A disheveled woman of indeterminate age opened the door. Wrinkles grew in concentric circles around her hooked nose. She reminded him of a witch trapped in a tree trunk. "It's about time you got here," she said. "Father Ryan, right?"

"Yes, and you are?"

"Maisy. I'm the only one up this late. I'll have to wake the stable boy for your horse. Anyway, Father Kyle's gone to bed. Too bad you missed dinner, but there's some leftovers, cold shepherd's pie."

Father Ryan suddenly longed for his delectable meals and vintage wines, served by the three plump widows in Wilkes-Barre. They'd loved it when he referred to them as three wise women bearing gifts. "It is late, but I haven't eaten since breakfast," Father Ryan said. "Perhaps there is someone else who could provide a more substantial dinner?"

"Ha, someone else?" she said. "I wish. Cook, maid, and nurse to Father Kyle: you're looking at her."

"The pie will be fine."

"It's on the sideboard. Help yourself," she said. "Probably best we both get some shut-eye. Your room is the first one at the top of the stairs."

She pointed the way and disappeared.

He found the pie—more gristle than meat—and decided not to bother. The dingy room at the top of the stairs consisted of a narrow bed, dresser, and chair. His stomach growled when he lay down. He meant to get up and change into a nightshirt, but drifted off to sleep, tossing about. Finally, just before dawn, he fell into a leaden sleep. He woke with a spasm in his lower back. It took several minutes to subside, and then he stood, vowing to acquire a more accommodating bed by nightfall.

After he'd shaved and changed into his only fresh cassock—he hoped his replacement in Wilkes-Barre would be kind enough to have his other garments delivered—he found his way downstairs. Father Kyle was already seated in the dining room, gumming a spoonful of grayish oatmeal. He indicated Father Ryan should sit while he fished false teeth out of a jar next to his plate. Father Kyle stretched his mouth over the dentures. "You're, mmmm, the, mmmm, new priest?"

"I am."

"So, the higher-ups in Philly at long last have listened." He clacked his teeth into place. "I've been telling them I'm too old—I can't hear confessions. I can't hear at all, for God's sake. Look at me. How am I supposed to say Mass or officiate at weddings or funerals with this dowager's hump?"

"I'm here now," Father Ryan said.

"What? Didn't quite get that," the priest said. "Oh, never mind. Just eat. Maisy will tell you what's what."

Maisy put a bowl of oatmeal and a cup of coffee in front of Father Ryan. He was starving and shoveled a heaping spoonful into his mouth. Chewy lumps floated in a viscous liquid. Suppressing the urge to spit it out, he forced a swallow.

"Maisy will tell you all about the parish. It's not a pretty story." Father Kyle's teeth moved independently from his jaw. "Ragamuffin kids. Tattered clothes, not much food, and manners are worse." Father Kyle sucked his coffee, seepage foaming around his mouth.

"Most of our men used to have jobs in the mine—all drunkards now," the old priest said, almost as if talking to himself. "You'll learn to spot the violent ones. Their wives show up at Mass peeking through veils. Not much we can do about the black eyes or split lips, but at least you know who to avoid."

"Sounds hard," Father Ryan said.

"What? Oh, doesn't matter," Father Kyle said. "Just remember I'm still senior priest. Last guy came up here tried to change things. Hope Monsignor made it clear. I make the decisions."

"I didn't speak directly with Monsignor," Father Ryan, "but now that you brought it up, I would like to discuss sharing duties. I see on the schedule that there is a daily Mass at seven and again at five, and confessions each afternoon. Do we have another priest available if the schedule becomes taxing for me?"

"See what I mean, Maisy?" Father Kyle held out his cup for more coffee. A bored Maisy poured without looking, missing the cup and drenching the carpet. "I'm not even sure what this new guy just said, but I'd guess he's another arrogant one. Come up here, think they know better how to run my parish. No changes. Got that?"

Father Kyle spit out the teeth and dropped them back in the jar. He picked up a newspaper, shook it open, and starting reading. Father Ryan managed to eat a few more mouthfuls and resigned himself to a piece of toast and the dishwater that passed as coffee.

After breakfast, Maisy helped Father Kyle out of his chair. "It's his nap time," she said. "Why don't you go on into the office? Father Kyle's desk is the big one, but there's a small table behind the door. Use that."

Father Ryan took a second cup of coffee—at least it was hot—into the small rectory office. The room smelled as if an animal had taken up residence between the walls. He numbly reviewed stacks of paperwork and examined the worn-out, filthy vestments hanging on a coatrack. He searched for ledgers or any signs of bookkeeping. Perhaps Father Kyle kept the list of donors and donation amounts to himself, or more likely, they didn't have any benefactors. He shook his head. Good thing I'm not supposed to change anything—wouldn't know where to start.

Maisy came in. "Fair warning, it's almost nine."

"What happens at nine?"

"You'll see," she said. He heard the rectory doorbell and discovered it hailed an endless stream of parishioners who took up his morning with a nonstop litany of troubles.

Maisy brought him bread and cheese at lunch. The loaf was stale, but the cheese was passable. "Here's a list of people who need visiting," she said when she came to pick up the tray. "Father Kyle has been unable to go for a while, so visits are backed up."

She handed him a folder. "Some of these folks live up the mountain, not easy to get up there. Takes a while, but you probably can see two a day and not miss afternoon confession. We'll have to see if one of the men around here can give you a lift."

"Thank you," he said. "Anything else I should know?"

"Breakfast at six tomorrow. Don't be late again. Father Kyle let it go today, but there's no sleeping in around here," she said. "And you have Mass at five this afternoon."

After Father Ryan said Mass for the three people who showed up, he walked to the dining room. Father Kyle was already gone for the night, as was Maisy, who had left him a plate on the counter. Father Ryan was so hungry he nearly inhaled the cold slab of meat, coated with either muddy breadcrumbs or congealed gravy. There was some rather tasty applesauce. He found a bottle of wine and opened it by himself. It was swill.

## Nanticoke, Pennsylvania, March 1884

Although he had not uttered the words since their first night together, Johanna knew En loved her. It wasn't the emotional turmoil of Thomas, popping up and disappearing, or the recurring disappointments of Connor. En was steady and loyal. Their love was solid. They still worked together during the day and shared a closeness during their evening planning sessions. The architectural drawings were complete. They would break ground on the new hotel by summer.

They had decided not to risk spending nights in the shed, just to make sure no one sought to prove Tilly's accusations. She missed him, their physical intimacy, but each night resisted the urge to go to him.

Finally, after several weeks, she decided to take the risk. It was a moonless night in March when she slipped out the back door and found her way to the shed. She felt for the door handle and twisted. En was on top of his bed, reading. There were two candles flickering on the bedside table. He sat up, put down his book, and stretched his hands out to her. "I knew you were coming," he said.

She undressed them both. She could manage it faster. Then he fell onto her.

Afterward, she lay with her head against his chest, his heart the same rhythm as her own. "Ever since I found myself in this country, I have been alone," she said. "Now, I have you."

"You do," he said.

"I feel so happy. I hardly trust it."

She waited, but En didn't say anything.

"En, how do you feel? Do you trust me?"

He didn't answer right away. She thought he might have drifted off to sleep, and she was disappointed that he would not stay awake for their first night together after so long.

Then he shifted to face her. "I lost my first family when I was so young," he said. "I only had to survive. I never chose Mai Ling or Rosie. I didn't know how important they were, and then they were gone. I didn't want to live after that."

"You are never the same after a tragedy. I understand," she said. "But I had hoped you were at least happier now."

"That's my point. I do know how important you are. This is the happiest I've been, perhaps in my whole life," En said. "But what I'm saying is I know I love you. I would ask you to marry me if I could, but in our situation, we have few options."

"I know, even if Connor is declared dead," she said. "It's not what I thought my life would be, but I am happy as we are."

"A happiness that is fraught."

"It's best we don't talk about it. I can't stand to be sad right now."

"We won't, not now," he said. "And perhaps I will never be able to call you mine, but we will grow together."

"We'll always have our shed," she said.

He pulled her closer.

"Now you see why I wanted to keep living here."

## Mountain Top and the Pocono Mountains, Pennsylvania, March 1884

The monsignor did not revoke Father Ryan's scheduled retreat, perhaps because no one brought it to his attention. A month into his tenure at Mountain Top, a replacement priest arrived to cover his week away.

Father Ryan had developed a routine. He learned that he could avoid Father Kyle if he skipped breakfast and ate dinner after evening Mass. The elderly priest spent most of the day in his room, rarely coming to the office. Without consulting the senior priest, Father Ryan reduced morning Mass to Mondays and Fridays. He offered confession on alternate days and held Wednesdays for visiting parishioners. After spending an entire afternoon digging himself and his volunteer driver out of deep mud, he decided to stop the visits until better weather made the roads passable. The parish was still falling apart, and he could spend Wednesdays working on resolving some of the more pressing issues. At least he could hand over a reasonable and ordered schedule to his stand-in.

Father Ryan went to his room to pack. He had not spoken with Father Neil since they passed one another that day in court. He was tormented about what Father Neil thought of him. He could barely tolerate the prospect of seeing his lover again, but worse would be if he never did. Father Ryan was closing his carpetbag when his cheeks started to itch. He looked in the hall mirror and saw his face was streaked with ... was it dried tears? Had he been crying?

He arrived at Pocono Mountain Monastery just before supper. He was not assigned his usual room. Although austere, his cell had always been on an upper floor where he could see the meditation garden through a narrow window. He had come to enjoy the sliver of blue sky and even a sunrise, depending on the time of year. Instead, he was escorted down endless stairs and found that his room had neither a window nor ventilation. It smelled like an outhouse.

The official retreat started the next day, but in the dining hall they were serving a meal for early arrivals. The priests were already in silence. Thank goodness he didn't have to make small talk. He couldn't stop himself from scanning the room. Father Neil was not there. His chest felt leaden. Walking back to his cell, he saw a buggy pull up the drive. He was too far away to see if Father Neil was among the arrivals.

Since his move to Mountain Top, Father Ryan had been plagued by insomnia. His bad back and the straw mattress made sleeping impossible. He got up at sunrise, the stench driving him outside before early morning prayers, and walked through the deserted garden. The dormant plants, curled up in surrender under decaying leaves, reminded him of his life. He sat on a bench.

A voice interrupted his misery.

"I thought you might have chosen a different week."

He opened his eyes. The man dearest to him in the world stood less than a foot away. "Are you really here?" Father Ryan said. "And you are speaking to me?"

"I believe we have a great deal to discuss," Father Neil said. "Tonight?"

Father Ryan nodded.

"Come to my room. It's the one you had last year," Father Neil said.

Although he yearned to go after him, Father Ryan forced himself to remain seated. He watched Father Neil walk away, the fringe of blond hair visible beneath his hat. He remembered stroking those curls.

The day stretched endlessly. Mass. Prayers. Meditations. Instead of saying the rosary, Father Ryan played out various scenarios—Father Neil's decision to stop seeing him; Father Neil berating him; going to the police. As his thoughts took root, each more hellish than the last, he felt shame. Father Neil had loved him and now would want nothing to do with him.

Father Ryan spent a torturous hour waiting for vespers to end. He arrived at Father Neil's door a few minutes before lights out and knocked once. Father Neil turned the latch immediately. Father Ryan stepped into the room. Father Neil's cassock was unbuttoned several inches below his neck. Pale hair peeked under the semicircle of his loose clerical collar.

"Are you well?" Father Neil said. "You look like you've lost a good deal of weight."

"Well enough." Father Ryan said. "Not as hungry as I once was."

They sat next to each other on the bed. Father Ryan could not remember a time they had ever been like this, fully clothed, as if discussing church business.

"They banished you. Mountain Top?" Father Neil put his hands on his knees. "Astonishing and cruel. You were doing a good job and building a formidable parish in Wilkes-Barre."

"Yes, but on lies," Father Ryan said. "I admit it. I have repented, but I will never be able to make amends for the sins I've committed."

"I've tried to piece it together," Father Neil said. "Would you have destroyed a woman who deserved our help?"

"Yes."

"Did you fabricate the will with that monster, Doyle?"

"I did."

"You know it would have made the mine bosses and Doyle even richer while taking food out of the mouths of Johanna's children and her employees?" Father Neil said. "You know that? You admit that?"

"I had my reasons, not all selfish," Father Ryan said. "The Church could have used that money and property to feed and clothe many in need."

"But the property didn't belong to the Church, nor would that have been Walsh's wish."

"I know," Father Ryan said. "Of course, I know." He knew it was useless to argue. There was no excuse for his arrogance, his greed.

"It was about pride." Father Neil looked so much older.

"It was despicable. I will never forgive myself." Father Ryan put his face in his hands. "What I've done is terrible; what my life is now … and losing you."

"You think you have lost me?"

"I know I have." Father Ryan held his breath. "Isn't that right?"

"I admit, your actions make me sick at heart," Father Neil said. "And angry. But aren't we in the forgiveness business?" Father Neil said. "Your behavior was … appalling. I'm still not certain you truly understand how wrong the betrayal of Johanna, Walsh, me—and most of all, your integrity—was. Can you even begin to comprehend?"

"Perhaps not, but—"

"And I was nearly forced to speak in court, to tell the world, about us."

"Was it you or Mother Agnes who told Bruce?"

"Does it matter?" Father Neil said. "Either way, I would have told the truth. And I would again."

"It might not have changed anything, only ruined us," Father Ryan said.

"I was certain you wouldn't let that happen," Father Neil said. "The better side of you would want to protect me, and I suspect all along you had your doubts about the morality of the entire scheme. The lawyer agreed with me, or at least he thought it was the best possible outcome. I gave you a chance to do the right thing because I knew you would."

"You are intuitive about people and a better man, a better priest, than I am," Father Ryan said.

"I am a weak man, too," Father Neil said. "We are all sinners, but I have seen the good in you. The person with a small sin is as guilty as one with the darkest heart. Redemption, it's the job God sent Jesus to do."

"You forgive me?"

"I forgive you," Father Neil said. "I want you in my life, even if it's just one week each year. I will confess it, as I always do, but I can't give you up."

He stood and opened his arms. Father Ryan gazed up at Father Neil and couldn't suppress the image of Christ on the cross. They embraced, and he could feel his lover's breath, warm on his neck.

They woke at the early bell. "Good morning," Father Neil said. "How are you feeling?"

"Forgiven?" Father Ryan said. "And unworthy."

"We all are." Father Ryan could feel Father Neil, soft and nestled against his thigh. He wanted to touch him, but he had not completed his confession.

"Are you awake?"

"Yes." Father Neil put his hand on Father Ryan's buttocks.

"Not quite yet, Father Neil," Father Ryan said. "I'm afraid there is more."

Father Neil took his hand away, rolled over. He rested his head on an elbow, waiting.

"One more burden, if I may?"

Father Neil nodded.

"Remember the man I told you about, the one I might have pushed?"

"You said he stepped off that bridge," Father Neil said. "You would have stopped him if you could have; I believe that."

"I let him drink too much, practically poured it down his throat."

"But you did not intend for him to fall," Father Neil said.

"No, but I keep wondering if I should turn myself in or at least tell the widow?"

"What does she think happened?" Father Neil said. "Does she know her husband is dead?"

"She … I don't know. She probably suspects he isn't coming back. I suppose she's glad to be rid of him."

"Is it Johanna?"

"It is."

"And everyone knows you challenged the will and then withdrew the petition. They might believe you had a reason to kill her husband," Father Neil said. "Did you?"

"Absolutely not."

"Did you intend to murder him?"

"Father Neil, what are you saying? Do you think I did?"

"I don't, and I'm glad to hear you say it out loud. I only met him once, at the boy's school, but many of my parishioners spoke of him. They characterized him as easily led and on a path to destruction. His jumping only sped up an inevitable death."

"Either way, shouldn't Johanna know the truth?"

Father Neil paused. "It wouldn't bring Connor back. It also might bring her the worst possible attention, just as she is getting her business running again."

"The truth does set one free."

"This may not be the best time for her to know she is free."

"You think if she were free, she would make bad choices? You don't believe Tilly—about En, I mean?" Father Ryan laughed. "You can't possibly think Johanna … with a Chinaman? Most people don't give in to lust as easily as we have."

"You and I have our secret. What makes you think others don't have them as well?" Father Neil said.

"Maybe you're right," Father Ryan said. "Sometimes I think more goes on than we hear about in the confessional."

"And we hear enough, don't we?"

"But Johanna and En … not possible." Father Ryan sighed. "But to the matter at hand, should I tell her or wait on God's judgment?"

"Mountain Top is a prison for you, so God has already taken care of your punishment," Father Neil said. "I would let God handle the rest, too."

Father Ryan thought about kissing Father Neil to signal the conversation was over, but Father Neil started to speak again.

"I believe that Johanna and the boys will do better if their world is not disturbed right now," he said. "Suicide is a mortal sin. Knowing that Connor may have taken his own life will not bring them peace, only more pain. You have caused enough adversity for that family. You must carry your own guilt, and what happened at the bridge, to your grave."

"Perhaps I'm being selfish, wanting absolution for myself. But this is a heavy burden."

"It is. I will carry it with you. It will be penance for us both."

"That and my banishment to Mountain Top. I predict great things for you; you are the bright, upcoming future of the Church."

"You know that doesn't matter to me," Father Neil said.

"That's why it's a great thing; you'll be a benevolent king. I've been put out to pasture and will likely remain there."

"Then you must find a way to serve the Lord where he has planted you," Father Neil said. "Open to the sunshine and rain that God bestows on that mountain and see what you might cultivate."

**Nanticoke, Pennsylvania, March 1884**

From her office behind the front desk, Johanna could see Sam Kress checking in. He was elegant: an expertly trimmed moustache, a perfectly tailored suit. Johanna always made a point of welcoming special guests. She came out of her office.

"Mr. Kress," she said, "so nice to see you again. Thanks to your Mr. Bruce, we are still here."

"I played a small part," he said. "And I refuse to accept the check you sent covering Mr. Bruce's legal work. It was my investment in you."

"I'm very grateful," she said. "I can return it to you, or if you'd agree, I'd like to invest it in something good for our community."

"I'm listening," he said.

"I made an offer on those old shacks at the edge of town. They were so run down the mine owners are happy to sell them. I thought we could restore them and make them available for families who need a place to live."

"Of course, wonderful idea," he said. "I trust you to make another real estate success."

"And when we do, you will receive your share of the proceeds."

"Thank you. I hope it's the first of many joint projects."

"Me, too," Johanna said. "And I see that your five-and-dime is almost under roof."

"That's why I'm here—working on build-out specifications," he said. "In fact, the local business community has a newly formed chamber of commerce. We want to start holding a lunch each month. I suggested we ask if we might meet here?"

"Mr. Kress, you are too kind," she said. "We would be honored and will do our best to present a luncheon that does you proud."

"The food here is delicious, and I hope your customers will become my customers." He smiled. "I must be off; someone will be in touch."

Johanna waited until Mr. Kress left the hotel before she tracked En down. He was in the garden. The plans for the new hotel were only on paper, but it was possible to start on the garden right away. En spent his free time constructing the beds and laying the paths.

"That's great news," he said, moving to hug her and then stepping back. They never knew who might see.

"And when the hotel is done, we can accommodate even more chamber events."

"They should ask you to join them," En said. "You are one of the town's most successful businesses."

"Perhaps, but I think the men rather like their own company," she said.

"Anyone making money, man or woman, that's good for the town," En said.

She left him with his garden and began to think how much she would like to be included with the town's business leaders, helping to make decisions that would impact the hotel.

What became known as the Kress Luncheon turned into an exclusive club that attracted interest from as far away as Wilkes-Barre. There were no other women members, but her mother used to say, "If you can't beat 'em, join 'em." Johanna was not formally asked to belong but was visible. She was the hostess, after all. She warmly met each guest and made sure she did none of the domestic work. She didn't want the men to see her as anything but an owner. The staff took the coats and provided all of the meal service. She asked questions designed to make each man feel important, laughed appreciatively at their jokes, and on occasion, flattered an ego. When the meeting began, she quietly left the room but returned as hostess until the last guest left.

After one particularly successful luncheon, the chamber president said, "We'd like to get the little lady's view on attracting more customers to greater Nanticoke. Why don't you sit in at the next meeting?"

A month later, Johanna was an unofficial member sitting at the table next to the president of the largest bank in the area. He was middle-aged and balding, his belly pushing out the vest of his three-piece suit. He refused to relinquish his bowler hat to one of her staff, so he sat with it on his lap. He ate with gusto, managing to keep up a running monologue between forkfuls of the roast beef, aspic, and buttered bread.

"We've studied it, at the bank, back in 'seventy-three. Those speculative bonds and overextension of credit to fund the construction of infrastructure led to terrible panic," he said. "Failure undermines people's confidence in Wall Street, you know. If big banks fail again, we're looking at another recession, but our bank has strategies—indeed, excellent ones."

Using his napkin like a towel, he patted away food particles clinging to his moustache. Johanna nodded and smiled. He liked to hear himself talk, which was fine with her. She let him drone on, enjoying her dessert and taking pleasure in sitting at the table, rather than working in the kitchen. She noted today's lemon poppy seed cake was moist and the icing a good blend of tangy and sweet. She had replaced Tilly after her day in court, and thank goodness the new cook could bake.

Johanna realized the banker was waiting for her to say something. He had been talking about railroads, so she ventured a question. "Do you think the Philadelphia and Reading Railroads will be able to stay afloat?"

"I do, and I can explain, my dear," he said. "At the bank, we know there is a lot of pressure, possibly even potential merger enthusiasm. Consolidation could shake up the industry and reduce the number of major railroads—not good for competition, which is why strategy is so critical."

One of the new maids cleared Johanna's plate. The girl dropped a spoon, and Johanna had to stop herself from picking it up.

"My apologies, madam," she said.

The banker was still talking. Johanna had another few minutes to herself as he enlightened her on currency disturbances. She wondered if he might ask even one question of her. Instead, he said, "And, of course, we have the knowledge and the services you could access if you wanted to move your accounts to us."

Oh, this is a sales pitch, Johanna thought. She sat back and let it sink in: her business was being courted by the biggest bank in town.

$$\infty$$

# CHAPTER FOURTEEN

# GARDENS

**Nanticoke, Pennsylvania, April 1884**

"I've never planted a garden before," Johnny said. His brow furrowed as he pushed the wheelbarrow uphill. En added force from the opposite side, shoving with his hip.

"It's only April," En said. "We could still have a frost. We'll turn the soil today and plant when it gets warm."

The ridged rows of brown clumps, still barren of foliage, would be ready for seeds to take root soon. It gave En more satisfaction than he had known in years. The garden materializing according to plans developed over the winter stood in stark contrast to his lack of agency. The garden was the only place in Nanticoke where he had authority. He had been honest with Johanna about his happiness with her, but he was reluctant to tell her just how much living here, imprisoned in this valley, constrained his spirit. Johanna's success established her in this community. He was neither servant nor man here.

En had always been strong and healthy. He had watched age impose physical limitations on his grandmother but never thought it would happen to him—at least in midlife. His ravaged hands and the need to calculate the pain of every task—even one as small as opening an envelope—was a constant frustration.

He gazed toward the chain of mountains around him. En wasn't a religious man but becoming a patient himself had unlocked an awareness of his own limited perspective, that in the vast unknown there was something boundless and abundant. At least nature did not differentiate. Fair or cruel, every farmer in the valley would be allotted the same measure of rain and sunshine. Cultivating a garden, he was equal to any man, woman, or child.

He now understood from the experience of knowing helplessness and agony what his parents used to say: that even when they were unable to cure, they could always heal. There was certainly more to medicine than curing. By relieving pain and offering hope, he could provide some measure of solace. En was ready to accept the imperfections and defeats of medical practice. He felt the presence of Mai Ling and Rosie, and he thought about the discoveries he could make that would give meaning to their deaths. If his parents were here now, he would ask them, "Help me. You once showed me the path. Will you guide me again?"

He had been cavalier in throwing away their legacy. Now that his dexterity was improving, he desperately wanted the use of his hands for one thing: to finish his medical training. The promise he'd made to his grandmother and his ancestors emerged as an unseen force driving his ambition to be a physician—a practitioner of both Eastern and Western medicine. Although science and medicine were his purpose, they both seemed out of reach—literally. The Běnshuài sent occasional letters, usually with stories about someone in the community, often a child, who had been refused care. He also asked En's advice about a new public health prevention effort that would benefit from a trusted medical doctor's leadership. He always included an invitation for En to return, finish school, and set up a practice in Chinatown.

"This summer, will we have carrots, pole beans, and corn?" Johnny said, breaking the spell of En's dialogue with the cosmos.

"That's the plan. We'll have to put up a stronger fence, or the deer will eat it up before we do."

Johnny took a hoe from the wheelbarrow and held it out to En.

"You always know just the tool I need," En said.

"That's my job." Johnny grinned, his ears red with the cold. "And, En, this summer I want to plant lots of the kind that are smelly, the ones we use for cooking."

"Herbs?" En pointed to dried stems jutting up in the soil. "Some of the mint and lavender lasted all winter, see over there?"

Johnny ran toward the tufts of dried brush and pulled up a handful. "One's for tea, the other for lamb roast." Johnny held the dried leaves and stems to his nose. "This one burns when I sniff, but the lavender smells nice, right?"

En's spine prickled before he saw the young men emerging from the overgrowth behind the hotel. He recognized Finn at once—taller, but still TC's mirror image. A burly fellow at Finn's side stepped dangerously close.

"Grab the Chink, Roy," Finn said, wiping his arm along his mouth, a line of dark saliva tracking against the sleeve.

"Will do. His kind do not belong here." In a flash, the man named Roy had pinned En's arms tight behind him, jacking up En's elbows. "Miners can't get work, and here you are, living off the Irish—playing house with our women and children when you should be cleaning up our shit."

"Johnny, go back to the hotel, now," En said, as pain ripped through his right shoulder. He tried to stand on tiptoe. Any more compression would tear his rotator cuff.

Johnny said, "I can't leave you alone."

En could barely hear the boy. "Go," En said. He wanted Johnny away from danger. It was cold and no windows would be open in the rooming houses or hotel. It was unlikely anyone would hear unless Johnny got to the hotel.

"Hey, Finn, grab the kid, before he squeals," Roy said.

"He's harmless. Let him run to mommy," Finn sneered at Johnny.

En watched from the corner of his eye as Johnny took off in a dead run.

The beating was vicious. Doubled over, his head sagging, En forced himself to remain upright. If he fell to the ground, they would do more damage with their boots, likely kick him to death.

Through a haze, En heard a shout, followed by a loud cowboy-and-Indian scream he remembered from playing with the boys. A force, or a person, barreled into him. Roy let out a whoosh as they toppled to the ground.

"Holy shit, the kid stabbed me," Roy said, rolling away from En.

En got on all fours and saw Roy holding his abdomen. A dark wet circle spread beneath his fingers. TC was above them, the dripping knife still in his grasp. En didn't have the strength to stand but watched TC circle Finn. They locked identical sets of eyes, taking careful steps in a gradually shrinking circle. Then, in a split second, TC bounded toward his enemy. Finn raised his arm. TC thrust the knife forward, slicing across Finn's palms.

"No," Finn said, instinctively batting the knife away. TC jabbed underneath, ripping through Finn's thin jacket, slicing the blade back and forth across Finn's torso. Finn stumbled backward. En could see Finn's shirt was shredded; rivulets of red spread toward his belt. He thought about helping staunch the blood, but before he could move, Roy and Finn were up and clinging to one another. Drops of blood, like seeds, dotted the furrows as the attackers hobbled toward the woods.

En stood, rested his hands on his knees, and tried to resist the nausea. He took deep breaths but was unable to avoid heaving bright red froth on the grass. When he could, En curled up on his side, too spent to move. Then, TC and Johnny were on either side of him.

"Can you stand, En?" TC said. En allowed the boys to steady him. In the distance, Johanna cried out, "Oh my God, what happened?"

"TC got 'em, Ma," Johnny said. "I wasn't supposed to tell that he had a secret weapon that he got all by himself—but good he did. My brother can sure use that knife."

"Who did this, En?" Johanna ducked under his shoulder and rested his body against hers.

"Finn did this," Johnny said. "He had another bad man with him."

En stooped forward and vomited again.

Mother Agnes welcomed the rare hours alone. She liked quiet and the luxury of contemplation. School had let out early, and some of her nuns were attending the Mass held on Fridays during Lent. A few nuns were elsewhere in the convent, but most had stayed in their classrooms, getting caught up on papers or decorating bulletin boards. Mother Agnes liked the children to have colorful and inspiring art around them. She would have preferred less sitting, but if the children did have to stare at walls, at least the teachers could use the space to teach and inspire. Rather than hanging a Bible verse in August and letting it fade until June, she set aside a special fund to encourage teachers to change the displays and rotate student papers. Attention meant so much to the children, many of whom had little reinforcement for good work.

Some of her most pious nuns—often those with the dullest classrooms—would remain in the sanctuary praying after Mass. She shouldn't judge, but they were nuns whose devotion to Catholicism, not always consistent with the love of Christ, taxed her patience. Not that she didn't appreciate the season of Lent: Palm Sunday and Easter were her favorite holidays—resurrection and new life. She particularly enjoyed Ash Wednesday, the day when the priest imprinted the shape of the cross on the forehead of believers with ashes burned from the previous year's Palm Sunday palm fronds. The ritual held great significance to her. Unlike the sacraments, which required baptism in the faith, receiving ashes was an ecumenical rite. A priest could bless anyone who sought redemption on Ash Wednesday.

She was also drawn to the concept of "dust thou art, and to dust thou shalt return," probably because she had to be reminded that all turned to dust. Raised in a wealthy family—something known only to her own Mother Superior—her parents had cultivated a love of beauty. She was an only child, and following the death of her husband, her parents held out hope that she would return to their large estate, remarry, and provide heirs. They believed the Church had stolen her away, never accepted her vocation, and made sure she could never assign any of the property to the Church. Legally, she still owned the house, filled with expensive furniture and art, the property bequeathed to her through an irrevocable trust until her death.

Long ago, she had hired an attorney to rent out the property, freeing her from the day-to-day burden of managing the estate. She didn't miss the mansion, but she still struggled to release her attachment to the antiques and paintings, even as she reminded herself it was all dust.

Over the years, as tenants moved in and out, she brought some of her favorite pieces to the convent. "Thou shalt not covet" meant she shouldn't crave what wasn't hers, and where once she had confessed this sin, as she matured spiritually, she changed her view. She came to believe that God desired her gratitude for the love and beauty that had surrounded her as a child. Appreciating creation was another way to honor the Creator.

The clock in the hall struck noon, and she wanted a cup of tea. On the way to the kitchen, she detoured into the foyer and delighted in her latest acquisition: a Queen Anne dresser, recently installed beneath the staircase. No one was around, so she grazed her palm over the inlaid burled wood. The intricate knot fascinated her: God must have taken extra care to get such delicate shading.

She was startled by a loud thump that sounded like something had fallen over on the porch. She opened the front door and found an untidy boy, streaks of blood on his face and his clothing askew.

"Is it you, TC? Oh my, you are a sight," Mother Agnes said. "Come in."

She ushered him down the corridor. He seemed uninjured, but his shirt and pants were soaked with blood. "This blood is not yours?"

"No, from guys who beat up En."

"Was anyone else hurt?"

"En, he was sick at his stomach. I didn't stay to see if he was hurt bad," TC said. "I mighta killed 'em … those two."

"Come into my study," she said. "Take a seat on the sofa."

Mother Agnes was relieved she had been near the door. No one else had seen TC. She could better protect him once she knew the facts. Who was around to help? It had to be a nun who was discreet. She went to the corridor and called to a trusted novice, "Sister Ann, please come immediately."

TC removed his wet socks and boots, also dark with blood. She helped lift his shirt over his head. He looked like a child getting ready for his bath. "Is that why you ran?" She wrapped a throw around him.

"Finn started it. Who will believe me? Only En and Johnny were there." TC wrung his hands. "I'm going to prison. Even if I see my da, I still don't want to go to the big house."

"Where did you ever hear that expression?" She couldn't help smiling. "And I don't think that is likely to happen."

Sister Ann entered. "Did you need something, Mother?"

"Please, bring us a wash basin, towel, and soap," Mother Agnes said. "And say nothing to anyone." She opened a cupboard where she kept extra clothes, mostly for the younger children who wet themselves but also for the handyman who was prone to getting himself coated in soot, mud, or paint.

Sister Ann returned and put a basin and towel on the table. Mother Agnes placed a large pair of pants and a shirt next to it. "Sister, let's leave this young man to change. He needs suspenders: the pants are too big." Mother Agnes pulled a metal box from her desk. "Would you go over to Kress Five-and-Dime and get suspenders or a belt?"

She handed the money to the novitiate.

"Yes, Mother," Sister Ann said.

She left but a minute later returned.

"Back so soon? Did you find a pair of suspenders among the sisters?" Mother Agnes asked.

"No, Mother," she said. "The police are here for you, in the foyer."

"TC, you stay here," Mother Agnes said. "Make sure you wipe off all the blood and hold up your pants until Sister returns."

She found the two policemen standing awkwardly in front of the highboy and escorted them into the parlor. They recounted a story similar to the one TC had just told her.

"You're saying that a skinny, ten-year-old lad overtook two men and stabbed them in broad daylight?"

A rotund policeman stared at his skinny partner and said under his breath, "Shut up, you're givin' away the case."

Mother Superior thought it was likely they had no case. She felt sorry for them. It isn't easy to arrest your own, but even so, she would not allow them to come after TC when she thought it likely he had acted in self-defense. She was an ace at intimidating good Catholic schoolboys, especially on her turf.

"I doubt we'll see them again," she said. "But perhaps TC or En will want to bring charges? I'm sure you know that TC is a student here—as I believe both of you were, some years ago? If I'm not mistaken, you spent a good amount of time here. Is it James?"

She watched the burly policeman's face take on the wide-eyed look of a six-year-old. "Yes, I'm James Madden, Mother."

"Of course, James. We used to read together."

Officer James's plump cheeks blushed crimson. "Yes, Mother."

"Well, I'll let you know if I learn anything more," she said. "Now, if there is nothing else?" She held the front door open for them to exit. "And, James," she said, "how is your dear mother's back?"

"You remember her sciatica?" he said. "She's about the same. Thank you, Mother."

"Please send her my good wishes," she said.

As soon as the policemen left, Mother Agnes hurried back to TC. She entered her office. White curtains flapped above the open bay window. The office was empty. So was the money box.

"I am leaving," En said.

It hurt to look at his bloated face. "En, your face is swollen. You can barely see. You're not going anywhere," Johanna said.

"I'm the target," En said. "You and the boys aren't safe if I am here."

She sat on the edge of his bed, where he lay beneath a quilt. Dr. Murphy had taped his shoulder, and she had bathed his broken face. The doctor said it was a miracle he wasn't more seriously injured. The ribs were going to hurt for a while, but the rest of him would mend.

"Finn has been a bad seed since they day we arrived. He was looking for TC, not you." Johanna said, shifting closer to him. "I'm certain TC has fled. The police think so too. I think they are a little sympathetic—or at least they don't want Finn starting trouble or fires."

"Maybe they wanted to hurt or kill TC," En said, "but they were also sending a clear message for me to get out of town."

"Perhaps, but it didn't work," she said. "They are the ones who are gone."

"But for how long?" En said. "And who else shares their view?"

"I don't think many," Johanna said, hoping it was true but sickened by the thought that some people hated themselves so much that they had to hate others. She shifted on the bed, and her hip accidently brushed against En's. He stiffened in pain.

"Shall I sit in the chair?" She loved this man so much: his loyalty, strength, what he had done for her and her sons. She couldn't bear to cause him any more pain. She could better protect him if he stayed close.

En said, "No, don't get up; I like you near." He closed his eyes.

It hurt to look at his face. She stared at the ceiling. This shed no longer felt like a place of refuge. She heard voices outside and the sound of someone opening a trash can lid. A heavy object landed with a thud in the bin. It struck her as odd, how life could go on as if nothing had happened.

"Why don't you try to sleep?" she asked. "That potion should make you groggy."

"I didn't include any narcotics in what I had you mix."

"En, this isn't the first time I've prepared herbs for you. I confess to slipping in a little of that white powder."

"You are a devious woman," En said. "It's one of the reasons I'm so taken with you. I like a woman who scares me."

"You don't scare easily," she said, slipping her hand into his. "Now, rest."

She sat with him until his breathing slowed. She took her hand away gently so as not to wake him, then reached over and lifted a tuft of hair away from his eyes. "I love you, En." She wasn't sure if he heard her, but she liked saying it out loud.

A bitter April wind whistled through the zigzagged crack in the window glass.

It didn't take long for Mother Agnes to find TC in the convent kitchen, likely lured by the aroma of garlic chicken and freshly baked rolls. The nuns ate only one meal a day during Lent. Mother Agnes believed that if they had to fast, at least that meal should be delicious. TC still had streaks of blood behind his ears and was holding his pants in a bulge, like a kangaroo pouch. She noticed half the rolls were gone from the basket. Father Neil was next to him, slicing a ham.

"I was in the sacristy and look who found me?" Father Neil said. "We got to talking about the best way to run away. Did you know, Mother Agnes, that my father didn't want me around when I was growing up? Not the way I am. Said he'd rather I was dead." He spread mustard on a roll. "Sometimes leaving is the only option, but you must be smart and take provisions."

TC looked on in disbelief, as if expecting Father Neil to change his mind and drag him off to prison.

"You are so right. Be prepared," Mother Agnes said. "And might I recommend a belt? Hard to run with your pants down."

"I'll be okay," TC said. He reached into his pocket and pulled out some bills. "Mother, please, here."

"Oh, no, TC, it's yours. You knew I'd want you to have it," she said. "And the police are gone. I expect those two hoodlums will skip town. The danger is over."

"You mean he doesn't have to run away?" Father Neil asked.

"No, I don't believe he does," Mother Agnes said.

"I can go home?" TC's eyes filled.

"Yes, of course," she said.

The boy didn't resist when she bent down to kiss his forehead.

"Father Neil and I will take you."

"Can I have that sandwich first?" he said.


The swelling around En's eyes receded. He could see the dragon patterns in the red silk hanging on the wall. His ribs still complained with each breath, but he was sitting up and with just one more shove would have his boots on.

"Dressed? And you're looking so much better." Johanna came into the shed with his dinner tray.

En wanted to tell her gently, so as not to blindside her, more about his desire to return to medical school. "I feel much better. I can see again," he said, "and my ribs are improved." He inhaled and pain circled his rib cage.

"Well, not quite yet, but you are doing remarkably well," she said.

He didn't know where to start, so he blurted, "I can't stay. They are going to come back."

"What? En, don't be silly. Not because of this," she said. "Two troublemakers?"

"The attackers made it clear I don't belong here," En said. "I put you, the boys, and the business at risk. The Chinese Exclusion Act has changed this country, and the politicians pander for votes, denouncing me, Celestials—all immigrants—as not even American."

"Thanks for the history lesson," she said, putting a plate on his desk. "Here's your dinner."

"I am leaving tomorrow." He sat on the bed and pulled her down to sit with him.

"En, don't be ridiculous. You can barely walk. Michael and his friends will keep watch. I agree; you need to move out of this shed for your own safety, but nothing is urgent."

"Those men have better things to do than stand sentry for me," En said. He looked at her. She was so dear to him. He wanted to stay, to build a life together. The boys were like his own children.

"The doctor said you need at least two weeks. And where will you go?"

"I have been back in touch with my old friend, the Běnshuài. He will make a place for me in Philadelphia."

She yanked back from him.

"It's not just that my being here puts you, everything, at risk," he sighed. "Johanna, I want to be a physician. I was furious that medicine failed Mai Ling and Rose, but thanks to you and being here, I can see that it's wrong to curse my lot in life when I have the capacity to spare someone else anguish. I acted like a petulant child, walking away from my training."

"You needed time to grieve," she said.

"I am grateful for being here and that the Běnshuài allowed me the time away, but I owe him," En said. "He has written that the need among my people is dire."

"You have been corresponding with the Běnshuài? Why didn't tell me about this offer?"

"I've turned him down twice."

"And when have these letters come?"

"Over the last few months. He had Michael's address. They were delivered there."

"And you have hidden this from me until now?"

"I don't want to leave you. We both have always known, perhaps feared, that this day would come," he said. How could he make her understand? He was content helping her with the properties, but his purpose was to heal.

"You decided without even talking with me?" Johanna turned away from him.

"If I leave, you can build the hotel and allow Michael and his friends to return to their own families."

"I keep telling you we don't know why this happened," she said.

"Johanna, we made plans for the hotel. We never made plans for us."

"I don't want to build anything without you."

He couldn't bear her sorrow. Maybe he should wait, but what would that solve?

"And the boys?" She stood and wiped her hands on her skirt, as if to be done with him. "What will we tell them?"

"That I am going back to medical school. That it doesn't mean I won't come back."

"Johnny will be shattered."

"I will explain."

He wanted to make it better, to tell her that once he graduated, she and the boys might join him in Philadelphia. Chinese men did marry Irish women, but he didn't know if it was legal. He had no prospects, and he had to offer more than false hope.

"I see. You will talk with my son before you break his heart but not give me any say about my own?"

One thing he knew about her: she might tolerate him hurting her, but she would never forgive him if he hurt the boys.

She walked the three steps it took to get to the door and was gone.


"En wouldn't listen." Johanna sat with Kathleen at the kitchen table, clutching a bottle of dandelion brandy. It had been dark for several hours, but neither of them got up to light a lamp. Johanna could make out only Kathleen's profile.

"Why don't you go back out to him?" Kathleen asked. "It's possibly your last night together for a while."

Johanna's anger cut through her gut. If En was going to make decisions unilaterally, he could spend this last night alone.

"Don't let the sun go down on your anger," Kathleen said.

Johanna felt a rising contempt and fought off an urge tell Kathleen that she didn't need her platitudes.

"I won't make it easier for him." She downed her drink. "And Michael, your husband, is the one taking him away."

"He's taking En to Philadelphia. You should be glad. There could be more trouble," Kathleen said.

"Glad? En is barely able to walk. And their escaping town could make it worse. Nothing is likely to happen if we let things go back to normal. We both know Finn will crawl under a rock," Johanna said. "Michael is my friend; you are my friend. How dare the three of you make this decision and leave me out of it?"

"I would have told you. Michael and En only talked today," Kathleen said. "It makes sense to go in the morning, to travel in daylight."

"He's running away. That never works. Thomas ran; Connor disappeared and is likely somewhere far away. Even Finn has learned to run. We have to stop acting like victims," Johanna said. "Let's believe better of people." She waved the bottle in the air, circling down toward her empty glass.

"You should stop. You're tipsy." Kathleen moved to put her hand over the rim, but it was too late. Johanna added two more fingers of brandy. "Johanna, you won on Walsh's will, based on God knows what. Don't underestimate the hatred against the Irish and the Chinese. You don't have a winning hand, and En's life is at stake."

"It's never going to get better?"

"Do you want there to be a next time for En?" Kathleen took the bottle. "No more brandy. Stop feeling sorry for yourself."

Stung, Johanna spit out, "You sure are high and mighty, supposed to be on my side."

"I am on your side," Kathleen said. "Calm down."

Johanna hated when someone told her to calm down, as Kathleen well knew. Those two words made her see red. How dare Kathleen and Michael act like they were in charge?

"I wish I could encourage your fantasy," Kathleen said.

Johanna didn't want to fight, but Kathleen wouldn't stop. "You don't know what you're talking about." She emptied the bottle.

"Maybe, maybe not, but can't you take comfort in knowing En will be safe, and perhaps even get a chance to get a medical degree?"

"Anything else?" Johanna said.

"You are still a married woman, the last time I checked. Even if Connor is declared missing or dead, you and En can't marry."

"Irish and Celestials do marry," Johanna said.

"Maybe in big cities, not here. Let him go. He deserves a new, free life in Philadelphia."

It was easy for Kathleen to banish En from Johanna's life. Kathleen had never known a day when she didn't have Michael since she was what, fourteen? It was always Johanna who stood outside the candy store, nose pressed against the glass—watching Kathleen gorging on sweets.

Johanna was done with Kathleen. "Please leave."

"We're trying to help."

"Well, you're not." Johanna turned her head away from Kathleen.

"I'll let myself out," Kathleen said.

Johanna sloshed the brandy in circles around her glass, sipping as if it were mother's milk, until there was no sweet liquid left.


Johanna woke up at the kitchen table. Johnny was at her side, shaking her. "Ma, are you sick?"

She must have fallen asleep. She sat up. Her back ached.

"Here, Ma." TC gave her glass of water. "You might have a cold or something."

"What time is it?" Her hair was sliding past her throbbing temples. She reached up to attach her braid. The hair felt like a bird's nest.

"I'll get Johnny ready for school," TC said, pulling his brother toward the back staircase.

"Ma, where's En?" Johnny resisted. "He's not in his shed."

"He had to go to Philadelphia," TC answered Johnny. "He is going to study in medical school."

"How do you know that, TC?" Johanna asked.

TC shifted his weight from one foot to the other. He wouldn't meet her eyes.

"TC, I asked you a question," she said.

"En came to my room last night when you and Aunt Kathleen were yelling. He said it's my job to take care of you and Johnny."

It wasn't possible for Johanna to feel more betrayed. How dare En put such an obligation on her son? "En was wrong to ask you," she said. "It's my job to look after you and Johnny, not yours."

"He's gone?" Tears poured down Johnny's cheeks. "And he didn't say goodbye?"

"Johnny, I know how sad you are," she said. "We are both sad."

Johnny buried his head in his hands. Johanna stroked his hair and watched TC carry the empty bottle of brandy to the bin. She couldn't think of the last time she'd had too much to drink. Her stomach roiled. If she wanted to help the boys, she would have to get herself under control.

"You two get dressed. I'll make toast," she said.


Johanna managed to get the boys off to school. She cleaned herself up and took a piece of toast to her desk. By midmorning, she was unable to stay upright and asked her assistant to cover for her. She went to her room and lay down. She woke up dazed and cotton mouthed. There was an incessant banging in her head. It got louder until she realized someone was pounding on the bedroom door. Before she got up, Kathleen burst in.

She was in no mood to see this woman. Couldn't she get over her perfect self and give Johanna some peace, or maybe just a few days to recover from what they had done to her?

Kathleen was half sobbing and grabbed Johanna by the shoulders, "They found them."

"What?" Johanna could feel her friend trembling. The fog of her hangover dissipated. "What's wrong?"

"Michael and En. They've been arrested. En for the knife attack and Michael … they are accusing Michael of helping En get away."

"That's not possible," Johanna said, knowing that it was entirely possible.

"They say they have a witness who saw En pull the knife."

"En doesn't own a knife, and Johnny said there was no one else. Who told you this?"

"A friend of Michael's. He came to my house a few minutes ago. He said we should go down to the jail right away. They are taking them to Wilkes-Barre for processing this afternoon and will keep them in that horrible city jail."

Johanna and Kathleen found the chief of police smoking in front of the one-story building that served as the Nanticoke City Hall. The holding cells were in the back.

"We've been expecting you." The chief took one last drag of his cigar, dropped it, and crushed the butt with his boot. "Follow me."

They went through the double doors of the station. A police officer sat behind a desk at the far end; rows of chairs lined the walls on either side. There were a few people clustered around a family member. Two men sat staring, looking stunned with shock or boredom.

"You're Irish, but I hear you're a pretty important lady in this town, so we thought to let you know, don't want to get on your bad side," the chief said. Nice words, but something about him mocked them. "We'll make an exception and let you see the prisoners, your manservant, or whoever he is, before we take him to Judge Doyle for arraignment."

Johanna guessed that selecting Wilkes-Barre as the jurisdiction was not an accident. And Judge Doyle could barely manage breathing—how was it possible he was still sitting on the bench? "And what are the charges against them?"

"As if you don't already know," he said. "We've learned that your boy's account of the fight was, shall we say, one-sided? We got a witness who says the Chinaman started it."

"But there were no witnesses," she said, incredulous that anyone would believe En was foolish enough to attack two men, not to mention with Johnny there.

"That's where you are wrong," the chief said. "If either of those boys that got knifed dies, we might even have a murder. Oh, I also want to speak with your older son, the one who was missing when we first stopped by. We learned he was covered in blood after the incident—likely an accomplice."

Johanna heard a woman shouting. She recognized the whiny high pitch. Mrs. Sullivan, sitting in a chair along the wall in the station's lobby, pointed at Johanna. Her clothes hung against a wasted body. How much weight had she lost? Her husband was next to her, stooped over, his face ravaged by age. What had happened to them?

"There's the mother. Her boy, TC, always after my Finn," Mrs. Sullivan stood and walked toward Johanna and Kathleen. "You want to pin this on my boy, too? Finn is an innocent, and we've had enough of your deceit. First sending him away, then throwing us out of house and home."

"What do you mean?" Johanna said.

"Never mind for now." The police chief took Johanna by the arm. "Mrs. Sullivan, we want to speak with you again, so please sit down; someone will be with you and your husband shortly."

He guided Johanna and Kathleen through a door. "We're moving the prisoners right after we take care of this courtesy, so let's go."

The cell block was at the end of a long corridor. A guard unlocked the door to the largest cell to allow Johanna and Kathleen entry. En was lying on an iron bed. Michael sat on the floor next to him. Michael got to his feet, smiled at Johanna, and took Kathleen in his arms. Johanna fell to her knees next to En's bed. His eyes were closed. She took his hand. His fingers were cold. The scar tissue had congealed and felt like wax. He was unconscious, barely breathing.

"What happened to him?" she said.

Michael's face was puffy, one eye blackened.

"Resisted arrest," the chief said.

"They both need a doctor," a man's voice called out.

Johanna turned and saw Sam Kress entering the cell block.

"Call a physician immediately, or I will personally see you are held accountable for use of deadly force."

The police chief blanched. "Mr. Kress, why is this any of your business?"

"This woman is my business partner, and by extension, both of your so-called prisoners are in my employ."

"They're due to be processed in Wilkes-Barre. They can see a doctor there."

"If you move these men and either one dies, I will hold you personally responsible," Kress said. "Get a doctor. Now."


Johanna stayed with En while Dr. Murphy examined him. "He shouldn't be lying flat," Dr. Murphy said.

One of the guards brought extra pillows. She and Dr. Murphy gently lifted En to a half-sitting position.

"His breathing is better. I'm going to give him something for the pain," Dr. Murphy told Johanna. He then treated the cuts and bruises on En's face and put ointment on Michael's eye.

"Neither of these men can be moved," he said, "and they need twenty-four-hour-a-day nursing care."

"All right," the chief said. "But the visitors must leave."

Before Johanna could object, Mr. Kress said, "Chief, you could be in trouble—police brutality, false arrest. We do not intend to leave them alone in your care."

"I need to speak with Mrs. Kennedy," the chief said. "Criminal police business."

"Then, Dr. Murphy, will you stay with them?" Kress said. "And, Chief, I understand you have a so-called witness. I believe there is information that Johanna and I can provide to clear this up, if you would be kind enough to find somewhere that we might converse in private."

It was not a question.

Although every part of her longed to cover his body with hers, Johanna had to leave En in order to get him out of jail. She was about to go when he groaned, opened his eyes, and looked up at her. "I'm fine, Miss Johanna."

It was reassuring that he used the "Miss" before her name, aware enough to hide their intimacy.

"May I stay too?" Kathleen said.

"I could use her help," Dr. Murphy said.

"Oh, what the hell," the chief said. "We won't be long."

Johanna pressed on her friend's arm as she left the cell. "Please." She could think of no other words.

"I will do everything I can," Kathleen said.

"I know you will," Johanna said. "And I'm sorry about last night."

"You had every right to your feelings," Kathleen said. "We won't worry about any of that now."

"We need you to come with us now," the chief said. "Mr. Kress asked that we begin with everyone involved, including Mr. and Mrs. Sullivan. Unusual, but what isn't today?"

The two police officers escorted them to a conference room where Mr. and Mrs. Sullivan were already seated on one side of the table. Mr. Sullivan looked exhausted. His indignant wife smirked at Johanna and Sam Kress.

The chief took a seat at the head of the table.

"I know your superiors will be glad that you have allowed us this conversation before you make more career-ending mistakes," Mr. Kress said.

"Now, calm down, everybody. You're making crazy allegations. All I want is to make sure we do things right," the chief said.

Johanna was always surprised to see how quickly a bully could be deflated.

"We'll hear you out, for the record," the chief said. "What information do you have on this matter?"

"I understand Mr. Sullivan says he witnessed the fight," Mr. Kress said. "May I ask him some questions?"

"I guess he can tell you what he saw."

Kress leaned close to Mr. Sullivan. The old man stared down at his hands.

"So, let's hear your story," Mr. Kress said.

"I was with them," he said, "the boys—Roy and my grandson, Finn. They were walking behind the hotel. Next thing I know, that Chinaman runs at my grandson. Knife blade pointing right at him."

"Pretty simple," the police chief said. "It's this fine man's word against those snot-nosed Irish kids and a Chink. Case closed."

"Just a minute," Mr. Kress said. "What's your name, sir?"

"Fred Sullivan," he said, picking at the broken skin around his bleeding cuticles. Johanna felt a surge of pity for the grandfather who wanted to save his grandson.

"And are you employed, Mr. Sullivan?"

"I used to be a miner. Then we kept a small rooming house."

"I understand you and your wife no longer rent rooms. You recently moved?"

"We did."

Johanna was unaware that the family was no longer in the big yellow house.

"Mr. Sullivan," Kress said. "Did you move to one of those remodeled cottages near the edge of town?"

"Cottage, ha, it's a hovel. And it's her fault we lost the house in the first place," Mrs. Sullivan raised a fist at Johanna.

"Johanna has no knowledge of the foreclosure," Mr. Kress said. "Your loan was with my company."

"You said you were business partners," the chief said.

"We are, but it's a different venture. I'm an investor in Charles Hanna's real estate company. They own a number of properties in Nanticoke. Johanna purchased those shacks from the mining company, as part of Charles Hanna's holdings."

"Thought they were out-of-town investors?" the chief said.

"No, the company is owned by En Charles and Johanna Kennedy. They have acquired a number of local properties. I am part investor in the so-called shacks where Mr. and Mrs. Sullivan now live because Johanna purchased them with money that I owed her. A growing community can mean less affordable housing for new immigrants and, like you, Mr. Sullivan, miners no longer working. She thought we both should give something back to the town."

"Always wondered how those shacks got fixed up," the chief said.

"Mrs. Kennedy desired a low profile, so she asked me to manage the renovations and establish guidelines for tenant selection. Mother Agnes and a few members of the community choose among new immigrants and destitute miners who gets priority based on need. It's true my company asked you to move out because you were more than a year behind in rent on that big yellow house," Kress said, "but the Charles Hanna Foundation allowed you to move into the cottage."

"You mean, it's because of her we got a roof over our head?" Mr. Sullivan lowered his head.

"Don't be ashamed, Mr. Sullivan. The mine owners want you to feel beholden, but we don't. I will take issue with Mrs. Sullivan's description of the cottages. I personally handled the renovation, and I think the former shacks are now nicely appointed homes."

Mrs. Sullivan took in a sharp breath. Her husband turned to her and said, "It's over. I can't do it."

"What do you mean?" the chief said.

"I wasn't with Roy or Finn. I don't know if En came at 'em or not."

"But it is possible, his word against the boys," the chief said.

"You don't got my word anymore," Mr. Sullivan said.

"There is more to it than that," Johanna said. "Mr. Sullivan, I know you love your grandson, but accusing En of crimes will not protect Finn from charges of arson—that was a year ago—and this recent assault on En. You can't keep protecting him. You might not be able to keep him out of jail, but you can keep him alive."

"I know." He gulped down a sob. "I don't know how he got this way, but if he doesn't change his ways, we're gonna lose him for good."

**Nanticoke, Pennsylvania, Spring 1885 (one year later)**

Johanna walked back to where En's garden was sprouting above the warming earth. Johnny had announced at breakfast that he would prepare the soil for En's visit later in the day. He had adjusted better than she thought to En's living in Philadelphia. En came for weekend visits more frequently now, about once a month. Johnny's level of excitement increased as the day grew closer. She was glad the garden would occupy him until En arrived. Johnny had volunteered the twins and their friend Riley to assist.

"Okay, see that great curly parsley, leave it be," Johnny said. "En will be so impressed these herbs came back up. Just pull the weeds."

The twins ran around the garden, yanking at emerging vegetation.

"Just pull only the weeds, you guys," Johnny yelled.

The twins' best friend, Riley, sat on a mound of dirt and watched.

Johanna supposed the poor little girl didn't have enough energy to skip about with her friends. Alone with grown-ups, Michael referred to her as "Riley the Ragamuffin." She was both ragged and small as a muffin. Riley, at eight, was around the same age as Johnny and the twins but the size of an elf. She had skinny legs, doe eyes, and, until Johanna and Kathleen started looking out for her, tattered clothing. Even now, unless she was with them, Riley likely didn't have enough to eat.

Riley was about five when her mother died, leaving a brand-new baby brother, Rufus, to his older sister's care. Her father was a miner. He spent his time working and, after he lost his wife, drinking. Rufus had become Riley's baby from the start. She fed and diapered him and tried to keep him clean. Now aged three, the boy was a dust ball always on the move. Michael had befriended their father, Kelly O'Conner, earlier in the year. Now most afternoons Rufus stayed at Kathleen's playing with Charlie. The twins and Riley played with Johnny in the open space that would soon be the construction site for the new hotel.

Although they were close in age, Johnny had never spent much time with the twins until Riley came along. She was the glue connecting the four of them. Johnny still had no interest in sports, so he didn't hang out with the boys. Riley, Mara, and Maeve filled the void after En left.

"Hey, we've done enough; my hands hurt," Mara said. "I want to play a new game."

"No," Johnny said, "You gotta clean up so we can show En the garden is ready for planting."

"Johnny, you are tiring your friends," Johanna called out. "En will be here soon, so how about I make you a snack to tide you over for dinner?"

"But, Ma," Johnny said.

"He'll be here for three days and will want to work in the garden with you," she said. "Leave some of the fun for him. And I have apple cobbler."

The twins raced toward Butterwort House. Johnny helped Riley up. He was such a sensitive child. Heartbroken over En, he'd found another needy person. Caring for her seemed to help.

Johanna had just served them when the siren blasted. All four children stopped eating.

"Is it trouble, Auntie Johanna?" Maeve said. "Our father is down the mine today."

"Is yours?" Johnny put his arm around Riley.

"Yes," she whispered.

"We don't know what it is yet," Johanna said. "Chances are it's a false alarm." She heard shouting and people running outside.

"I need to go to Rufus," Riley stood up.

"I'm sure he's fine; Kathleen is with him."

Riley walked to the door. "I need to go to Rufus. We always wait for Da together."

"I'll take you," Johnny said.

"Let's all go," Johanna said. "Put your jackets on."

The Farrells' kitchen was full of people when they arrived. Kathleen had the older girls reading books to the little ones. She grabbed Johanna's arm with ice-cold hands.

"Michael is down there," she said. "So is Riley's father."

More people arrived. Johnny saw En among them and raced to his side. "You're here!"

En hugged Johnny. His eyes held Johanna's. "Do you know anything?"

"Not yet."

She came to him and they embraced. She no longer cared what people thought.

"You're here, for an entire weekend," Johnny had his arms around En's middle

"One year down, two more to go," En said.

The siren blasted again. Kathleen stumbled into a chair, making a feeble attempt to hide her anguish.

"I have to go to the mine," En said.

"I know," Johanna said. "Godspeed."

En took off for the mine. There was a crowd held behind makeshift barriers. He saw Michael near the mine's entrance, shouting directions as two men, carrying a stretcher, surfaced.

"Put him down over there, next to the others," Michael shouted.

En called to Michael, who was covered in coal dust but apparently unhurt. Michael strode toward him and pulled him through the crowd. "Got a doctor here, make way."

"Never been happier to see you." Michael took En's arm. "We've got medical supplies; Dr. Murphy is on his way. Where do you want to start?"

There were five bloody piles laid out on the ground. The men's faces were blackened; two of the piles were open flesh and torn clothing. It was hard to see a person—only raw meat.

"Get a doc over here," someone shouted. "This guy's still alive."

En threw off his coat as Dr. Murphy ran up.

"En, you're back in Nanticoke—good timing."

He pointed to one man, "Take that one."

En knelt next to a man whose breathing was labored and checked the pulse on his one good arm. The other half of his body had been crushed. He guessed the man's lung had collapsed. Someone opened the bag of medical instruments for him. En cut a small hole in the man's side, inserted a glass tube, and blood poured out. The man gasped and his breathing eased. En applied tourniquets and pressure to staunch the bleeding and splinted his broken limbs.

En had done all he could for now. Dr. Murphy was still with his patient, so En moved on to the third man. He made the same assessments, stabilizing broken bones and dressing wounds. He had no idea how much time passed before stretchers arrived.

"We got it from here," Dr. Murphy said, wiping his bloody hands on a towel. He walked over to En. "These three can make it to Wilkes-Barre; the others never had a chance. You saved at least one of 'em."

"They are going to have a long recovery," En said.

"Likely never work again," Michael joined them. "And the mine. They won't pay for their care or take care of their families."

"They're going to need a lot of help for a long time," Dr. Murphy said. "Fortunate you were here, En—how is it you're back?"

"Just for a long weekend," En said. "Two more years of medical school ahead."

"I retire next year. I sincerely hope you will come back; these folks will need you," Dr. Murphy said. "I'm heading out with the wagons. Hope to see you again, En, under less inconvenient circumstances."

"You sure you got this?" Michael said. "We can ride along."

"No need. They send nurses with the transport wagon," Murphy said. "It's been hours. Get home to your families. They are likely worried about you."


It was midnight when En and Michael returned. They had sent news that Michael was not injured, but Johanna and Kathleen sat in the parlor together, too anxious to sleep. Johanna had barely seen En and longed to have him close.

When the men, covered in mud and dried blood, arrived, Johanna had never seen either of them more downcast. Michael embraced Kathleen. En took Johanna in his arms.

"We heard a mine shaft collapsed?" she said.

"It did," Michael said. "An elevator went into free fall. Five men were crushed. Took time to bring them up. En and Dr. Murphy saved three of them. If En hadn't arrived, I doubt Dr. Murphy could have taken care of all three fast enough."

"And the other two?" Johanna said.

"They didn't survive," Michael said.

"Thank God En was there," Kathleen said. "I hope you see how much this town needs you, En."

Johanna was grateful for Kathleen's show of support in encouraging En back to Nanticoke. She was tempted to add her own words, but he looked so exhausted she remained quiet.

"Those two men didn't have a chance," Michael said. "The rope should have been inspected—it just snapped."

"There is no excuse. It was obvious; the pulley frayed the rope—if only they had checked," En said. "And the support beams should have held. They were moving too fast to get to the next chamber."

"How awful," Kathleen said.

Johanna hoped for an end to the Molly Maguires, but as long as mine owners exhibited callous greed and utter disregard for the workers, she doubted things would change.

"Anyone we know among the injured?"

"Jake Fallon, two of his buddies—don't think they live in Nanticoke," Michael said. "But let's sit down."

Uneasy, Johanna and Kathleen sat next to each other on the sofa.

"Kelly O'Conner was one," Michael said. "Riley and Rufus are orphans."

A small voice asked, "What's an orphan?" Riley O'Conner, dressed in one of the twin's too-big nightshirts, was standing halfway down the staircase.

Kathleen got up and scooped her up. "Let's get you back to bed," she said. "We can talk about it in the morning." Riley didn't make a sound. She nestled into Kathleen's arms, nearly lifeless.

Johanna thought of this poor child and the other families who had lost providers. "So much hardship … that child lost her father, and the mine bosses won't help those children."

En took Kathleen's place next to Johanna. "I will help," he said, putting his hand on her shoulder. "I will come back."

"Oh, En," she said. "Those words bring me joy in the midst of this horror, but you must be sure. Tonight isn't the night to make a decision."

## Nanticoke, Pennsylvania, Spring 1887 (two years later)

Johanna wanted to scream but instead pasted on a smile as she entered Mother Agnes's office. Mother Agnes lay still, barely inhabiting her fragile body. The nuns had moved her bed in front of the bay windows, so she could gaze at her beloved garden. Outside, Johanna watched the pale yellow and lime greens of spring come to life. Inside, the only color on Mother Agnes's ashen face was a deep lavender beneath paper-thin eyelids.

"She is peaceful," Sister Ann whispered. "In and out of sleep."

"I'm not asleep and not peaceful in the slightest." Mother Agnes's eyes shot open. "Johanna, dear, you look lovely."

Johanna had taken care with her appearance, knowing that it made Mother Agnes happy when Johanna looked well. She took a chair by the bed.

"I will leave you to visit privately," Sister Ann said, closing the door.

"Maybe you can get that blasted nun to let me decide whether I want to go in peace."

"And I take it you do not?" Johanna gave her a rueful glance.

"I'm quite unhappy. I want to stick around, at least until the clinic opens."

"En has to finish medical school first," Johanna said.

"He's been gone nearly three years. Isn't it time?"

"He's coming back from Philadelphia later today," Johanna said, "but he has to return for just a few more weeks, until he graduates in June."

"I doubt I'll make it until June."

"You seem strong enough today."

"No, Johanna, I'm not." Mother Agnes tried to sit up, her face contorted. "I expected many more years. I'm furious with God."

"You once told me I should use my anger."

"And it was good advice. Your anger got En and Michael free and Finn behind bars."

Her voice was shaky, but she continued. "Where once this town wouldn't have allowed En his humanity, he's going to finish medical school in Philadelphia, and they are going to welcome him back, as their doctor no less. I know that has been your plan all along."

"You see right through me. And I want you at the opening, cutting the ribbon."

"That's in God's hands," Mother Agnes said. "At least we raised enough money. There is no resistance, right?"

"Nothing. I think it will work. Charles Hanna owns the clinic building, and that helps. Plus, the care will be free," Johanna said. "I think the people of Nanticoke will accept En as their doctor, rather than having no medical care. It's certainly in their best interest."

"We can't minimize the backlash toward the Chinese," Mother Agnes said. "Newspapers are painting Chinese immigrants with the brush of ugliness and lies. Weak politicians are fearmongering and justifying the failure of their ignorant constituents who feel better when tyrannizing others."

"En said the only time Americans were happy with the Chinese was the day they laid the Golden Spike."

"Indeed. Even after the great war for freedom, it will take generations for negroes and new immigrants to find a rightful place here."

"Most of them came for opportunity and just want a peaceful life." Johanna decided to speak more openly than she had during previous visits. "Mother, I'm certain you are aware, from our many conversations, that En and I ..." Johanna noted that Mother Agnes was now wide awake. She wondered if the nun had been anticipating the topic. "Do you think En and I can make a life here?"

"You are in love?"

"Yes," Johanna said.

"A brave love."

"But not a complete one. We've been separated for so long. En chose medicine over staying here these last years."

"Before he left, En came to see me," Mother Agnes said.

"You never told me that," Johanna said.

"There was no reason, but I don't think he would mind my sharing it with you now. Of course, he felt his staying in Nanticoke made you and the boys vulnerable to more trouble. He said he owed it to his ancestors too," Mother Agnes said. "He wants to be a physician. And it was a wise decision, giving you both some time."

"All I know is he chose to leave, and I am still angry," Johanna said. "I will say that each of his visits gets better, and there seems to be no pushback."

"En chose to leave, but he hasn't left you, my dear. He did what was best at the time. His coming back for visits shows he wants to live here eventually. It's been a hardship for him too."

"I'm just so tired of waiting. I've yet to learn what happened to Connor, but I suppose he is dead. He would have come back to see Johnny. And now I worry that En will decide to stay in Philadelphia."

"Life is hard. You've had a lot of pain but had many miracles, too. You won the properties free and clear, the insurance came through, and you have turned a small hotel business into a real estate company that now owns how many houses?"

"Charles Hanna has about twenty-seven properties between here and Wilkes-Barre. The security is nice, but it doesn't make up for the fact that my boys are growing up and their home life has always been so precarious."

"They've had you," Mother Agnes said. "Both boys stayed in school."

"That's true, but they have missed time with En—especially Johnny."

Johanna thought about how she wished it had been different. "I couldn't stop yet another man from disappearing from their daily life."

"I have some other thoughts," Mother Agnes said. "Would you like to hear?"

"I'm going to hear regardless, right?" Johanna smiled.

"Only if you agree."

"Then, yes, please."

"I agree it has been unfair," Mother Agnes said. "But anger is a powerful emotion, as you noted. Continue to use it as fuel."

"I thought you were going to tell me to forgive."

"A waste of time," Mother Agnes said.

"True, I am one of the least forgiving people I know. It seems to come so easily to you."

"That's not what I meant. Forgiveness isn't easy for anyone, possibly more so for those of us wearing the cloth," Mother Agnes said. "It's reasonable you can't let go. You've endured so much. Part of your bravery is your willingness to mourn loss but keep going. En loves you, but he, Kathleen, and Michael had to do what they thought was right."

"I've tried, but it's never been the same. I know it's unfair of me; they have done so much for us. I love them all, I do, but I can't get over the three of them making decisions without me, and bad ones at that. En and Michael could have gone to jail and died there if Fred Sullivan hadn't admitted the truth."

"People disappoint. What turned it around was your generosity of heart. You offered your enemy charity. Your love disabled their hatred," Mother Agnes said. "To answer your question, I think it's possible for you and En to be together."

"You do?" Johanna felt like crying.

"Not that there won't be challenges," Mother Agnes said.

"Finn was charged as a juvenile. He'll be out soon," Johanna said, "and possibly come after TC, Johnny, or En again."

"True, but that is for another day, and beyond your control. And I believe in forgiveness, but before you can even think of forgiving anyone else, start with yourself."

"I'd better stick with the anger formula for the time being."

"Perhaps some gratitude as well?" Mother Agnes said. "Can you think about being grateful for what you do have? Accepting good?"

"For a change?"

"Yes, a change for the better," Mother Agnes sighed. "And speaking of change, you know my time is coming."

"No, you will cut the ribbon when we open the clinic," Johanna said. "Promise me."

"The Bible says there is a time to be born and a time to die. I can only promise you that God has perfect timing, even if it angers us mortals."

"I don't know how I will go on without you," Johanna said.

"You will. I've watched you manage without En—you've never been stronger," Mother Agnes said. "Finn might still be out there, harming others, and himself, if you hadn't made sure he was held accountable. The boys and the business are in good shape, and you've added the clinic's construction to your workload."

"I want to finish what we started together," Johanna said.

"And create a place for En to land. I admire you. It's difficult to be a businesswoman and make it in a man's world. Your hard work empowered you in a way we could never have foreseen. You saved yourself and your family," Mother Agnes said. "Your boys love you, your friends and this community respect you, and somewhere En's love will find you. My love as well."

Johanna didn't feel very powerful. If only she could keep Mother Agnes here, with them. "I will try to be more grateful. I truly don't know how I will go through life without you."

"The love we share is eternal, always know that." Mother Agnes closed her eyes, "and now, I'm sorry, dear. I need to close my eyes."

"Of course," Johanna said. "May I sit with you for a while?"

"I'd like that," Mother Agnes murmured.

Johanna thought Mother Agnes was asleep, but then the nun, her eyes still closed, smiled and said, "And soon, I will see real power."


She always felt better after seeing Mother Agnes, even if she feared it was one of the last visits her beloved friend would manage a conversation. Johanna wasn't concerned about a new Mother Superior interfering with the clinic. No one but Mother Agnes could have helped her found it, but now that it was established, Johanna could sustain it. Once the clinic opened, the community would get behind it too.

What broke Johanna's heart was contemplating the loss of this unique woman. Johanna had never been able to predict what Mother Agnes would say or do, and there was a gaping void the minute she left the convent. She hoped to keep the vibrancy of Mother Agnes—her wisdom and wry sense of humor—alive. She hated the way imperfect memories set in the minute she wasn't with the nun. She didn't want to make the woman into a caricature, but that's what would happen. She vowed to come by every day and spend as much time as she could with the real person until—dear God, no—until she died.

Johanna exited the brick walls that shielded the convent from the church and school. The day had warmed, and the forsythia hedge shot spikes of yellow at odd angles. She breathed in the perfume of rebirth.

She gazed across the courtyard. He was standing there. He wore a suit and tie, black overcoat, and something new: a bowler hat. He looked learned and sophisticated, much less like a railroad worker or house servant and more like he belonged in Philadelphia. She hoped he would belong in Nanticoke soon.

She ran toward him, not caring who saw their embrace. His wool coat scratched her check. His lips were soft on her hair. He wrapped his arms tight around her.

"You're early," she said.

"I'm right on time."

COMING SOON

A Sequel to *Irish Luck, Chinese Medicine*

Sample the first chapter of the next book in the Mulberry Chronicles series:

**IRISH MEDICINE**

En turned away to absorb the meaning of the letter. He didn't want Johanna to see his face. They were in the paneled study of their Philadelphia home. The room was furnished with the latest in Victorian décor. He didn't care about things like that, but he was glad she could enjoy the fruits of her labor. Their place in the community, however precarious in the past, appeared secure, at least for now.

"What are you reading that you don't you want me to notice?" She was smiling.

He shouldn't have been surprised that she picked up on his mood. They knew each other so well now that she often guessed what he was feeling, sometimes before he did.

Not trusting his voice, En handed her the thick stationery, Hahnemann Hospital embossed across the masthead. His keeping correspondence a secret from her was a sore spot and caused them both anguish in the past. Johanna would surely understand why he wanted to spare her from this futile endeavor and why he had been compelled to continue it. There was never any news; why burden her with his nightmare? He'd arranged for a private post office box when they moved from Nanticoke three years ago, just in case.

"Is it good or bad?" Johanna reached for the paper he held out to her.

"Both." En turned away, afraid she would be angry and hopeful that she might help him figure out what to do next.

August 10, 1893

Dear Dr. Charles,

This letter regards your continued inquiries about the passing of your wife and daughter, Mai Ling Chang and Rosie Chang, respectively. Unlike previous years, I may have some news, although I expect it will not entirely resolve the matter.

We discovered a box of old records during a recent move. Although we did not routinely treat Chinese patients, it appears your wife was seen here at the peak of the typhoid outbreak in 1882. Apparently, one of our doctors made an exception to the policy. I am enclosing a copy of a death certificate for Mrs. Mai Ling Chang. There was no record for a child with the surname Chang, and as you know from my previous letters, we do not have hospital records in either name.

As we have discussed, and you sadly know only too well, the epidemic was sudden and taxed the hospital beyond capacity. We can now affirm, and as the enclosed death certificate shows, Mai Ling Chang was indeed treated and died here.

It is also possible the child was treated and may have died here as well, but her death was never recorded. We did find a separate note in the files referencing approximately thirty children, deemed orphans after those confusing weeks, who were remanded to the state. While we have no further information, I understand that these children were likely sent to Catholic Charities and placed for adoption under records sealed by court order.

Yours sincerely,
William Reynolds, MD
Physician in Chief

There was a handwritten note at the bottom of the page.

*En,*
*Likely your Rosie is not among these orphans. I would advise your chance of finding her alive is extremely remote. Perhaps there is less anguish in making peace rather than continuing a fruitless search?*

*I am deeply sorry. Yours truly,*
*W Reynolds*

Johanna held the letter in one hand and placed her other on her heart. She met En's eyes for a long moment. He could see she was upset, but she kept her composure. Why hadn't he told her that he'd been searching? He knew her mistrust after Connor and Thomas. Even his correspondence with Woo and unilateral decisions left her easily wounded. He'd always believed he could make her understand his reasons if the time came. It had arrived.

She stood up, folded the letter, and handed it back to him. Her skirt rustled as she walked across the room and into the marble foyer. She stopped by the foot of the staircase.

"You're going upstairs?" he said. "Don't you want to talk about this?"

"Let's not delay, En," she said. "I think we should start with Monsignor Neil. He will have access to Catholic Charities files."

"But Dr. Reynolds recommended that I stop," he said.

"What does he know? We aren't looking for thirty children, just one, and if she is out there, it won't be that hard to find her. She will look like you."

# ACKNOWLEDGEMENTS

Thank you for reading my novel. Born in my writing group, *Six Great Books*, the appreciation of my fellow writers kept me at it. Admiration and thanks to David Bonck, Kristin Battista-Frazee, Kelly Hand, Janet Hall Werner, and Donna Drew Sawyer.

Thank you to my publisher, Create Cache, founded by Donna Drew Sawyer, my dear friend, who has won book awards and a devoted following for her novel, *Provenance*. We shared our creative process, and if we could invite our characters to dinner, I predict lively conversation. Donna is my Irish Luck.

And thanks to my Chinese Medicine muse, Edison Liu, MD. Dr. Liu is a renowned oncologist and genomics trailblazer who shared his considerable expertise and wisdom. Conversations with him sparked my interest about Chinese and Irish laborers working side by side and his question, "Will the physician be Irish or Chinese?" ignited my imagination.

Chinese language scholar and traditional Chinese medicine practitioner, Henry Buchtel, capably reviewed the book for accuracy on acupuncture and cultural literacy, adding rich detail and, as he would say, "reasonable treatment plans." He provided well-researched and detailed knowledge about acupuncture and anything incorrect in the depictions is my error in translation.

Sherry Hatcher introduced me to Henry, an example of the gifts dear friends and early readers bring. I am indebted to other valued friends and pre-readers for sharing their insights, ideas, and encouragement including Patricia Broullire, Sandy Davis, Barbara Faculjak, Patti Kelly, Anne Kendall, Karen Leggett, Ann McDaniel, Larry Matthews, Jill Scharff, MD (who saved the day,) and Lise Van Susteren, MD.

I also want to thank editors Mandy Campbell Moore, Patricia Henley of the Chesapeake Writers' Conference (and Conference Director, Jerry Gabriel, a role model and admired author,) and my "closer" editor, Ginny Glass of A to Z Editing, for wonderful teaching that included gems like: "Readers understand things like moments of weakness, anger, even being cold or distant to protect a broken heart, but they only know what you show them." Carole Freund generously agreed to final stretch review, and I am grateful for her careful reading, expertise, and friendship. My talented designers include the great folks at JERA Publishing, Kimberly Martin and Jason Orr.

I'm blessed with an extraordinary family. My mother, Gertrude Kennedy Mahoney, whose stories about her grandmother and her childhood at Lake Nuangola take wing in this novel, and my father, Daniel Joseph Mahoney, whose memories of the Molly Maguires are the backdrop for the book. Both parents nurtured me and my sister, Sharon Mahoney Williams, to grow up creatively exuberate, appreciative of faith and the Church, and with healthy perspective that inoculated us against indoctrination. And with my sister, they also gave me a lifelong playmate and best friend. It is no surprise she would champion this book and encourage (insist) her book group, *The Sun Valley Bookettes*, invite me to join them. (It was wonderful and I'll come 'round the Idaho mountain again.)

I also have a second sister by marriage, Elizabeth Phillips, my muse, sidekick and confidant, also an early reader, who gave me excellent guidance, as always.

Thanks to my cousin, Peggy Weir, who gave me a joyful boost because she has lived some of the stories, people, and places that inspired the book—and found it credible and fun.

Much of what I have learned from my children and grandchildren is reflected in the strengths of the characters, especially the young people in the book. I've been blessed to have a front row seat watching the bravery, humor, competency, loyalty, and generosity of heart of my children: Jim, Courtney, and Daniel and of those by marriage: Victoria, Colleen, and Bill. And for my five granddaughters, Ella, Grace, Mara, Olivia, and Isla—all dancing through life bestowing joy, originality, and creativity to the world, LYSM. (Love You So Much.)

The book explores challenges I've faced in life, including understanding and receiving healthy male energy. I'm thankful for the men in my life, even when we didn't live happily ever after. And then there is my husband, Lewis, with whom it's happily ever after most of the time. As Tom Jones' lyrics from *The Fantasticks* say,

*All my wildest dreams*
*Multiplied by two*
*They were you. They were you. They were you.*

Gratefully,
Molly

## ABOUT THE AUTHOR

Molly Mahoney Matthews grew up dreaming of becoming anything but a writer, so this book is a surprise and a career re-invention. She spent many years as a businesswoman, built a company, and to encourage other entrepreneurs, decided to write a book: *Job-IQ: How to Find a Job, Create a Career, Build a Business.* While working on the manuscript, she joined a writer's group. Everyone else was writing fiction, and as a lark, Molly experimented writing a few pages of what would become *Irish Luck, Chinese Medicine.* She discovered she loved channeling stories from her characters. Now, they won't stop talking! She is currently working on a prequel, *Chinese Luck,* and a sequel, *Irish Medicine.* Molly and her husband live in Fort Lauderdale, Florida and Bethesda, Maryland.